The rain had stopped outside and a warm wind teased the tent flap, bringing with it the green smells of spring. Lavinia stretched and took a deep breath.

"Lovely," Captain Clay whispered. "Unbelievably so."

Lavinia smiled and brazenly kept her gaze locked to his, not shying from the sight of his strong, bare chest. She almost made him laugh with pleasure. This was no shrinking Southern violet. Lavinia Rutledge was all woman.

Before Lavinia could think, Damien Clay's arms were around her, pulling her tight against his bare chest. Then he pressed his lips firmly to hers—tasting sweetly, devouring hungrily, as Lavinia settled close to him, feeling her senses swirl like a pink cloud of desire. . . .

Fawcett Gold Medal Titles
by Becky Lee Weyrich:

CAPTIVE OF DESIRE
RAINBOW HAMMOCK
TAINTED LILIES

SUMMER LIGHTNING

Becky Lee Weyrich

FAWCETT GOLD MEDAL • NEW YORK

A Fawcett Gold Medal Book
Published by Ballantine Books
Copyright © 1985 by Becky Lee Weyrich

Library of Congress Catalog Card Number: 85-90696

ISBN: 0-449-12797-4

Manufactured in the United States of America

First Edition: August 1985

To my new grandson,
Jonathan Henry Walter

My Dear:

I have to inform you of the sad fate which awaits your true friend. I am to suffer death this afternoon at 4 o'clock. I send you from my chains a message of true love, and as I stand on the brink of the grave I tell you, I do truly and forever love you. I am ever truly yours.
M. Jerome Clarke

(Written in the hour before his execution on Wednesday, March 15, 1865, at the Louisville Military Prison, by Marcellus Jerome Clarke, alias Sue Mundy)

Chapter One

March 1862

The hoary live oaks wept with rain, and fog off the Savannah River shrouded all traces of the early Georgia spring in a chill mist. Beyond the forest clearing lurked impenetrable, rumbling darkness and the constant threat of the unknown. But within the feeble circle of orange light, Company K of the Wiregrass Rifles took their ease. One lone figure remained tense, however, flinching at the slightest sound and darting suspicious eyes at the others.

"Hey, Sarge," Private Grundy from Clinch County called, making the solitary soldier jump, "iffen we had us a gal or two in camp, we sure could hoot 'n' holler fit to kill tonight! Reckon why us Johnny Rebs don't have none of them *patriotic ladies* following us into battle like I hear tell old General Joe Hooker's been bringing along for his boys' pleasure?" The drunken private passed the crockery jug on to his burly sergeant.

The big man took a swig but kept his attention on the young soldier who had segregated himself from the others. He just couldn't make the kid out. It wasn't natural for a feller going off to war not to be buddies with his squad.

Private "Vinnie" Rutledge, late of Thunderbolt Plantation near Savannah, knew Sergeant O'Dell was watching her. She pulled her kepi down farther to shadow her face and the blanket

1

closer around her rain-soaked Zouave's uniform. Pretending to stare into the sputtering campfire, she kept one eye on the rowdy men. They had consumed the last of the spirits they'd received as farewell gifts when the regiment marched out of Savannah three days before and were making fast work of several jugs of confiscated moonshine. Now, besotted as shantymen on a Saturday night, they were restless, querulous, and hell-bent on mischief.

Lavinia had to admit to herself that for once in her life she was just plain scared witless. She'd fared all right so far. No one knew she wasn't just another green recruit fresh out of the South Georgia swamps. But all this loose talk about women . . . Had some of them guessed?

She'd cropped her long red hair, whacking it off as best she could with her skinning knife. But its natural curl and the night's rain had kinked it to a fine, fiery fuzz framing the pretty oval of her face. She'd chosen a Zouave's scarlet and green uniform especially because of its loose shirt, bolero, and full pantaloons. She'd stitched every seam herself, adding extra fullness to conceal her blossoming womanhood. Still, had the men—that surly sergeant from Waycross in particular—recognized some telltale female softness in the depths of her large green eyes? Had they wondered at the translucent luster of her beardless cheeks? Had they noticed the delicacy of her hands, her slender feet?

And this damn rain! she thought. It plastered her shirt to her bosom.

"Hey, you! Swamp boy!" Sergeant O'Dell growled. "You not so good at holdin' your liquor—or are you just downright unsociable? You'd best be making friends with these here boys if you want some of 'em saving your hide once we face down them Yankees." When Lavinia didn't answer, Sergeant O'Dell turned back to his men with a broad wink. "Maybe this boy just figures on sitting the war out, dreamin' of home and his mama's sugar tit?"

The dozen or so soldiers in the clearing added their own guffaws and lewd comments. Even after hearing their coarse language for three days, Lavinia still blushed, but she tried to ignore them. Sergeant O'Dell, in particular, had been looking to cause her trouble all night, even forcing a swig of rot-gut whiskey down her earlier, claiming it would keep away the grippe in this soggy weather, but laughing his fool head off when she choked on the foul stuff.

Her stomach still clutched in horror at the mere thought of the fiery liquor. She had sipped champagne at balls and even tasted brandy from her brothers' glasses once or twice, but that white lightning from the still they'd come across earlier in the day was pure poison!

"You hear me, boy?" The big black-bearded man approached the rotten log where Lavinia sat huddled alone by the fire.

She cringed inside the wet blanket as his shadow fell over her. Her eyes stayed focused on the ground while every nerve screamed a silent plea for help. But her five brothers, unaware that she had sneaked off to join their troop, were farther up the line in another camp, no doubt fast asleep and dreaming about their father and sister back home at Thunderbolt.

Lavinia sighed wearily. Right back to Thunderbolt was where they'd send her if they found out she meant to go to war the same as them.

She sat up taller on the log and squared her slim shoulders defiantly, thinking about what they'd say to her when they discovered she was here. Jake, the eldest, would call her "a gall-durned little fool" and tell her war was "man's work." The twins, Elijah and Earl, would sulk and accuse her of trying to steal their thunder and remind her she ought to know her place and stay in it. Mallard would get high-and-mighty with her and inform her that his betrothed—that prissy Sammie Sue Effingham—would never make such an unladylike spectacle of herself.

Only her closest brother, Josiah, the one she loved most of all, would understand and take her side no matter what. He realized how badly she wanted to be just like her brothers and he never teased her about it. Josiah shared her feeling of being more at home on a horse's back than in a dancing partner's embrace. He liked her in britches better than in sissy girl-things.

Yes, he'd compliment her on the fine uniform she'd made and tell her what a brave thing she tried to do. He'd assure her that she was just as good as any man—even Papa!

Papa! she thought suddenly. He'd be the worst! Rambeau Rutledge would be in a towering rage by now—storming around the house, kicking the furniture, the hunting dogs, and any servant that got in his way. Then Lavinia smiled. Give Papa one more day, though, she thought, and he'd be all tears and forgiveness when she did get home. There were ways to get around that man—*any man!*

Her thoughts far away, Lavinia hadn't noticed that Sergeant O'Dell was glowering at her. Suddenly, hurtful fingers clamped down on her shoulder, making her jump. She stifled a cry of pain. The terrifying thought struck her that maybe this was one man she couldn't twist around her little finger.

"On your feet, Rutledge!" the sergeant ordered. "When I speak, my men jump!"

Lavinia rose quickly, but on legs that felt limp as last week's laundry. Sergeant O'Dell towered over her, a powerful man with a body as thick as the cypress trunks in the Okefenokee and a face as dark and ominous as the Trembling Earth itself.

"Well, boy? What have you got to say for yourself?" O'Dell boomed.

"Nothing, sir!" Lavinia answered in the deepest voice she could muster—one that cracked, making all the men laugh.

"Go easy on the the lad, Sarge," Private Grundy pleaded. "Can't see as he's done nobody no harm—just settin' there starin' off into space. Reckon he's probably got a gal on his mind, same as the rest of us."

"No, sir!" Lavinia barked.

Sergeant O'Dell's threatening expression softened, then he broke into a wide grin. "No, sir!" you say? Do I take that to mean, Private Rutledge, that you ain't got no gal?"

"No, sir, I mean, yes, sir . . . no," Lavinia stammered, her cheeks nearly as red as her hair.

"Ever had one?"

"No, sir!" Lavinia choked out the words.

"Why, that's a downright shame, son," O'Dell drawled

sympathetically. "Going to war, and you ain't never had a woman? Goddamn! Makes me near want to bawl. You know, you could get gut-shot the first time out and *never* know what it's like holding a big-breasted woman against your bare chest or sinking in deep when you need relief so damn bad you feel like you're gonna die from it."

The sergeant closed his watery blue eyes, savoring the pleasurable thoughts, and let out a gusty sigh. A moment later he grabbed Lavinia by the shoulders and said, "Jesus, boy, we got to do something about this! A man can't fight till he's seasoned!"

"Yeah! Right now! Tonight!" The chorus of male voices disturbed an owl's peace and it hooted resolutely.

"Won't go into battle alongside no goddamn virgin!" a hulking private from Homerville growled, and the others agreed.

"Reckon that settles it, Sarge," Grundy added. "Can't let the sun come up without that boy's dipped his wick."

"Please!" Lavinia cried, panicked by the alarming turn the discussion had taken.

Sergeant O'Dell was all business now. "Don't have to beg, son. We know what's ailin' you. And I swear to you, if there's a woman to be had in these parts, you'll have her this very night! Spread out, men! Search the woods. If we don't find one roaming around, we'll hike over to the first crossroads and have a look-see."

The men charged off in all directions, whooping and hollering. They had found their sport for the night. The liquor might be gone, but not one of them could resist the excitement of a woman hunt in the dark, rain-soaked forest.

Lavinia slumped back down on her log and sighed out loud. At least they were leaving her alone. They'd never find a woman foolish enough to be out in middle of nowhere, especially on a night like this.

A quarter of a mile from the camp, Captain Damien Clay cursed his horse, the rain, the meandering Savannah River, the unfriendly gods of night, and the entire Union army. But most of all he used up his vocabulary of profanity on the calico skirt he wore over corset and petticoats. Whatever possessed women to submit to wearing such uncomfortable, outlandish gear?

He gave a low, disgusted snort, then mumbled to himself, "The real question is how John Hunt Morgan—*that clever bastard*—ever coerced me into this."

The ride south from Murfreesboro, Tennessee, had seemed longer than usual. The Smoky Mountains were still cold, with snow and ice in some passes. His day spent riding through the Piedmont hadn't been too bad. Spring was definitely breathing its first sweet kisses across the plateau. But the marshy areas along this river were a pure hell of stagnant pools, treacherous quagmires, and never-ending cold rain.

"And this stupid dress!" He slapped the thick thigh muscle beneath the calico.

Suddenly, voices ahead alerted Clay that he was nearing an encampment. He could tell by the Cracker accents that these were the Georgia boys Colonel Morgan had sent him to find. Tugging at his saturated bonnet, he spurred his tired horse through the mud toward the noise.

Around a bend in the narrow, weed-choked road, a pine knot torch flared, startling the animal. It reared, nearly unseating its rider, but a dozen hands came out of the darkness to gentle the bay and help Damien Clay down.

"Lordy, ma'am, you gave us a fright!" Private Grundy said. "We done found you at last, then you go and almost break your pretty neck. Wouldn't do! No, sir! Wouldn't do a-tall, not with us needing a woman back at the camp so desperate."

This was the part of his job Damien Clay enjoyed. More often than not he'd come across men who didn't recognize him as one of their own gender. It pleased him. After all, his mission depended upon his success at deceiving people. But the looks on the soldiers' faces when he revealed himself! It was almost worth the parasols and petticoats!

Clay, who had been an actor before the war, cleared his throat, searching for the proper, high octave, then asked, "Is someone ill, soldier?"

Suppressed snickers rippled through the group. "You might say so, ma'am," the private replied. "Could you oblige us by coming along? We got a right fine tent so's you could get out of the rain."

Damien Clay gave his long, dark hair a practiced feminine stroke before he said, "Well, I just think you are all real gentlemen. I've been riding around for hours, trying to find my way to Augusta, but in this rain and all, well, I'm just soaked clean to the skin and shivering cold."

"Reckon we can find you some dry duds, ma'am, if you ain't too particular."

"Anything . . . *anything*! Just to get out of this wet dress would be heaven!"

A general wave of laughter followed Clay's words before Grundy said, "I reckon our minds are runnin' on parallel tracks, ma'am. If you'll just follow me and the boys."

Damien Clay didn't like the scheming look in the private's bloodshot eyes or the tone of his voice. He'd heard that lecherous whine many times before. He had ways of dealing with this sort. But he decided to go along, just to see what was up. No danger, he thought. His official credentials were safely tucked away inside the ruffles sewn onto his bodice.

Lavinia heard voices. Good! she thought. They've given up this insane mission! She stood up and strained to make out what the returning soldiers were saying. But what she heard was not reassuring. The men's tones had softened and all curse words had been dropped from their speech.

"What was *that*?" she gasped. *"A woman laughing?"*

Unconsciously, she backed away from the approaching voices. Her stomach made rumbling sounds of fear and her mouth went dry as jerky. Where could they have found a woman? And what was she going to do now?

With a delighted oath Sergeant O'Dell barreled into the clearing from behind her. At the same moment Private Grundy and his band of grinning cohorts led a hard-ridden horse into the firelight's glow. Lavinia swallowed hard to force down her panic when she saw the dark-haired woman on its back.

"Dammit all, Grundy, if you don't deserve a field promotion for this! Reckon I'll make you corporal in charge of procurement from here on out," the sergeant crowed.

"Warn't nothing, Sarge," Grundy said, flashing a sly smile at Lavinia.

Sergeant O'Dell doffed his cap and offered the visitor an exaggerated bow. "How do, ma'am? Mighty fine to welcome you to our humble camp on this stormy night. Name's O'Dell, Sergeant O'Dell, Ware County."

The bedraggled rider slid gracefully from the horse and offered a limp hand, which O'Dell patted solicitously.

"You must be in charge here, Sergeant," his guest said with a flutter of thick black lashes.

"Sure am," he replied.

"Well, I just want to say that your boys should receive medals for saving a poor lady alone from the terrors of this place. Why, I could have run slap into a passel of Yankees! I can't thank your men . . . and you . . . enough."

Captain Damien Clay was enjoying his performance immensely. The blustering sergeant was tongue-tied. The other soldiers stood gaping as if they hadn't seen a woman in years. What fun it was going to be to reveal the disappointing reality to them all!

Damien glanced about the clearing. One of their motley number didn't seem to be pleased with his unexpected appearance in camp. The boy was young, handsome. Almost pretty, he thought. But the look on his adolescent face was one of stark terror. Damien stared around the circle of liquor-bright eyes. An air of nervous anticipation surrounded them. Something was afoot! All the men kept looking furtively from him to the boy in the ridiculously oversize Zouave's uniform. And the lad kept edging farther from the gathering, until he stood in the shadows at the verge of the forest.

"Ma'am, might we ask your name?" Sergeant O'Dell inquired politely.

Damien fluttered a hand, then giggled in a practiced manner. "Oh, how silly of me! I am Mistress Annie Flowers from Kentucky. You must forgive my manners, Sergeant. It's been such a dreadful ride!''

"Surely, ma'am, I mean, *Miss* Flowers." O'Dell's conscience was pricking him slightly. The woman wasn't married. But, hell, any proper lady wouldn't be out traveling alone and at night. Maybe she was one of those "hookers" Grundy had been mouthing off about.

It didn't matter, O'Dell decided. Wasn't no way his men were going into battle with a virgin fighting in their ranks. If Miss Annie Flowers valued her virtue, she shouldn't have been out roaming around just asking for trouble.

O'Dell cleared his throat. "Beggin' your pardon, Miss Flowers, but this being a military camp and all, I got to ask you a few questions."

Damien Clay's well-tutored hands fluttered to his trembling lips. He produced a deep blush. "Oh, Sergeant O'Dell, you aren't going to search me, are you?"

Damien's hands were serving a special purpose. They covered the twitch of his mouth that threatened to spread into a wide grin. He'd been through the search-and-seize routine before. It was his favorite, because it was the biggest shocker to his captors.

O'Dell harumphed nervously. "Well, no, of course not, Miss Flowers. But there are some things I have to know. You are a loyal Confederate?"

"Oh, heavens, yes!"

"Do anything for the Cause?"

"I'd give my life, I promise you, Sergeant O'Dell!"

"Well now, we won't be asking that. It's just . . ." O'Dell let his gaze travel to the quivering figure still hiding in the shadows. "Well, you see, Miss Flowers, it's a matter of honor and bravery. We men are the ones asked to lay down our lives for the Cause. You ladies . . . well, there's other things you can give."

Damien Clay was trying to follow the sergeant's disjointed thinking, but he couldn't figure out what he was about to be asked to do. Obviously, it had something to do with the shy boy who had not entered into the group to welcome him. *The boy!*

Oh, God! Suddenly, he understood. What a story this would be to tell to Morgan and the others! He could hardly wait!

Lavinia had been watching the woman carefully. Her first thought had been to make a run for it, but that would never work. Now her mind was more conniving. Surely, the woman would be no more willing to submit than she would under the same circumstances. Perhaps the two of them could work something out together—something that would fool the men. Yes, that was it! She and this Annie Flowers would accept the offered tent for the night. They could fake some sort of action to satisfy the men—a few moans and groans. She knew the sounds to make from hearing her brothers when they brought the upstairs maids to their rooms.

The idea bolstered her courage. She strode to Miss Flowers' side and took her arm, smiling up into the woman's deep brown eyes.

"Sergeant O'Dell, if you don't mind, I'll get straight to the point with the young lady. Miss Flowers, I need a woman. You seem to be the only one available in this wilderness. And a charming one, I might add."

Damien Clay gulped down a rumbling laugh. He was looking into the most innocent face he had ever come across belonging to a uniformed soldier. This would be even better than he had anticipated. He knew the universal superstition about taking a virgin into battle. It was like having the proverbial Jonah on a ship. Obviously, Miss Annie Flowers had been chosen to rectify the lad's innocent state. How interesting!

Damien, never forgetting his role for a moment, cast a pleading look about the circle, but met stern gazes.

"I'm sorry, miss, but the boy speaks God's own truth," O'Dell said. "We set out to get him a woman tonight and you're the one we found. Now, if you and Private Rutledge will just go on into the tent and . . . well, tend to this business."

"Ow-w-w, no-o-o!" Damien gasped, but Lavinia Rutledge had a firm grip on his arm, leading him determinedly to their place of assignation.

Their gazes met for the briefest instant. Damien Clay experienced a moment's discomfort. He had never looked into eyes so much like liquid green fire. The feeling unnerved him.

Lavinia, at the instant her gaze met the other woman's, felt something stir deep within her but acknowledged it as relief. Once inside the tent, away from the prying eyes of the soldiers, she could explain everything to Miss Annie Flowers. They would find a way to get themselves out of this mess.

Her one danger was being discovered by Sergeant O'Dell and the others. But surely, Miss Flowers wouldn't betray another woman.

Would she?

Chapter Two

The moment they entered the dark confines of the tent, Damien Clay shrank away from his ardent swain, determined to act the innocent maid to the end of this charade. He huddled in a back corner, letting the lad know that Annie Flowers would not be easily bedded. He could hardly wait to see what the callow youth would do with a hysterical woman on his hands. This assignment was turning into a real acting feat . . . and a damn fine diversion on such a cold, wet night.

A tense silence stretched between them. Damien stood his ground, waiting to see how Private Rutledge would approach him. The soldiers outside had hushed their raucous conversations to focus all attention on the sound of any action from the tent. Only the howl of the wind off the river relieved the deadly quiet in the clearing.

When Vinnie took a step forward, Damien whimpered, "Please," holding his hands before him as if for protection. "You can't mean to do this, sir. I'm spoken for."

Lavinia hesitated but, annoyed by the woman's cringing manner, growled, "You heard 'em. I got to!" Shoot, she thought, getting caught up in her own make-believe, she didn't make a bad-looking Zouave. Why was the woman getting so beside herself? She ought to consider it an honor to be deflowered by a noble son of the Confederacy! "Come here, Miss Flowers!" she ordered.

12

"No! Please."

"Jesus H. Christ!" Lavinia swore, using her brother Jake's favorite expression and trying to imitate his oft-heard speech. "You sound just like Sammie Sue Effingham!"

Damien smiled to himself in the darkness, considering the private's statement a compliment to his acting abilities. "I don't believe I've had the pleasure of making your friend's acquaintance, sir, but I'm sure I'd like the lady very much," he answered primly.

"I'm sure you would! The two of you are cut from the same bolt. You'd have a fine time, whining and crying all over each other. And I bet you'd rather dance than hunt, just like her!"

Damien Clay drew back in mock distaste. "*Hunt?* You mean shoot poor little animals?" He made a sound in the dark that let Vinnie know he was shuddering at the very idea. In truth, he did recoil at the thought of shooting *little* animals, but he was a crack shot who never missed or felt a twinge when he aimed at a mountain lion . . . or a Yankee.

Lavinia Rutledge felt only disgust for the other woman. How very fortunate that she herself had been raised in a household of men! She was almost sorry for girls like Annie Flowers and Sammie Sue Effingham. She had female cousins who preferred needlepoint to riding, and would sip lemonade for hours on the veranda, talking about the silliest things with those sissified boys—the ones who didn't enjoy a romp with the hounds. Lord, Lord! she thought. I'd die if I had to spend just one afternoon entertaining that bunch of pantywaists!

Damien Clay couldn't see Vinnie's face. The light from the campfire, glowing through the tent flap, was directly behind the young soldier's dark silhouette. Subtle light filtered through the damp Zouave's uniform, making Damien even more aware of the lad's youthful and less-than-muscular build. Private Rutledge stood with hands on hips, revealing slender arms that would have been considered pleasingly shapely on a woman. And the lad's waist, even swathed in the bulging sash, was obviously little wider than the span of Damien's fingers. He wondered if the young man had ever considered acting. With a figure like that he'd make a smashing Juliet.

Lavinia was getting nervous. What would the woman do when she confessed her subterfuge? Well, it didn't matter. They were wasting time and the soldiers would start getting restless pretty soon if they didn't hear some action.

"I said come here, Miss Flowers!" Vinnie said rather louder than she'd meant to. To her surprise a smattering of applause from outside the tent reached her ears.

Damien advanced only a step or two. "Oh, please, I know I can't escape this, but at least give me your promise that you'll be gentle with me. I've heard such awful tales of ruthless men who have no understanding of women . . . men who defile their virgin lovers in the most shameful and painful manner." He smiled, pleased with himself, knowing he was making the young soldier squirm. "You won't treat me like that, will you, Private Rutledge? I couldn't bear it!"

Vinnie moved forward, ready to reveal her own sex to the woman, but Damien Clay, wanting to prolong his amusing role, dashed away from her, sobbing and moaning.

"Dammit, woman, get over here right this minute or, so help me, I'll tie you down and force you to submit!" Vinnie was frustrated, and yelled at the top of her lungs as she made her threat.

Loud cheers sounded around the campfire.

"Attaboy, Rutledge! Give her hell!"

"Go to it, Vinnie!"

"Yeah, tie 'er up and toss those skirts!"

The shouted encouragement from the soldiers shocked Lavinia back to reality. What did she think she was doing? If she got the woman so scared she couldn't think straight, she might not be able to cooperate even is she was willing.

"I'm sorry, Miss Flowers," Lavinia whispered in her own voice.

Damien Clay squinted in the darkness, thoroughly surprised by the lad's change of tone. He sounded exactly like a woman. Yes, Juliet would be the perfect role for him if he could soften his voice like that at will. There were few enough actors who could master such vocal control.

"I've got to talk to you, explain some things. And the men

outside mustn't hear what we say," Lavinia continued in a nervous tone. "We're in something of a fix here, but if you will just listen and do what I say, I think I can get us out of it."

"Really?" Clay said, so fascinated by the private's voice that he nearly forgot to disguise his own. He caught himself in mid-word so that his voice cracked in a peculiarly Southern fashion.

Outside, the rain continued to fall, making the men around the campfire shiver in their misery. The lack of whiskey further shortened their tempers. They gave up their silent wait to exchange stories about exploits in various bordellos they had frequented. Their lewd conversations, rather than helping to pass the time until Private Rutledge made his move, only primed them all the more for some action.

"What's that damn kid doin' in there, Sarge?" Private Grundy whined. "Hellfire, I done beat the bushes to find him a woman, and now he don't have the slightest idea what to do with her!"

"Give him time," Sergeant O'Dell answered. "I reckon it's been too long for any of you bucks to remember, but the first time takes a while workin' up to."

"Hell! Didn't take me no time a-tall," the big soldier from Homerville said, punctuating his remark with a well-aimed stream of tobacco juice spit into the fire. The gob sputtered and hissed, attracting all eyes for a few seconds, then the men's attention focused once more on the tent.

"I reckon they are dawdling a bit," the sergeant admitted. "Grundy, go give 'em a shove."

Approving cheers echoed in the clearing.

Lavinia Rutledge had worked up her nerve at last. She had her mouth open to announce that she, too, was of the female persuasion, when suddenly the tent flap flew back and a loud voice snarled, "All right, swamp boy! This is it! You ain't even done anything. Look at her. She's still got all her clothes on! I swear, boy! What's the matter? You too shy or just can't get it up?" Grundy didn't give Vinnie a chance to answer, but rushed on with his threats. "I tell you what—you either get on with your business in the next five minutes or me and the boys are gonna help. We'll pass her around amongst us, and as for you, Rutledge, I ain't got no aversion to good-lookin' boys myself! I reckon, if you don't fancy women, there's another way we can break you in.''

Lavinia's heart was thundering. She rushed forward to grasp Annie Flowers in her arms before Grundy backed out of the tent.

"That's better!'' the private growled, leaving the pair to the business at hand. "And don't be so goddamn quiet about it,'' he added. "Me and the boys got a stake in this too, you know.''

Damien Clay's smile broadened to a grin he could feel but Vinnie couldn't see. She hadn't realized yet that he was acting the part of a woman, but he knew for certain now that the soft, lilting voice she'd used earlier was a charming reality. He understood, too, the reason for the oversize uniform. All that material was needed to camouflage the ripe, heaving breasts, which at this moment were trembling tantalizingly against the ruffles of his own bodice. He let his hands slip around her back, pulling her even closer to him. Had it not been for his petticoats, she would have been aware of his most unladylike arousal.

Lavinia came suddenly to her senses. Private Grundy's wild threats had nearly scared her to death, but now she was aware of a strange warmth and excitement rushing to flood her veins. What on earth was happening to her? Maybe it was only a protective feeling. Annie Flowers was clinging to her as if for her very life. The other woman's body heat was welcome in the chill of the damp night, but there was more to this feeling than simple warmth. She tried to pull herself out of the woman's grasp, but Miss Flowers held her in a grip that would have been worthy of a strong man.

Panic began to rise in Lavinia's breast. Though she was tall for a woman, Annie Flowers topped her height by several inches and outweighed her as well. Lavinia's attempts to struggle free were to no avail. When she felt the other woman's hand seize her chin to tilt her face upward, she began to tremble, then fought all the harder.

No! This couldn't be happening! The tables were completely turned, with Miss Flowers the aggressor and Lavinia fighting for her virtue. Suddenly, full, demanding lips came down hard over hers. Lavinia pounded her clenched fists against the other woman's breast, but Annie Flowers only tightened her grip and increased the pressure of her mouth. Vinnie felt strange fires lick at her when a tongue teased her lips. She weakened slightly, giving in to a mysterious sensation of languor. But when a hand snaked between their bodies to find Lavinia's breasts within the heavy folds of her shirt, she tensed again. Jerking her mouth away, she felt the scrape of beard stubble against her cheek.

At that moment all the pieces of this outrageous puzzle fell into place. She'd been so caught up in her own role-playing that she hadn't realized she wasn't the only actor in this drama. Miss Annie Flowers was a man! A cheeky, conniving . . . virile man!

She freed one hand and brought it back to slap his face, yelling, "Bastard!" But he caught her wrist, all the while laughing low in his throat, and brought her open palm to his lips.

"Let me go!" she demanded, her voice trembling with rage.

Someone from the group around the campfire heard her and called out, "That's the boy, Vinnie! Show her what it's all about!"

The man in woman's clothing was leaning down to capture her lips once more. She tried to resist until he whispered in sarcastic mimicry, "Dammit, woman, you wouldn't want me to tie you up and force you to submit."

"You wouldn't dare!" she gasped.

"I've dared far more for much less, Private Rutledge! And, besides, you tormented poor Miss Flowers in the same fashion when the dainty slipper was on the other foot. Some might say I'm only avenging the fair maiden's honor."

"You're being ridiculous!" she ground out through her teeth as his moist lips teased her earlobe, sending little shivers running through her. "I couldn't have done anything—not anything like *that*—to her . . . to *you*." He was confusing her, robbing her of the absolute control she always took such pride in.

"Ah, but I'm not so unfortunate as you. I can back up any threat I make with action. And, I assure you, I *am* a man of action, Private Rutledge!"

"Lavinia." She sighed, feeling her whole body go limp and quivery as he whispered his warm words directly into her ear.

"Lavinia, is it?" he asked, holding her away now at arm's length. "You should be promoted to the rank of major general at least. It's a shame to waste such a beautiful name on a common soldier."

She took advantage of her release from his close embrace to clear her head and senses, breathing deeply before she replied with a haughty laugh, "My father and brothers would take you apart for even suggesting that there might be anything *common* about Lavinia Rutledge, sir!"

For several moments they stood glaring into each other's eyes, unable to read any true emotions in them through the darkness. Still, the contest of their wills was nearly a tangible force in the air, striking back and forth between them with the intensity of lightning flashing out of a boiling purple summer sky.

The recognition of her true feelings struck Lavinia just as fiercely, unexpectedly dividing her emotions as quickly and cleanly as summer lightning splits a pine. The last thing she'd ever wanted was to succumb to female weakness by letting a man take possession of her heart. But it had happened . . . in one shattering instant. And there was no way she could fight it. Whoever this man was, she wanted him! She would do whatever was necessary to make him hers. And as all Southern belles knew, the way to catch a man you really and truly wanted was to make him think you couldn't care less.

He was chuckling softly as her scheming mind turned cartwheels. "No, I'd say that Miss Lavinia Rutledge—in or out of a Zouave's uniform—is a most *uncommon* lady!"

"Damn your hide, Rutledge!" Grundy roared from outside. "I'm comin' back in there!"

Damien Clay reacted quickly, ripping the shoulder of his

gown and crying in the high-pitched voice of a seemingly hysterical woman, ''Help me, oh, please, someone! You brute! Unhand me!''

A roar of applause rose from the campfire and Sergeant O'Dell's voice was unmistakable, saying, ''See, Grundy, I told you. It just took the boy a little while to get wound up. But he's one helluva stud. I'd lay odds on it. Them swamp boys know how to plow a furrow deep and true.''

The man in the calico dress—the man Lavinia Rutledge had decided to marry—amused her for the next few minutes, acting out both parts of a highly energetic double devirgination. One moment, he was Annie Flowers, crying and pleading with her young stallion to be gentle. The next moment, he was Private Vinnie Rutledge, snorting like a wild boar in rutting season and making the most horrible threats if the woman didn't shut up and cooperate. Lavinia had to cover her mouth with both hands to keep from laughing out loud. But the soldiers outside the tent probably wouldn't have heard her anyway. They were overjoyed at the sounds coming from the tent and lost in their own erotic fantasies.

However, the final act of Damien Clay's little drama left Lavinia blushing from her boots to her kepi. With a burst of zeal he took both of his characters to simultaneous orgasm—Miss Annie, keening her ecstasy while she sang her lover's praises, and Private Vinnie, grunting and groaning as if he might expire from pure bliss at any moment. The sounds went far beyond anything Lavinia had ever overheard coming from her brothers' bedrooms.

A cheer rose from outside. A number of the men voiced their lewd praise of their young comrade's entry into manhood. Again Lavinia found herself blushing. Now she was the one tucked far back in the corner of the tent, acting the nervous virgin.

The two of them waited in silence until they were sure from the snores they could hear outside that the men had settled down for the night. Then Damien moved to where Lavinia had taken a seat on the sergeant's low cot. Without saying a word he reached down and took her hand in his.

"That would have been much more enjoyable with *two* actors playing the scene. But now that you've heard the lines read, shall we try the action?"

Although his voice sounded teasing, Lavinia thought he might be serious. The idea intrigued her. But no . . . She drew her hand from his grasp and shook her head.

"Then perhaps you'd like to explain what this is all about, now," he said quietly.

"Seems to me you're the one who should do the explaining. I don't even know your real name," Lavinia countered. "And what kind of man goes traipsing around the countryside wearing a dress?"

She could tell he was controlling his laugh—keeping it low so they wouldn't wake the soldiers.

"Well, Miss Rutledge, I suppose you're right. I should introduce myself. Captain Damien Clay, CSA, on assignment."

She lit the lamp by the bunk and eyed him suspiciously. "I've seen all kinds of uniforms in this man's army, but nothing to compete with that tacky gown, Captain. If you insist on dressing like a woman, you might at least show better taste. You must let me give you the name of my seamstress."

"I'd like that," he whispered, sitting next to her and leaning so close that she could see the lamp's glow reflected deep in his warm brown eyes. His hand moved up her arm to the collarless neck of her shirt and he stroked her throat as he said, "I'm sure your seamstress could tell me secrets about you I'd love to find out for myself."

He unhooked the top button of her shirt, but Lavinia drew away. "Captain, *please*!"

He laughed. "I know the rest of that line. It goes: 'I'm not that kind of a girl!' Just what kind of girl are you, Lavinia Rutledge? I must confess, I've never met a lady wearing Zouave's drawers before. I'm at a bit of a loss as to how I should act, but I admit to being aroused by your peculiar attire. You seem so much more *accessible* dressed that way."

"That's *not* my intent, I assure you, Captain Clay! It's very simple. My five brothers are with this company. I plan to follow them to battle."

"Didn't you realize you'd never get away with your deception in this?" He fingered the sleeve of her outlandish uniform, then captured her hand once more. "It's nonregulation. Besides, it wouldn't be long before someone singled you out. In that carnival costume you stand out like a sentinel among the butternut boys of the Wiregrass Rifles."

Lavinia shrugged and sighed. At least he hadn't given her the tired old lecture about a woman's place being at home and war being men's work. She had realized immediately that she had the wrong uniform, but she figured if anyone asked she'd just say she'd gotten separated from her unit and joined up with the rifle company when they came along.

"Never mind the way I'm dressed," she snapped. "What are *you* doing decked out in petticoats and pantalettes?"

Damien laughed and slapped his knee. She certainly was an outspoken young woman. Never had he heard a lady mention female undergarments to a gentleman. But then, was Lavinia Rutledge a lady? Her hands were delicate and soft beneath the recent calluses she must have gained from work around the camp. His guess was that she'd never before been required to use her hands, except perhaps to play the piano or balance a dainty teacup. Yes, Miss Rutledge looked and talked like a thoroughbred. And Damien Clay was an expert on thoroughbreds—horses *and* ladies!

"The reason is very simple," he answered. "I'm in this damn dress at the order of my commanding officer."

"Oh, yes! That explains everything," she said sarcastically. "Only who is your commanding officer? An escaped lunatic?"

Damien threw back his head and laughed loud and long at this. When he recovered himself, he replied, "I've often thought so, Lavinia."

The rain had stopped outside and a warm wind teased the tent flap, bearing the green smells of spring. A few birds sang their first sleepy, morning songs in the woods, and a stream of rose-tinted gold caught the canvas tent in its embrace. The air was fresh, as if the whole world had been washed and renewed in the night. Lavinia stretched and took a deep breath of the sweet spring dawn.

"Lovely," Damien whispered. "Unbelievably so!"

She smiled sleepily at him and her eyes seemed to send out a soft challenge. Never taking his own eyes off her, he stood slowly and stripped away the ruined dress, the muddy petticoats. Lavinia brazenly kept her gaze locked to his, not shying from the sight of his strong bare chest. She almost made him laugh with pleasure. This was no shrinking Southern violet! No, Lavinia Rutledge was all woman—and, he guessed, quite passionate.

When Annie Flowers' clothes were scattered about the tent floor and Damien Clay was down to his riding britches and boots, he motioned to Lavinia and said, "Move over."

She sat up quickly, her eyes wide. "What?"

"There's only one cot in the tent. I'm beat. I have to get some sleep. I didn't think you'd mind sharing with me since we are in the same army and all." He noted her shocked expression. "You don't have to worry. I'm too worn out to get amorous."

Lavinia shifted slightly on the narrow bunk to make room for him. She wondered why his statement had left her vaguely disappointed. She knew, had he tried anything with her, she would have fought him tooth and nail.

She closed her eyes, trying to calm her conflicting emotions as she felt the thin mattress sag under his weight, his warm body sliding her toward him until their hips touched. She'd never fall asleep; she knew it. Her mind was painting all sorts of shameful pictures of the two of them lying side by side in her own wide bed at Thunderbolt. She could almost smell the lavender sachet scent of the silk sheets against her skin. And she could see his dark hair spread over one of her pale, lace-edged pillows. A peculiar though not unpleasant throbbing moved from her heart, suffusing her body as it traveled ever lower, warming her from the inside out. She shifted restlessly. He seemed to be sleeping already. Cautiously, she reached out and touched his lips with her fingertips, remembering the wonderful warmth of his kisses.

Before Lavinia could resist, Damien Clay's arms were around her, pulling her tightly against his bare chest. His lips stopped just before they met hers. He smiled and whispered, "I forgot to tell you, Lavinia. I'm incorrigible . . . can't be trusted."

Then he silenced his own lips, pressing them firmly to hers, tasting sweetly, devouring hungrily, mingling his own life's breath with hers. Lavinia settled close to him, feeling her senses swirl in a cloud of desire.

Yes! she thought to herself. Captain Damien Clay is my man!

She returned his kisses with a fervor of tenderness, aware of the danger and of his growing desire, but too overwhelmed to deny her own need for him.

Chapter Three

Lavinia Rutledge awoke in an uncertain daze. She was not in her own bed. For several moments she lay tense, not daring to move on the sun-warmed cot. Her back was to the tent's entrance, so her first waking vision was of an unrelieved expanse of canvas wall. Everything including the warm, pleasant tingling she felt inside seemed strange and unfamiliar. Where was she? What had happened?

Bit by astonishing bit the previous night's events returned to her mind. She realized with a start that the slight, pleasant breeze ruffling the hair at the back on her neck was, in fact, Damien Clay's even breathing. And, shifting her startled gaze downward, she found that the weight pressing against her hip was the captain's arm thrown across her body in a casually possessive manner. She could feel heat radiating from his wonderfully lean and muscular body, though several inches separated his chest from her back.

She lay very still, not wanting to wake him, wanting to luxuriate in the lovely memories of last night. She stared down at his hand, the long, tapered fingers curled in relaxation against the scarlet fabric of her trousers. That hand, she thought with a kind of wonder, had touched her breast last night, had stroked her, fondled her, made her whole body ache deliciously. She'd never guessed that anything as unremarkable as a man's hand could be such an instrument of pleasure. She felt her nipples

24

hardening with desire just thinking about it, and a liquid warmth flowed through her.

Cautiously, she let her own hand stray down to touch his. With one finger she traced its firm flesh. His hand twitched and moved, clasping her own. She closed her eyes; his touch felt so warm, so good. Unconsciously, she snuggled closer, until her back settled into the curve of his body. She sighed with pleasure.

Then, without warning, his arm clamped about her waist, pulling her tight to him, and his lips found the nape of her neck. His tongue touched the spot that only his breath had teased before.

"You're in dangerous territory for this time of the morning, Private Rutledge," his sleep-husky voice warned her.

She made no move to pull away, but answered, "Enemy territory, Captain Clay?"

"Hardly," he replied, and his hand slipped up to cup her breast, sending a thrill through every part of her.

For some moments they lay quietly, enjoying the unexpected intimacy of their waking. This was a new experience for Lavinia Rutledge, but she vowed that it would not be the last time she awoke to Damien Clay's embrace. Her father had been trying to persuade her to choose a husband for the past two years. Well, now she had chosen. All that remained was to get him to chase her until she caught him. Of course, she could use the age-old ploy of announcing to him that she was pregnant. But somehow that didn't seem sporting. Still, it was a thought to keep in mind if all else failed.

Her mind had strayed to how lovely it would be to have Damien Clay's baby, when he turned her slowly toward him, until they were looking into each other's eyes. Lavinia wasn't a shy person, but she felt suddenly embarrassed by the depth and intensity of his brown eyes as he held her gaze. It seemed as if he were looking beyond her face into her very soul. And something in that deep part of her quivered with a new kind of desire.

"Kiss me good morning?" he whispered.

"Um-m-m" was her only reply as she closed her eyes and offered him her parted lips.

She felt his breath before physical contact was made. This phantom kiss—a foreshadowing of the real kiss to come—made her shiver with delight. When flesh pressed flesh Lavinia felt as if she were melting into him. He kissed her ever so tenderly at first, then as his desire grew and fed hers their lips did passionate battle. He drew away at last, but only slightly. Once again she felt his breath mingling with hers, and now he nipped at her tender lips in a way that sent quivers through her until she writhed ecstatically in his arms.

When he knew she could stand no more of his love play, he held her close and searched the sweet softness of her mouth with his urgent tongue while one of his hands pleasured her aching breasts.

Lavinia Rutledge had never known such delicious torture.

He pulled away quite suddenly with a deep, rumbling laugh. "I warned you, young lady. This is getting dangerous."

She stared at him, not understanding. "What's wrong?"

"If you don't know, you're more innocent than I thought. I should have my head examined for getting myself into this. All five of your brothers will probably be waiting in line to test me on the field of honor."

He rose from the bed and Lavinia noticed a frighteningly unnatural bulge in his tight britches. Blushing instinctively, she cast her eyes down.

Damien laughed, turning his back to her while he adjusted his minimal attire. "You'd better climb out of that sack, too, Lavinia. Sergeant O'Dell and the others are going to want a full report soon," he warned her.

Lavinia had completely forgotten about the soldiers. From the moment of their first kiss last night, the rest of the world had been wiped from her mind. She had thought only about her plans for herself and Damien Clay. She had imagined everything in straightforward, uncomplicated terms. She wanted to marry this man and she would. There was no doubt in her mind. She always got what she wanted. Never mind the soldiers, her brothers, the war. To hell with them all!

"What now?" she asked, rising from the cot and tucking in her voluminous shirt.

He walked toward her, smiling, and cupped her defiant little chin in his hand. "Now, young lady, we will find someone to escort you back to Thunderbolt, where you belong, and I'll ride back north to join Morgan's Raiders on the Green River. But I'll carry along some very pleasant memories of a certain red-headed private I met in my travels."

The red hair he mentioned came accompanied by a fiery temper. And his words lit its fuse.

"No!" she yelled at him. "I won't go back! I'm going with you!"

He was amused. "I'm sure you'd be an asset if we could bottle that temper and use it against the Yankees, but be that as it may, Miss Rutledge, I'm sending you home . . . *today!*"

"Try it!" she dared.

"I intend not only to try it but to accomplish it." He was maddeningly calm, walking about the tent, picking up his gown and petticoats, which were strewn about as if a whirlwind had come through.

She sat down on the cot and looked at the earthen floor. Damien Clay mistakenly took her new attitude for one of submission. In fact, Lavinia was merely plotting her next move.

"It's the best thing, really," he said, pulling on his shirt. "The war's ugly, Lavinia. No place for a woman. And your father must be half out of his mind worrying about you by now. Maybe we can get one of your brothers to see you home. I'm sure their commanding officer will understand the situation and make allowances. I'll speak to him about it myself. You'll be on your way before noon and home where you belong by tomorrow night."

"I *am* where I belong," she said quietly.

"Lavinia," he warned in a don't-start-that-again tone of voice.

Suddenly, she sprang up from the cot and threw herself into his arms, a fountain of well-worked-up tears streaming down her cheeks. Clasping him around the neck, she sobbed, "Damien, you can't send me away. *I'm going to have your baby!*"

He stared down at her, stunned. Anger flooded through him, then changed suddenly to mirth. He had been right about her. She should be on the stage. What a little actress!

"My dear Lavinia," he said, laughing as he forced her arms down to her sides, "if you are carrying my child, this will be the first virgin birth in almost two thousand years!"

She looked the way she felt—as if he'd struck her. The high color drained from her face and real tears replaced the ones she had forced to her eyes moments before. She was suddenly gripped by a soul-deep horror. Of course she realized it was too early to know for sure if she was pregnant, but she *could* be. Hadn't he kissed her deeply and repeatedly last night and this morning? Did he think she was a perfect little fool not to know what could come of such kisses? Her brothers had told her all about it. And if anyone should know about such things, they certainly would. They'd told her they didn't want her getting into any trouble. And up until last night she'd been very careful not to allow any of her beaux more than a quick peck at her cheek. What a cad Damien Clay was to take advantage of her and then refuse to acknowledge any responsibility for his actions!

"Lavinia, are you all right?" he asked, frowning.

When she didn't answer, he came to her and took her cold hand in his, stroking the back of it with gentle concern.

"I shouldn't have laughed at you. I'm sorry. But no one is that naive, my dear. Even if I had performed the act unconsciously while I slept, I'm sure I would remember." He paused and frowned down at her. "You and I both know nothing happened last night."

She opened her emerald-colored eyes wide at his words. Her lips trembled as she hissed, "What do you mean, nothing happened? I let you kiss me! And you touched me and . . ." Her voice broke off in embarrassment and she blushed deeply.

For a moment Damien Clay was too stunned to speak. He could only stare at her in amazement. Surely, she didn't believe . . . but she must! Oh, God! What had he gotten himself into?

"Lavinia, listen to me, please," he said as gently as he could. "Believe me when I tell you that there is no chance you're pregnant. If there were, I'd marry you in a minute and be grateful to have such a beautiful and spirited wife. But, my dear, it simply doesn't happen that way.''

"How, then?'' she challenged, a rebellious tone in her voice once again.

Damien rolled his eyes heavenward. What the hell was he doing in a conversation like this? And how could he possibly explain the facts of life to her without embarrassing them both dreadfully? How had he learned? He paused for a moment, trying to remember. Oh, yes! The recollection brought a smile to his face. On his fifteenth birthday his foster father had given him a special present. He'd taken him to the finest bawdy house in Huntsville, Alabama, and turned him over to a lady named Maude. What he hadn't learned from her wasn't worth teaching. But how did girls find out such things? Of course. From their mothers. And Lavinia had told him during the night that her mother had died long ago.

He took a deep breath. "Sit down, Lavinia. We'll talk.''

"Rutledge, by God, are you planning to stay in the sack all day?'' Sergeant O'Dell yelled from outside the tent. "I know it's hard to dismount once you've broke a new mare to the saddle, but us foot soldiers have got to be movin' out, boy. There's a war on, remember?''

Damien Clay silently blessed the rough sergeant for the interruption. He hadn't known what he was going to say to Lavinia anyway. Probably something dumb about birds and bees and lambs being born in the spring. He certainly hadn't relished the task.

She caught at his hand, pleading silently with wide eyes.

"Don't worry about it, Lavinia. Once you're married, your husband will explain everything to you. Now we'd better get out there and explain a few things to Sergeant O'Dell.''

"What'll they do to me?'' she asked, suddenly dreading the coming confrontation.

He grinned at her. "Well, if you really were a private, they'd probably set up a sawhorse and make you ride 'Morgan's mule' for the rest of the day as punishment. But since you're a lady—and a very lovely one,'' he added, bowing slightly to her, "I imagine they'll do exactly what I've proposed and send you home. Come along now, Lavinia. Time to expose our double charade to the soon to be astonished multitudes."

She panicked then—not because she was about to face the soldiers but because these might be her last moments alone with Damien Clay. She had to think of something fast. She couldn't let him get away!

"Damien," she said, clutching his arm. "When will I see you again?"

He brushed her cheek lightly with his lips. "Possibly never, my dear. But don't let that upset you. I'm sure you have more beaux back at Thunderbolt than you can count. And my guess is you'll be married very shortly. You're ripe for it."

"I'm not going to marry!" she announced.

"Then it will be some unlucky soul's great loss. You have much to offer, Lavinia."

"And if I offered it to you?"

He smiled indulgently but shook his head.

A sudden frown crossed her face as a thought crossed her mind. "You aren't married already, are you?"

He laughed at her worried expression. "I'm afraid the woman hasn't been born who could put up with my idiosyncrasies. Besides, I'd look rather foolish going courting in my calico dress, wouldn't I?"

"Please, Damien, be serious."

"I am, Lavinia. Ever so serious. I think you've just been swept off your pretty little feet by a chance encounter in the midst of all this chaos. You'll have forgotten all about me a week from now. You'll be in love with someone else by then."

She tossed her head and replied tartly, "I never said I was in love with you!"

"Good!" he answered. "Let's leave it that way. It will be easier for both of us."

He started to turn away from her, toward the tent flap, but she caught his arm. "Damien . . ."

He looked down into her dewy green eyes. There was such emotion, such naked honestly there, that he felt himself drawn to her once more. She seemed to be pleading silently for some assurance that she hadn't been just another fleeting encounter for him. She needn't have worried about that. He knew he would taste her kisses in his dreams for many nights to come, all the while wishing that her lovely pliant body were pressed against his. There was something about Lavinia Rutledge that got under Damien's skin, that made him want to hold her, protect her, make passionate love to her, and turn her over his knee for a good spanking all at the same time.

Slowly, he bent his lips to hers. Again her mouth parted under his tender assault. For a long time they stood with only their lips touching. Then with one strong arm he drew her to him. Lavinia easily fitted the contours of her body to his and gloried in the rich, unexplained feeling that his touch sent through her blood.

How could she let him go? The answer was simple: she couldn't!

"Well, I'll be a blue-eyed, three-legged hound dog!" Sergeant O'Dell breathed as he threw the tent flap back to find Private Rutledge and a stranger in a clinch. "What the hell's goin' on here?"

"Diversionary tactics, Sergeant," Damien Clay replied. "I was just giving the private here a lesson in secret military strategy."

"Leapin' Jesus!" O'Dell responded when Lavinia stepped away from Damien and her unbuttoned Zouave's shirt displayed the soft cleavage between her breasts. "Y-you . . ." the sergeant stammered, pointing a finger at Clay and then at the rumpled calico gown that lay on the cot. "And you . . ." he said, turning back to Lavinia, tongue-tied in amazement.

"Yes, Sergeant O'Dell?" Damien asked, his lips twitching into an amused grin.

"Well, hellfire! I ain't never seen nothin' like this in all my born days!" Then the sergeant's confusion turned to anger. "Where'd you come from, girl? And what call you got to be tagging along with my unit? The major's going to hear about this!"

"Indeed, he will," Damien answered. "Miss Rutledge will

need an escort back to Thunderbolt Plantation. I intend to speak to the major about it myself.''

"Right cocky bastard, ain't you?" O'Dell fired at Clay. "Just who the hell are you, anyway? There's names for growed men that go traipsing around dressed up like they was women."

"The name for this one is Captain Damien Clay, Sergeant, and I'll thank you to keep a civil tongue in your head in front of the lady."

The sergeant's eyes widened. "*The* Damien Clay?"

"If you refer to the one who rides with John Hunt Morgan, then I am your man, O'Dell."

"By doggies!" the sergeant enthused, offering his hand. "I've heared tell of you, all right. Who-o-ee! They say you put on that dress and ride out all alone and hold up Yankee supply trains, rob their banks, steal their mail, not to mention all the Yankee generals you've took prisoner single-handed. And they don't never guess nor figure out who you are 'cause they think some pretty gal has 'em by the balls."

"I'm afraid that's a bit more than I can take credit for, Sergeant," Damien answered with a shy smile. "But those are some of the tales they tell about me."

Lavinia was staring up at Damien with new respect and a definite sense of awe. He'd told her the dress was his uniform, but she hadn't thought to ask exactly what activities he was involved in. To think that this brave hero was going to be her husband. Yes, she had chosen well! The two men talked on while Lavinia got lost in her own thoughts, imagining herself at Damien Clay's side, riding out to whip the Yankees. They could pretend they were cousins. No, *sisters*! They would ride together every day, bedeviling the Union forces, then spend their nights making wonderful love to celebrate their triumphs. Oh, it was going to be a grand war! she decided.

"Well, Lavinia," Damien said at last, interrupting her exciting fantasies. "It's time we found your brothers and made arrangements to get you home."

She started to protest, but changed her mind. A plan was forming. For the time being she would go along with him and not make any trouble. Her big scene would come once they located her brothers. After all, she needed a suitable audience.

As they exited the tent into the bright spring morning and faced the confounded soldiers of the Wiregrass Rifles, Lavinia felt a sudden thrill of anticipation at what she was about to do. Smiling, she waved at the men who had been her comrades for the past few days. After their initial shock they gave her a hearty cheer of farewell.

"So long, boys," she called out to them. "Take care of yourselves and whip those Yankees!"

"That's more like it, Miss Rutledge," Damien whispered. "I knew you would finally come to your senses."

"Yes, Damien," she answered submissively.

As they walked toward the horses he couldn't see the sly smile on her full pink lips or the scheming lights dancing in her summer-green eyes. He assumed he had seen the last of her temper.

Damien Clay had assumed too much, too soon.

Chapter Four

A mockingbird sang from the upper branches of a white-blossomed dogwood as Damien Clay mounted his bay horse and leaned down to give Lavinia a hand up. To the bright-eyed young woman, close to her man once more, spring seemed a living entity, filling her senses and stirring her blood with new hope and marvelous expectations. All of these centered around the man whose strong arm was now circling her waist.

The horse clip-clopped along at a pleasant gait through the late March verdure of the forest of water oaks, pine, and red cedar. Indian azaleas blazed in their startling pink glory through the woods, and bright splashes of sunlight filtered down through the tall trees, highlighting gay streamers of jasmine and scarlet trumpet vines festooned in celebration of the season.

All seemed peaceful, sweet-scented, warm, and soft to the touch. Even the morning air felt like a gentle caress on Lavinia's cheeks. She leaned her head back against Damien's shoulder and breathed deeply, then sighed.

"Isn't it a glorious morning?"

"Fitting," he answered, "on the heels of such a night."

His words puzzled Lavinia. Did he mean that the night had also been glorious because they'd been together? Or was he merely referring to the hours of cold rain, such a contrast to today's welcome warmth? She smiled. She wouldn't ask him which he meant. She would simply allow herself to assume that he was thinking of having shared the narrow cot with her.

"According to Sergeant O'Dell, we should find your brothers about a mile ahead. You'll be quite a surprise visitor, Lavinia."

She said nothing, but thought to herself what a surprise she had in store for Captain Damien Clay. She really hated being devious, but desperate situations called for desperate measures. She assured herself that this was just such an occasion. And, too, he might be shocked and angered by the action she was about to take, but in the long run he would come to understand. He might even thank her for it . . . someday.

Though they were following the Savannah River's northwest path, they stayed well away from its marshy banks. But from time to time Lavinia caught glimpses of its glimmering waters through the trees. And the river sounds—the lazy slap of water on the banks, the cries of herons and coots, and the quiet whisper of the marshes—brought pleasant thoughts of home to her mind. She could hardly wait to show Thunderbolt Plantation to Damien. He would love it as much as she did, she was sure.

"You aren't very talkative this morning, Lavinia," Damien said, interrupting her reverie. "Tell me about your brothers. You said there are five of them. All older than you?"

"Yes. Jake's the eldest and when Papa's not around he tries to boss us all. Makes me so mad sometimes, I could just spit!"

Damien smiled, amused by her sudden flares of temper and the way she had of lapsing into the most unladylike speech and behavior at those times.

"Jake's okay, I guess," she went on in a quieter voice. "He's ten years older than I am, so I suppose he's always figured he had a right to lord it over me."

"That would make Jake twenty-five?" Damien asked, his voice completely serious, though his grin was wide, anticipating her reaction to his question. He was not disappointed.

Lavinia turned until her eyes were blazing up into his and hissed, "He's *twenty-eight*, I'll have you know! And that makes me eighteen—full grown and not to be tampered with!"

Damien made a clucking noise with his tongue and feigned

surprise. "*Eighteen?* Such a shame. You're far too pretty to be an old maid, Lavinia. But then, I suppose your temper may have something to do with it."

"An *old maid*, is it?" She was in a rage now, her soft cheeks flaming angrily. "I'll have you know, Captain Damien Clay, that I've had plenty of offers! I could have married a dozen times over."

"I'm impressed!" he bantered. "But if that's the case, what are you doing decked out for war and running around like a wild little hellion? You should be home with a baby on each knee and a loving husband at your beck and call."

"You paint a fine picture of marriage with your fancy words. But think about it. If I were married now, with children to take care of, I'd undoubtedly be tending them alone. My husband would be away, fighting this ridiculous war with all the other men. You called me an old maid. I'd rather be that a thousand times than be tied down yet all alone."

"*Touché!* You have, indeed, made your point, *Miss* Rutledge. Now tell me about your other brothers."

"After Jake come Elijah and Earl. They're the twins. The two of them are like a couple of overgrown sheepdogs. When Jake tells them to jump, they ask, 'How high?' But they can be meaner than all tarnation when they get riled. They're good boys, though. I love them, truly." Her soft voice changed abruptly. "Mallard is quite another matter, however. Overbearing, pompous, conceited! Oh, he just purely boils my blood. He's always comparing me to that prissy Sammie Sue Effingham he's engaged to. Of course, I come off lacking in every detail. Damned if I'd want to be like her, though!"

Lavinia had worked herself into such a state, talking about her brother Mallard, that she had to pause for a few seconds to collect herself. Damien used the quiet moment to gain control over the laughter trying to escape him. She was something when she got angry!

"The best comes last," she continued. "Josiah is just a year older than I am, and he and I think alike on most things. I almost told him about my plan to slip off to join the army, but decided it might get him in trouble with our other brothers. He would have approved, though. I just know it.''

''Well, it looks like you'll be finding out what Josiah thinks in another few minutes.'' Damien pointed over her shoulder to the line of horsemen several yards ahead of them. ''If I'm not mistaken, that's the cavalry unit we're looking for.''

Lavinia remained silent, preparing herself for what she was about to do. Everything—her happiness, her entire future—depended upon her actions in the next few minutes. She couldn't make a slip. This was far too important to her.

''There they are!'' she cried out suddenly. ''See the five big men, riding together?''

Damien stared. *Big* seemed an ineffective adjective when applied to the Rutledge brothers. He saw immediately that Lavinia's height was a family trait. The five men towered in their saddles over the other mounted officers around them. He certainly hoped he never angered any of them. Anyone who engaged one of the Rutledge brothers in fisticuffs would have to be either mad or suicidal. And, besides, Damien Clay was not a man who enjoyed physical combat, preferring instead to use his acute mental powers and cunning to defeat his enemies.

Suddenly, a shrill whistle split the air and the Rutledge men simultaneously reined in their mounts so quickly that the horses pranced and reared. Damien looked down, amazed to see Lavinia, two fingers between her teeth, producing the ear-splitting signal. Was there no end to the girl's talents?

''Come on!'' she ordered, sliding easily down from her perch in front of him. ''They heard me.''

''I have no doubt of that! I imagine that offensive noise you just made was heard in at least four states. Did you learn that at finishing school?'' he asked sarcastically.

''Shoot, no! Jake taught me when I was just a tad. He said if I was ever in trouble just to give a whistle and they'd all come running. And they always do. See?''

Sure enough, the five horses, spurred by their riders, were pounding down on them at breakneck speed. When they spotted Lavinia standing beside Clay's horse, they gave a chorus of wild yelps and reined in once more. In a moment she was sur-

rounded by five laughing, shouting men, her smaller figure ob-
literated by their massive hulks.

Not one of them even looked in Damien Clay's direction. He
studied them, trying to figure out which one was which. Elijah
and Earl were easy to identify. The twins were identical—big-
boned redheads with grins parting their freckled faces from ear
to ear. Josiah wasn't difficult to spot either. He looked much
younger than the others—an extremely handsome lad who
carried his height with almost elegant ease and whose coloring
was identical to his sister's. The remaining two looked very
much alike, though the premature silver at Jake's temples
plainly proclaimed his seniority to the dark-haired, somber-
faced Mallard. Yes, Clay could see why Mallard would not be
Lavinia's favorite. Even now he seemed to be standing apart
from the others and staring at her with marked disapproval.

"Dammit, girl, how'd you get here?" Jake demanded at
last, his jubilant welcome turned to serious concern. "And
what are you doing in that crazy getup?"

Before she could answer Jake, Mallard broke in. "Running
away, no doubt. You're a disgrace, Lavinia Rutledge! I hope
Papa takes his buggy whip to you when you get home. It's high
time you learned to act like a lady. Why, my Sammie Sue
would never—"

"Shut up, Mallard, for chrissakes!" Jake boomed. "Let
Vinnie talk."

When all five men hushed at once, the silence seemed deafening. Damien watched as they stepped back, all staring at
their little sister. He felt a pang of sympathy for Lavinia. How
could she possibly explain her wild escapade to her brothers?
He was sure that if she were his sister he would turn her over
his knee and whale the daylights out of her.

Lavinia took a deep breath. Her moment of truth had come.
She'd better make it good! She stole a quick glance at Damien,
smiled, then turned back to face her brothers. The next instant,
she gave a convulsive sob and covered her face with her hands.

Consoling murmurs sprang to her brothers' lips and they
converged on her to give comfort. Damien's momentary concern for her faded when he saw that her tears had reduced the

men to towering masses of jelly. He guessed her sly objective. Undoubtedly, Lavinia Rutledge had used her arsenal of emotional weaponry effectively on her brothers in the past.

"Tell us who's made you cry, Lavinia," Jake growled. "We'll take care of him for you."

Damien felt suddenly unnerved by the fact that all eyes had turned on him. Instinctively, he pulled on the reins and his horse backed a few paces away from the glowering brothers. At the same moment, they began their advance toward him, murder in their collective eyes.

"No, wait!" Lavinia cried out. "It's not his fault. He *can't* marry me with the war and all. He's a really important man, *the* Damien Clay."

"I don't give a good goddamn if he's *the* Stonewall Jackson!" Jake declared. "Nobody messes with my little sister and then refuses to marry her!"

Damien sat stunned, unable to believe what he was he hearing. Lavinia had carefully diverted the entire conversation from her unexplained arrival in the wilderness, her strange outfit, and her chopped-off hair to a discussion of imaginary wrongs committed by *him*. He watched, dumbfounded, as she threw herself against the side of his horse, her arms spread wide as if to protect him from her brothers' angry assault.

"No!" she sobbed. "Don't you dare hurt him. I love him! Even if he doesn't want to marry me, I won't let you harm the father of my child!"

"Lavinia!" Damien groaned.

"You just keep your trap shut, mister!" Elijah snarled, waving a threatening fist at Damien. "Ain't no sorry sonuvabitch gonna do my little sister wrong! Me and Earl'll take your hide off inch by inch. Skin you like a damn rabbit!"

"No! Let's hang him," Earl put in, yanking the rope from his saddle.

"If you'd just let me explain," Damien offered.

"It seems to me there's no explanation that would rectify this wrong you've done. Lavinia may be a spoiled, impetuous girl, but that still doesn't give any man the right to take advantage of her!" Mallard put in, his face as dark as the thunder-clouds now threatening over the river.

"Just hold on a minute!" Damien growled back at the lot of them. "I brought your sister here this morning to see which of you wants to take her home to Thunderbolt. There is *nothing* between us! You have my word on it."

Damien Clay's level tone made the brothers look once more to Lavinia. It was obvious that their confidence in her tale had been shaken.

"Well, Vinnie? Is he telling the truth?" Jake asked.

She took a long time to answer. When she finally spoke, Damien could almost feel the noose tightening around his throat.

"It's partly true," she said. "He did think I should go home. I wanted to follow him to battle. That's why I cut off my hair and made this uniform. But he said it was too dangerous, especially now that . . . we've *been* together."

Ten murderous green eyes swung their gazes back to Damien Clay.

"So it's true about the baby," Jake said with finality. "You no good, lying sonuvabitch! You were going to just dump her back at the plantation and go on your merry way. Just like that!"

"Hold on a minute, Jake." The youngest of the brothers, Josiah Rutledge, spoke up for the first time. "Can I talk to Vinnie alone?"

The other four exchanged wary glances, but finally Jake nodded his consent. Damien still sat his horse, surrounded now by the four armed men, while Josiah led his sobbing sister a short distance away.

"Now, Vinnie," Josiah said quietly, "you've got to stop crying and talk to me. If you love this Damien Clay, you'd better give me some answers fast. Otherwise Elijah and Earl will string him up from the nearest tree and you know it."

"Yes, Josiah," Lavinia answered, calming herself immediately. "What do you want to know?"

"I want to know if it's the truth about you and him."

Tears rushed to her eyes again. "Do you think I'd lie about such a thing, Josiah? I don't know for sure if I'm carrying his child, but I've shared his bed. Don't look so shocked. I love him. And I do want to marry him. He's all I've ever wanted."

"Damn!" Josiah cursed softly. "I was hoping you'd made the whole thing up. I really can't understand you getting yourself into such a mess, Vinnie, but I guess in wartime these things just happen."

"Then you'll help me?" she asked hopefully.

"I don't know what kind of help you want."

"I want to marry Damien Clay. I *have* to!"

Josiah draped his long arm around her shoulders affectionately while he thought about the situation. At last he said, "What if *he* takes you home? You'll have some time to talk things over on the way. When you get back to Thunderbolt, you can discuss all this with Papa. He'll know what to do."

She threw her arms around his neck and hugged him soundly. "Oh, Josiah, I love you so! That's exactly what I hoped you'd say. He'll marry me. I just know he will!"

"All right. Calm down, Vinnie. The main thing is to get him out of here before anything happens to him. Fuses are shorter than ever around the camp after the past few days of rain and bad rations. Let me talk to this Clay fellow, and I'll square everything with Jake and the others, too."

By the time Lavinia and Josiah rejoined the group, Damien Clay figured his last moments were close at hand. Never before had a few stolen kisses gotten him into such a tight spot. He had to hand it to Lavinia, though. When she set her mind to something, it was "Katy, bar the door!" Damn, she was a strong-willed woman for all her fragile looks, a real iron butterfly.

No wonder she hadn't married. What man wanted a woman who could outthink, outcuss, and probably outfight him? Certainly Damien Clay would never consider marrying such a willful female. So what if her kisses tasted of sweet innocence! So what if the feel of her ripe breasts against him sent his blood pumping! So what if he was cussing himself even now for not taking her while he had the chance! Lavinia Rutledge was not his type and that was that! When he married—*if* he married—he wanted a sweet-tempered, mild-mannered, prim and proper lady.

Of course, it might be interesting, he mused, to wake up to that fiery red hair on the pillow next to his every morning . . . to look into those hot green eyes first thing, then pull her close and tarry there in bed a bit. He closed his eyes, imagining.

Certainly life with Lavinia would never be boring. But no! Boring he could live with. Marriage to Lavinia would be a second War Between the States. And that he couldn't take!

Josiah motioned his brothers away from Damien's horse. They left him grudgingly, casting threatening glances back over their huge shoulders. Lavinia stood alone, to one side, her fingers demurely laced before her and her eyes downcast. The perfect victim, Damien thought.

There was grumbling from the tight knot of brothers, then nodded agreement all around. Damien strained his ears to see if he could catch their words, but with no luck. He noticed, though, that Lavinia was smiling now. Apparently, she understood and approved of the meeting's outcome.

"Mr. Clay," Josiah said as he approached.

Damien noticed the lad's lieutenant's insignia and corrected in a commanding voice, "*Captain* Clay!"

"Sorry, sir," Josiah replied. "You aren't in uniform and I thought—"

"I don't give a damn what you thought! I'm with John Hunt Morgan's brigade," Damien told him. "I rode down here to bring information to your commanding officer. You may have noticed that your column has altered its course this morning. I relayed my information to Sergeant O'Dell of the Wiregrass Rifles and he sent it on up the line."

"Yes, well, I had no idea." Josiah seemed momentarily flustered by the other man's seniority and importance—exactly as Damien had hoped he would be. But he got quickly back to the business at hand. "My sister tells me that the two of you have shared a bed."

"I won't deny that," Damien answered. How could he? "But I assure you, since it seems I must, that it was all perfectly innocent."

Josiah gave him a hard look, obviously not believing that

any man could spend time in bed with his hot-blooded sister and not take full advantage of her charms.

"Well, I don't know where you're from, Captain, but around these parts there's a certain code of honor."

"See here, Lieutenant. If you mean to challenge me to a duel, you can forget it. Already the Confederacy has lost more officers to duels among themselves than to the whole Union army. It's a barbarous practice and illegal to boot. I'll have no part of such 'gentlemanly' nonsense!"

"That was not my intent, Captain Clay. What I'm asking you to do is see my sister safely home. Once you reach Thunderbolt, you may stay or go, as your conscience dictates."

"I assure you, Lieutenant Rutledge, my conscience is perfectly clear where your sister is concerned."

Josiah frowned at him. "I may have to challenge you yet, Captain. Are you calling my sister a liar?"

"A gentleman would never call a *lady* a liar, sir," Damien answered, carefully skirting the truth himself.

"Then you agree?"

"I agree to see Miss Rutledge safely home. No more."

"That's all we're asking, Captain," Josiah said.

Damien Clay found himself both furious and amused at the turn of events. He thought to himself that if Lavinia Rutledge were at the head of the Confederate forces, the Yankees wouldn't stand a chance.

As they remounted—Lavinia on a spare horse provided by her brothers—and headed south, Damien was still peeved with her. But how could he stay angry with such a vivacious, unpredictable, effervescent female? Her tears were long gone, and her face glowed with the very love of life. She approached her return to Thunderbolt as yet another great adventure.

"Do you suppose we'll meet any Yankees along the way, Damien?" she asked with a hopeful note in her voice.

"If we do, God help them!" he answered with grudging admiration for her wily victory over him. "You'll have them begging to become your prisoners with one flash of those green eyes."

"I'm awfully glad you aren't mad at me, Damien. I knew you'd understand why I said all those things."

He laughed out loud, but with little humor. "You absolutely baffle me, Lavinia Rutledge! Never before in my entire life has any woman accused me so unjustly. You could have got me hanged! Do you realize that?"

"Oh, I wouldn't have let my brothers hang you, Damien. How silly!" Her laughter trilled through the quiet forest, startling a red-winged blackbird from a palmetto thicket. "Of course, if you hadn't gone along, I might have allowed them to *persuade* you."

Her flippant attitude was beginning to make him angry all over again. For God's sake, didn't the woman realize she was interfering with his very life and breath? Damien Clay—free spirit, soldier, bon vivant—was being manipulated shamelessly by a woman! He only hoped his fellow officers never found out about this demeaning episode. But for now, he must endure. He would return her to her home as quickly as possible and then offer prayers of thanksgiving that she was out of his life forever!

By the time the sun started to set, turning the river into a pearly ribbon of glowing golds, reds, and purples, they were both weary and ready to stop for the night.

Damien, wanting to keep his distance and his temper, had ridden ahead of Lavinia most of the long afternoon so that little conversation was possible between them.

Fine, she'd thought. Let him act the injured martyr if he liked. He couldn't possibly spoil her good mood. And as the sun sank, her hopes soared higher. Once again they would be all alone together in the night. The situation offered limitless possibilities.

He found a sheltered glen of cedars and, without consulting Lavinia, settled on the place as a suitable campsite. Silence stretched between them as they unsaddled their horses, found wood for a fire, and performed the other mundane tasks necessary to make themselves comfortable during the coming hours until dawn. When all else was done, Damien unpacked a frying pan and coffeepot and set about frying fatback and heating water.

"Let me do that," Lavinia offered.

"Cook? You?"

"Of course, I can cook!" She tried to wrest the pan from him, but he moved it quickly away.

"Never mind. I don't want to have to worry about being poisoned," he said sharply.

Lavinia sat back on her heels, pouting. "You're still mad at me?"

He didn't answer. He wasn't sure how he felt. He knew it was nice to be gazing at her across the fire. The flames cast a coppery sheen on her skin and made her eyes dance with reflected lights. It was good to have her with him to hear the quiet sounds of the night—the owls hooting in the trees, the nighthawks diving with great splashes into the river, the chirping sound of the peepers along the shore. But then, anything good was always made better by having someone to share it with, he thought. It wasn't just *her*.

"I could ride on alone from here, Damien. Thunderbolt isn't that far. I know the way. I could travel the road at night—even blindfolded."

"Don't be silly," he answered. "I've come this far; I'll see it to the end."

He lapsed into pensive silence once more, trying to force his mind away from the lovely firelit image she presented.

He seemed so far away that it made Lavinia nervous. She'd hoped her offer to go on alone might bring a more emphatic reaction from him. She'd hoped a lot of things. But it was beginning to look as if she'd only manufactured a pile of pretty dreams for herself. So he didn't want her! Who cared?

She was about to give up, and tell him that she wasn't hungry and was going to sleep, when he said, "Lavinia, did you really think you might be pregnant after last night?"

She jumped at his unexpected question, then smiled a bit nervously and stared into the fire to avoid his gaze.

"A kiss won't do it, you know." His voice was very gentle.

"There's a lot more to making love . . . and babies. So you needn't be afraid when a man kisses you from now on."

"Is all the rest just as nice?" she asked quietly.

"Oh, much nicer! You'll see one day."

"Will I? I wonder," she answered in a wistful tone.

"A pretty girl like you? Sure you will."

She looked up at him and smiled. He was trying to make up. She could tell. And she was glad. Even if she never saw him again after tomorrow, she didn't want them to part enemies.

"You're very sweet to say that, Damien. But I'm not so sure I'll get my chance. Who knows how long the war will last? All the beaux I had are gone—some killed already. No, the old maid's fate you mentioned may well be what's in store for me." She wiped a tear from her eye. A real one this time, Damien could tell.

He rose and went to her, taking her in his arms gently. "Lavinia, don't start that again. There's really nothing to cry about."

"Oh, Damien," she said, "I'm such a ninny!"

"You're no such thing!" he answered fiercely. "I won't let you talk about yourself that way."

Neither of them knew exactly how it happened, but in another instant their lips met. All the delicious fires of the night before returned in their hot-burning fury. Lavinia shuddered with the impact of his kiss. It was as if all the emotions, good and bad, of the long day went into the passion of their feelings. They clung together, swaying slightly, their bodies warming to each other.

Slowly, never releasing Lavinia's lips, Damien eased toward the blanket he had spread for the night. With slight pressure on her shoulders he maneuvered her down onto the soft bed of pine straws. He felt his desire growing with every passing moment. Lavinia's heart thundered in her breast, beating its tattoo against his own.

With urgent hands he pulled her shirt out and sought the warm flesh beneath. Lavinia quivered and moaned into his open mouth as his fingertips found one naked breast, stroking the nipple until it stood erect and aching with a burning need.

She lay on her back, feeling the world melt around her into a frantic maelstrom of desire. His hands seemed everywhere at once—caressing her face, her throat, her breasts once more. His lips followed the same path down her neck and into the deep V of her unbuttoned shirt. Then he was tugging at the fabric, pulling the last barrier away until the cool night air teased her breasts, causing a new and delicious sensation. She twisted her fingers through his long hair, begging wordlessly for something . . . she wasn't sure what.

Her whole body went rigid when his moist lips closed over the hot tip of her breast, bursting open new floodgates of longing. He sucked her deeply, seeming to draw some silken thread through her body from its innermost parts.

"Damien, *darling*!" she gasped.

He raised his head and found her lips again while one hand strayed down, stroking her quivering thighs and belly through the satiny fabric of her trousers. She felt such a throbbing heat that she thought she might faint. What was he doing to her? How could his touch bring such pleasure and painful yearning all at the same time?

He drew away slightly, staring down into her wide eyes. His own looked hot with desire. There was a need in his gaze that transmitted itself to her. She tried to speak, to reassure him that whatever he wanted would be his, but found that her voice failed her. Then his eyes unfastened from hers and she saw them travel down to her breasts. Never before had a man looked at her body with such naked hunger. She could feel her bare flesh quivering under his searching, longing gaze. Slowly, he bent and touched his mouth to her peaked nipples, first one and then the other. The gentle pressure was like a fiery brand. She arched her back, longing for him to draw her flesh between his moist lips once more. Instead, he raised his head and looked back at her face.

"Lavinia," he whispered, "do you want me to show you the rest?"

Her deliciously jumbled mind snapped back to reality at his words. Her body cried out for her to tell him yes, but she couldn't do that. She had tried to trick him into marriage already. But he had been too smart to be taken so easily. Now he was offering to present her with the very bait for her trap. But no! She loved Damien Clay too much. When and if they married, she had to know that he loved her, too. She would never know for sure if she accepted what he was offering now.

"Lavinia?"

His voice was urgent in her ear, his hands equally urgent on her body. She longed for him, ached for him. But ever so gently she pushed him away.

"Just hold me, Damien. Kiss me."

They fell asleep far into the night, their lips still touching, his warm, gentle hands still cupping her sweetly aching breasts.

Chapter Five

Colonel Rambeau Rutledge jerked suddenly awake and squinted hard at the footpost of the big, carved rosewood bed. Damn! It was still there. Blurred, but right where it had been for the past two nights and a day. He could see it almost plain as day.

"Helen-of-Troy?" he bellowed. "Helen-of-Troy! Goddammit, you lazy no-account wench, move your ass when I call you!"

"I's comin', Colonel!" the huge black housekeeper yelled back from down the hall. "Fast as I can. And ain't gonna do no good, you gettin' foul-mouthed about it. Me and *Arthur Ritis* both got to travel on these two poor old crippled-up legs. I's fast enough, but him, he's slow as molasses in January."

She opened the door to Thunderbolt's master bedroom, filling the wide space with her enormous, white-aproned black bulk.

"What you yellin' about now?" she demanded, her hands on her widespread hips and a disapproving scowl on her round face.

He pointed a shaking finger at the bedpost and his big white felt Sunday-go-to-meeting hat perched at a jaunty angle atop it.

"I can still see it. And till my Lavinia comes home or I'm so drunk I can't see that hat, I'm staying put," he whined. "Bring me another jug. Right now!"

49

"I ain't going to do no such thing, Colonel Rutledge!" Helen-of-Troy stamped her wide, carpet-slippered foot for emphasis. "That moonshine'll rot your innards."

"Well, they're *my* innards!" he yelled back.

Helen-of-Troy, born fifty-eight years before at Thunderbolt, the same year as Rambeau Rutledge—used to his tantrums—sniffed haughtily before she turned to go.

"Wait!" he called. "You can't leave me like this!"

"I'll leave you any way I want! I got a heap of respect for the colonel, but I got none a-tall for a crazy man! You want to drink yourself to death, you go fetch your own poison! Never heard of nothing so dumbheaded in all my life!" she muttered. "Gonna drink hisself blind so's he can't see his hat on the end of the bed, all on account of his darlin' Lavinia done run away. Reckon she'll stay away now that her pappy's lost what little sense he ever had! Don't blame her neither, not one bit! She comes home, Helen-of-Troy is going to say, 'I's powerful sorry, missy, but your old daddy's plumb tetched. Ain't no need you stayin' around here. Might as well go on back wherever you been, you poor baby!' "

"You wouldn't!" he said, raising himself from the bed for the first time in thirty-six inebriated hours.

"Swear to God!" she answered, and he knew she meant it.

"Well, maybe it was a dumb idea," he mumbled, climbing out of bed and pulling on a robe over his wrinkled shirt and drawers. "But, hellfire, what am I supposed to do?"

"You might try bathing, shaving, and pullin' yourself together 'fore she gets home."

Rambeau Rutledge's bloodshot eyes widened. "You reckon she's on her way, Helen-of-Troy?"

She grinned. "Sure as rain." Then she whispered, after glancing left and right, "I done had me a vision, Colonel."

"A vision! Well, by damn, woman, why didn't you tell me?"

She shrugged as if her second sight were a matter of course. "Didn't figure you'd care one way or t'other—you bein' set on drinking yourself blind and all."

"When?" he demanded.

"Oh, three, four this mornin'. Don't rightly remember the exact hour."

"No! When's she coming?"

"Oh, that! Could be anytime," she answered nonchalantly. "But if I was you, I wouldn't waste no more time staring at the dumb old hat."

The colonel danced a jig about the bed, then laughed. "Helen-of-Troy, I could kiss you!"

She backed out of the room, a dark scowl on her face. "Don't you dare!" And she was gone.

There was a different sort of charge in the atmosphere between Lavinia Rutledge and Damien Clay as they rode toward Thunderbolt that morning. Neither of them referred to the night before, even though their thoughts centered on little else.

The handsome captain, his long hair tied back and his shirt opened in a deep V to allow the warm sun on his chest, felt oddly bewildered. Occasionally, he glanced sideways at the calm, smiling woman riding beside him. And she *was* a woman, he'd decided. After last night he would never think of Lavinia Rutledge as a mere girl again. Something about the proud tilt of her chin and the confident way she sat her horse this morning made him feel as if he'd lost some sort of battle. But there had been no hostilities between them last night. Far from it! Short of surrendering entirely to him, she had been totally yielding and loving. She had come into his arms with a warmth and passion he'd never known from another woman. He experienced a throbbing in his loins just thinking about it.

Yet he was glad she had denied him, as much as he had desired her and still did. Had she allowed him to make love to her last night, she would have given him a hollow victory. He would probably have ridden with her as far as Thunderbolt, left her in the safekeeping of her father, and forgotten about her in short order. Now, however, the passionate challenge still existed between them. He had to admit to himself that her very refusal the night before had heightened her appeal. He wanted Lavinia Rutledge and, by God, he would have her come hell or high water.

Lavinia, riding in silence, was aware that Damien kept glancing at her surreptitiously. The day before, his odd expression and silent contemplation would have worried her. But not this morning. She had gained a new confidence in herself. She no longer felt the need to employ tricks and deception in order to assure her future. She felt as if during the night she had passed through some invisible veil that marked the boundary between adolescence and womanhood. The transition made her feel remarkable—capable of accomplishing anything she set out to do.

In fact, the whole world seemed new and fresh to her this morning. The narrow oyster-shell road, which was leading them the last few hundred yards to the entrance of her father's plantation, seemed to glow with a dazzling brightness in the spring sunshine. The wild honeysuckle growing around the oaks at the sides of the road gave off a fragrance sweeter than she'd ever smelled. And the man riding so somberly beside her was like a different person, closer, even dearer to her than he had been before.

"Oh, look, Damien!" she cried suddenly. "There's the house!"

They turned a sharp bend and he saw in the distance a rambling white structure with purple morning glories clinging to trellises along the wide sunswept veranda. A green expanse of lawn lay before it, where a small black boy tended a flock of sheep. The animals moved lazily, cropping the lush grass.

The sudden clanging of a bell told Lavinia that their approach had been noticed.

"That's old Agamemnon announcing our arrival," she said excitedly. "He'll be waiting at the gate for us."

Damien Clay felt suddenly like a fumbling boy. "Perhaps I should let you go on alone from here. I mean, your father's probably not expecting guests. I don't want to put anyone out."

She turned a glowing smile on him and reached out to touch his hand. "Don't be silly, Damien. Papa will want to meet you. And Helen-of-Troy is always ready for company. She'll spoil you half to death; just wait and see."

Damien couldn't deny his pleasure at the invitation. What in hell had gotten into him? he wondered. This time yesterday he'd been trying to get out of seeing her home, and here he was eager to stay for a while. Still, he reasoned, he had made good time so far, and Morgan could survive without him for a few more days.

"You're sure?" he asked her cautiously.

"Of course you'll stay. As long as you like."

Any further discussion was forgotten in the hubbub of noise and activity suddenly swirling about them. A dozen or more small black faces grinned up at them and a pack of spotted hounds yipped and frolicked with the children. Agamemnon, an ancient soul with a woolly cap of white hair, waved his old straw hat toward the house, yelling, "They's here! The baby-chile and her gentleman's come!"

Their progress up the shell drive to the house looked something like a circus parade, Damien thought, with the slave children, dogs, a gaggle of honking geese, some of the sheep, and a noisy assortment of chickens and guineas all falling in line and shouting, barking, bleating, or squawking to announce their arrival. Ahead of them, waiting and waving from the veranda, he saw an enormous black woman and an elegantly clad white-haired gentleman, obviously the patriarch of the Rutledge clan.

Lavinia and Damien were hardly given time to dismount and say hello before the two of them were whisked away to separate rooms by servants to "fresh youselves and dress for dinner," as Helen-of-Troy explained. Damien, feeling as if he were caught up inside a tornado, followed a servant to the room assigned to him, wondering which act would come next in this circus of a family.

Lavinia peeled off her dirty uniform as soon as she entered her peach-and-gold bedroom.

"Lordy, Helen-of-Troy, I hope you've got a bath ready for me!" she exclaimed. "I'm wearing half the sod between here and Augusta."

"Gonna marry him, are you?" the big servant said with a grin. Helen-of-Troy, as always, got straight to the point.

"Maybe," Lavinia answered with a noncommittal smile.

"Don't you go trying to put nothin' over on me, missy. I seen the way he looked at you—like you was one of them fancy pastries and him with a sweet tooth that couldn't wait!"

"Oh, hush up, Helen-of-Troy!" She hugged the servant as she spoke. "Just help me out of these boots and into that tub. I don't want to keep him waiting."

Lavinia scrubbed her skin with violet-scented soap until anything she might have picked up during her short stint in the army was only an unpleasant memory. She washed her short hair several times, letting Helen-of-Troy pour a final rinse of fresh-squeezed lemon juice through it until it was squeaky clean and bright as a new copper penny.

"Is Papa mad at me?" she asked as the servant toweled her gleaming body dry.

"Shoot, honey, that man can't stay mad at you. You know that. Oh, he bellowed like a old bull soon as he found out you was gone. That didn't last long, though. Next come his cryin', whinin' spell. That's the part I hate the most. After that he come up with a plan to drink hisself blind." She shook her tignoned head in awe. "The colonel sure can put it away. I ain't never seen a man could drink so much and still stand on his two feet."

"Oh, that makes me feel awful!" Lavinia cried. "Is he still drinking?"

Helen-of-Troy grinned her wide grin. "Don't you worry about that none. He done drank the still plumb dry, and I told Agamemnon I'd put him out to stud in the wenches' cabin if he whipped up any more of that rot gut. Ain't nothin' scares that old fool like the thought of having to get it up for a woman at his age. Won't be no more moonshine 'round these parts for a while!"

Lavinia giggled, thinking of poor old Agamemnon, who claimed to be a hundred and two years old and the father of seventy-odd children, cringing at Helen-of-Troy's threats. When he'd reached his centennial birthdate, he had announced to them all that he was "swearin' off women." She remembered her brothers howling and slapping their knees at the same time that her papa choked on his bourbon and branch water. She hadn't realized what was so funny at the time, but now she laughed aloud, remembering the scene and the defiant, determined look on Agamemnon's face as he made his announcement. Several of the young servant women had fled from the birthday party in tears.

"Chile, you better quit your dreamin' and get into this dress," Helen-of-Troy scolded. "Them men are going to be waitin' on you."

Damien Clay could hardly believe his eyes. The guest room was actually a suite, with bedroom, study, and a dressing room complete with copper bathtub. The furniture, of the finest and most expertly carved mahogany, gleamed from hand-polishing. The study offered an impressive library of fine leather-bound works. Miraculously, a superb suit of clothes, exactly his size, appeared while he was bathing. Also, for his comfort and enjoyment, wine, cheese, and fruit were placed on the desk by some phantom hand.

So this was plantation life! A far cry from what he'd been used to. Orphaned or deserted at birth—he'd never known which—he had grown up in the back alleys of Huntsville, Alabama, scavenging to keep from starving. At last, in his early teens, he'd had to resort to out-and-out stealing. Lucky for him, he picked the right victim, a wealthy but compassionate man. Where another might have had him jailed or even hanged, Cyrus Clay had taken Damien into his own home and treated him like a son. He even paid to send him off to Transylvania College in Lexington, Kentucky, where Damien had been a classmate of John Hunt Morgan. But even the fine old Clay mansion in the Twickenham section of Huntsville couldn't compare to Thunderbolt Plantation.

And still, there was something of his poverty-stricken youth that clung to him the way the stench of a jail clings to a prisoner. Servants made him nervous. He thanked Colonel Rutledge's valet for his offered help, but asked that he be left alone to dress himself.

As he donned the rich clothes, he felt his thoughts wandering back to Lavinia. He remembered the warm softness of her lips, the welcome swell of her breasts against his chest, the way she used the most delicate touch of her fingertips to arouse him. Smiling into the mirror, he noticed the tiny red marks on his neck where she had nipped him with her teeth sometime during the night. He adjusted his neck scarf to cover her love bites.

"Just wait till our wedding night! I'll do a bit of nipping myself!" he told the face in the mirror.

He stepped back suddenly as if he'd been hit. *What was he saying?* Just when had he decided to *marry* her? Oh, no! That wasn't part of his plan. He meant to have her, yes. But marriage to that hellion was out of the question!

During "dinner," as the noon meal was called at Thunderbolt, Damien could hardly taste his food. Lavinia Rutledge filled all his senses. Never had he seen such a transformation. She was gowned in the palest pink organdy dress, its neckline low enough to give him a delicious glimpse of the snowy slopes he had scaled and clung to so lovingly the night before. Without the bulging Zouave's sash her waist was unbelievably tiny and made to look even narrower by the wide ruffles of her skirt. Somehow her short hair had been miraculously restored to look its full length, smoothed neatly into a chignon adorned by tiny pink roses. She looked as dainty as a china doll, as sweet and lovely as a virgin bride. No one would ever suspect she was Private Vinnie Rutledge.

"Captain Clay, we'd be mighty proud to have you stay on a bit with us," Rambeau Rutledge said, snapping Damien out of his trance.

"That's very kind of you, sir. If you're sure it's no imposition, I'd like to stay—very much."

"Oh, good!" Lavinia said, smiling so brightly that Damien felt a new ache in his groin. "I want to introduce you to my dressmaker."

Colonel Rutledge drew his shaggy white brows together

showing his bafflement. Why in hell would this young man care a tinker's damn about meeting that old nag down in Savannah who charged him a fortune to keep Vinnie in fine feathers? But then, whoever knew what Lavinia was talking about or thinking? He loved her dearly, but, by all the saints in heaven, he sometimes wished she'd been another son. He would never understand women!

The colonel cleared his throat to hide his confusion. "Lavinia, you've had a caller while you were away."

A delighted smile lit her face and Damien Clay realized suddenly that he was frowning.

"Oh, how nice! Who was it, Papa?" she asked.

"Randolph Wentworth. Seems he took a shot in the leg and he's home at Mulberry Hall recovering. Said he'd sure admire seein' you before he has to go back to the war."

"Oh, poor Randy! I hope his wound isn't serious," she cried with more concern in her voice than Damien enjoyed hearing.

"Reckon he'll be using a cane for a time, but he'll recover."

"This Mr. Wentworth is a *good* friend of yours?" Damien could have kicked himself for asking, but the thought of Lavinia with another man sent a twisting snake of jealousy slithering through him.

"My very best friend," Lavinia replied. "Why, the first time he asked me to marry him I was just ten years old. He really is a dear person. I'm so upset that he's been wounded."

Wounded! Damien thought. *I'm the wounded one! Sitting here bleeding from the heart all over the goddamn table!*

"He rode over again this morning just before you got here," the colonel continued. "Helen-of-Troy was so sure you were coming home today that I told him he might drop in again this afternoon. I hope you don't mind, darlin'."

"Mind? Why, I'll be thrilled to see dear Randy again!"

Suddenly, Damien found his frown had vanished. The idea that had just popped into his mind unbidden was absolutely fiendish. Terrible! he told himself. Despicable, malevolent, malicious! He *loved* it!

"Damien," Lavinia said, touching his hand gently across

the table and smiling apologetically, "you won't be offended if I have a caller this afternoon, will you?"

He smiled back and answered, "Not at all, Lavinia. I may just go up and lie down for a while. After the past two nights I really could use some sleep."

Lavinia was still blushing from his reference to their nights in each other's arms when Damien excused himself to go upstairs. She was puzzled by his actions and quite disappointed. She'd hoped the attentions of another man would spark some response in him. He'd seemed to have more on his mind than an afternoon nap, but she couldn't imagine what.

Chapter Six

Damien Clay had a strange, fluttery feeling deep in the pit of his stomach. He always got butterflies before going onstage. It was a good sign. This slight edge of nervousness honed his talents to a fine sharpness and kept his performance at its peak.

He chuckled softly to himself as he hurried up the broad staircase at Thunderbolt and muttered, "Let's face it, old boy, this may be one of the most important performances of your life!"

Earlier, while he was preparing for dinner, he had explored his guest suite, curious as any visitor in a strange place. One ornate armoire was filled with lovely gowns. He guessed that they were available for the convenience of guests who might snag a ruffle during a ball or burst a seam during more strenuous entertainment with the brothers Rutledge. Now he entered his room and headed straight for the large cedar-lined cabinet.

He chose the perfect ensemble—a spring-green dimity with a high neckline and long, sheer sleeves. The covering of light material would hide the slight but very unladylike sunburn he had carelessly acquired earlier in the day.

He shaved again to be on the safe side, then quickly donned petticoats and the other necessary underthings also provided in the armoire. The dress came next. A perfect fit! Stockings stuffed into the bodice gave him an alluring silhouette.

Carefully, with an artist's unfaltering hand, he applied powder, a touch of rouge, and the faintest blush of lip paint. This highlighting erased any rough male edges, leaving in their place the soft fresh glow of a pretty maiden's face. Even to Damien himself the transformation was astonishing. He could quite lose his heart to such an attractive girl.

He smiled at the lovely young woman, whose dark flashing eyes laughed back into his, and went to work creating a suitably becoming hairdo to complete his disguise. Happy with the final results, he dabbed on some honeysuckle toilet water, draped a fine lace shawl about his shoulders, and went to his window to watch.

He didn't have long to wait. A shiny green buggy drove up, its matched bays prancing merrily in the bright afternoon sun. The driver and only occupant wore a spanking new lieutenant's uniform, the brilliant CSA on his belt buckle flashing and buttons gleaming. Damien felt a sudden twinge of envy. Surely even the damned war would be easier to take wearing a sharp-looking uniform instead of calico and lace.

The officer, Randolph Wentworth, eased himself dramatically down from the buggy. Whether out of necessity or for effect, he leaned heavily on a gold-headed cane when his mirror-polished boots touched the ground. He was a tall man with a shock of chestnut-colored hair and a handsome, squarish face.

Damien stiffened as he watched a bright flurry of pink organdy ruffles and outstretched arms rush at the stranger and embrace him with such zest that Wentworth nearly lost his balance.

"Oh, Randy my darling!" Lavinia's words drifted up to the window, causing Damien to growl low in this throat.

"Lavinia, love, where *have* you been?" Wentworth demanded in a tone that reeked of possessiveness.

"No explanations right now, Lieutenant Wentworth! Just you wait till we get you inside. Why, I won't have you standing out here in this broiling sun and you with a near-mortal wound! We've got to take care of our brave boys," Lavinia gushed.

Damien rolled his eyes and murmured, "Deliver me!"

Lavinia, her arm clutching Randolph Wentworth's gold-sash-swathed waist while his draped about her invitingly bare shoulders, led her "brave boy" up the front stairs. The hardest part for Damien came as they vanished from his line of vision. He could hear Lavinia's pleased, flirtatious laugh, but he couldn't see what Lieutenant Wentworth was doing to elicit such delight from the lady. His blood boiled as his imagination went on a rampage.

His big, silver railroad watch in hand, Damien counted off the seconds, allowing Lavinia precisely five minutes alone with Wentworth before he put his plan into action. As the sweep hand inched toward four minutes and fifty-nine seconds, he strode for the door. The moment he opened it he was greeted by more of Lavinia's pretty laughter. He headed for the stairs with more haste than was proper for a lady and all but flattened Helen-of-Troy as she came around a corner with her arms full of linens.

" 'Scuse me, ma'am!" the servant said, then took a second look and gasped.

"My fault entirely," Damien replied, forgetting to disguise his voice to match his appearance.

Helen-of-Troy backed away, her eyes like twin white moons in a night sky. She was shaking, gulping for breath.

"De good Lord have mercy of dis poor old soul!"

Damien reached a gloved hand toward the terrified woman. "Helen-of-Troy, I didn't mean to startle you."

"Don't you come near me! I know who you is . . . *was*! And I ain't never bad-mouthed you like everybody else. Not one word has Helen-of-Troy ever spit out her mouth about Aunt Josie Rutledge! Now you go way and leave me be! You got no cause to haunt me!" She turned and hustled down the hallway in the opposite direction, muttering, "I swear, some haints got no respect for decent folks. Might of knowed, though, if I's to meet a ghost slap in the middle of the afternoon, it'd be old crazy Aunt Josie! Lordy, Lordy, that woman was bats!"

Damien thought about going after Helen-of-Troy and explaining, but he was wasting valuable time. And how would he explain himself anyway? She was probably better off thinking she had seen a ghost than trying to deal with the real truth of the matter. He dismissed the servant from his mind and concentrated solely on the lilting laughter coming from below. Even more distressing now, Lavinia's periods of mirth were punctuated by long, suspicious silences. Damien quickened his slippered step.

He fluttered gracefully into the parlor where Lavinia was entertaining her gentleman friend. The sound of the door opening startled the pair, who quickly put a respectable distance between them on the rosepoint love seat. Lavinia stared, wide-eyed, her lovely, infinitely kissable mouth slightly agape while Randolph Wentworth sized up the intruder with what Damien had come to recognize as instant interest from one of his own sex. The officer stood and bowed, awaiting his introduction to the charming creature poised at the door.

"Oh, Cousin Lavinia, how rude of me!" Damien said in his most seductive voice. "I purely forgot that you had a caller this afternoon."

Lavinia's voice seemed to have exited by the same door that Damien had entered. She could only sit and stare dumbly. Damien, taking full advantage of her uncharacteristic silence, approached Lieutenant Wentworth, gracefully dropping a curtsy. The handsome officer's eyes met those of Damien Clay. He smiled a blatant invitation. Damien fluttered his eyelashes in a practiced manner and cast his gaze down demurely.

"Cousin Lavinia, where *are* your manners, dear?" Damien chided. "You must forgive her, Lieutenant Wentworth. I'm sure she's quite overcome with seeing you again, especially after your dreadful experience. My, you are a brave soldier!"

Wentworth, enchanted by the vision before him, was all clearing of throat and appreciative glances.

"I'm Lavinia's Cousin Ra-bey-ah-ca." Damien masterfully pronounced *Rebecca* in the exaggeratedly drawn-out, four-syllabic manner in which Alabamans spoke the name. "I'm from Huntsville, and it's been ever so long since I visited my cousins here at Thunderbolt."

"Miss Rebecca," Wentworth said in a worshipful voice. "I've always loved that name. It's so . . . so biblical!"

With a smile to break hearts, Damien replied, "Oh, I do quite agree, Lieutenant. Or may I call you Randy?"

"Please!" Wentworth rasped.

Randolph Wentworth had wanted Lavinia Rutledge since before he actually knew what boys wanted girls for. He had been delighted when he found out the intricacies of human mating, for Lavinia seemed to possess all the proper attributes to make such an intimate process the ultimate rapture. Still, there was something very appealing in a different sort of way about Rebecca Rutledge. He couldn't quite put his finger on it, but she seemed worldly and sophisticated at the same time that she was lovely and fresh.

"Won't you sit here with us, Miss Rebecca?" Wentworth offered.

Damien smiled, nodded, and squeezed in between them. He was immediately aware of Lavinia's thigh pressed close to his, though a tidal wave of petticoats separated flesh from flesh. He was even more aware of the angry green flash of her eyes. She hadn't quite recovered from the shock of his appearance yet, but when she did . . .

"Cousin Rebecca, *darling*," Lavinia drawled with murder thinly disguised beneath her words, "I thought you meant to nap after dinner. You know you're exhausted after your trip."

What the hell did Damien Clay think he was doing? She'd hoped Randy's visit would bring about some action from Damien but she'd never expected this! Lavinia was fit to be tied! But damned if she'd let him get away with this. She'd seen a lot of nervy people in her day, but never before had she seen one man go to such outrageous lengths to be rid of another. Damien Clay was actually *flirting* with Randolph Wentworth! And Randy—*blast him*!—was eating it up, falling for every shy smile and flutter of an eyelash! Well, if Captain Damien Clay thought he could outfemale Miss Lavinia Rutledge, he had another think coming!

"Actually, Cousin Lavinia, it wasn't the trip that fatigued me so. I haven't been sleeping well lately—not for the past two nights anyway." As he spoke, Damien Clay slipped an unseen hand under their skirts and squeezed Lavinia's thigh with strong fingers through the fabric of her dress, smiling as he watched a blush creep into her face.

"Really!" Lavinia gasped, but quickly cut off her words. In a calmer tone she went on. "Really, Rebecca, you look like you need some rest. Why, dear, you've got circles under your eyes that go clear down to your *chin!*"

"Lavinia!" Randolph Wentworth objected. "I think you're being most uncharitable toward your cousin. Why, she looks fresh and lovely as a peach blossom to me."

Damien turned an absolutely melting smile on the man. "Thank you, Randy. You're ever so kind to say so."

"Not at all, dear lady," the smiling officer purred. "I'm sure Lavinia's only teasing you."

Oh, God! How much more of this could Lavinia stand? She rolled her wide eyes heavenward, silently pleading for intervention from on high.

Damien turned back to Lavinia and grinned broadly at her, saying, "Oh my, yes, she is a tease, Randy! Why, every now and again I think I'll just go right out of my mind if she goes any further with it! She just gets me so fired-up sometimes with her teasing that I want to jump right on her and tear her pretty clothes off for being so mean."

Wentworth coughed, then cleared his throat, embarrassed suddenly.

"Oh, well, I wouldn't really," Damien replied, crossing his fingers beneath the folds of Lavinia's dress.

"Of course you wouldn't, Miss Rebecca. Not a fine lady of class and breeding like you."

"She's a breed all her own, all right," Lavinia muttered under her breath, her own hand now under the skirts, trying to fend off Damien's playfully arousing attack.

It was no use. Damien Clay simply refused to behave. She would have to try a more direct approach.

Lavinia feigned a sudden attack of dizziness as an excuse to lean her head on Damien's shoulder and hiss into his ear, "Get out of here! Make your excuses and leave us!"

"I wouldn't dream of doing such a thing, Cousin Lavinia! There's your virtue to be thought of!" Damien whispered back in his own husky voice. "We'll just see if your brave lieutenant is up to handling two women at the same time."

"I'll get you for this!"

"You will, indeed," he promised. "Maybe sooner than you'd expected."

"My dear young ladies!" Wentworth said abruptly and in a loud voice as if he'd just been startled out of a trance. "I do hate to leave you both, but I promised Mater I'd be home in time for tea. Some of her lady friends are joining us and you know how mothers are about showing off their lads in uniform. I mustn't disappoint her, much as I'd like to stay to dinner."

Pompous bastard! Damien thought. Who asked you to stay?

"Oh, Randy," Lavinia simpered adorably, "I hate for you to leave so soon! I'd hoped we'd have more time together *alone*." She gave Damien a withering glance.

"Well, there's still the ball at Mulberry coming up." He looked painfully solemn suddenly. "I'll be going back, you know, the very next day."

"So soon?" Lavinia asked, aware once more of Damien's hand exploring her thigh, making her furious but arousing her dangerously at the same time.

"I'm afraid so." Wentworth replied. "But let's not think about that. Let's just concentrate on the ball. I hope you two lovely young ladies will both save me a dance that evening!" He gave them a broad grin that flashed at Lavinia but came to glowing rest on Cousin Rebecca.

Fury boiled through Lavinia Rutledge's blood. Never before had she found herself in such a mystifying position, livid with jealousy over one beau's interest in another. The pure idiocy of the whole situation made her head spin.

"Lavinia dear, are you feeling all right?" Wentworth asked.

She had put a hand to her forehead in the time-honored manner of a delicate lady about to swoon. "I'm really not sure, Randy darling. It must be your mention of going back to that dreadful war."

Randy, all concern now, came to kneel before Lavinia, chafing her wrists to aid her circulation.

"There, there. You mustn't think about that. You poor, poor

dear. I was an oaf even to bring the subject up in front of you, especially with all your brothers away fighting. Forgive me, Lavinia.''

Her eyes were closed, but she let a slit of light in to see where Damien was. She'd felt him rise from the love seat beside her. She spotted him standing next to the kneeling lieutenant.

"Don't worry about Cousin Lavinia, Randy. I'll see her up to her room. I'm sure she only needs to rest a bit," Damien said.

Wentworth rose immediately and bowed to Damien. "You are a dear lady, Miss Rebecca. I'm sure Lavinia couldn't be in better hands.''

Lavinia lapsed into a fit of coughing, but "Cousin Rebecca" kept a straight, concerned face as she replied, "I intend to see that she's well taken care of, Lieutenant. You can count on it!''

Without further ado Lieutenant Randolph Wentworth bade the pair a good afternoon, insisting that he would see himself out.

The silence in the room after he left was nearly deafening. Lavinia still sat on the sofa, her eyes closed and head back, as if she really had fainted. Damien stood for several moments watching her, smiling with the usual satisfaction that always followed a superb performance on his part.

"Well?" he said at length.

It was as if that single word or perhaps its smug delivery in his own voice, not Cousin Rebecca's, lit a spark to set off an explosion. Lavinia fairly flew at him, arms and fists flailing and curses hissing off her tongue. But he easily captured her, pulling her close and subduing her. His lips came down hard, shutting off her colorful flow of words, turning her oaths to sighs.

If Lavinia had thought she might faint before, the threat of swooning was even greater now. He held her in a grip that almost stopped her breathing. It was as if, having been faced with the challenge of another man, he intended to bind her so closely to him that she could never stray again. She found the crushing weight of the embrace comforting and unusually arousing. He was punishing her with his love—almost bruising her arms while he tortured her lips with hot, wet kisses that all but took her breath away. This was different from the two previous nights. Then, he had held her, caressed her, made her ache with a strangely unfamiliar longing. But now his body laid claim to hers, branding her within and without as if he were certain of ownership. She couldn't have fought off his loving aggression if she'd wanted to. With knowing hands and forceful lips he drained away the last ounce of strength she possessed. But it didn't matter. The furthest thing from her mind was to fight him.

"There, my fine lady!" Damien growled. "What do you think of Cousin Rebecca now?"

Lavinia smiled, her moist lips parted and inviting, her eyes closed, as she said in a dreamy voice, "I think she's the cousin I'd most like to share my room with when she comes to visit. But I wouldn't want to have to share my beaux with her. Poor, dear Randy! You had him in quite a state, you know."

His lips were touching hers again, but very lightly so that she felt and tasted as much as heard his whisper. "And you had me in quite a state! I've never been a jealous man, Lavinia. Not until now, that is. I want you! I might even consider marriage if that's the only way I can have you. *Poor, dear Randy* can go find his own woman!"

Lavinia pushed back away from him, staring into his face. Had she heard him correctly? His expression showed no hint of humor. A stern and serious Damien was very visible now beneath Cousin Rebecca's painted façade. But still . . .

"Are you asking me to marry you, Damien Clay?"

"No!" he answered with blunt force. "I'm not asking anything, Lavinia. I'm just telling you that something odd's happened to me. I'm not the same man I was a few days ago. I keep getting crazy, dangerous notions in my head. And you're the one putting them there! There are two things I've never had to resort to to have a woman—rape and marriage. I'm warning you now, Lavinia, that with you I might be tempted into either at the drop of a hat. So you'd better just watch yourself!"

"Well, I never!" she gasped, trying to pull herself free from his embrace, outraged by his words at the same time that his commanding voice and touch reduced her to quivers.

He only caught her closer and whispered warm, moist words into her ear. "Maybe you never have before, but you're going to soon enough, darling."

"Damien . . . oh, Damien," she sighed. She caught his cheeks between her palms and brought his lips down to hers, letting the tip of her tongue tell him with its fluttering motion what she wanted. He responded to her invitation and for a long time they held each other, mesmerized with touching, tasting, feeling. Lavinia Rutledge was learning that each new encounter with Damien Clay brought with it new heights of sensation. And now that she was sure he would be hers—for good and always, sooner or later—she could allow her mind to indulge in all the delicious fantasies about him that she had carefully avoided in the past days.

"Damien," she whispered at last. "Come to my room tonight."

He drew away, wary suddenly of being pursued. It was one thing for him to plan and scheme to have her, but quite another when she offered herself so willingly.

"I'll do no such thing, Lavinia. And I'm surprised you'd suggest it!" He'd planned to suggest it himself. How dare she bring it up before he had the chance! It was damned unladylike of her.

"Well, you want me, don't you? You said so yourself." She paused, but he didn't reply. "I'm only being honest. I want you, too!"

"Good God, Lavinia!" he burst out suddenly. "You should be ashamed of yourself!"

"Why?" she demanded, glaring at him.

"Because . . ." he began, but couldn't finish, realizing that his male beliefs would be impossible to explain to a straight-spoken, free-thinking woman like Lavinia Rutledge. "Just *because*!" he finished lamely.

Now Lavinia's angry blush was of a scarlet hue. She was infuriated by his reaction. "Well, you don't have to get huffy about it, Damien! It's just that I had this *vision*, I suppose you'd call it. That very first night. I imagined how you would look in my . . . my bed," she blurted out. "I just thought maybe it was like Helen-of-Troy's visions and it was supposed to come true." She lowered her eyes and her voice. "I figured if fate was willing it, we ought to cooperate."

He couldn't have laughed at her; she was too dear in her forthright honesty. He did smile, though, just before his lips brushed hers tenderly.

"That does sound nice, darling," he said softly. "Mighty nice indeed!"

"Damien Clay—darn your hide!—I think I'm in love with you!" she said, burying her face against his shoulder. She was fixing to cry. It made her so mad!

Damien put one finger under her chin and raised her face, then leaned down to kiss the tears away. "It's all right to cry once in a while, honey. You don't have to hide it. Not from me."

She sniffed and gave him a fierce look. "I bet I'd make a damn good wife!"

Damien threw back his head and laughed loud and long. "I'll just bet you would, Lavinia Rutledge! And I don't imagine you and your husband would ever know a dull moment, not if you lived together a hundred years."

"*Two* hundred," she answered, and kissed him soundly. "Two hundred and *fifty!*"

His dark eyes took on a dreamy, mesmerizing quality and he drew her close once more, whispering, "Hell, you'd live it all yelling, fighting, scratching, throwing chairs at each other— and the rest of the time you'd be occupied doing this."

All talk and laughter ceased. The room fell still. Only the hum of the spring insects as their isinglass wings fluttered on the balmy air, the mingled small sounds from repeated kisses, and the rapid beat of two hearts marred the perfection of the silence.

Chapter Seven

Rambeau Rutledge spurred his big stallion, Tarnation, and sailed over the split-rail fence that separated the cotton field from the mulberry grove.

"Damn silkworms!" he muttered, shaking a clenched fist at the gnarled mulberry trees, one of his more expensive horticultural mistakes. "Ain't worth your keep, you miserable little bastards!"

His mood was as black as his horse, but unproductive silkworms weren't the main cause of his present agitation. Something mighty suspicious was going on under his very roof, and damned if he'd have it! After all, he was the master of Thunderbolt, and his say was law! He meant to put his foot down *but good* once he figured out what was hatching!

"But, hellfire! I ain't got a notion what's got everything so stirred up," he complained to his galloping steed. "Vinnie acting so galldurned peculiar, prim, and ladylike all the time around that Captain Clay. Always smiling like she was the cat that just lapped up the cream. And Helen-of-Troy seeing Aunt Josie's ghost. Damnation! Last time that happened the crops purely shriveled up in the field. And why in hell hasn't that young buck Wentworth popped the question to Lavinia yet—and him leaving to go back to war in just a couple of days? I swear, it don't make no sense a-tall!"

He headed Tarnation into a narrow trail through a cane

thicket in search of a producing still. Helen-of-Troy might have laid the law down to Agamemnon, but if Rambeau Rutledge was any judge of men—and he prided himself on being one— that old, woolly-headed scamp had a batch brewing somewhere. And he meant to find it. How was a man supposed to puzzle out a problem with a head so damn clear and purified that he couldn't think devious?

Tarnation came to a jolting halt, almost unseating his pixilated rider. "Whoa, boy!" Colonel Rutledge commanded belatedly just in case anyone happened to be nearby. He certainly didn't want people thinking that on top of everything else he'd lost control of his horse, for God's sake!

Horse and rider sat very still. Tarnation, his big head raised to the wind and his flanks quivering, whinnied with nervous excitement. Rambeau Rutledge sniffed at the breeze, trying to catch the malty scent of moonshine, but all he smelled was warm manure from the fields, the hot horseflesh under him, and the pervading aroma of river mud.

"What is it, boy? You sniffed one out? Hot dang! You're better than a divining rod for turning up firewater. Go to it!"

Rutledge let the horse have his head. Tarnation turned toward the river and plodded slowly, still testing the air with flared nostrils. After a short time they crashed out of the cane brake into a field of scrub palmetto and broom grass. Colonel Rutledge could feel his mouth getting drier by the minute, just thinking about that still bubbling away nearby.

"Come on, Tarnation. Find it, boy!"

The horse was still trying to make up his mind whether to head north or south when Rambeau Rutledge spotted two people in the distance. He forgot all about his parched throat and the imagined still waiting for him.

"*Tarnation!*" Rutledge swore. His horse neighed in response, assuming he was being addressed. "Well, if that don't beat all!"

The two figures he was watching had at first appeared to be one, so closely had they been clinging to each other there in a copse of spicy bay trees some distance away. But now he could see clearly that there were two of them—a man and a woman.

Then as he continued to watch, they merged into one again, kissing each other in a manner he'd never witnessed before outside one of those sporting houses up to Savannah. Certainly, he'd never kissed his Lyda Beth that way. Why, it would have been downright shameful! His wife had been a decent, God-fearing woman, not given to venery in any form unless out of absolute necessity to procreate.

Even while the sight of the passionate pair repulsed him intellectually and spiritually, his baser instincts responded with an accelerated heartbeat and a downward pulsing of blood. He strained his eyes to identify the couple, but the shadows in the grove were too deep for him to see their faces. Figuring it must be the sharecropper's daughter, and, having heard interesting tales about her, Rambeau Rutledge settled back to watch. What he saw made sitting a horse damned uncomfortable, and that swelling discomfort brought with it a new wave of thirst.

He wondered suddenly if the Widow Wentworth over at Mulberry might have a drop of something to wet his whistle. And while he was there, maybe the two of them could . . .

"Stop it, you old fool!" he growled at himself.

Still, his mind lingered for a bit on Randolph Wentworth's comely mother. She wasn't a bad-looking lady—a full head of mahogany-colored hair, a nice cushiony figure, "And all her teeth still her own, I'd be willing to bet!" he added out loud. She'd been alone these past ten years and he'd been without the right kind of woman for nigh onto twenty. They weren't getting any younger. He'd soon see sixty, God willing, and he calculated her age at near forty. It made sense that the two of them should comfort each other in their declining years.

He was nodding his head, agreeing with himself, when he thought of his plans and dreams for Lavinia. Sudden resolve gripped him. He was, indeed, an old fool! How would Vinnie take it if he and Sara Wentworth got into the thick of it? No, sir! It wouldn't work! Only one match could be made between the Wentworth and Rutledge clans, and he meant for that to be between young Randolph and his Lavinia!

He was about to turn Tarnation back toward the house when the couple in the bay trees broke their prolonged embrace and stepped together, hand in hand, into a pool of bright morning sun. Rambeau Rutledge's jaw went slack, his chin drooping down so low that his white goatee brushed his shirtfront.

"Saints and little fishes!" he swore. "The fornicating son-uvabitch!" He shook a fist at heaven and raged. "This is all your fault, Josie Rutledge! You come sneaking around and there's trouble every time." It struck him suddenly that his long-dead younger sister with her loose morals and peculiar ways probably wouldn't be found among the heavenly hosts. So for good measure he shook his fist in the other direction. "*My* Vinnie! My dear, sweet Vinnie. And you, you *scarlet woman*, had to come back around haunting to corrupt her!"

Lavinia could only just barely imagine what it would be like to be married to Damien Clay, but with every hour that passed she wanted it more and more. She clung to him, there in the bay grove, feeling her very spirit tingle as he kissed her for so long and so deeply that she thought going to heaven in a fiery chariot couldn't feel a bit better.

"Lavinia," he whispered, still keeping his lips close to hers, "I don't like having to sneak off to the woods to be with you."

She was too giddy with the taste and feel of the man she loved to make much sense out of anything. Nuzzling his ear with her lips, she sighed, "You could always dress up like Cousin Rebecca and come sleep in my room."

He gave a frustrated snort and answered, "I don't think either of us would get much sleep. But then, I haven't been getting much anyway. All I do is lie awake at night thinking about you down the hall. God help me, I almost sneaked down there and slipped in with you last night."

"Hm-m-m," she purred, letting her long fingers knead his hips, "that sounds wonderful. Why didn't you?"

Damien held her away at arm's length and shook her slightly. "Lavinia, you're playing with fire, I warn you! I'm not a man to go wanting. And I've never wanted anything in my life as much as I want you."

She smiled to herself and pressed closer to him, fanning the very flames he warned her of. He had yet to say he loved her

. . . only that he *wanted* her. And marriage was a subject they only joked about, although she was dead serious. She'd about decided the only way she was going to get Damien Clay was to force him into making her surrender. Not too willingly, of course.

"*Lavinia*!" he cried as he felt her nails dig into his sides, sending mild pain and a fresh wave of dangerous desire through him. "I'm not a saint! If you keep this up, I can't be held responsible for my actions."

"Oh, Damien," she whispered against his neck, "don't be such a tease. I know you'd never harm me."

Her fingers crept beneath his shirt, up his sides, then to the front of his chest. Damien went rigid, sweat pouring down his face as she stroked him with a light and agonizing touch.

"*Me?* Harm *you*?" He gave a choking laugh as his jaw muscles tightened with strain. "Never! Why, everyone knows that I am strong, handsome . . ." She was counting his ribs. He was gasping. ". . . loyal . . ." She ran a nail down the center of his chest. He shivered. ". . . kind . . ." She pinched his paps and he cried out, "*Trustworthy*!"

Lavinia giggled. "And you make a damn fine-looking woman, to boot!"

"You little witch!" he growled, forcing her teasing hands from his chest and pulling her into his arms none too gently. "Let's see how you like being tortured!" In one swift movement he undid her bodice. Freeing her breasts, he taunted her nipples as she had his.

Lavinia gave a little cry of surprise and pleasure and closed her eyes. Leaning back against his arm, she let her breasts strain upward as if daring his bold hand to try to conquer her. But instead of punishing her as he had been punished, Damien lightened his touch. Slowly, barely brushing her flesh, he drew phantom circles around her nipple, setting up shock waves of sensation coursing through her whole body. She moaned softly.

He bent and touched his lips to hers ever so tenderly. She quickly encircled his neck with her arms, deepening their kiss. She could feel the heat of their bodies mingling. She was aware of a strange pulse throbbing against her thigh. He cupped her buttocks, raising her to him.

"Oh, Lavinia! I need you so!" His voice was a warm, moist echo in her ear. She felt his words in the deepest part of her.

"I want you *now*, my darling!" he whispered hoarsely.

Feeling his hands kneading her flesh, tempting her nipples to aching erections, Lavinia was lost in a strange and aphrodisian world. She was weak with need, hot with longing. She might well have given herself to Damien Clay then and there. Lord knows, she wanted to! But the sight of the horse and rider off in the distance stopped her cold.

"Damien, no!" Lavinia said, pushing his lips away and buttoning her blouse in a panic.

"He can't see us," Damien protested.

But the spell was broken by the intruder. Lavinia felt as if the whole world were suddenly staring at them. She was embarrassed beyond words. Though she could still feel the tingle of Damien's fingers and lips caressing her flesh, she shyly took his hand and led the way out of the copse. He was right. She was, indeed, playing with fire. She had decisions to make and they must be made soon. Damien Clay wouldn't stay at Thunderbolt forever. Nor would he be put off much longer.

"We have to talk, Lavinia," Damien said firmly.

"I know." She couldn't bring herself to look at him. "But, please, not right now."

"You aren't nervous, are you?"

She laughed. "Nervous? Who? Me?"

Damien didn't press her. The time they'd just spent together had affected him deeply. If he had a lick of sense, he'd go back to the house, pack his bags, and take off. But he knew he wouldn't. There was something about Lavinia Rutledge. If he left right now, he'd be cussing himself for the rest of his life. He'd always wonder what it would have been like with her. But *damnation*! It scared the pants off him the way the thought of marrying her kept creeping into his mind.

* * *

Colonel Rutledge, his fine-boned face bright crimson with rage, stormed the veranda of Thunderbolt with a fury he hadn't exhibited since the battle of Buena Vista in Mexico.

"Helen-of-Troy!" he bellowed, slamming through the front door. "Dammit! Where are you, woman?"

Muttering under her breath, the obese housekeeper moved from the pantry at the back of the house through the dogtrot to the front hall with all the slow, stately grace a woman of her size could manage. She was determined to be neither hurried nor harried this morning. If the colonel was set on bursting a blood vessel over some trifling annoyance, that was his privilege. But Helen-of-Troy had no intention of getting her finely preened feathers ruffled on such a glorious spring day.

"You called?" she asked in a maddeningly calm voice.

"Damn right, I called!" He was yelling, though she stood not three feet away from him in the cool, quiet entrance hall. "Do you know what I just saw? Well, *do you*?"

Helen-of-Troy took a step back to avoid being struck by his wildly gesticulating hands. "You going to wake the dead, Colonel! Now how in the ever lovin' would I know what you just seen?"

"You always know *everything*!" he answered sarcastically. "You're always having visions! Seeing ghosts!"

His last statement succeeded in shaking her determined calm. "Oh, Colonel, you ain't run into Aunt Josie's ghost too?"

He shook his head and answered, "Might as well have. I just saw some of her devilment." He squinted a suspicious eye at his housekeeper. "Have you seen her again?"

"Well . . ." Helen-of-Troy twisted her spanking white apron in nervous hands, not wanting to answer.

"Well?"

"I ain't sure, Colonel. It was her, right enough, that I ran slap into the other afternoon up in the hall, but I only *suspect* I may have seen her later."

"Hell's fiery caldrons, woman! Either you saw her again or you didn't. Which is it?"

"Well, I reckon I did! It was just for an instant. She went

scooting into Captain Clay's room later that same day. But I only caught a glimpse . . . couldn't be sure my old eyes weren't playing tricks on me.''

Colonel Rutledge groaned and slapped his forehead with the heel of his hand. "Lord, help us all!" he moaned. "That explains it!"

"Explains *what*?" Helen-of-Troy demanded.

"I just saw Captain Clay playing fast and loose with our Vinnie down in the bay grove. I was ready to take my shotgun to him. But if Aunt Josie's ghost was messing around in his room, I reckon he can't be faulted for his actions. She's put a conjure on the poor man for sure.''

Helen-of-Troy, her eyes saucerlike, made a sign to ward off evil spirits, but she had a feeling it was too late. She'd been determined not to let Colonel Rutledge spoil her lovely day, but she hadn't bargained on more mischief from Aunt Josie's ghost. Suddenly, the bright sunshine seemed to fade and the spring flowers festooning the garden lost some of their glorious riot of color.

"What we going to do, Colonel?" she whispered.

"I'll have to talk to him, explain everything. It's plain he's not in his right head. Still in all, I can't allow what's been going on to continue. No sir! I won't have it!"

Lavinia and Damien appeared at the front door at that very moment. Lavinia wondered as she came in and kissed her papa on the cheek if she'd missed a button on her blouse or if he could tell by the flush on her cheeks what she'd been up to. Both her father and Helen-of-Troy gazed at her so oddly.

"Morning, you two!" she said with a forced smile. "My, my, both of you look as if you've seen a ghost!"

Helen-of-Troy threw up her hands, rolled her eyes, and muttered something Lavinia didn't catch as she hurried off down the hall.

"Papa, what *is* going on?" Lavinia insisted.

"Never you mind, daughter. You just go on up to your room. Me and Captain Clay have some talking to do—*alone*!"

Lavinia cast an uncertain glance at Damien. He was frowning, but he said, "Go on, Lavinia. Do as your father says."

She hated to leave them alone. No telling what her papa was up to. But somehow, with the warmth of her lover's kisses still tingling her lips, she knew he could handle anything that came up. Damien Clay, in her opinion, could move mountains, win battles single-handed, and even change winter to summer, she was sure! So why should she worry that he couldn't deal with whatever was bothering her papa?

"Come into the library, son."

Damien felt a nervous prickling along his spine. Something was up! Maybe the old man had guessed that he and Lavinia were more than casual acquaintances and was about to lay down the law to him. Then again, maybe the colonel had invited him in to have a friendly sherry and a man-to-man talk. No, that wasn't it. Some flicker deep in Colonel Rutledge's eyes told Damien he was about to catch hell.

The library was a man's room with its hand-hewn cypress paneling, plantation desk, and leather-bound volumes. The trophies on the walls—deer, wild boar, and assorted fish and fowl—attested to the proficiency of the Rutledge clan with bow and arrow and rod as well as rifle.

"Have a seat, Captain Clay," the colonel offered, indicating a large, overstuffed leather couch. "Can I pour you a pony of bourbon?"

Damien, not a man to drink in the morning, started to decline. But when he saw that Colonel Rutledge was fixing one for himself, he decided he'd better accept, just to be sociable.

The colonel paced the room for some moments in silence. He seemed to be grappling for the proper words. Finally, he turned, his face solemn and lined with worry. Damien was confused by his expression.

"Dammit, Clay, this is a hard subject to get into! Lavinia's the only daughter I've got, and I promised her dear mother I'd do right by her. I just can't have strangers coming in here and tampering with her affections!"

"Please, sir," Damien interrupted, "I don't think Lavinia considers me a stranger. And I've hardly 'tampered,' as you say."

The colonel waved a silencing hand. "Don't interrupt me

when I'm sailing under a full head of steam, boy! You see, it's like this. There's a sort of understanding between me and Randolph Wentworth. He's done right by my Vinnie all these years—stayed clear of other women, shunned the bottle, learned the plantation business top to bottom. He would have made her a fine husband. Yes, indeed! But now . . ."

All of a sudden Damien Clay remembered the rider they'd seen from the grove, and he got the colonel's drift all right. Colonel Rutledge had been spying on them this morning, the old scoundrel!

Damien felt his collar choking him and ran a finger inside to loosen it. The conversation was proving even more difficult than he'd anticipated. He eyed the shotgun over the fireplace, expecting Colonel Rutledge to reach for it and send for a parson all in one move. If, in a weak moment, he decided to marry Lavinia on his own that was one thing. But *damned* if he'd be forced into it!

"According to my last will and testament, my boys inherit Thunderbolt after I'm gone. People might look askance at me if I left a part of it to Lavinia, her being a girl and all. But by marrying Wentworth she'd come into plenty of land. He's the only child, so all of Mulberry will go to him and his wife and heirs." The colonel paused and downed the rest of his drink. "Yep! I had her future all set till you came along!"

"But, Colonel, I really don't see what difference my coming has made. As for Lavinia marrying Wentworth, I'd say that's her decision to make."

Colonel Rutledge turned suddenly and leveled a hard, piercing stare at Damien, ignoring his words completely. He sank into a chair as if the weight of the world were forcing him down. "Only one thing could mess up my plans for my daughter. And it appears to me that you've been doing your damnedest to accomplish it, Captain! Vinnie's a *good girl*! I mean to keep her that way till she's wed legal and proper! Are you getting my drift?"

Damien rose to his feet, giving him a visual advantage over the seated man. When he spoke, his voice boomed with authority. "Colonel Rutledge, your daughter, as far as I know, hasn't any present plans to marry Lieutenant Wentworth or anyone else. I'm very fond of Lavinia, as you may have guessed. If I had more time to stay and court her in the proper fashion, I might one day be asking for her hand. But I only have a few days, not long enough for either of us to make a sensible decision in the matter of marriage. If I come through this war in one piece, and if Lavinia isn't married by that time, I plan to come back here and try to win her.''

Damien paused, dumbstruck. Just when had he made that decision?

The man offered him a cold, offended stare. ''You young folks nowadays!'' he snorted. ''Stubborn, bull-headed, got to decide everything for your own selves! It wasn't that way when I married Lavinia's mother, I can tell you!''

''But times change, sir, and people must change with them.''

Damien steeled himself for the colonel's explosion, but it never came. Instead the older man said quietly, ''You don't know what you're saying, lad. She got to you, just like Helen-of-Troy said.''

''On that point, sir, we do agree. She got to me the first time I laid eyes on her. Any man would be affected by her charms.''

''I knew I was right,'' the colonel said, frowning. ''This is all Aunt Josie's doing!''

Damien stared in silence. He wasn't sure how or when, but somewhere along the way he had lost control of this conversation. He had no idea what Colonel Rutledge was talking about now.

''Beg pardon, sir? Who's Aunt Josie?''

Lavinia had gone upstairs, determined to wait it out while the men talked below in the library. But the more she paced, the smaller her room seemed to become. She felt like a caged animal. She couldn't sit still. She couldn't lie down. *What* were they saying? *When* would she know?

She went to her open window, hoping that their voices would carry up to her on the hot breeze. But the only sounds were the mockingbirds on the lawn below and the hum of bees gathering pollen from the flowers on the trellis.

As she stood, straining her ears, she realized suddenly that the warm morning had turned into sultry noontime. Even the hot wind dropped. The whole world seemed to be left sweltering in the stillness. Perspiration made little tickling rivers down her sides and between her breasts. She decided a cool rinse-off and a fresh frock would help her feelings tremendously. And maybe by the time she was bathed and dressed, her father and Damien would be finished. So resolved, she rang for Helen-of-Troy.

The big servant still wore a solemn face as she bustled into the room, huffing under the weight of the water pail.

"Helen-of-Troy, I declare, you look sour as an old pickle! What's ailing you?"

"Never you mind," the woman answered, pouring the fresh spring water into the porcelain pitcher and the gold-rimmed bowl.

"Don't you 'never mind' me! I know when something's amiss around here." Lavinia stripped out of her rumpled blouse and cooled her breasts with a damp cloth. "What's Papa so eager to talk to Damien about?"

The servant remained grim-faced and silent.

"You don't approve of Captain Clay, do you?"

"Ain't up to me one way or t'other. But whatever Aunt Josie's got a hand in is powerful apt to go wrong and that's a fact!"

Lavinia had finished washing and was slipping into a cool muslin dress sprigged with tiny lavender flowers. "Oh, my Lord! Don't tell me you and Papa have been seeing ghosts again!" Her laugh brought a dark scowl from Helen-of-Troy.

"Ain't nothing to be laughing at, missy! You know what happened last time she come poking around here."

Lavinia uttered a weary sigh and said, "There was a drought that year, for heaven's sake! *Everyone* lost their crops. We weren't the only ones, and poor Aunt Josie certainly had nothing to do with it!"

"*Poor* Aunt Josie, my hind foot!"

Lavinia turned an accusing look on her servant. "You *aren't* about to speak ill of the dead, I hope!"

"Nary a word!" Helen-of-Troy answered quickly, then muttered under her breath, "But I can think as ill as I like!"

Lavinia sat at her vanity, pulling her silver brush through her hair with angry strokes. "There are no such things as ghosts, but even if there were, what does Aunt Josie have to do with the way I feel about Damien Clay?"

"She's put a conjure on him, that's what. And me and your papa both know it! We can't have a man that's not in his right mind courtin' you, honey. The colonel's down there putting things straight with Captain Clay right this minute. No, siree! Ain't gonna have no man that's been tetched by a spirit foolin' with my lamb!"

Lavinia whirled from the mirror. "*What!* You mean Papa's down there telling Damien to leave because of some asinine notion about Aunt Josie's ghost? Well, we'll just see about that!"

She was out of the room and halfway down the stairs before Helen-of-Troy could react. The servant ran after her, shouting, "Miss Vinnie, honey, you come back here!" But it was no use. Lavinia's mind was made up. She would put an end, once and for all, to all this nonsense about ghosts!

Sure enough, when she reached the door to the library, the first words she heard were "Aunt Josie." She flung the door wide, confronting the two surprised men with a determined jut to her chin and a flash of angry green fire in her eyes.

"Vinnie dear, what are you doing here?" her father asked. "This is man talk. No place for a girl."

"I'm *not* a girl, Papa. I am a woman! And since Aunt Josie is included in your discussion, I see no reason why I shouldn't be!"

"*Lavinia*," the colonel said in a warning tone.

She ignored him and turned to a confused-looking Damien, demanding, "Just what has he been telling you?"

Damien gave her a half smile, taking in her fresh-scrubbed skin, tumbled hair, and unslippered feet in one desirous glance. "Frankly, I'm not sure."

She marched over to where her father sat and stood before

him, hands on her hips and one bare foot tapping angrily. "There are no ghosts at Thunderbolt, Papa! And, quite frankly, *if* there were such things as ghosts, and *if* Aunt Josie decided she wanted to leave her grave and go traipsing about the countryside, I imagine that Thunderbolt would be the *last* place she'd want to visit! She wasn't treated very kindly here, from what I've heard."

The colonel drew himself up, determined as his daughter. Damien Clay marveled at the sight of their faces, so alike in battle with their stubborn jaws, angrily blazing cheeks, and flashing eyes.

"I'll have you know, young lady, that Helen-of-Troy ran slap into her in the hallway upstairs the day Randolph Wentworth came calling! And later she saw her going into Captain Clay's room, bent on mischief!"

Suddenly, all the pieces fell into place for Damien. He didn't know who Aunt Josie was, but he did remember Helen-of-Troy's mutterings during their encounter in the hallway. It wasn't any wandering spirit Helen-of-Troy ran into! He chuckled to himself, thinking that he must have used too much rice powder on his face if he'd looked pale as a ghost.

Lavinia and her father were still snapping at each other, exchanging verbal jabs, when Damien broke in. "Please, I think I can explain all of this."

Throughout Damien's explanation of how and why he sometimes dressed as a woman, Colonel Rutledge's expression vacillated between relief and astonishment. The old soldier's eyes went wide with interest when Clay detailed John Hunt Morgan's daring raid of Lebanon, Kentucky, in January, and how they had destroyed Yankee supplies, whipped the Federal-held town to a panic, then donned confiscated blue coats for their daring dash southward through enemy lines back to safety, bringing along prisoners for good measure.

Colonel Rutledge, caught up in the excitement of the tale, slapped his knee, his face beaming, and said, "John Hunt Morgan! I knew him when he was still wet behind the ears. Tall, good-looking lad, with sandy hair and a smile that broke the ladies' hearts. We saw action together at Buena Vista in the Mexican War. Damn fine soldier!''

Lavinia had taken a seat near Damien. She was smiling, too. What a marvel this man was! He'd taken her angry, superstitious, disgruntled father and turned him into a sweet-tempered ally in only a matter of minutes. She could have yelled her head off all day and it would have been like arguing with a fence post. She never had been able to get around her papa once they got head-to-head on something. But Damien knew just what to say. She looked up at him with love fairly brimming in her eyes. They were going to have a fine marriage!

"Papa, I'm glad you and Damien get on so well. That'll make it all the easier for you to say yes when he gets around to asking for my hand." Lavinia hadn't meant to blurt it out; she'd meant to let Damien bring the subject up of course. Still, time was running short. She could feel it slipping away while Damien fooled around, balking at the harness like an old mule.

Both men stared at her in shocked silence. Damien drew slightly away. What was Lavinia saying?

When Colonel Rutledge finally spoke, his words came like cannon shot—unexpected and point-blank.

"I'm sorry. My answer will be *no*!''

Damien breathed his relief.

"No?" Lavinia cried, jumping out of her chair. "What do you mean, *no*?''

"Lavinia!" Damien said, catching at her hand. He felt suddenly like a fox with his leg in a trap. "I don't know what's going on here, but I think I deserve some say in the matter.''

She was near tears, panicked because she knew she'd made a tactical error. Of course, Damien had a say in this. He had the only say. What did she think she was doing, announcing that he was going to ask her to marry him? A move like that could scare off the most eager suitor. And her hold on Damien Clay was tenuous at best.

Damien, meanwhile, was squirming in discomfort. He was about to voice his objection to this entire discussion and insist that he'd better be going—back to Tennessee—when the colonel said, "You asked about Aunt Josie, son." Rambeau Rutledge cast a penetrating glance at his daughter. "It's time you knew the whole truth as well, Lavinia."

Both Damien and Lavinia forgot all else for the moment. They sat silently, side by side, giving the colonel their full attention.

"Aunt Josie, my younger sister, tried to take you away from me, Lavinia, when you were no more than a baby!"

Lavinia gasped softly. She didn't remember Aunt Josie. She'd always thought of her as a rather pathetic character, the misunderstood black sheep of the family. She had no idea the woman had been a kidnapper.

"Josie was high-strung and capricious, never happy with what she had. When she was about your age, Vinnie, she ran off with our daddy's overseer. Oh, it was a terrible scandal! Word had it he left her in one of *those* houses up to Savannah." Colonel Rutledge cleared his throat, embarrassed to be mentioning such a thing in front of his daughter. "Then about the time your mother was coming due with you, we got a letter from Josie. Said she was sick and destitute. My Lyda Beth, God rest her soul, was a good and tender-hearted woman. I wasn't for allowing Josie back on the place—sister or no. But Lyda Beth wrote to her and told her she could come home. Well, Josie showed up a few days later, bag and baggage. The only sickness she had, though, came on her every morning, if you get my meaning."

"You mean I've got a cousin I don't know about?" Lavinia asked.

The colonel shook his head and said, "Let me finish, child. My Lyda Beth worked herself into her grave waiting hand and foot on Josie. But Josie gave birth to a stillborn son just a day before Lyda Beth's accouchement. But by that time Lyda Beth's strength was gone. She gave birth to you, Lavinia, and then she passed on." The colonel stopped for a moment to wipe his eyes and blow his nose. His voice was a gravelly whisper when he continued. "With her dying breath my Lyda Beth asked me to let Josie stay on and take care of you. I promised her I would. It was the only thing I could do to ease her passing."

Damien could feel the tension radiating out of Lavinia's body. He felt for her. He knew what it was not to remember one's mother.

The colonel shook his head sadly. "Josie was *bad* to the core. Twice, honey, she took you off. I was frantic till I found you. Josie hated me for bringing you back to Thunderbolt. I told her to go on her way finally, but she refused, said you were *her* baby, that Lyda Beth's was the one that had died. She got crazier and crazier.

"Then I got real sick, a mighty peculiar ailment. If it hadn't of been for Helen-of-Troy, I wouldn't be sitting here today. She recognized the signs and knew what was ailing me. Seems somebody'd put a conjure on me—a death wish. Now, folks can laugh all they like about black magic, but I've been through it. I know! Helen-of-Troy not only suspected; she *proved* that Josie was the one doing it. Josie was meeting back in the woods with a bunch of Satan worshippers and taking you! Helen-of-Troy caught them red-handed. And lucky for me, she knew what to do to counteract the spell.

"Soon as I could put my feet on the floor again, I figured on running Josie off the place for good. But I never got the chance. Mary Lou Satterfield, whose family had owned Oak Harbor plantation, caught Josie in her own bed with her husband and blew the both of them to Kingdom Come! Then the poor woman turned the gun on herself." Colonel Rutledge sighed wearily.

"So you see, honey," he continued, "even if that wasn't Aunt Josie's ghost we saw *this* time, she's still about the place and up to her mean tricks. How am I supposed to know what crazy notions she might be putting into your head?"

"I'm sorry for all your troubles, Colonel," Damien said. "It's truly a sad tale. But I think Lavinia is about as normal and red-blooded a woman as I've ever met. I see your point. You think Aunt Josie might have cast some sort of black magic over Lavinia. But I think you're wrong. I'd marry her in a minute. . . ."

Lavinia never let him add his intended qualifier to the statement. "Damien!" she cried, throwing her arms around his neck. "Oh, Damien! We'll announce our engagement at the ball!"

"Well, if you're sure, son, and Lavinia's willing," Colonel Rutledge said with a broad smile.

What could Damien do? Even Aunt Josie's ghost couldn't help him out of this one. He kept his silence and let Lavinia go on kissing him and telling him how much she loved him. There was no way out . . . *at the moment*!

Chapter Eight

Lavinia took special pains with her appearance the following day. Helen-of-Troy had prepared a concoction of grated horse-radish and sour milk. Every two hours all day the servant applied this preparation to Lavinia's face, muttering bitterly as she tried to remove the faint hint of freckles sprinkled across her mistress's nose and cheeks. Lavinia's hair was washed in frothy egg whites and allowed to dry stiff before being thoroughly rinsed with rum and rosewater. She had had doubts all her life that Helen-of-Troy's home beauty treatments really worked, but she endured it all in happy silence, willing to go to any lengths to make herself irresistible to the man she loved.

"Which do you think, Helen-of-Troy?" Lavinia asked as the hour of the Wentworths' ball neared. "Should I wear the ashes-of-roses silk or the emerald crepe de Paris?"

Helen-of-Troy stood back, her face one broad smile and her eyes sparkling appreciatively at her young mistress. "Don't much matter, Miss Vinnie. Ain't a soul at that fancy ball gonna notice what you wearing. They gonna be looking at your face! I declare, I never seen one glow like yours tonight. That Captain Clay must be some kind of man."

"That he is, Helen-of-Troy! And he's about to be *my* man for good and always!"

Lavinia held up one gown and then the other, trying to decide. The ashes of roses gave her face a pleasing, reflected blush, but she chose the richer, more provocative emerald gown. The deep color made her skin look pale and delicate as ivory and brought out the verdant hue of her eyes. The bodice dipped low, showing a charming shadow of cleavage between her ripe breasts. Below her nipped-in waist the skirt billowed like an expanse of storm-tossed sea. Gold lace gleamed at her shoulders and spiraled into glittering medallions low on the skirt. These medallions were repeated in a miniature pattern on her white silk stockings and matched the gold kid dancing slippers that replaced her army boots of a few days before. The final touch, a gold lace fan, and she was ready for the ball.

"Lordy, Miss Vinnie, if you ain't a sight!" Helen-of-Troy enthused. "That Captain Clay is purely going to swoon when he lays eyes on you!"

But it was Lavinia who felt near swooning when she reached the parlor where the colonel and Damien were waiting to escort her to Mulberry Hall. Her captain had spared no effort in preparing himself for their special evening. He presented a princely vision like none she had seen before in his dress uniform. The bluegrass green of his coat and britches matched the emerald color of her gown. And the gold lace trim she wore was repeated in the shining epaulets at his shoulders and the double row of brass buttons on his blouse. Knee-high cavalry boots, polished to a mirror finish, and a rakishly plumed felt hat completed the uniform of the former Lexington Rifles, now the Second Kentucky Cavalry—Morgan's Raiders.

For some moments the two of them stood motionless, as if frozen in a tableau. Only their eyes moved, acknowledging their appreciation and desire for each other. Slowly, Damien raised his hand to Lavinia. She placed her fingers in the warm hollow of his palm. He squeezed gently and she felt the pressure all the way to her heart. Nothing . . . *nothing* could spoil the enchantment of this evening! She had waited all her life to know this feeling. And now that her heart was singing and her blood pulsing with excitement, she would hold on to these sensations—and to this man—as if for life itself.

Had Lavinia been able to read Damien's thoughts through his smoldering brown eyes, she might not have been so light of

heart. Having given the matter of their "engagement" some
thought the night before, Captain Clay had decided to do the
only gentlemanly thing to his way of thinking. He would attend
the ball, let Lavinia announce their coming marriage, then ride
off into the thick of the war, never to be seen or heard of
again—presumably lost on some bloody battlefield. It was his
only honorable course of action. He could not disgrace Lavinia
by refusing to allow her to make her announcement. He really
did care for her and he didn't want to see her hurt. But on the
other hand, he was his own man, and not even this most desirable lady was going to trap him before his mind was made up.
So, under the existing circumstances, he thought it prudent to
spend one last, innocent evening with Lavinia Rutledge and
then say good-bye . . . *forever*!

The colonel cleared his throat to remind them that he was
still in the room. "Ajax is bringing the carriage around now.
Shall we go?"

"Yes," Lavinia and Damien answered as one. But they remained locked in each other's gazes, neither seeming inclined
to make a move.

"Lavinia dear, I don't think I've ever seen you looking lovelier," Colonel Rutledge said. "Don't you agree, Captain?"

Damien tucked Lavinia's hand possessively into the crook of
his arm and smiled down at her. He did, indeed, agree. He
would have a hard time, as delicious as she looked tonight,
keeping his resolve to leave her a virgin when he went away.

He warmed Lavinia's heart anew when he replied, "I've
never seen any woman look lovelier, Colonel. Either I'm truly
the luckiest man on earth or this is a dream and I'm going to
wake up shortly and be sorely disappointed."

Lavinia leaned close, feeling Damien's warm breath against
her cheek, and whispered, "This is no dream, darling. And I
promise never to disappoint you."

The glow from Mulberry Hall could be seen a mile away
through the forest of moss-draped oaks that surrounded the old
Wentworth plantation. Candlelight gleamed from within while
bonfires in the slave quarters turned the moonless spring night

into silvery twilight. The incessant March winds had turned hot, in anticipation of the approach of April, and sweet with the season's profuse flowering. Occasionally, a bird trilled softly with its final sleepy tribute to the day, but otherwise the coach swayed along the shell-paved road in silence.

Lavinia sat next to Damien, feeling as if she had been transported into some magical realm. She was fully aware of his nearness, his masculine warmth. Her right hand lay concealed beneath a fold of her voluminous skirt; before they were many minutes into their ride, Damien's hand had found hers and caressed it secretly. His fingertips, tracing intricate designs on the back of her hand, sent little thrills of pleasure up her arm. Then gently, he turned her hand, repeating similar delicate patterns on the soft palm. She sat rigid and tight-lipped, afraid she might sigh aloud at the wonderful feeling and give away their hidden intimacy.

"It's not far now," Colonel Rutledge said. Though the pair in the carriage with him were too lost in their own world to notice, the colonel's voice had taken on a wistful tone. He, too, was caught up in the romance of the evening, thinking of the comely Widow Wentworth, her gentle smile and the pleasing timbre of her voice. Now that Lavinia had decided to marry Captain Clay, he felt free to make his own feelings known to Sara Wentworth.

"Evening, Colonel!" the Wentworths' smartly liveried footman said in greeting as the carriage rolled to a stop in front of Mulberry Hall. Their hostess swept onto the veranda immediately, smiling her welcome and taking the colonel's arm. Neither Lavinia nor Damien could miss the amorous gleam in his eyes now. Romance was in the air.

Lavinia squeezed Damien's hand excitedly. "Isn't it beautiful?"

He had to agree. The old planter's cottage was a handsome home, indeed, with its wide porches stretching around the house and the vine-covered chimneys at either end. Mulberry was not as immense as Thunderbolt, and the style was of low-country design, less formal than the Rutledges' residence. But this was obviously the home of a wealthy family—well-built and immaculately cared for.

"Colonel Rutledge! Miss Lavinia!"

Damien recognized the voice hailing from the veranda. Randolph Wentworth stood before the wide front entrance, resplendent in his butternut and gray dress uniform. Damien smiled in spite of himself. The gallant lieutenant was riding for a fall tonight. He felt a sudden burst of triumph swell his heart. This skirmish was over already and he had emerged the victor, with the charming Lavinia clinging to his arm.

But when she hurried up the broad stairs to embrace Randolph Wentworth, Damien felt jealousy overwhelm him once again. He followed her at quick-march and recaptured her arm.

"Oh, Randy, this is my friend, Captain Damien Clay. He's on leave from his war duties and staying with us at Thunderbolt for a few days."

The two officers exchanged challenging glances before Wentworth, holding Lavinia's other arm, said, "We're always happy to welcome strangers to Mulberry, sir. I'm sure you'll find the ladies overjoyed at the prospect of another unattached male in their midst."

"Thank you, Lieutenant Wentworth. I'm pleased to be here. But I'm afraid I'll have to disappoint the ladies. You see, I'm *very* attached at the moment." He drew Lavinia closer to his side to emphasize his point.

Lavinia looked from one to the other and gave a nervous laugh. Before she could explain Damien's words to Randy, her striking captain had whisked her away from their host and into the house, his grip on her arm too tight for comfort. My, he could be masterful when he set his mind to it! His forceful manner thrilled her through, but she decided not to let him know it.

"Damien, you were rude to Randy!" she protested. "Whatever are you thinking?"

As the other guests stared and twittered, he ushered her into an unoccupied sitting room and shut the door after them. When he turned to face her, Lavinia saw the anger in his sable eyes.

"What I'm thinking, Lavinia, is that the sooner you tell Lieutenant Wentworth you're spoken for, the better off we're all going to be! I don't intend to spend the whole evening having to cut you out of the pack just to be near you!''

"Damien Clay, how dare you talk to me that way? Randy and I are old, dear friends that's all!''

"From the way he looks at you, I'd say he thinks of you as more than *dear*!''

Lavinia's face took on a slow smile, which started deep in her eyes, then turned up the corners of her mouth into a coy grin. Soon she was laughing softly.

"My darling Damien! Why, you're *jealous*!''

He blustered for a moment, fumbling for excuses, but finally admitted, "*Damn right I am!* I won't have it, Lavinia! I'm giving you fair warning. I have a short fuse, and I wouldn't want to do our host any damage before the night's over. But if you continue to act like a butterfly bent on kissing every flower in the field, I can't be held responsible for my actions!''

Lavinia's Southern-belle affectation melted away. When she spoke again, her voice was rich and husky. "You're too much man to be jealous, Damien.''

"And you're too much woman to have to play silly female games. Come here!''

Lavinia started to take a step toward him, but his approach was much swifter. In an instant he had her in his arms, crushing her so close to him that the buttons on his blouse bit into her flesh through the tight bodice of her gown. His warm mouth came down on hers, parting her lips expertly. One arm locked her willingly in the embrace while his other hand traversed the bodice of her gown, finally settling between her breasts to fondle one and then the other. Lavinia felt a welcome languor seep through her blood. She pressed closer to the warmth she so desired. Her arms slipped up his back until her fingers laced behind his head, twining through his long hair.

Damien damned himself for a fool even as he kissed and caressed her. His loins were getting the better of his brain! If he kept up this madness, he'd have her stripped of her pantalettes before the night was over. He'd warned her about the danger of these intimate moments between them; now, mentally, he repeated that warning to himself.

"Miss Lavinia!" The outraged voice from the doorway came like a shot, tearing their embrace asunder. "Sir, I will see you in the grove at dawn tomorrow! The choice of weapons is yours, of course," Randolph Wentworth barked.

He advanced on Damien, removing a glove for the customary slap. But Lavinia jumped between the two men, barring Wentworth's way.

"No!" she cried. "This is all my fault. I should have told you as soon as we arrived, Randy. Damien and I are engaged to be married. There will be no duel on my account!"

Wentworth's face paled before it went scarlet with a mixture of rage and embarrassment. But he managed to recover some measure of composure and said, "I believe this is a trifle sudden, don't you, Miss Lavinia?"

"Everything in wartime happens suddenly out of necessity, Lieutenant Wentworth," Damien answered smoothly. "And love, in particular, has a way of striking like summer lightning."

At Damien's mention of love, Lavinia's heart gave a sudden happy lurch. This was more than she had dared hope from the evening. The vision she had been harboring for so long now blossomed to fullness in her mind's eye.

Wentworth stood silent and solemn, allowing tension to build in the room. Lavinia held her breath. She hoped he wouldn't make a scene. She really hadn't planned to hurt Randy. And she certainly hadn't wanted him to find out about her engagement by walking in on such a compromising situation.

"I'll wish you both my best, then." He bowed smartly, still unsmiling. "Miss Lavinia, you know I've always wanted nothing more than your happiness."

She pressed his hand for an instant and smiled. "I know, Randy, and I thank you for that."

"You'll be joining the other guests shortly?"

"Very shortly," Lavinia answered.

"Then I'll leave you to your . . ." He paused, embarrassed, and cleared his throat. "I'll go."

When they were alone once more, Lavinia quickly insinuated herself back into Damien's embrace. He hadn't meant to hold her again, but the passionate electricity that had built between them was only slightly diminished by Wentworth's interruption. Damien's arms and lips still ached for more. But after a brief kiss he put Lavinia away from him. His lips curved into a warning smile.

"Would you care to dance? We're getting into dangerous territory again."

Lavinia sighed deeply. "It may be dangerous, but it's *so* lovely. Can't we just stay here?" She slipped her arms around his waist again and rested her cheek against his chest.

"Enough of that, Lavinia!" Damien said, removing her encircling arms. "Pardon my bluntness, but there comes a point where pleasure turns to torture. Especially when one is wearing tight britches!"

Still, Lavinia refused to let him open the door. She clung to him and whispered, "The only torture for me will be when I have to let you leave."

He brushed her lips tenderly, trying to ignore the guilt he felt at her words. "We won't think about that now. I have a little while left. We'll cram that time full of happy memories, I promise you!"

The happy memories Damien promised began the moment they entered the ballroom arm in arm. A general gasp went up from the other guests. Lavinia and Damien had no idea what a striking picture they presented in their matching green and gold costumes. And Randolph Wentworth had spread the word of their engagement. Not a young woman in the room—and they outnumbered the eligible males four to one—could deny her envy of Lavinia. Who knew how long the war would last or how many sweethearts would be lost on far-off battlefields? And here was Lavinia Rutledge, lovely and flushed with the very glow of happiness, entering on the arm of her handsome betrothed. Could there possibly be a more romantic scene?

Damien bowed to his partner a bit stiffly, feeling all eyes on the two of them. Lavinia answered with a deep curtsy. Then the pair were in each other's arms, whirling about the shining floor. The other couples parted for them as Lavinia's full skirt dipped and billowed, from time to time offering a glimpse of shapely ankles clad in gold-flocked stockings.

Captain Clay proved light on his feet as he swept his partner along through the intricate steps. Lavinia had never enjoyed dancing so much in her life. She felt as if she and Damien were floating some inches above the polished white pine floor. She lost herself in the sensation of oneness created by their flow of movement. His eyes, so dark and deep, held hers with a kind of magnetic force. She felt her throat growing tight with emotion. They were so completely one at this moment. It was almost as if they were making love right there with the other guests watching. She never wanted this dance or this feeling to end.

A sudden, thunderous pounding of hoofbeats on the drive distracted the guests. A moment later boots thudded heavily across the veranda and someone banged the brass knocker on the front door. A ripple of curiosity traveled through the crowd in the ballroom. The music stopped, leaving Lavinia feeling light-headed as she still clung to Damien's arms.

"Captain Clay," Randolph Wentworth called from the foyer. "There's a messenger here to speak with you."

Damien was gone only a moment. But when he returned to the ballroom, it seemed to Lavinia as though he had traveled miles away from her. Gone was the look of abiding love from his eyes, the soft smile from his lips. He held a mud-smeared paper crumpled in his fist. She stared at the communiqué, terrified, as if it were a poisonous snake coiled to strike.

"Damien?" she said in a bare whisper.

"I think we'd better thank our host and take you back to Thunderbolt now, Lavinia." The serious tone of his voice confirmed all of her worst fears.

"The message?"

"I'll tell you later. . . when we're alone."

For a moment their gazes locked in intimate combat, her eyes pleading, his demanding her instant obedience. Without further conversation, he took her arm and steered her toward the door.

Lavinia, stunned by the sudden change in Damien, felt numb with shock. How could her beautiful evening end this way? She glanced up at his face, stone-hard now, his eyes cold and fathomless. She knew in her heart what the message meant. He didn't have to tell her.

Damien had needed only a glance at the mud-spattered, travel-weary rider on the veranda at Mulberry to know what the message must be and who had sent it. Now, riding back to Thunderbolt with Lavinia clinging desperately to his arm, he felt as if he had been yanked out of a lovely dream world and back into the cold, cruel light of reality.

The sudden realization came as a harsh blow. All this time he'd been plotting—trying to think of a way to get out of Lavinia's clutches. Now Morgan and the war had provided him with a convenient escape, but he didn't want it. He wanted Lavinia instead. And time had run out.

Damn Morgan! he thought fiercely, then corrected his curse. No, damn this war!

John Hunt Morgan couldn't be blamed. He was a man in similar straits, torn between duty and his affection for a woman. And Morgan's pretty Martha Ready was having to wait just as his own Lavinia was about to be called upon to do.

Damien was brought up short by his own thoughts. He hadn't intended to ask Lavinia to wait for him. Oh, no doubt she would wait for a while of her own accord, painting pretty pictures in her head about the two of them and their marriage to come. But those fantasies would fade with time. She'd find someone else, fall in love all over again, and be happily married before he saw the end of this conflict.

If this coming battle proved as critical as Morgan believed it would be, he certainly didn't want to go into it with the extra burden of Lavinia Rutledge's high hopes and sultry promises weighing on his heart and mind.

Yes! Damien thought. Damn this awful war!

"Damien, please tell me what's going on," Lavinia begged. "It's bad news, isn't it?"

They were alone in the carriage. Colonel Rutledge, totally involved in the wooing of the Widow Wentworth, had urged them to go on without him. He would borrow a horse and ride home later, unless, of course, their hostess invited him to stay the night.

Damien cupped Lavinia's cheek in his hand and felt the wetness of her tears.

"Please don't cry, Lavinia."

"I'm not crying!" she snapped, going rigid beside him.

He took her hand and said gently, "The time for tears won't come until—"

"Until *when*, Damien?" she demanded. "You're going to leave me, aren't you? I knew it the moment you walked back into the ballroom."

He kissed away her tears and whispered, "You knew this was coming—that I had only a short time to stay with you, darling."

She steadied her voice before she dared to answer. "Yes, I knew. But now part of that time has been stolen from us." Her arms went around his neck and she hugged him fiercely. "Oh, Damien, I can't bear it! I won't let you go!"

The sound of pain in her voice cut him to the quick. How could he have done this to her? He held her close and silenced her with his lips. Suddenly, he remembered why he had never allowed himself to become close to a woman before. Love was a wonderful emotion, until the parting came. And his life had required one parting after another.

She drew her face away and said, "At least I know now that you'll be back. That we'll be married after the war." Her tone almost challenged him to deny it.

"Lavinia, listen to me," he whispered. "You told me not long ago that you didn't plan to marry, that you couldn't bear the thought of having the man you loved taken from you. Maybe you were right. Maybe we should just be satisfied with what we've had and forget—"

"No, Damien!" she cried, clinging to him, her mind set now on her course of action. "It's too late to forget what you mean to me. And, I vow, I won't let you go! Not yet!"

"I don't have a choice, Lavinia."

"But I do!" All tears and weakness were gone from her voice. Stubborn, determined "Private Vinnie" was back.

All night she had been pondering this momentous decision. At first it had been something to add the final touch of excitement to the evening. Now, however, the plan seemed far more important to her, the direst necessity. There must be more between them than words before Damien rode away. Lavinia would never consider such a move if there weren't a war raging. But there was!

Her mind made up, she parted the curtain at the carriage window and called up to the driver, "Ajax, take us to the summer house, please," and the carriage immediately changed course.

Damien, guessing her intent, took her hand and caressed her cold fingers tenderly. He knew that, given the opportunity to have her, he would be powerless to refuse. He had made a vow to leave before this could happen. He didn't plan to marry her. He had no right, therefore, to accept what she was about to offer. Still . . .

"Lavinia?" he whispered with a world of uncertainty in his voice.

She answered him softly and simply. "I want you, Damien."

Chapter Nine

Damien's lips found Lavinia's in the darkness and warmed her through. There was bridled passion in his kiss and a promise of things to come. Lavinia vowed silently that at least for this one night she would make time stand still and banish the war and their coming parting from their minds and hearts.

Tall azalea bushes bursting with pink blossoms bordered the narrow drive up to the summer house. The tiny guest cottage was of rustic design but comfortable, with a welcoming look of weathered wood and wide, curtained windows. Beyond the house the Savannah River shone like a silver ribbon running through the night.

"We're home, darling," Lavinia whispered, her voice trembling slightly at the enormity of what she was about to do.

Damien hesitated before opening the carriage door. He felt obligated to give her one last chance to back out. "You're sure we shouldn't go on to Thunderbolt?"

"Damien dear, I'm not sure of anything at this point. I only know what I feel . . . what I want. . . ."

He leaped down from the carriage and lifted Lavinia into his arms, then strode toward the cottage door. Neither of them noticed as Ajax waved, grinned, and clucked to the horses, urging them homeward.

Damien Clay and Lavinia Rutledge were alone and of like mind and nothing else mattered.

They entered the cottage, aware of the musty smells of dampness and wood fires of long ago. For a time Damien stood in the center of the main room, still holding Lavinia in his arms and paying homage to the sweetness of her lips. When at last he bent to set her on her feet, his eager mouth found the soft hollow between her breasts. Lavinia's tense fingers caught in his hair and held him there, feeling her heart race at the sensation of teasing lips upon forbidden flesh.

"Please, Damien," she whispered at length. "Let me catch my breath."

He released her and laughed softly. "Would young Private Vinnie Rutledge have allowed his maiden such a courtesy? I doubt it very much. I believe his exact threat was to tie poor Miss Flowers and toss her skirts. What a surprise that maneuver would have produced!"

Lavinia found herself blushing at the same time she joined in Damien's laughter. Suddenly, their glum moods were banished. She could deal easily with the present as long as she could force the uncertain future out of her mind.

"Ah, sir, make light of poor Private Rutledge if you will, but tonight he gets his second chance at Miss Flowers. We'll just see what happens!"

Abruptly, Damien stopped laughing and pulled Lavinia into his arms. "Indeed we will, Private Rutledge," he said, breathing warmth into her bodice until her breasts quivered and ached.

"Damien, no!" she gasped as his strong fingers tugged at the thin fabric.

But her protest fell on deaf ears as he freed her breasts from their tight green prison and sought an erect nipple with hungry lips. Lavinia leaned back against his supporting arm, feeling the strength drain from her legs to be replaced by a quivering heat. Slowly, tantalizingly, Damien drew wet circles on her taut flesh with the tip of his tongue until she moaned aloud and begged him for mercy.

Lavinia took several gasping breaths. She shook her head, trying to make her eyes focus. But she felt as near to swooning as she had ever been in her life. She and Damien had not been together like this since the night before they reached Thunderbolt. But the consciousness of her longing had been with her every hour, waking or sleeping, since that night on the trail. Now, to have him suddenly take her, playing her emotions as if they were the chords of a fine-tuned instrument and he the perfect maestro of passion, left her achingly breathless yet yearning for more.

"You're right, darling," he said at length, never shifting his gaze from her naked breasts, "we should take it a bit slower. After all, we have all night."

"Only this ni—" She checked the word before it could pass her lips. She would not allow her thoughts to travel beyond the present instant.

"Do you suppose there's any wine about?" he asked, lighting a lamp near the fireplace.

At the flare of light Lavinia instinctively covered her bare breasts with her hand and arm. Damien glimpsed her action out of the corner of his eye and turned a stern look on her. He shouted no command, issued no order except with his eyes. Slowly, feeling a blush creep into her cheeks, Lavinia lowered her arm. She was keenly aware of her breasts heaving, of the rise and fall of her very erect nipples. Never had a man looked at her the way Damien was gazing at her now. There was such a naked expression of desire on his face that it made her tremble. He walked to where she stood, stopping so close that she could feel his warm breath on her exposed flesh. The shock made her gasp and she drew away, but only for an instant.

"You are quite the loveliest woman I've ever laid eyes on, Lavinia Rutledge," Damien said in a husky voice that held an underlying tone of humor. "I do believe that if we were married and had our own home, I would instruct your seamstress to cut the bodices from some of your gowns so that when we were alone, you could go bare-breasted as the fabled beauties of ancient Crete." He fingered her gently, smiling. "Yes, I would enjoy that!"

Lavinia was feeling weak again. His very gaze was taking its toll on her. "Damien, don't make fun of me," she begged.

He reached out with both hands and lifted her breasts in his palms, kissing one and then the other. Looking into her eyes, he whispered, "Make fun, Lavinia? Never! Make *love*! That's what we're here to do, isn't it?"

Suddenly, she felt panic-stricken. Once, when she was a child, she had run away from home after a severe scolding from Helen-of-Troy. But when darkness descended and she was out of sight of the safety and security of Thunderbolt, she had become terrified, alone and miserable, longing only for home and family, the known as opposed to the unknown. Now she felt the same way. She wanted Damien Clay. She wanted his love, his passion. She wanted with all her heart and soul for him to make her a woman. But still, he represented the terrifying unknown. The known quantity, innocence, was infinitely easier to live with than the passionate caresses of this man—this *stranger*.

Quickly, Lavinia pulled the bodice of her gown back into place and said, "Damien, I think we'd better go on to the house now. It's only a short walk. Papa may be home and worried about me. This really wasn't such a good idea after all." Her words rushed pell-mell from her lips, tumbling over one another in a panic.

"Your papa is well occupied for the evening, Lavinia. We have plenty of time." He reached out for her once more to take her in his arms.

"No, Damien, don't!"

He stepped back, his face a mask of puzzlement. "You're serious, aren't you!"

"Yes?" Her uncertain reply was more question than declaration.

Damien gripped her upper arms and captured her lips in a brief but bruising kiss. "It won't work, Lavinia! You don't lead a man on and then push him away at the last moment. You're trying to play games again, and I won't have it. I won't deny that I've been thinking of this from the first moment I held you in Sergeant O'Dell's tent. Lord, how I wanted you that night! You were so soft and warm there beside me. I held myself in check, though. But coming here tonight was your idea, Lavinia. I never would have suggested such a thing, as much as I wanted it. Now that we're here alone, there's no turning back. I won't be refused!"

She pulled out of his painful embrace. Hands on hips, she glared at him. "And I won't be pawed, sir! You'll act the gentleman or be damned!"

The laughter burst from Damien's throat. He couldn't help himself. She was so lusty and adorable when she got angry. There she stood, her bright red hair mussed, her full breasts straining out of her gown so that the dark nipples still peered at him like half moons rising out of the sea, and the rage of a thousand demons etched on her pretty face. He felt a whole new rush of desire for her.

"I fail to see any humor in this situation," Lavinia said haughtily, her chin at a proud angle. When his laughter continued, she stamped her foot and yelled, "Damn you, Damien Clay, don't laugh at me!"

He tried, but he couldn't stop. Lavinia got madder by the minute. When she rushed at him with a feline cry and fists flailing, he grabbed at her to save himself from bodily harm. Tangling in her swirling skirts, he tripped, and in falling bore her beneath him to a nearby couch. His body covered hers, putting an end to her frantic attack. She struggled to free herself, but his lips pressed against hers soon took the last of the fight out of her.

Lavinia felt her anger transformed into a very different but equally fierce emotion. Her whole body, pressed down under his weight, flamed with a raging liquid fire. In their tumble her skirts had slipped up so that now only her thin pantalettes protected her from his bulging heat. At the feel of his body throbbing against her thigh, instinctively her hips arched upward in a premature thrust.

"Slowly, my darling," he whispered into her ear. "We don't want to rush things."

Suddenly, she became very conscious of how little she knew of all this. "I'm sorry, Damien." He hardly heard her soft words.

"You have nothing to be sorry about."

"Yes, I do. I'm such a ninny about . . . about these things. I don't even know what I'm expected to do beyond kissing you."

He almost said, *I have experience enough for both of us!* but thought better of it. Instead, he remained silent while he worked at the fastenings of her gown. When she was wearing only her thin basque and pantalettes, he sat up and removed his blouse and white linen shirt. She stared up at him with wide, frightened eyes.

He shrugged, laughed softly, and bent down to kiss a tiny beauty mark on her right shoulder. "There's really nothing to fear, Lavinia, other than breaking our necks when we tumble off this settee. Is there a bed in this place?" he whispered.

Lavinia nodded and pointed toward a door at one side of the fireplace. He lifted her from the couch and made for the bedroom. The tall tester there was an inviting sight after the narrow couch. Turning back the covers and laying her gently in place, he noted that a decanter and two glasses were on the table beside the bed. The absence of dust told him that they had only recently been placed there. By whom? Lavinia? Had she planned this all along?

As if reading his thoughts, Lavinia answered, "Helen-of-Troy brought the wine. I guess she knew we'd be coming. She has visions."

Damien raised an eyebrow at Lavinia's matter-of-fact tone. Visions were not a part of his everyday routine. But then, nothing at Thunderbolt, including Lavinia Rutledge, was.

He poured the deep red wine into two glasses and handed one to Lavinia. She drank thirstily, poured more, and drank again, then replaced the glass, and leaned back among the pillows.

"There!" she said with a slightly thickened tongue. "I'm ready!"

"Are you indeed, Miss Rutledge! You sound like a patient at the tooth doctor's announcing that you've had enough spirits to dull the pain before he extracts a molar! By God, I won't make love to a woman who's in that frame of mind!"

Lavinia cursed herself silently. She wasn't doing anything right tonight. She caught his arm as he started to rise. "Damien, please . . ."

"Get dressed," he snapped. "I'm taking you home!"

Damien left the bed and stalked back into the main room. Was he really angry with her now or only manufacturing excuses to soothe his conscience for having allowed himself to get into this situation in the first place? He couldn't decide. But it was probably just as well that nothing had happened. In a few hours dawn would come and he'd be safely out of Lavinia Rutledge's life.

He picked up his green blouse discarded hastily on the floor, and withdrew the handwritten message from the breast pocket, letting his eyes scan the page. He could almost see John Hunt Morgan perched on Black Bess's back, his right leg slung over the saddle horn so that the top of his cavalry boot formed a writing surface as he'd scrawled the quick note.

16 March 1862
Headquarters in the Saddle

My dear Miss Flowers,
    You missed all the fun, my friend! Shortly after you removed yourself from our midst to commence your southward trek, the Second Kentucky undertook a daring night raid behind Federal lines into Nashville, successfully firing the steamboat Minnetonka *tied up at the wharf.*
    Yesterday, took time out from my pleasurable pursuits with Miss Ready at Murfreesboro to strike a blow at the Louisville & Nashville Railroad, putting locomotive out of operation, firing 13 freight cars, burning water house, and destroying machinery for sawing wood and pumping water. All in all, left Gallatin depot a shambles!
    But now to the business at hand. General Johnston has decided we might catch Grant with his trousers down the first week in April by advancing north from Corinth. Make haste, my friend, lest you miss the grandest battle yet.
                Ever respectfully,
                John Hunt Morgan
                Colonel CSA

Damien was still frowning at the paper in his hands, puzzling over Morgan's words, when he heard a sound behind him. Trained by months of battle that a hairbreadth instant could prove the difference between life and death, he crouched and swung toward the sound as he reached for the pistol he wasn't wearing.

Had Lavinia Rutledge been a Yankee sharpshooter, he realized, he would have been a dead man. But as it was, his heart only stopped for a moment when he caught sight of her. She stood like a statue in the doorway to the bedroom, the cream satin spread from the bed wrapped in Grecian fashion about her obviously naked body. The shiny fabric was pulled taut across her high, full breasts and draped over one shoulder, leaving the other temptingly bare. The glow of the candle behind her on the bedside table showed him once more the roundness of her hips and the tiny span of her waist. One long, shapely leg escaped her satin toga. The sight of that exposed limb brought a new throbbing heat to his body.

"Damien," she said in a husky whisper.

He tried to force his gaze away, to refuse the invitation in her voice, but it was no use. He was powerless even if he'd wanted to turn away. Morgan's words haunted his mind—"the grandest battle yet." That would translate, he was sure, as the bloodiest and most dangerous battle yet. A man about to face death could not afford to let what remained of life slip from his grasp simply for the sake of honor and propriety. He wanted Lavinia Rutledge. By God, he *loved* her! And she shared both the emotion and the need. He opened his arms to her and she came quickly, willingly, passionately into his embrace.

"Damien, Damien," she crooned as he held her face in his hands and kissed her forehead and eyelids. "Don't let's fight anymore. Please! I can't bear it!"

"No more! Never, I promise," he breathed into her mouth.

Lavinia could feel the trembling urgency of his hands on her body. He kneaded the satin covering her breasts until it slipped from her shoulder and down about her hips. Slowly, feeling her own fingers quiver with nervousness at her urgent need, she forced the covering down from her hips until she stood before him unclothed and unashamed.

He took a step back, letting his eyes devour the sight of her. Her pale body glistened in the lamplight, making her seem to glow from within. Never in his most vivid and expansive dreams had Damien ever imagined that there could be a woman so beautiful. She looked almost unreal to him—almost too lovely and fragile to touch.

"Come to me, Damien," she whispered, holding out her arms to him. She was trembling all over—not from cold; still she needed his warmth next to her.

"My darling!" he said hoarsely, and pulled her into his arms.

The satin spread made a bed for their love. In moments Damien lay in his love's arms, as naked as she. Lavinia, with senses sharpened so that tastes, smells, feelings, and even her eyesight seemed more acute, drank in the visual impressions of his body. Never had she dared try to imagine what Damien or any man looked like from the waist down. But now she gloried in the wonderful sight of her stallion. It was the only word fine enough to fit him.

For a long time they lay together, feasting their senses on each other's bodies, feeling the delicious pain of need rise with the pleasures of touching, kissing, tasting. Damien's hand strayed along the curves of her hips and down over her smooth belly, making her writhe beneath his knowing touch. When his fingers moved lower to stroke the fiery down between her thighs, she gasped out his name. Exotic new thrills spiraled through her.

"If I die tonight, I will have lived enough!" she sighed.

Damien lowered his body to cover hers and whispered against her ear, "You have only begun to live, my darling."

The next instant she felt him enter her and it was as if she were being reborn. The sensation was extraordinary. His heat seemed to sear her tender flesh, and the fullness in her body made the ache of her need ever stronger. Suddenly, he raised his chest, placing his hands on her shoulders to hold her in place. His eyes looked glazed, but burned like a hot, dark flame.

"Now!" he said fiercely, gripping her shoulders with strong fingers.

He gave a mighty thrust. Lavinia cried out at the tearing pain within her but soon lost all consciousness of the discomfort as their bodies settled into a matched rhythm of movement and she felt only the pleasure of flesh stroking flesh. It seemed that she had lived her whole life for this moment—to be made a woman by this one man. To know his needs and to offer her body and soul to him alone. The feeling brought great contentment and release.

But no sooner had Lavinia decided that she knew the best there was to know in this world than Damien opened up a whole new world for her. Quickening his thrusts as he kissed her deeply, he aroused new depths of sensation. Lavinia felt that she was climbing a huge hot stairway that led far up into the stars. Each step she took upward brought increased awareness and waves of pleasure. She couldn't be sure what waited for her at the top. She only knew she must keep climbing, must reach the pinnacle. And then she knew her goal was in sight. A warmth bathed her legs and a stirring vibration seemed to run through her body. In a burst of heat and light and a flood of liquid ecstasy inside her, she was there. Damien gave one last, shattering thrust and gripped her close to him, gasping her name between heaving breaths.

A moment later they lay quiet in each other's arms. Lavinia's entire body felt as if it had been bathed in magical waters. All her nerves tingled and she was sure she could hear the blood coursing joyfully through her own veins. This, she was sure, had to be the most wonderful moment in her life.

"I'm sorry I had to hurt you," Damien whispered, letting his still-trembling fingers caress her damp thighs.

"Hurt me, darling? No! You've made a woman of me," she answered.

"*My* woman!" He leaned down and kissed her lips lightly. "The woman I love more than life itself."

"Oh, Damien!" Suddenly, Lavinia was crying. Tears spilled out of her eyes and poured down her cheeks. "I love you, too, Damien! And I don't want tonight to end. I want you to hold me and love me for as long as we have left. Please!"

Damien lifted Lavinia into his arms. Her tears, which refused to be checked, flowed down his chest. Again he took her to the soft bed and poured her a glass of wine, but this time he didn't leave her. Until dawn filled the room with its rose-gold glow, he held her and made love to her in the tenderest fashion.

Lavinia spent the long night in ecstasy. There was no more pain for her as he rode her gently and caressed her to new heights of sensation. Only with the morning light did the new pain come. As Captain Damien Clay arose from the bed and donned his uniform to return to the war, Lavinia Rutledge knew a pain like none she had ever experienced. It was as if her heart were being torn out.

"You aren't leaving this morning?" she finally worked up the courage to ask.

He kissed her gently, then answered, "I have to."

"But you're going back to the house first?"

"Only long enough to collect my things."

"Then I'll go with you."

Lavinia threw off the covers and started to get her clothes, but Damien pressed her back down and tucked the covers up only as far as her waist.

"No. Please don't, darling. It will be easier for me to leave you right here." He sat down on the edge of the bed and smiled into her eyes. Tenderly, his fingertips fondled her breasts. "I want to remember you just like this, my last vision of you like some pagan goddess of love."

"Oh, Damien, I can't stand it!" Lavinia sobbed, clutching him close as if she never intended to let him go. "Can't I go with you?"

"That's impossible, darling," he answered gently. "And I want your solemn promise that you won't come traipsing after me. It's not safe."

She looked away, unable to meet his eyes. Damien put his fingers under her chin and raised her face to his so that she had to look at him.

"Promise me, Lavinia!"

"Oh, I promise!" she said reluctantly, but he couldn't see her fingers crossed behind his back. "Where will you be going?"

"I'm not sure. I'll be heading somewhere north of Corinth, Mississippi, where the army has its headquarters at present. I imagine I'll meet up with Morgan and the others along the Tennessee River. If I miss them there, I'll go on to Murfreesboro. That's where Morgan has his unofficial headquarters—at the

Ready residence on Main Street. There's a certain young lady there who has vowed she'll be Mrs. Morgan as soon as she can get the colonel off his horse long enough to marry him!''

"And when will you be back?"

Damien offered her only a ghost of a smile. He wasn't sure he'd ever be back. Certainly, until last night he'd had no intention of ever returning. But he couldn't tell her that now.

"Your guess is as good as mine, darling."

She hugged him fiercely and kissed him, then held his cheeks between her palms a moment longer, trying to memorize his face.

"Damien, do take care! If anything happened to you . . ."

"Now, no more of that, Lavinia!" he said in a stern voice. "I want no tears, no heartbreak, no worrying about things that can't be helped. Understand?"

She put on a brave face and even managed a smile for him. "I understand," she whispered. "That sort of thing won't do anyone any good."

"That's my girl! Now, kiss me, darling, and I'm off."

She kissed him. Oh, how she kissed him! A kiss to last them both until they should be reunited. And afterward she smiled for him and told him how much she loved him. He assured her of his own affection, then departed. When he cast a last glance over his shoulder at the little cottage, Lavinia, still smiling, was standing in the doorway waving, the satin spread draped about her.

This was the vision he would carry back to war with him. He'd never know of the rivers of tears she shed after he was out of sight or of the scheming going on in her mind to join him in Tennessee.

For the rest of the day Lavinia lay on the rumpled bed, which still smelled faintly of his body, alternately crying and making her plans for the trip.

Chapter Ten

Damien Clay's horse went lame a day's ride shy of a little Methodist meeting house called Shiloh in Tennessee. Due to this quirk of fate, he missed his rendezvous with John Hunt Morgan the first week in April, and so missed the bloodiest and fiercest battle yet waged between North and South. In lines drawn up around the rustic log church and a nearby flowering peach orchard, the untried armies met on the warm Sunday morning of April 6 and learned the whole terrifying truth about war. One fourth of the hundred thousand men engaged in the battle did not answer roll call the morning after the conflict ended.

Four hours before Damien finally caught up with the Confederate Army, now retreating south back to Corinth, he had been made aware of the great battle by the boom of cannon fire and the pall of black smoke inking the sky in the distance. His frustration mounted with each passing moment until he spotted his comrades off toward the west, bringing up the rear of the Rebel retreat. Mounted on Black Bess, his powder-singed plume waving like a battle flag, John Hunt Morgan was not hard to pick out of the group.

"Colonel!" Damien called. "Colonel Morgan!"

Morgan wheeled his mount at the sound of his shouted name and stood high in the stirrups, searching the distance. When he saw the lone figure leading the limping horse, he urged Black Bess out of the column and raced across the field.

"By the Eternal, Clay, I thought you were dead!" Morgan said in greeting.

Damien noticed at once that his commander's face was drawn beneath the black powder and grime of two days' battle. His grayish-blue eyes, usually lit by a mischievous sparkle, held only a glazed, vacant look, as if he'd just seen something his mind couldn't grasp. Morgan's normal broad smile was absent, and he seemed to sit his horse with less exuberance than was customary. All in all, this bitter taste of war had taken its toll on the newly promoted colonel.

"Not dead," Damien answered, "just down on my luck. My horse tossed a shoe a day and a half ago. It's been boot-to-sod since then. You wouldn't happen to have a spare mount, would you?"

Morgan's scowl deepened. "I'm afraid I've more than one riderless horse after Shiloh. The full count's not in yet. But General Johnston is gone, shot in the leg and bled to death before he even realized he was seriously wounded."

"My God!"

Morgan shook his head. "He's only one of thousands. I don't know how any of us came through it. I tell you, Clay, I've never seen such fighting!" He glanced back toward the battlefield, out of his sight now, but his mind seemed to be wandering its scorched and bloodied ground. He said, as if trying to total the dead count by naming the casualties one by one, "We lost James West."

Clay lowered his head in respect and said, "A good man."

"He was that. They were all good men. My brother Charlton caught a bullet, but he was one of the luckier ones. Basil Duke, my sister Henrietta's husband, took a minié ball through his shoulder. Both gravely wounded, but they'll recover to fight again. Here"—Morgan leaned down and offered his arm—"let me give you a hand up. You can ride Basil's horse. He'll be out of action for some time, I suspect."

When the two men riding Black Bess entered the ranks, Damien was horrified by the looks of shock and bewilderment on

the faces of his comrades. Hardly a man was without a battle
scar, and it was obvious that their mental wounds would be
even longer in healing.

"It must have been ghastly," Damien said as much to himself as to Morgan.

"There's not a word in our language awesome enough to describe what it was, Clay. Those of us who survived will carry
the bloody sights and sounds of Shiloh with us to our graves,
and maybe on beyond!"

Up ahead in the slowly moving column, Damien spotted
three riders who sat head and shoulders above the others. A
buzz of recognition sounded in the back of his brain, but intent
as he was on listening to Morgan's account of the Second Kentucky's movements over the past few weeks, he paid no imme-
diate attention to it. Not until they broke ranks to camp for the
night did he realize the tall riders were three of Lavinia's brothers.

"Those Georgia men," he said to Morgan. "What happened to their two brothers?"

"Those big fellows, you mean?"

"Yes. The Rutledges."

"Damned if I know, Clay. They could be dead, deserted, or
captured by the Yankees. Are you acquainted with them?"

"Yes," Damien answered. "I know their sister, Lavinia."

He walked off to talk to the Rutledges, leaving Morgan staring after him in wonder. The taciturn Clay had spoken volumes
with his tone.

"Well, by damn!" Morgan muttered. "I never thought the
woman was born who could domesticate Damien Clay. Miss
Lavinia Rutledge must be something!"

The three Rutledge brothers had built a fire slightly away
from the others and were stretched out on the bare ground, their
heads propped on their saddles. They lay in silence, staring fix-
edly into the flames. When Damien approached, Jake alone
looked up.

"Howdy," he said in a toneless voice. "You get Lavinia
home safe and sound?"

Damien nodded, squinting through the near darkness to see

if he could identify the other two. Elijah and Earl, he saw at last.

"Where are Josiah and Mallard?" he asked.

"What's it to you?" one of the twins—Clay wasn't sure which one—snarled.

"Natural concern," he answered. "Your sister and I have become . . . very close."

"How close?" the other twin growled, rising as if he meant to throw a punch.

"Hold on, Earl!" Jake warned. "We got no say in this. Lavinia said she wanted him. I agree, there's no accounting for her taste, but if he's the one she picked, the least we can do is be civil to her man."

The twins, grumbling, settled back down and both shoved their hats forward over their eyes. In minutes they were snoring.

Damien squatted next to Jake and asked again, "What happened to your other brothers?"

Jake gave a low whistle through his teeth, then let out a long sigh. "I reckon you weren't here for the battle."

"No. My horse went lame. I just hooked up with Colonel Morgan a while ago."

"Well, you wouldn't be asking what happened if you'd been a part of it. I tell you, I've never seen such a slaughter. Men as thick as ticks on a hound dog and all shooting and yelling at once. The smoke so heavy you couldn't breathe. Lordy, it was like hell on earth!"

"Then they're lost?"

"Josiah is."

Damien had been praying silently that Lavinia's most loved brother would be safe. The news left an empty feeling in the pit of his stomach.

"You're sure he's dead?"

Jake sat up and squinted hard at Damien. "Mister, I ain't *sure* of *nothing*! When you got twenty-five thousand dead and wounded strewn over a couple of square miles and the enemy trying to fill your tail with grapeshot while you light out, you don't stop and look for somebody, not even your own little brother!''

"What about Mallard?"

"He stopped a couple of bullets in the first charge. He wouldn't of been anything but buzzard bait if he'd stayed around, so the major told him to head on home. He'll be all right to fight again in a month or so. Mind if I get some sleep now? It's been a right long three days.''

Before Damien could answer, Jake Rutledge was snoring in chorus with his two brothers. For a long time Damien stayed where he was, staring into the fire and thinking about the war, Josiah Rutledge, and Lavinia.

If it hadn't been for an uncommonly heavy line of thunder squalls that moved in from the coast, delaying Lavinia's secret plans, she would have missed Mallard's homecoming. As it was, she spotted him before anyone else as she paced the veranda, searching the skies for some sign of a letup in the storm.

The rain, coming down in silvery-gray sheets, reduced visibility to such an extent that she didn't see Mallard until he was halfway up the drive. And even then she couldn't tell which of her brothers was returning unexpectedly from the war. Ignoring the drenching downpour, she raced out to meet the approaching rider. He sat crouched in the saddle, a bloodied sling supporting his right arm and another bandage wound about his upper thigh. Shielding the rain from her eyes with one hand, she caught the horse's bridle in the other and led the animal to the veranda steps, then offered her arms to help her brother down. Mallard slid, near-unconscious, out of the saddle, almost knocking his sister over with his weight.

"Papa!" she yelled over the crashing thunder. "Ajax! Come quick! It's Mallard and he's hurt!"

Immediately, Ajax was beside her, lifting Mallard from her protective arms.

"It's all right now, Miss Vinnie. I'll get him up to bed."

"No, Ajax. He can't take the stairs. I'll have Helen-of-Troy fix him a bed in the parlor. Just get him in out of the rain for now."

The veranda, deserted only moments before except for Lavinia's lone vigil, now became a beehive of activity. Helen-of-Troy hurried out with blankets to warm Mallard, then bustled back in to make his bed. Rambeau Rutledge hovered over his injured son, asking a battery of questions that Mallard was too weak to answer. Lavinia, drenched to the skin, went for brandy. Word spread over the plantation by the slave grapevine and soon the curious people came to the big house to see "the young master, home from the war."

The dark afternoon had turned into a black, stormy night before Mallard, bathed, his wounds dressed, and tucked into bed, came around enough to realize where he was. Lavinia sat beside his bed, cooling his fevered brow with a damp cloth. He looked like death, she thought. His bearded face was the color of ashes and his eyes, when he finally opened them, were bloodshot and jaundiced.

"Mallard," she whispered, "can you hear me?"

"Vinnie?" His voice was as thin as a cobweb. "Vinnie, is that you?"

"Sh-h-h! Don't try to talk. You're home, Mallard. You're going to be all right now."

Rambeau Rutledge, hearing Lavinia's voice, came into the room. "He's awake?"

"Just barely," she said softly. "I think the fever's broken. He needs to sleep now. In the morning we can ask him about the others."

All night Lavinia stayed with her sick brother. He had terrible nightmares, thrashing about and sometimes crying out without waking from his torment. Near dawn his sleep deepened to a more peaceful level and Lavinia was able to nod off in the chair beside the bed. She dreamed, as she did every night, of Damien—the warmth and security of his arms about her, his lips on hers, his gentle, fondling hands on her body.

"Lavinia? Lavinia!"

Her whispered name seemed a part of the dream. A hand was touching hers. She sighed and smiled as the clouds of sleep parted to let in the light of day.

"Lavinia, have you been here with me all night?"

Her eyes shot open suddenly and she saw not Damien's face but her brother's. The shock jolted her.

"Mallard!" She shook her head to clear it. "You're better this morning."

"I don't feel like I'm better. My whole body aches as if I'd been dragged behind a team of horses." He tried to move his injured leg and groaned loudly.

"You must lie still! Do you feel up to seeing Papa? He's so eager to talk to you."

"Yes, of course. And Sammie Sue. Could you send Ajax over to Heather Hill to fetch her?"

Lavinia tried to cover the grimace she felt coming on. Sammie Sue Effingham would undoubtedly move right in and try to take over. Well, never mind! Let the little wimp nurse Mallard back to health. That way, Lavinia would feel free to leave all the sooner.

"Of course I'll send for Sammie Sue, Mallard. Can I do anything else for you before I go get Papa?"

"No, thank you."

She rose to leave, but Mallard caught her hand. "Wait, Lavinia. I'd better tell you before Papa comes in. You're going to have to be strong to help him through this."

Lavinia's heart gave a sudden lurch. She took a deep breath, steeling herself for bad news. "What's happened, Mallard?"

"It's Josiah."

"Oh, God, no!" Lavinia cried. She'd been ready for almost anything, but not this. The tears rushed to her eyes. Her whole body began to tremble.

"Lavinia, stop it!" Mallard ordered. "That won't help. Your hysterics will only upset Papa. I shouldn't have said anything until Sammie Sue got here. She'd know how to handle this situation."

Certainly, she would! Lavinia thought, squaring her shoulders and quelling her tears. Sammie Sue would faint dead away, making herself the instant center of attention and throwing the whole place into a greater panic.

"I'm all right now, Mallard," she replied stiffly. "How was he killed?"

"My dear girl, as usual, you've jumped to silly female conclusions. I never said Josiah was dead!"

Lavinia stared at her brother, trying to deny her urge to strangle him. How dare he give her such a terrible shock, then act as if nothing had happened!

"If Josiah is still alive, where is he?" she asked in a deadly calm voice.

"That's just it. We don't know. Nobody's seen him since the start of the battle. He's simply unaccounted for."

If Mallard hadn't been wounded already, Lavinia was sure she would have taken the gun down from over the mantelpiece and shot him herself at that point.

"No one is *simply* unaccounted for, Mallard! What happened to him? Where is he?" Her voice had risen to an angry shout, which brought both the colonel and Helen-of-Troy running.

"What's wrong?" Rambeau Rutledge insisted. "Is Mallard worse?"

Worse than what? Lavinia felt like asking. But instead she answered as calmly as she could manage, "No, Papa, in fact he's quite fit this morning. But Josiah is missing in action."

The colonel slumped down in the nearest chair and Helen-of-Troy rushed to pour him a restorative brandy.

"And the others?" he asked quietly.

"Jake and the twins were fine the last I saw of them," Mallard answered.

"Thank God for that!" the colonel sighed.

"Well, you never know. I left after the first day. I'm sure the battle raged for some time. So my accounting is hardly valid at this point."

Colonel Rutledge paled and Lavinia shot her brother a look fit to kill. She hurried to her father and put her arm around his shoulders. "I'm sure they're fine, Papa. And we'll find Josiah! Don't you worry!"

"How, daughter? He could be anywhere. We may never see him again."

"Oh, we'll see him again! As for how we'll find him, I'm going after my brother!"

"Lavinia!" the colonel and Mallard chorused.

"I don't want any arguments! Damien told me where John Hunt Morgan's headquarters are. I'll go to Murfreesboro. Someone there is bound to know what happened to Josiah."

"Lavinia, you can't strike out alone like that!" the colonel said.

"She ain't going alone, Colonel!" Helen-of-Troy put in. "I'll be right alongside her, driving the buggy and looking after our lamb."

Lavinia turned toward the woman to object, but the expression on Helen-of-Troy's face told her that the matter was settled.

"When will you leave, child?" Colonel Rutledge asked tiredly, knowing there was no use debating the matter once Lavinia's mind was made up.

"As soon as the rains stop, Papa."

"According to the ache in these old bones," Helen-of-Troy said, "that'll be about half after dawn tomorrow."

Sammie Sue Effingham arrived an hour later, rustling, bustling, and weeping her way through the house. Her pudgy fingers dabbed convulsively at her tear-webbed lashes, which resembled nothing so much, Lavinia thought, as a nest of black widow spiders caught in a deluge. Gowned in black bombazine, her chosen costume until the war ended, she hovered over Mallard, drowning him with tears and maudlin sympathy.

"My darling boy, how could they have done this to you?" Lavinia heard her croon between sobs. "But don't you worry yourself a moment longer, my precious love! You will rise from your bed of pain to walk once more. From this instant on, you shall not be out of my care or out of my sight!"

Lavinia covered a sadistic smile with her hand, wondering what Sammie Sue would do the first time her *darling boy* needed to use the slop jar Helen-of-Troy had placed under the edge of the bed for his convenience.

"My own sweet Sammie Sue," Mallard sighed. "How I've missed you, my dear!"

"And I you," she replied, clutching his fingers to her lips and closing her eyes in ecstasy.

"Ahem!" Lavinia cleared her throat to alert them to the fact that they were no longer alone.

Sammie Sue quickly deposited Mallard's well-kissed hand back atop the bedclothes and said, "Just as I suspected, Lieutenant. Your pulse is quite weak. I'll instruct Helen to fix blood pudding and oxtail broth to build up your strength."

"Thank you, Miss Effingham," Mallard responded formally.

"I'm sorry to interrupt, Sammie Sue, but Ajax is about to come in and help Mallard . . ."

"Oh, no!" Sammie Sue shook her head so furiously that the tight blond curls about her face bobbed like golden springs. "Whatever Mallard needs, I'm here to take care of it!"

"If you'll please let me finish, Sammie Sue. I was about to say that Ajax will help Mallard get on the slop jar." Normally, Lavinia would have used a less explicit term—chamber pot, or even johnnie—but she couldn't resist using the servants' name for the squat earthenware jar just to see the prim Miss Effingham's reaction.

She was not disappointed. Sammie Sue's hands flew to her thin lips and her face turned scarlet. She literally fled the room, her skirts flapping out behind her like starched ravens' wings. Mallard scowled at Lavinia, but she smiled sweetly, ignoring his expression.

"Shall I call Ajax now?"

"Not until you apologize to Sammie Sue for embarrassing her, Lavinia! You know she's a very delicate and refined lady. Not at all like you!"

Lavinia turned angrily toward the door, then paused and tossed Mallard a quick smile over her shoulder. "You'll have been begging for the slop jar a long time before I apologize for anything, brother dear!" And then she was gone, Mallard shouting after her in his rage.

Helen-of-Troy caught up with Lavinia as she swished furiously up the stairs. "What you mean getting your poor brother riled like that, Miss Vinnie? And him all stove up the way he is!"

"Well, why don't we just leave it to dear, sweet Miss Sammie Sue to unstove him!"

"Miss Vinnie! For shame, you talking that way. That chile's only trying to help."

"By the way, Helen-of-Troy, that *dear sweet chile* is about to instruct you to fix blood pudding and oxtail broth for her patient. You'd better hurry along to the kitchen so you don't keep her waiting."

"Blood pudding! Oxtail broth!" Helen-of-Troy sputtered. "Well, I never! I ain't killing no ox just to make broth out of his tail! Haven't I been taking good care of my lambs all these years? And that woman thinks she can just march right in here and start giving orders. Not to Helen-of-Troy, she can't!"

Lavinia smiled. "There. You see, I'm not the only one under this roof with a temper. And things around here are going to get worse before they get better. I say we pack our bags and hit the road for Tennessee, Helen-of-Troy. Right now!"

The servant was frowning and considering her words when a call came from the hallway below. "You there, Helen!"

"It's *Helen-of-Troy*, ma'am!"

"Whatever," Sammie Sue snapped impatiently. "Come down here this minute. I have a special menu made out for my patient. You must see to it at once!"

"Do we leave *now*?" Lavinia asked.

"Right now!" Helen-of-Troy agreed.

Lavinia hated to abandon her father with Sammie Sue Effingham in the house, but these days he was spending most of his time over at Mulberry Hall at Sara Wentworth's invitation. He would be fine.

As for Mallard, he was too ornery not to get well. Besides, as long as he was bedridden he would have to endure Sammie Sue Effingham around the clock. To Lavinia's way of thinking, that sort of incentive would make the sickest man well in jigtime.

The rain was still falling as she and Helen-of-Troy pulled

away from the veranda of Thunderbolt late that afternoon. But the storm had passed. This was a gentle spring rain that would turn the fields green and carpet the woods with fragrant violets. Lavinia wiped the last of her good-bye tears from her eyes and took a deep breath.

"The air even smells promising, Helen-of-Troy. We'll have a good trip."

"You reckon, Miss Vinnie?"

"I know so!"

The two women settled into companionable silence and watched the road north unfold before them. The only thing on Lavinia's mind now was that at the end of that road Damien would be waiting.

Wouldn't he be surprised to see her!

Chapter Eleven

The drive across the state of Georgia proved a wonderment to Lavinia and Helen-of-Troy. Never before had they crossed the demarcation line that signaled the end of South Georgia's rich black loam, giving way to blood-red clay and gently rolling hills.

"Would you look up there!" Lavinia said, leaning forward and pointing ahead. "The dogwood looks like it's piled in drifts up the side of that hill. And the rebuds just coming out are like puffs of pink smoke. I never!"

While the beauties of nature occupied Lavinia's mind, Helen-of-Troy kept a sharp eye peeled for Yankees. Up till now all they'd run across were a few scattered dirt farmers who had assured them that the going was safe as far as they knew. But Helen-of-Troy trusted her own instincts over the say of strangers, and the prickling of the hair on the back of her neck meant trouble, sure as shootin'.

Lavinia realized after a time that the other woman was no longer responding to her enthusiastic chatter. Instinctively, she hushed and listened. What greeted her ears was an unearthly silence. Not a bird chirped in the woods around them. Nor was there any soft scurrying of a rabbit or fox in the brush.

"What's wrong, Helen-of-Troy?" she whispered.

"Don't know. But reckon we'll be findin' out soon enough."

Ahead of them the rutted road wound around the base of a small mountain. Tall trees covered the trail like a dark canopy, their tortured branches clutching at one another and tangling into a gray-black mass that blocked all daylight from the road.

Helen-of-Troy pulled back gently on the reins and murmured to the horses, "Whoa, boys!"

Both women scanned the darkness ahead, squinting to try to make out any signs of movement. But the pass lay still and deserted as far as they could see.

"What do you think?" Lavinia asked.

"I think we either got to go ahead or backtrack. And I ain't never been no good at getting horses to back up."

Lavinia felt under the seat for one of the pistols she'd brought along just in case. That *in case* might be about to present itself! She was a good shot, though she'd never aimed at another human being. But if push came to shove, she could and would shoot. She put the gun in her lap, her finger steady on the trigger, and covered the weapon with her shawl.

"Let's go," she told Helen-of-Troy.

The horses started up again with a jerk but soon settled into a slow, steady clip-clop. The packed earth of the road gave way to a rocky surface so that the metallic ring of the horses' shoes echoed loudly through the woods with each step. The farther they got into the dense forest, the more Lavinia's skin crawled. She knew they were being watched. But by whom? There was not the slightest movement about them. Still, someone was out there—somewhere. She could feel it. She shifted uneasily on the buggy seat. Even the sound of her petticoats rustling against the muslin of her skirt seemed startlingly loud in the silence.

"You see anything, Helen-of-Troy?" Lavinia whispered.

The servant shook her head in answer.

"Me neither, but I can sure feel something."

"Sh-h-h!" the other woman warned.

They rode on slowly, every nerve in both their bodies straining to pick up on the slightest sight, sound, or smell that might mean imminent danger. Lavinia ached with the kind of tension brought on by fear and prolonged immobility. She almost wished the someone or something that was out there would present itself. Nothing could be more terrible than this waiting and not knowing.

Up ahead loomed a turn in the pathway, overhung with dense vines and low, tangled branches. Beyond that bend the twilight they had been traveling through would turn to deepest night. Lavinia clutched the pistol tighter and sent up a silent prayer for their protection.

Helen-of-Troy rolled her eyes heavenward and muttered, "Lord, You get me out of this place and I *swear* I ain't never leaving Thunderbolt again!"

"Hush!" Lavinia cautioned. "Did you hear that?"

"Hear what?"

"I'm not sure . . . branches breaking, leaves rustling. A deer, maybe?" She looked at her servant for reassurance.

" 'Tain't likely."

Both horses began to whinny nervously. Their flanks twitched and they shied, breaking their measured rhythm.

"Whoa, boys! Easy! Steady on down!" Helen-of-Troy soothed them. "Whatever's out there ain't far away now," she whispered.

Suddenly, a grating cry split the dead silence. The horses balked then reared in their traces. Lavinia cried out, feeling her heart leap to her throat. She pulled the gun from beneath her shawl, firing aimlessly into the branches ahead. A second shot from off to the right followed hers, then a breaking of branches and a thud. Directly in their path a large shape lay flapping and gurgling its death cry.

"Damned old turkey buzzard!" Helen-of-Troy observed. "You got him with your first shot, Miss Vinnie!"

Lavinia's eyes weren't on the dead buzzard in the road. She was scanning the side of the mountain for signs of movement as she answered, "I only fired *one* shot!"

"Must be a echo in these parts, then, 'cause I know I heard two."

"Down that way, Caleb!" An unmistakably male voice drifted to them. "You sure you didn't fire off that piece of yours?"

"Never got the chance," a second man answered.

"Well, I coulda swore somebody else shot that turkey before I pulled back on my trigger. I heard it, too."

"You lapped up too much of that moonshine, is all, Jedediah. You're hearing things and you ain't seeing too well neither. That wasn't no turkey, I tell you. It was a buzzard!"

"The hell you say! 'Sides, the men won't know no difference. They sent us out to shoot something for supper. Meat's meat, ain't it?"

"Turkey's one thing. Buzzard's a whole 'nother!"

"Aw, hell! Leastwise we ain't had to resort to eating rats yet like some of them poor bastards!"

Lavinia and Helen-of-Troy sat in silence, both following the two voices down the hillside and watching the spot where they expected to see the men come onto the trail at any moment.

"What we gonna do, Miss Vinnie?"

"Don't worry. I can handle these two. They're probably just a couple of our soldiers sent out to forage. They won't give us any trouble. They may even be able to show us the shortest route to Murfreesboro."

Just then the two men broke out of the underbrush. Their attention turned immediately from the dead buzzard to the buggy and its two female occupants. Lavinia's calm assurance faltered when she saw that the pair were not wearing the Confederate gray she'd expected but were clad in Federal blue, which looked much the worse for wear.

"Miss Vinnie?" Helen-of-Troy whispered in a frightened tone. "They's *Yankees!*"

"Well, how do, ladies?" said the older of the pair, a tall, thin man with a dark stubble of beard. He tipped his battered felt hat and offered them a snaggle-toothed grin.

The other soldier, a lad of perhaps nineteen, gawked at the two women but said nothing. He stood shyly behind the older man, absently picking at a pimple on his chin.

"Good afternoon, gentlemen," Lavinia answered in a voice she forced to be both calm and authoritative. "I wonder if you can tell me if we are still in Georgia or if we've crossed the line into Tennessee."

"Come from the south, did you?" the thin man, Jedediah, inquired.

"Yes. I'm looking for my brother."

Jedediah squinted hard at Lavinia and his smile vanished. "A Johnny Reb, mayhap?"

"A wounded boy!" Lavinia snapped. "Does it matter the color of the uniform he wears? I've come to find him and take him home!"

"Well, now. The color of his clothes does make a mite of difference when you come traipsing through Federal lines. We can't be too careful of spies."

"*Spies?* That's ridiculous!" Lavinia cried.

Suddenly, a horseman appeared, riding out of the gloom ahead. He sat tall in the saddle, and even though Lavinia couldn't see him clearly, she identified him as an officer by the hat he wore and the saber gleaming at his side. As he rode nearer she saw his empty right sleeve. He carried a rifle at the ready in his left hand and held his horse's reins between his teeth. The two soldiers stepped back out of his way as he guided his horse toward the buggy, never taking his eyes off Lavinia. He circled their wagon, then brought his mount to a halt beside her. She could see those eyes now—the ones that had been undressing her with their ice-blue stare. A new kind of dread shivered along her spine when she saw the tortured lines of his granitelike face.

"Did I hear you men say you've captured a spy?" he demanded in a voice as deep as it was cold.

"Could be, Major Coltrain, sir," Jedediah answered. "We was fixing to bring her on along to camp for questioning."

Lavinia tightened her grip on the hidden gun. They weren't taking her anywhere without a fight! She was just about to raise her hand and fire through the shawl when the one-armed officer swung his horse over and leaned down, grabbing shawl, hand, and gun all in one expert movement. Lavinia cried out as his strong fingers crushed her own and dug into her thighs.

Slowly, the major raised her weapon, aiming it directly at Lavinia's heart. She was conscious of the cruel smile playing over his face as he taunted her.

"You men meant to bring me an *armed* captive? Meant to let this one kill me, did you?"

He swung the pistol away from Lavinia, pointing it at his own two men. They shied away, all color draining from their faces.

"No, sir, Major!" Jedediah managed through his terror. "We didn't know she had a gun!"

"I ought to shoot you both on the spot," Coltrain growled, cocking the pistol, toying with his cowering soldiers as a cat plays ruthlessly with a mouse.

"Please, Major, sir!" Caleb whined. "We ain't done nothing!"

Coltrain lowered the pistol, threw back his head, and laughed a sinister, humorless laugh. "On that score, at least, you are correct, soldier! No need to waste good bullets on such a worthless pair."

He shifted his strange, psychotic eyes back to Lavinia, devouring her with his cold blue gaze. She watched what looked like pain twist his features. He grabbed at the empty sleeve and bared his teeth in sudden anguish. Sweat broke out on his forehead.

Jedediah jumped toward the major's horse, putting his hands up in case his superior should slip from his saddle. Coltrain kicked him away in a rage.

"I was only going to get your medicine out of your saddlebag, Major."

"Not now!" Coltrain growled. "I need a clear head to deal with this spy."

"I'm not a spy!" Lavinia cried, but the angry look he turned on her silenced her immediately.

"Escort them back to camp," he ordered the soldiers. "Bring this one to my tent. You men take charge of the nigger wench."

Taking the reins between his teeth once more, Major Coltrain wheeled his devil-black mount with such a jerk that the animal reared and cried out in alarm. Then he was off, charging away into the murky gloom.

Both the soldiers expelled pent-up breaths of relief as Major Coltrain disappeared around the bend in the trail ahead.

"Jesus H. Christ!" Caleb swore. "That man's plumb crazy!"

"You watch your mouth, boy! You say *crazy* and let him hear it and you'll find yourself dancing at the short end of a long rope! Besides, he ain't always been this way. It's that stuff he takes for the pain makes him mean as a rattler with his tail in a knot. Just step easy around him. There won't be no problem."

Lavinia had heard every word they said. Now her mind whirled as Jedediah clamped a hand onto one of the horses' bridles, urging the team on along the path. When he paused to snatch up the dead buzzard from the roadway, she said, "Jedediah, you aren't really going to turn the two of us over to that madman, are you?"

He grinned back at her and chuckled, poking a joshing elbow into Caleb's ribs. "Hell, no, ma'am! Why, I wouldn't do a thing like that. I'm only gonna turn *you* over to the major. That nigger of yours is gonna cook this here bird for me and the fellers!"

Lavinia and Helen-of-Troy both gasped. For the rest of the ride they sat rigid and silent, not knowing what to expect when they reached the Union encampment. Lavinia worriedly turned over in her mind dozens of stories she'd heard about Federal soldiers' treatment of women spies. Most of the tales had come from the men of her old unit, the Wiregrass Rifles, and were not reassuring. Never mind! she thought. There was no way they could prove that she was a spy. On the other hand, there was no way she could prove that she wasn't!

By the time they reached the camp on the far side of the mountain, dusk had dwindled to full dark. Cookfires glowed among the tents, but from the smell of parched corn pervading the air, Lavinia could tell that the men were low on victuals. The cheers that went up when Jedediah raised the dead buzzard for all to see bore that out.

Her captors halted the buggy before a tent that was larger than the others in the clearing. Warm light glowed through the canvas and the delicious odor of stewing beef wafted from inside. The major obviously did not share his men's meager rations but kept a separate well-stocked larder for himself.

"Major Coltrain, sir," Jedediah called.

A prolonged silence followed. Jedediah shifted his weight impatiently from one foot to the other but did not call a second time. Lavinia's fear began to give way to annoyance, then anger. The black clouds that had been hugging the peak of the mountain all afternoon now opened up. She was not only being kept waiting by this impertinent man; she was being kept waiting in the rain. After traveling all day she was bone-weary. And the smell of the major's stew was making her stomach rumble with desire. No matter if the man was insane, she wouldn't mind tasting a bit of his stew.

"Maybe he didn't hear you," she finally said to Jedediah.

"He heard. He'll let us know when he's ready."

"Call him again," Lavinia demanded.

Jedediah answered her with a hard look.

Lavinia gave it a few more seconds but finally lost all patience. Standing suddenly, she shouted, "Major Coltrain! *If you please!*"

Immediately, the tent flap flew back and a dark face peered out at them. "What you mean disturbing the major's dinner? You shush out here till he's ready to receive!"

"I will not shush!" Lavinia shouted back at the officer's black servant. "You may inform Major Coltrain that Miss Lavinia Rutledge of Thunderbolt Plantation will be joining him for dinner. Now!"

The servant's head popped back in the tent flap for an instant, then out again. "The major, he say, 'Do tell the lady to come in!' "

"Thank you!" Lavinia answered haughtily.

"Miss Vinnie, what am I going to do?" Helen-of-Troy asked.

"You're going to come with me," Jedediah informed her, "and pluck this bird and cook him."

"I ain't never cooked no turkey buzzard in all my born days, and I don't plan to start now!" But her protests were in vain as

Jedediah plopped the ugly creature into Helen-of-Troy's plump arms and started to usher her away.

Just before she entered the major's tent, Lavinia offered Helen-of-Troy a pleading glance that she hoped would be reassuring as well.

"Well, this is a surprise!" the major said, rising from his heavily laden table as Lavinia entered his tent. "I hadn't expected such a charming guest for dinner. Roscoe, another plate! Quickly, boy! Then you may leave us."

Lavinia eyed Major Coltrain suspiciously. He looked and acted different now. On the trail she'd thought him a hard, fierce man, filled with bitterness and cruelty. But now, washed and combed for dinner, he might even have been called handsome in a rough-chiseled way. His thick black hair was combed back from his high forehead, and the harsh lines about his full mouth softened in the lamplight. Only those frigid blue eyes still retained a hint of malice.

The tall, undeniably attractive man stood back stroking the pointed goatee on his chin, measuring Lavinia with a new kind of interest.

"So you're a spy, hm-m-m?" he mused.

"I am not!" Lavinia answered.

"Well, now . . . Miss Rutledge, was it? I'd hardly expect anything other than a denial out of you. We've had more than our share of trouble from Rebel undercover agents. And more often than not, they come in the guise of charming young ladies, even though some wear trousers underneath their petticoats. Only last week I had such a male impostor hanged for his chicanery. A pity, too, for he wasn't a bad sort."

Lavinia thought suddenly of Damien. Was he the only Confederate soldier who sometimes masqueraded as a woman, or were there others? She felt the blood drain from her face suddenly as the word *hanged* echoed in her brain.

"My dear Miss Rutledge, you've gone quite pale." He came toward her, reaching out with his hand as if to steady her. "Have I touched a sensitive spot, perhaps?"

Suddenly, his hand shot up, closing on her neck and chin in a painful grip. His mad eyes flared at her. Lavinia wanted to scream, but swallowed her pain instead. She could not let him know how afraid she really was. Still holding her, he ran a rough finger over her lips, then brought his mouth down hard on hers. Lavinia struggled against him, but the man had obviously practiced his one-handed grip. She could not get away without breaking her own neck.

"You don't kiss like a spy," he said with a low laugh. "Most of them use their first opportunity to work their feminine wiles on a man—any man. But you resist me, Miss Rutledge."

"As I would resist any man who tried to take advantage of me!" she snapped.

"Ah, the 'death over dishonor' school of thought!" he said sarcastically. "I was once a victim of such distorted thinking. You see my badge of honor—an empty sleeve and a shattered life!"

Lavinia was torn suddenly between feeling sorry for the man and hating him for what he was and what he was doing to her.

"Pardon me, Major, but at least you still have your life. That's far more than some can boast. My own brother may be lying dead somewhere at this very moment and my fiancé—" She broke off, fearing to bring Damien's name into the conversation.

The major bowed to her slightly. "My apologies, Miss Rutledge, and my condolences. I do tend to get maudlin from time to time. You're perfectly within your rights to remind me that there are others less fortunate than I. Now, if you'll kindly unbutton your blouse for me, we can have done with all this and get on with dinner."

"I beg your pardon!" Lavinia said, taking several stumbling steps back from him and clutching at her bodice.

"Oh, come, come, *Miss* Rutledge! Please don't insult my intelligence by trying to play the innocent. Either you are a woman or you aren't. I'm only trying to save you some embarrassment."

Lavinia was fuming. "You'll pardon me if I don't thank you for your kind consideration, Major, but I really can't see how you plan to *save* me anything!" She spat at him.

"On the contrary, Miss Rutledge." He moved toward her again, clasping one hand behind her neck and bringing his lips dangerously close to hers while his wild eyes burned with the feverish light of madness. "The alternative would be to call my sergeant in to strip you naked. I'm quite certain the soldier would enjoy that—if you are indeed a young lady, as you claim. However, you might not find the experience as pleasurable as he."

"You are *insane*!" Lavinia gasped, realizing he knew full well she was a woman, and was just toying with her.

Immediately, Major Coltrain's demeanor changed. His lips strained into a thin, hateful line and his eyes narrowed to dark slits. She watched his hand, fascinated with horror as he flexed his fingers in a clawlike fashion.

"Insane, is it?" he said in a tone chillingly controlled. "If that's the case, then you have all the more to fear from me."

"I'm not afraid of you!" Lavinia said, as much to reassure herself as to convince him.

His strangely mobile features softened. "I'm glad. Most people do fear me. But I like you, Miss Rutledge. I'd like for us to be friends."

Lavinia allowed herself to relax slightly. "That might be pleasant, Major Coltrain, in different surroundings, under different circumstances."

"I agree," he answered calmly. "So why don't we finish this business at once. Open your blouse!"

Lavinia stood staring at him for a moment, trying to decide what to do. She could make a dash for the tent flap and get away from him. But the momentary escape would be futile. His men were right outside. They would only recapture her and return her to the major. She had no doubt that he would have her stripped then, possibly humiliated before all his men, as punishment. She'd heard of such shameful things happening when women defied these godless Unionists.

"I must play on your sympathy now, Miss Rutledge," he said after a time. "My arm is paining me like the very devil and my temper is growing short. Please don't make me do something that we'll both regret. Shall I help you?'' He made a move toward her and reached for her laces.

''No!'' she cried, and resignedly began undoing her bodice. A moment later her muslin dress gaped open to the waist. Lavinia stared at Coltrain defiantly, not wanting him to know the shame and degradation she felt. He came to her with his one hand and parted the fabric. He needed only a glance for his proof, but his hand lingered on her bare breasts. The heel of his palm brushed her nipple and she felt her body respond. He stared at her with hungry eyes that held both threat and promise. When he leaned so close that she became conscious of his breath teasing her flesh, Lavinia felt heat rise in her body and blood rush to stain her burning cheeks.

''I'm quite satisfied that you're all woman now, Miss Rutledge. Thank you.'' He turned his back on her abruptly. ''If you'll see to your laces, we'll dine.''

Lavinia, quickly and with a great sense of relief, fastened her bodice. She felt almost triumphant, as if she'd just done some great service for the Cause. She knew it was silly, but she had faced down the enemy and sacrificed something of herself for the Confederacy. It was almost as if she were sporting her first battle wound. The crazy thought that crossed her mind was *Damien will be so proud of me when he finds out*! Then her sensible side took over, warning her that Damien must never know of this encounter with Major Coltrain. Still, she felt quite pleased with herself when she turned, ready to sit down to dinner.

But Major Sam Coltrain was not sitting. He was waiting to intercept her. Surprising her and taking her off balance, he pulled her hard against his chest, once more seeking her lips. Lavinia fought to get out of his grasp, but the major's one arm was like a steel band around her. His lips came down savagely, imprisoning her mouth with his. Her struggling seemed only to encourage him. After a time she forced herself to stop resisting, though she did not respond to him in any way.

''There, you see,'' he said, releasing her at last, ''you'll come around in time. You *all* do!''

She felt stunned, light-headed. ''What do you mean?''

"You camp followers. If you aren't a spy, then surely you're a 'hooker,' as the men call you women. Well, Miss Rutledge, you'll be happy to know that you have a place here with me, at least for the night."

He took his seat again at the table and motioned Lavinia to join him. She sat, but kept a cautious eye on her host.

"If you want to know the truth of the matter, I'm damn sick of this war!" he said. "I left a thriving timber business in New Hampshire to join the army. I left a woman I planned to marry, who I later learned didn't wait for me. I left everything pleasant, happy, and civilized behind me. And now I've left my arm buried in a trench outside the surgeon's tent on some bloody battlefield I've tried to forget. The only future I see is whatever pleasure I can eke out minute by minute, day by day." He reached across the table, took Lavinia's hand, and brought it to his lips. "And you, my dear lady, are my pleasure for this moment."

His words gave Lavinia a strange feeling. She'd never thought about the other side of the war, the sacrifices the men in blue were forced to make. Her only concern had been for the Confederate soldiers. She still considered Sam Coltrain the enemy, but she also saw him as a man, much like any other . . . even Damien Clay.

His stew was delicious and she was famished. For a time she didn't talk to the major but ate her fill greedily. He sat in silence, too, smiling as he watched her consume a generous portion.

"All of you come into camp half starved," he observed. "I've never seen anything like the way you women can eat. Don't you bring provisions along with you when you set out to find us?"

Lavinia laid her silver fork across the top of her cleared plate and wiped her mouth daintily with her linen napkin. "I'm not one of the women you keep referring to, Major. I'm neither a spy nor a camp follower. And I certainly didn't set out to find *you*! I'm looking for my brother. He's a lieutenant with the Confederate Cavalry. He was unaccounted for after the Battle of Shiloh."

A dark look crossed the major's rugged face. "Shiloh," he echoed. "That's a name we'll all be a long time forgetting."

"You were there, then?" Lavinia asked hopefully.

He nodded and looked at her with clouded blue eyes. "I was there."

"Then you might have seen Josiah!"

"I might have. I might even have killed him!"

The major's words dropped like a heavy weight on Lavinia's heart. He was right, of course. This whole mission to find her brother might be futile. Tears brimmed in her eyes.

"I'm sorry," he whispered, taking her hand in his. "I shouldn't have said that. There's no need for me to upset you needlessly."

"I'll have to go to the battlefield, I suppose. It's the only way I'll know for sure."

"No!" he said vehemently. "You can't do that!"

"It's not safe?"

"Oh, it's safe enough now. But you don't want to see it. Take my word for it."

His voice was so grim that Lavinia hardly dared ask him why not. But she had to know.

"Miss Rutledge," he answered, "have you no concept of this war? Thousands of men were killed at Shiloh! The battlefield, in time, will be a boneyard, but right now . . . so soon after . . ." He paused, not wanting to finish the thought, but seeing her determined expression, he rushed on. "There were too many casualties for the burial detail to do a decent job. You'd best turn your buggy south and go back home."

Lavinia was near tears again, thinking of the possibility of Josiah lying unburied on the battlefield. "No, I can't do that," she whispered.

"You aren't going to Shiloh?"

"No. I'll go on to Murfreesboro. I have the name of a friend in that town. Perhaps I'll hear some news when I get there. I can't go home. Not without knowing."

Feeling that her mission to find Josiah was all but impossible, Lavinia's thoughts turned suddenly back to Damien. Fear clutched at her once more.

"The spy you said you hanged, Major, what was his name?"

Sam Coltrain's eyes narrowed with suspicion. Perhaps the whole story of a missing brother was mere fabrication. It was the sort of trick these Rebel spies used to throw a man off his guard.

"Why so interested, Miss Rutledge?"

"No reason. Female curiosity." She tried to sound unconcerned but failed.

"Oh, come now, dear lady! Don't take me for an idiot. We've established the fact that you are a woman. But we have yet to determine whether or not you're a spy. Were you in this area, perhaps, expecting to pass information on to someone else—maybe even a man with long dark hair and a face and figure transformed by his artistic cunning?"

Lavinia cringed at the change in the major's voice and the description of the hanged man—so like Damien.

"No," she whispered. "I'm not carrying any information. I'm not a spy. I'm only a woman looking for her lost brother and her lost—"

"Yes, Miss Rutledge? Go on with it!" he demanded. "It's completely within my power to brand you a spy and order your execution. Finish your last statement or I swear to you . . ."

"My lost lover!" she yelled at him, tears rushing to flood her eyes. "There! Are you satisfied? I'm trying to find the man I love. The man I plan to marry!"

Sam Coltrain rose suddenly and came to her side of the table, where he stood glaring down at her. In a surprise move he grasped her arm and pulled her up to him. His lips almost touching hers, he said through clenched teeth, "Oh, I think you have a very good reason for all these questions! I don't like being made a fool of, Miss Rutledge. Your *poor brother*! Your *poor lover*! How well you Southern women lie! Who are you working for—Mosby, Morgan, or Lee himself?"

"No," Lavinia cried. "I told you, I'm not a spy!"

Sam Coltrain laughed low in his throat, an ugly, humorless sound, then said, "You've come to the wrong place for information, my dear. We've been cut off from our unit since Shiloh." He laughed again. Actually, you could say we severed the ties ourselves. Coltrain's men are operating toward their own ends now. So, you see, you'll get no information here. My men and I are staying as far away from Federal lines as possible."

"Deserters?" Lavinia gasped.

"You might call us that. I prefer to think of myself simply as a sane man in a world gone mad. But I'll give you something to tell your superiors so that your little foray won't be a total loss." He clutched Lavinia to him, crushing her lips with his. After a prolonged kiss, he held her close and whispered harshly into her ear, "You can tell them that Sam Coltrain was not only an excellent soldier but an unsurpassed lover as well!"

"No!" She cried, beating her fists against his strong chest.

She fought him tooth and nail but could not tear out of his grasp. He covered her face and throat with hot, hungry kisses even as she slashed his neck and face with her nails.

"Damn you!" he yelled, throwing her to his bunk. "I wish you were a spy! They'll go to any lengths to save themselves and, frankly, I need a woman badly right now, Miss Rutledge. What I do not need is more pain!" He pulled a bandanna from his pocket and wiped the blood from his face and neck. "Will you accept money?"

Lavinia stared at him, dazed and confused. "What?"

"Money, woman! Federal gold in payment for your favors?"

Suddenly, his meaning came to her all too clearly. And topped by that realization the cruel weight of her fears for Josiah and Damien became too much for her. In all likelihood they were both dead. She fell back against the pillow, sobbing. Sam Coltrain had said he couldn't take any more pain. Lavinia Rutledge had more at the moment than she could bear. She lost herself in it, wanting nothing more than to be able to vanish from this terrible world of war and madness and death.

When Sam Coltrain, bewildered by her hysterics, came close to lay a comforting hand on her arm, she screamed at him, "Why don't you just go ahead and hang me if you think I'm a spy?" In her anguish she half hoped he would take up her challenge.

But then his fingers were smoothing the tangle of hair back from her brow. A moment later a glass of brandy touched her lips and she drank slowly, deeply. The warmth of the wine burned her mouth and throat, but swirled through her body with an anesthetizing sweetness. A wonderful languor settled over her. She seemed to be floating some distance above her own body. She felt the weight of her grief removed, replaced by no emotion at all, only a pleasant vacuum of sensations.

She lay on her back, staring up at nothing. She was aware of Sam Coltrain fumbling at her laces, but her limbs were too heavy to resist. Besides, what did it matter? What did anything matter anymore?

He undressed her slowly with his one hand. In her present state she offered no resistance. As he stripped away each garment, he lingered over the uncovered flesh—fondling, kissing, tasting. Somewhere deep inside, Lavinia knew that her breasts and thighs were being stroked, that her lips were being kissed, that the most intimate parts of her were being explored by an urgent and searching hand, but her conscious mind ignored him completely. Instead, she painted pleasant fantasies of herself and Damien together at the river cottage.

"More brandy before . . . ?" a man's voice seemed to ask from a great distance.

She rose slightly to accept the drink, then sank back into her pleasant euphoria as the scorching liquid sent out new probing fingers of warmth to fondle and arouse her.

Suddenly, the insistent pressure of a knee between her legs snapped her back to her senses. Her eyes shot open to stare, startled, into Sam Coltrain's. He hovered over her, naked and ready to take her.

"I'm glad you're back, Miss Rutledge," he whispered. "You should get some enjoyment along with your fee."

He counted out twenty gold pieces, letting each clink down,

making a pile on her belly. The touch of the cold coins came like a shock wave, jolting her, repelling her. Suddenly, her eyes danced with angry green fire.

"No!" she screamed, pushing him away from her. She scooped up the coins and flung them at his head.

Coltrain, his face pale with fury, drew back to strike her, but something in Lavinia's expression stopped him. He recognized a certain pride and valor in her demeanor that had once lived in his own heart. To violate such a woman would destroy what little self-respect he still possessed. He lowered his threatening hand and took a step back from her. But he couldn't force his gaze away from her magnificent form, her full breasts heaving wonderfully with rage and indignation.

"Hang me!" she said in a deadly voice. "I'd rather that than this. The only way you'll ever have me is to kill me first!"

"I've killed my last man and hanged my last spy in the right-eous name of the Union." Coltrain replied. "And until to-night, Miss Rutledge, I have never tried to force myself on a woman. If anyone needs hanging, it is I!"

He turned away and began pulling his clothes on.

She stared at him in shocked amazement. "Then why . . . ?"

"Why did I try to take you? I don't know why. Probably be-cause you're the most desirable woman I've been with in a very long time. Because I just found out there's no one waiting for me back home and I'm mad as hell and needed to take out the hurt on a woman—any woman." His angry tone softened al-most to a whisper. "No, that's not it! The minute I saw you out on the road I knew I had to have you. I thought I could persuade you one way or another. I suppose I thought I might frighten you into submitting." He stopped talking for a moment, as if searching for the right words. "You hate me now, Lavinia Rut-ledge. I know that and I'm sorry for it. I don't know where you came from or where you're headed, but our paths will cross again. And when they do, you'll come to me willingly. When you're ready for it, I'm going to show you the meaning of love as no man ever has before or ever will again!"

Lavinia tried to deny that his words had any impact on her. She loved Damien and no other. Certainly her only feeling for

Sam Coltrain was hostility. Still, there was something about his words that touched her.

He leaned close and captured her lips again, searching her mouth deeply. Lavinia drew away and stared up at him.

"You sleep now," he whispered. "I'll watch over you."

Lavinia did sleep, almost immediately. But at intervals during the night she was awakened by Sam Coltrain's lips upon hers. Each time, as soon as her eyes fluttered open, he would go back to his chair, take his seat, and sit staring at her with those strange, cold blue eyes that shone with a mixture of love and hate.

All night the lamp burned inside the tent. It was still burning when she awoke just after dawn. And her first waking vision was of Sam Coltrain, wide-awake in his chair near the cot. She sat up and stared back at him.

"You didn't sleep at all?" she asked.

"You'll be leaving this morning. I can sleep after you're gone. I couldn't waste a minute while you were here, Lavinia Rutledge. I have to remember you so I can keep you in my memory until I find you again."

"Sam," Lavinia said softly, using his given name for the first time, "I told you I love another man. I'm going to be married soon."

"I'm surprised you aren't already," he answered matter-of-factly. "It won't make any difference. We'll meet again someday."

Lavinia was beginning to feel more than casual discomfort in Sam Coltrain's presence. She rose to find Helen-of-Troy and be on her way. His eyes never left her as she dressed, but he made no move to touch her. Then as she was about to leave the tent he jumped up and barred her way.

"Lavinia," he said in a pained, pleading voice, "before you go . . ."

She looked into his face—the tortured eyes, the ugly scratches on his cheeks where she had clawed him the night before, the full lips that she now knew so well.

"Yes, Sam?"

He raised his hand slowly, tentatively, to her cheek, cupping it gently. Then his fingers slid down her throat, hesitating when his hand reached her shoulder. She made no movement to resist his touch. He cupped her breast, closing his eyes as he fondled her. Lavinia bit her lip, trying to hold back unbidden tears as she thought of the way Damien's hands felt upon her. Would she ever feel his touch again?

"You wanted to know the name of the spy I hanged," Sam whispered as if he had read her worried mind. "It was Whit Bradley."

Lavinia covered the hand on her breast with trembling fingers in a gesture of gratitude. "Thank you, Sam Coltrain. I won't soon forget you."

He laughed and kissed her lips quickly. "I won't give you a chance," he answered. "We've an appointment to keep—sometime, someplace!"

As Lavinia rode out of camp with Helen-of-Troy beside her still grumbling about having had to cook a buzzard, Major Sam Coltrain called after her, "I mean to have you, Lavinia Rutledge. If not in this life, in the next!"

"What's that man yammerin' about?" Helen-of-Troy asked. "And what did he do to you last night?"

"Oh, nothing much," Lavinia answered evasively.

"He acts plumb crazy!"

"Maybe he is," Lavinia answered. "And then again, maybe Sam Coltrain is the only sane man left in the world!"

Lavinia rode through the hills of southern Tennessee all day in silence, thinking about her strange experience of the night before. What had it all meant? And how had her meeting with Sam Coltrain changed her, if at all? Finally, she gave up trying to work it all out and forced her thoughts ahead to Murfreesboro and Damien. That was one thing she didn't have to puzzle over—her love and need for him.

"Touch those horses up, Helen-of-Troy!" Lavinia commanded suddenly, an edge of excitement in her voice.

"Child, you in a powerful hurry all of a sudden."

"I surely am!" Lavinia answered, smiling at the thought that each clip-clop was bringing her closer to the man she loved.

Chapter Twelve

The big old two-story house on Main Street, just off the public square in Murfreesboro, hummed with activity. Everyone in town noticed the servants scurrying in and out, beating rugs, washing windows, sweeping the wide front porch. And the smells of turkey, ham, and fruit pies cooking drifted on the spring wind clear to Stones River. The excitement emanating from the Ready house infected the whole town. So much hustle and bustle could mean only one thing.

"Morning, Charlie!" the mayor called as his buggy rumbled down Main Street. "Reckon Jack Morgan must be coming to pay a call on Miss Mattie."

"Reckon so!" Charles Ready answered from behind a copy of the *Daily Rebel Banner* as he sat on his front porch, an island of calm in the storm.

Everyone in Rutherford County, and, indeed, all of Middle Tennessee, knew and respected the Honorable Charles Ready, prominent attorney, gentleman farmer, and statesman of no small repute. But in spite of all his other accomplishments, at this point in time his greatest claim to fame seemed to be that he was Martha Ready's father.

Although his other two daughters, Mary and Alice, received their share of suitors, too, Mattie's romance with dashing Colonel Morgan was the most talked-about love affair of the war.

"My dear!" Mrs. Bascomb exclaimed over the pickle barrel

145

at the general store to old Mrs. Colter, who was hard of hearing and used an ear trumpet. "You know he's sixteen years older than she is, don't you? And a widower! His poor wife Becky's hardly cold in the grave."

"Eh? Speak up, Lizzie. You say she was lost in a cave?"

"Cold in the grave! Spent years just withering away after their poor little boy died. Now, boom! He's going to up and marry Mattie!"

"Eh?"

"Marry Mattie Ready!"

"Who married Mattie?"

"John Hunt Morgan!"

"I declare! I didn't even know he'd asked her yet!"

He hadn't, but this morning as Mattie Ready sat before her mirror, brushing her long brown hair, her gray eyes danced with a certain expectant sparkle and her cheeks were high with excited color. Her thoughts, of course, were all of Jack Morgan.

"Mattie, are you going to primp in front of that looking glass all day?" Alice's pretty head bobbed around the doorjamb, a teasing frown on her face. "Colonel Morgan will come riding up the street and want to sweep you right off your feet and I'll have to say, 'Why, I'm so sorry, Jack darlin', but Mattie's still not fit to be seen. Won't I do?' " A twisting of curls around a finger and a fluttering of eyelashes accompanied Alice's speech.

In the mirror Mattie made a face that reflected back at her younger sister. Taking down the felt hat she'd adorned with an ostrich plume in imitation of the one Morgan wore, she set it at a rakish angle on her head. She held her hairbrush beneath her pert nose to simulate his mustache, and in a suitably deep voice said to her sister, "I'm right sorry, Miss Alice. But my heart, soul, and body belong to Mattie!" Martha swaggered about the bedroom, imitating Morgan's bold stride as best she could in her long pink skirts. "You see, Miss Alice, though you're a comely enough *child*, my Mattie's *all woman* and fits me like a glove."

Alice squealed in embarrassed delight and gasped, "Martha Ready! Shame on you for saying such naughty things!"

Mattie dropped her disguise, winked, and whispered, "I think them all the time. I might as well say them aloud. But only to you, and to my diary, of course, Alice. I'd never let Jack know that I want him . . . not *that* way."

"Do you think he'll ask you to marry him this time?"

Mattie's heart gave a sudden thump. She removed the hat and stared at it as if she were looking at the man himself and might read an answer to Alice's question in his beloved face. She hardly dared hope for such a miracle. The first Mrs. Morgan, God rest her, hadn't been gone quite a year. Propriety dictated that he hold off on making any such commitment. Still, because it was wartime, some conventions were being broken. Mattie herself had been about as brazen as a girl could be in order to catch John Hunt Morgan's attention, spreading the word before she ever even met him that she planned to become his wife.

Her initial statement had come out of a burst of heartfelt patriotism. As the war had divided North and South, so had it severed the romantic ties between Martha Ready and her most ardent suitor in Washington, Illinois Representative Samuel Scott Marshall. When he chose to don the Federal blue, Mattie had bidden him a fond farewell, telling Alice afterward, "It's a good thing, for it would have been more than I could stand, with him on one side and brother Horace on the other."

Back in middle Tennessee, Mattie staunchly embraced the cause of the Confederacy. She made clothing, rolled bandages, helped raise money, and sewed battle flags inscribed "Victory or Death." When Fort Henry fell, Mattie and her sisters wept. Then the war moved to their very doorstep and along with it came the dashing Captain John Hunt Morgan. The Readys opened their home to the officers stationed nearby and it became unofficial headquarters for General William J. Hardee and his staff. The lovely Ready sisters acted as their charming hostesses.

One evening General Hardee brought one of Morgan's men to dinner. Seated next to Martha, but confused by how much she and her sisters all looked alike, he said, "Pardon me, but may I ask your name?"

Martha, her heart burning with patriotic zeal from hearing the latest exploits of Morgan's Raiders, replied, "My name is Mattie Ready, but, God willing, you may soon call me Mrs. John Hunt Morgan!"

The young officer, impressed and somewhat in awe that he had sat next to the lady who would soon wed his commander, spread the news about camp upon returning. Morgan was amused and curious when word of his bride-to-be reached his ears. He mentioned the gossip to General Hardee, who immediately saw his chance at matchmaking. Calling one of his messengers, the general said, "Tell the Readys that I'm bringing the famous Captain Morgan to dinner. And be sure to tell Miss Mattie that he's a widower and a little sad. I want her to sing for him."

So Miss Martha Ready sang for John Hunt Morgan, and before she knew what was happening, Mattie found herself in a whirlwind wartime courtship with the most desirable officer in the Confederate Army. Jack Morgan proved the typical southern aristocrat—seemingly shy, soft-spoken, and modest in the drawing room, his calm demeanor belying his daring recklessness in battle. But his appearance alone, from shining spurs to plumed hat, proclaimed him a hero of the South. Every woman who saw him fell perfectly in love in an instant. But only Martha Ready could claim his heart. He had been courting her for some time now. All that remained was the actual bending of his knee, the saying of *I do's*, and then . . .

"Mattie Ready, you're a million miles away!" Alice complained. "You'd better get yourself back here before he arrives. And you haven't answered my question yet. Do you think he'll ask you to marry him?"

Mattie made a sudden rush at her sister, embracing Alice so tightly that the younger girl squealed in protest.

"Oh, dear God, I pray he will!" Mattie cried.

By the middle of the following morning Lavinia Rutledge could see the end of her long journey just ahead. The trip had been grueling but blessedly uneventful since her skirmish with Sam Coltrain. The man's words and the strange fire in his eyes still haunted her, but her heart beat for Damien Clay alone.

"I reckon that must be Murfreesboro up the road," Helen-of-Troy said with a relieved sigh. "Lordy, these old bones ain't never gonna be the same, Miss Vinnie!"

Lavinia sat up taller, arching her aching body and rubbing the small of her back with both hands. "I know what you mean, but we'll be fit as a couple of fiddles after a good night's sleep in a bed. A decent meal won't hurt any either! I'm so hungry I could even eat that old turkey buzzard about now."

"You shush that, Miss Vinnie! You know good and well a lady don't never get hungry!"

Lavinia said nothing but smiled to herself. After all they'd been through on this trip—facing down Yankees, hauling the wagon out of muddy streams when it got stuck, sleeping in the wild, and last night, taking a Saturday-night bath naked in a river so she'd look halfway respectable when she presented herself to the Readys—Helen-of-Troy still thought first of what was and wasn't proper! It made a person want to giggle right out loud, but Lavinia stopped herself. Helen-of-Troy would only tell her that giggling wasn't ladylike either.

Lavinia's thoughts were interrupted by the sudden sound of thunder. Instinctively, she glanced up, but the morning sky was an unmarred expanse of brilliant blue. Still, the thunder rolled.

"Lordy, Miss Vinnie!" Helen-of-Troy screamed. "They're coming right down on us! Giddap, you horses! Move it!"

Jerking her head toward the rumbling sound behind them, Lavinia saw a cavalcade of horsemen pounding the road to a thick cloud of dust. They were soldiers; she knew by their company banner and the sounds of their sabers clanging. But soldiers from which army? The swirling dust obscured the riders. Her heart pounded in time with the thudding of the oncoming hooves.

The horses pulling the buggy, frightened by the noise and Helen-of-Troy's angry admonitions, pitched and reared but refused to turn off the road. Just as Lavinia was sure the approaching troop would overrun them, a tall officer riding a black horse called a halt. She watched in amazement as the column of Confederate Cavalry stopped in orderly fashion some yards away. Their leader, his coal-black mount prancing prettily, approached alone. He sat erect in the saddle, the plume in his hat waving jauntily. By the time he reined in next to the buggy, Lavinia's eyes were wide and her pulse racing.

"Ma'am," he said, sweeping off his hat and inclining his head toward her in gallant fashion. "I hope we didn't frighten you. Allow me to present myself. I'm Colonel . . ."

"Morgan," Lavinia breathed. "John Hunt Morgan!"

A delighted smile, showing even white teeth, spread itself between his full mustache and clipped beard. A twinkle of amusement flashed in his clear gray-blue eyes.

"My notoriety rides before me," he said with a warm chuckle.

"I heard all about you before we left Georgia . . . from my fiancé."

Morgan quickly added up the clues—she'd come from Georgia, she was young and beautiful in her crisp yellow frock, and there was no mistaking the family resemblance to the five brothers who had fought with him at Shiloh. "Ah, Miss Rutledge," he surprised her by saying, "what a delight to meet you!" He reached for her hand and brought it to his lips while Lavinia stared in awe. "Captain Clay has spread your fame far and wide."

She gave a little cry of excitement and turned to look back at Morgan's men. "Damien! Is he here?"

"Not at the moment. But I'll send one of my men back to camp to summon him immediately." He turned and waved a hand, calling, "Hawks!"

One of the soldiers rode forward to join them. He was a handsome young lieutenant who reminded Lavinia very much of Josiah. She smiled, thinking of her brother. Lieutenant Hawks returned her smile and, tipping his hat, said, "Good morning, ma'am."

"Miss Rutledge, may I present Lieutenant Henry Hawks," Morgan said formally. Then turning back to his aide, he ordered, "Ride back and find Captain Clay. Tell him his fiancée . . ." He paused, grinning mischievously, and winked at Lavinia. "On second thought, Hawks, don't tell him anything except that I need him in Murfreesboro right away. Tell him to come to the Ready residence as quickly as horseflesh can carry him. And, Hawks," he called after the courier, who was already on his way, "whatever you do, don't mention Miss Rutledge to him."

Lavinia's spirits soared. She joined in with Morgan's pleased laughter as they watched Lieutenant Hawks spur his mount to more speed and soar over a stone fence to cut across a field.

"Is that a prerequisite for becoming one of Morgan's Raiders, Colonel?"

"Fine horsemanship, you mean, Miss Rutledge?"

"No, Colonel. That's not what I mean! Are all your men required to be as refined and handsome as you and Lieutenant Hawks . . . *and* Captain Clay?"

His eyes glittering with merriment, Jack Morgan brought her fingertips to his lips once more. "Ah, my dear lady! Were I not on a special mission to win the heart of my own true love, I would steal you away from my good friend Damien at this very moment. You are, indeed, a treasure!"

Mattie Ready had spent a horrendous night tossing, turning, and jumping nearly out of her skin at the slightest sound. When she did doze off for a moment or two, she awoke in a sweat, terrified by dreams of what might be happening to John Hunt Morgan. Now as she dressed to go to church with her family, she moved about her room in a daze, each motion taking extreme effort.

Where could he be? What could have happened? The message he'd sent on ahead had stated that she should expect him on Saturday. Now here it was Sunday morning already and not a sign of him, not a word to ease her mind and heart.

"Mattie dear?" her mother called from the hallway. "The buggy's around front. We're all waiting for you."

"Coming, Mother," she answered, but still she hesitated. What if he came while she was in church? Worse yet—what if he sent a message and the courier found no one at home? She might spend days waiting and worrying needlessly.

A small black slave scurried past her open door, trying to catch Alice's cat, Stonewall. The sight of the little boy sparked an idea. Mattie hurried to her door and called, "Bo-Bob, you come here!"

The tiny servant, struggling with the fat yellow cat in his arms, hurried to her. "Yessum, Miss Mattie?"

"I'm going to give you something really important to do this morning."

"I done got ole Stonewall, Miss Mattie!" Bo-Bob announced proudly. "He ain't so smart as he thinks!"

"That's very good, Bo-Bob, but this is even more important. You put Stonewall out, then I want you to sit on the front steps while we're at church. If anyone comes by looking for me, you take his message and scoot right over to the church. Tiptoe in and give it to me. Do you understand?"

"Yessum, Miss Mattie. I'll do that very thing."

She watched as the boy, still struggling under Stonewall's protesting weight, strutted down the hallway, impressed with his important mission.

"Mattie, *please*!" her mother called again.

"Coming right now," she answered.

But before she headed for the stairs, Mattie Ready removed the little white hat trimmed with silk cherry blossoms she'd planned to wear to church and put on her plumed felt instead.

Just for luck! she told herself, giving the broad-brimmed hat a pat as she hurried down to join her family.

Their usual slow Sunday drive to church was quick this morning, since Mattie had almost made them late. As they hurried inside, she was very conscious of everyone staring at her. The faces all seemed to register accusation, as if it were her fault Colonel Morgan had failed to appear at the appointed time. Martha Ready set her beplumed head at a proud tilt, squared her shoulders, and walked down the aisle like a queen. Let them think what they would!

But her lofty spirits flagged as the service dragged on and Bo-Bob failed to appear with the hoped-for message. As Mattie's optimism faded, her mind wandered. She lost her place in the prayer book, forgot the words to her favorite hymn, and try as she would she couldn't concentrate on the reverend's sage admonitions about the wages of sin.

"Mattie!" Alice poked her and hissed under her breath, "Stand up!"

Mattie came out of her mental meander with a start and looked around to see that the entire congregation was on its feet. Only she and old Mrs. Colter with her ear trumpet and cane remained seated in their pews. She stood quickly and then her heart all but stopped. There, two rows down, she saw Bo-Bob, a folded paper in his little fist, searching for her everywhere.

"Bo-Bob!" she whispered loudly. Heads turned and Mrs. Bascomb, her huge bosom heaving with righteous indignation, shushed her loudly.

The boy offered his young mistress a wide grin of relief and hurried to her. "A soldier done brung this, Miss Mattie," he said, handing her the note.

"Thank you, Bo-Bob! You run along home now."

She tried to finish singing the hymn, but her mind refused to focus and her lips were trembling so that she couldn't form the right words. When they sat down again, she unfolded the note, immediately recognizing Jack Morgan's bold black scrawl. He would arrive by noon!

"Alice," she whispered. "I have to leave!"

"What? Are you ill?"

"No. Jack's coming. He may be at the house this very minute." Mattie was half out of her seat before she finished speaking.

"I'm coming with you!" Alice insisted.

There was no time to argue. Mattie hurried out of the church with Alice in her wake and every eye in the sanctuary following them. Once outside, Mattie broke into a run.

"Slow down!" Alice protested, but found herself helpless to stop her sister's flight. Checking first to make sure no one was watching, Alice lifted her skirts above her ankles in imitation of Mattie and broke into a trot. In no time at all they were home.

When Alice came puffing up behind her, Mattie was standing dead-still, her skirts still caught up in her gloved hands, staring at the deserted front porch with a look of devastation on her pretty face.

"He's not here!" she cried, her shoulders quaking from exertion and pent-up emotion.

"Oh, Mattie, I'm so sorry. But maybe . . ."

Just then the quiet Sunday morning was disturbed by the sound of horses' hooves thundering down the street. Mattie and Alice hurried up the porch steps to get a better view as two dozen Texas Rangers galloped past. This advance procession had hardly gone two blocks before Morgan's Raiders came into view. As if to signal John Hunt Morgan's approach, the church bells began pealing in the distance, and out of the quiet houses people hurried, laughing and shouting, toward the Ready residence to welcome him.

The reverence of the Sabbath gave way to a carnival atmosphere. Cheer after cheer went up from the throngs of townspeople. Men tossed their hats into the air and gave the Rebel yell. Women waved their handkerchiefs and called out to their favorites among Morgan's men.

But Mattie Ready saw only one man. He rode his trusty steed, Black Bess, with a certain style that set him apart. Bareheaded, the sun sending golden sparks from his hair and beard, Morgan came down the street in stately pomp, his right hand held high, waving his plumed hat to the excited crowd. Even from a distance, though, Mattie could see that his eyes never left her. His gaze caressed her through and through, making her heart beat so fast that she felt faint.

"Jack . . . my darling Jack," she murmured, wiping happy tears from her eyes.

"I wonder what, or *whom*, he's brought us this time," Alice said.

Mattie smiled, thinking that he never arrived without a surprise. Once he'd brought thirty-eight captured Union soldiers, more than the number of men riding with him that day. Other times his surprises had been less spectacular, but no less welcome—mail from friends and family in distant towns, newspapers from other areas, foodstuffs, which he knew were running low in Murfreesboro, or a special bottle of wine for her father.

She thought how little any of that mattered to her so long as her Jack was here himself, safe and sound and about to hold her in his arms once more.

"Oh, look!" Alice cried excitedly. "He has a buggy in tow. A fine buggy and two women!"

"What's that you say?" Mattie demanded, shading her eyes against the noon sun to get a better look.

What she saw was not reassuring. This was no refugee Jack had rescued along the way. The red-haired woman was a beauty! And the well-fed servant handling the matched team attested to the stranger's wealth and position. Martha Ready felt a sudden, undeniable stab of jealousy.

"Ladies!" John Hunt Morgan's booming voice rang through the clear spring air, hushing all else.

Mattie looked up at him and her heart swelled anew. He was so handsome, so dashing, so wonderfully commanding.

"Ladies," he repeated, "I bring you a guest!" Turning back toward the buggy, he motioned toward Lavinia. "Miss Rutledge of Thunderbolt Plantation in Georgia, soon to wed to our own Damien Clay."

Having made his announcement, Morgan dismounted and took Mattie's hand. For the longest time they stood staring at each other.

"My precious one," he whispered, bringing Mattie's fingers to his lips.

"My darling Colonel Morgan!" It was all Mattie could manage through the happy tears caught in her throat.

Lavinia watched the two of them and felt their emotion in her own heart. Soon she would be repeating a similar scene with Damien Clay.

"Miss Rutledge, welcome! I'm Alice Ready. My sister Mattie should do the greeting, but she seems to be struck quite dumb at the moment.'' Alice giggled and Lavinia liked her immediately for it.

"In my opinion, Miss Ready, she has good cause for her neglect!"

"Oh, how true!" Alice sighed. "I only wish that I had a beau like Colonel Morgan."

Lavinia glanced about the crowd to catch every marriageable girl and woman present staring with longing at the touching reunion between Mattie and her Jack.

"It would seem that you're not alone in that wish, Miss Ready. I'd guess that there's not a woman here who wouldn't change places with your sister in a minute."

"Even you, Miss Rutledge?" Alice asked with a teasing laugh.

Lavinia paused as if considering before she answered. "Well, now, I think I've found my man. He's no John Hunt Morgan, mind you! But as Damien Clay himself once told me, he's strong, handsome, brave, trustworthy, loyal—"

"I am, indeed!" a familiar male voice said from behind her. "Every bit of it and more!"

"Damien!" Lavinia cried.

But she was given no opportunity to say more. The next moment she was in his arms. His lips sought hers hungrily and she answered his tender assault in kind. Lavinia wasn't conscious of the shocked oh's and ah's from the crowd or the outraged "*Miss Vinnie!*" that burst from Helen-of-Troy's lips. She heard only the singing of her heart as it beat in time against Damien's.

"You *promised* me you'd stay at Thunderbolt," he said between kisses.

"I lied!" she whispered against his lips.

"I'm glad!"

All other talk was forgotten for the moment, swept away by a warm, soft whirlwind of desire.

Chapter Thirteen

"Well, Clay, I see Hawks found you!" Morgan said with a laugh. "I was going to save Miss Rutledge as a surprise. Now you've gone and ruined everything by showing up too soon!"

Jack Morgan, one arm possessively encircling Mattie's waist, walked over to the other couple, who were still locked in their hungry embrace. His interruption finally brought their kiss to an end. Damien released Lavinia's lips but continued to hold her close in his arms.

He laughed and winked at Lavinia. "If this is ruination, I'll take downfall over salvation every time!"

Morgan slapped him on the back and said, "You'd better watch this young man, Miss Rutledge. He's totally incorrigible!"

"So he's told me," she replied, smiling up into Damien's eyes. "I wouldn't have him any other way."

"You young people, come on in the house. Dinner's on the table," Mrs. Ready called from the front door.

The four of them headed inside, but a last cheer from the assembled crowd made them turn and wave. Soon the whole town headed home, excited, with much to talk about over their Sunday fried chicken and fresh peach pie. The dining-table conversation at the Ready home proved especially lively.

"We've been hearing rumors that you'll soon be on the

move again, Colonel,'' Mr. Ready said as he carved thin pieces of white meat from the huge turkey before him.

"That we will, sir!'' Morgan answered. "Something like that is hard to keep a secret what with all the preparations required. There's been a lot to do after Shiloh—cleaning equipment, shoeing horses, oiling the guns, and laying in supplies. I've a fat war chest from General Beauregard to finance this expedition—fifteen thousand in gold—so we're finally ready to ride.''

Both Mattie and Lavinia looked up, their smiles fading. They hadn't missed the significance of his last words.

"Ready. *now*, Jack?'' Mattie asked quietly.

Lavinia missed the intimate look that passed between the colonel and his sweetheart. She was staring up at Damien. Had she come all this way, found him again, only to lose him so soon? He read her expression and squeezed her hand under the table.

"We set out for Kentucky the last week in April, Mattie,'' Morgan continued.

"But that's only . . .''

He nodded. "That's very soon, my dear. But the sooner we move out, the sooner we'll return.''

"I know that, Jack. I'm not complaining. It's only that I'd hoped we'd have time to talk and catch up on things this visit.''

"We *will* talk,'' Morgan said with a meaningful look. "That's been my plan all along.''

Lavinia noticed the warm flush that crept into Mattie Ready's cheeks and the nervous smile playing at the corners of her mouth. Something important had just passed between the two, but she wasn't sure what. She didn't have time to ponder the mystery, however. Damien's hand under the table was demanding her undivided attention. Once again she felt the familiar warmth flood through her that only his touch could summon. The rest of the meal took far too long. The turkey, dressing, turnips, and spring peas were probably delicious, but though she ate some of everything, Lavinia tasted nothing. She could think only of the precious minutes slipping away. She wanted to be with Damien *alone*!

"A fine dinner!" Morgan said to Mrs. Ready at last. "I thank you kindly, ma'am. Now, if you will excuse us, I'd like to take Miss Mattie riding."

"On such a hot afternoon? After this heavy meal?" Mattie's mother objected.

"My dear!" Mr. Ready cautioned, frowning meaningfully over the tops of his wire-rimmed glasses at his wife. Then he turned a smile on his daughter and her beau and said, "Enjoy yourselves."

Morgan rose and held Mattie's chair for her. "Care to join us, you two?"

Lavinia and Damien exchanged uncertain glances. In truth, Lavinia did not want to be with anyone else. But she could see that they would have very little privacy in the Ready house. Even now a Sunday caller was coming up the front walk. Better to be out in the open countryside with Mattie and Colonel Morgan, she thought, than trapped in the stuffy parlor enduring equally stuffy conversation.

"Sounds like a fine idea, Colonel!" Damien made the decision for both of them.

"Come along with me, Lavinia," Mattie said. "I have some riding things that might fit you."

Once the two women were upstairs in the bedroom, Mattie Ready cleared up the mystery for Lavinia. "This promises to be a very special outing! I'm sure you'll understand how eager I am to have Jack Morgan put his intentions into words." Mattie rummaged through her armoire while she talked, looking for something that would fit the taller Lavinia. "He's told me he loves me, of course. There's a certain understanding between us. But until a date is set, I won't feel right in my heart. Undoubtedly, Damien must have put you through the same ordeal while he stalled around and made you die inside with worry. Ah, this should do!"

Mattie handed Lavinia a riding ensemble of palest dove gray. The skirt, narrow at the waist and hips, flared becomingly at the shot-weighted hem. A trim jacket and white linen blouse completed the outfit.

"Yes, I do understand, Mattie. I thought I'd lose Damien for sure in the beginning.'' Lavinia smiled conspiratorially at the other woman. ''But I finally chased him until he caught me!''

They both laughed, understanding the female logic behind the strategy that Lavinia confessed to.

''Exactly!'' Mattie answered. ''Colonel Morgan has caught me; of that I'm certain. All that remains now is for him to realize that the chase is up. And I do believe this very afternoon he will admit that the fox has gone to earth! So, after we are away from town, Jack and I will part company with you and Damien. Understood?''

''Understood!'' Lavinia answered thankfully.

The two women dressed quickly, Lavinia in the gray suit, which was just short enough to show a hint of well-turned ankle, and Mattie in an ensemble of the brilliant green that Lavinia had come to recognize as the favored color of Morgan's Raiders. The ostrich-plumed hat completed Miss Ready's fashionable ensemble.

Lavinia's excitement rose with each passing moment. Her last time alone with Damien had been the most wonderful of her entire life. She'd never imagined that a woman could know such happiness. All her life, until Damien Clay happened into it, she had thought of love and marriage as something a woman was *forced* into. She'd longed for the freedom a man had to choose the paths he took. But now she realized that love was a far cry from her earlier conception and that marriage was a much-prized goal if the right man was involved. And Damien Clay was the right man. Of that she was certain! He had only to look at her to cause the quivery sensations she knew so well. His lips on hers alternately becalmed her and turned her wanton. And when he made love to her it was like . . . it was like nothing else she had ever experienced, so it was beyond the words she possessed to describe such exquisite grandeur.

''Ladies!'' Damien and Jack Morgan chorused, both bowing gallantly as Lavinia and Mattie came down the broad stairs.

The men had changed, too. Both were out of uniform now, wearing open-necked linen shirts and tight buckskin britches that disappeared into the tops of their cavalry boots. They were a handsome pair, Morgan with his golden good looks and cool blue-gray gaze, and Damien with his long dark hair tied back and the mysterious fire burning deep within his eyes when he looked at Lavinia.

"Damien and I thought we might ride out the Nashville Pike to Stones River," Morgan said as they ushered the ladies to the mounts waiting at the hitching rail out front.

"Oh, yes!" Mattie said with a broad smile. "You'll love it there, Lavinia. The river is so nice and the cedar groves dark and cool. It's my favorite spot."

"I'm sure I will," Lavinia answered, but she didn't need a picturesque river or tall, cool trees. Already she was in her favorite spot—next to Damien Clay.

"You look quite fetching in that short skirt," Damien whispered for her ears alone. "I do love a woman with a bit of daring!"

"Then I'd better have Helen-of-Troy shorten all of my skirts immediately, if that's all it takes to make you love me."

His hands were about her waist, sending thrills of pleasure through her as he assisted her into the saddle. He answered with a devilish grin, "Have her lower the bodices as well and you can count on my undivided attention and affection at all times!"

Lavinia flushed deeply and cast a quick glance at Mattie and Jack to see if they had heard. But they were lost in their own intimate conversation.

She flashed Damien a hot look and scolded, "You *libertine*!"

"Why, thank you, ma'am!" he said with a laugh as he mounted his horse. "You're not only daring and exotic but a keen judge of human nature as well."

"You're impossible, Damien Clay!"

"No, Lavinia," he said in a voice suddenly turned serious. "Not impossible, only impractical." He turned and looked at her oddly. "We're a pair, aren't we? Misfit, mismatched, and misunderstood. What are you doing here anyway, Lavinia Rutledge? Why aren't you back at Thunderbolt, where you belong?"

She didn't like the change in his tone or the way his easy

smile had vanished. She'd thought he was glad to see her again. Could she have misread him? Could something have happened in the time they'd been apart? Had he changed his mind about marrying her?

"Damien?" She turned a worried expression on him.

"Not now, Lavinia. We'll talk when we get to the river." He sighed, then said under his breath, "Yes, indeed we will!"

They rode the rest of the way in strained silence. Lavinia, sure that something was very wrong, could think of nothing else. Her mind cast about wildly, searching for some offense she had committed, some wrong turn she had taken in the strange road she'd been traveling with Damien Clay. Surely he couldn't have heard of her encounter with Sam Coltrain! The thought jolted her.

Finally, she saw the river winding ahead of them. Morgan and Mattie turned slightly in their saddles and waved, then galloped off into one of the numerous cedar groves.

"Let's dismount and tie the horses over there under those trees." They were the first words Damien had uttered in nearly a half hour.

She got down stiffly from her dapple-gray horse, not because the riding had made her sore but because his strange silence had lashed her into uncomfortable uncertainty. She felt, as Helen-of-Troy would say, as if she were tiptoeing barefoot through the chicken yard. Lavinia had always had difficulty handling the displeasure of others when she did wrong. But to have Damien upset with her and not know the source of his irritation was almost beyond her endurance.

He tied their horses without speaking to her or looking at her. Finally, after making a great production of that task, he stood back, hands on his hips, staring at her. He still wasn't smiling. Lavinia had plunged from the heights to the depths. She felt physically ill with discomfort and uncertainty.

"I'm sorry," Lavinia whispered, not knowing what else to say but unable to endure the silence between them any longer.

"Oh, are you?" he shot back at her in a cold tone.

She was fighting back tears now and the very thought that she might break down in front of him made her furious. Not with herself. No! She was furious with Damien Clay! Just who did he think he was, treating her this way, spoiling what could have been a wonderful afternoon for both of them?

"And just what are you sorry for? I'd like to hear the full list! It seems you've been quite busy since I left you. Was I off your father's land before you started packing to come after me? There's a war going on, in case you haven't noticed, Miss Rutledge! There's no place here for adventurous young ladies!"

Slowly, her head, which had been lowered at a submissive angle, rose. She faced him, her eyes, wide in anger, like twin beacons of fox fire. Deep inside, she could feel a rumbling, as if her whole body were a volcano about to explode.

"Damn you, Damien Clay! I'm not sorry for anything!" she said in a voice gone cold with rage.

"Good!" he replied coolly. "Keep thinking that tomorrow when I'm gone and you're left to your own devices once more. Remember the good times we've had and also remember that I warned you to stay where you belonged—back home at Thunderbolt! If you had, we wouldn't be having this argument right now! I have a job to do. And I can't look after you and perform my duty at the same time. Maybe one of these days you'll learn to follow orders!"

"You bastard!" she cried, rushing at him, her nails like talons. "Nobody gives Lavinia Rutledge orders! I do as I damn well please and you'd better not forget it. Besides, I didn't come here just to see you. I'm looking for Josiah, you conceited son of a . . ."

He caught her wrists an instant before she could claw his face, holding them in a bruising grip at the same time that he pulled her body up against his. Even through her riding skirt she could feel the hot bulge in his britches. The thought that he wanted her even as they struggled against each other, even as he tried to reject her verbally, gave her a perverse satisfaction. She pressed her body closer, rubbing against him, but never stopped trying to wrench her hands free to tear at his grim face.

Damien felt defeated. He was losing both battles, the one against Lavinia and the one against his own body as well. In defeat his anger rose. He wanted to hurt her, to make her cry and go running back home to safety. But first he wanted to make love to her, possess her totally and ease the pain in his loins that had raged for her since the moment he rode away from Thunderbolt. Damn, she'd put him through hell these past weeks! Now here she was, at it again, manufacturing more torture than he could endure.

So nobody gave Lavinia Rutledge orders, eh? He ground his teeth, stilling the growing urge to wrestle her to the ground, turn her over his knee, and pound her lovely bottom until she begged for mercy and promised to behave. Her behavior at the moment was both shameful and tempting. He'd known prostitutes who weren't as skilled at arousing a man's lust as the prim and proper Miss Rutledge. Right at the moment she was driving him wild!

"I return your curse, Lavinia Rutledge!" he said between clenched teeth. "Damn *you*, for the passionate bitch you are!"

Even as the last of his hot words scorched her, his mouth came down hard over hers. This wasn't the way she had imagined it or wanted it to be. She'd been so sure that Damien would take her into his arms tenderly the moment they were alone, that he would rekindle the flames of rapture they had felt at the cottage by the Savannah River. But now he was forcing her lips to part, probing her mouth with a fierce, punishing hunger. Her body ached with the strength of his arms crushing her against his hard frame. One of his hands tangled through her long hair, pulling her head back, molding her mouth and body to his. But even as she struggled against him, her desire was on the rise. This was a new, violent side of Damien Clay, a side she'd only imagined lay smoldering within him, thinly disguised beneath his placid façade. Still, she possessed the same savage need deep down. She wanted him now as she had never desired him before. Her hands snaked up his back, and the talons that would have clawed his eyes moments before now dug into his shoulders, urging his wildness with her own.

"I brought you out here to tell you good-bye," he said into her open mouth.

Her lips captured his and stopped his words. She clung to him, kissing him passionately, wantonly.

"The day you say those words and mean them, Damien Clay, will be your last day on this earth!" she hissed into his ear.

"It would be for your own good."

"I'll worry about what's good for me, thank you!"

Their jousting conversation continued between brutal kisses. "What if I told you that I don't really love you, Lavinia?" he asked.

"I'd call you a damn liar!" she replied, biting his lower lip until he shied away in pain.

He bit back, sinking his teeth into the tender flesh of her earlobe. She gasped softly. His tongue soothed the spot he'd bruised, then trailed along the contours of her ear, finally teasing the inside and causing her to shiver and sigh.

"You're making this difficult, Lavinia," he breathed into her ear. "Don't you know when you're not wanted?"

In answer, her hand sought out his throbbing buckskin-covered bulge and she repeated, "Liar!"

He groaned in answer to her touch and drew her down to the ground with him, holding her fondling hand in place. His head went back, his eyes closing as if he were in mortal pain. Lavinia's hand pressed harder, rubbing up and down.

"Oh, God!" he groaned, and quickly caught her fingers in his to stop her sweet torture.

Lavinia was experiencing her own hell, one of desire and confusion. The very fact that she feared he might thrust her away, order her back on her horse, and leave her aching with need made her want him all the more.

"Damien?" she said cautiously.

He was still stretched out on the bed of soft leaves beside her, his eyes shut and a look of near-anguish on his handsome face. In answer, he reached out, drawing her to him, fitting their taut bodies together. For some moments he held her close, rocking slightly, breathing into the soft hair at her temple. It was as if he were waiting for some pain to pass. Then slowly, he slackened his hold. His eyes came open and searched her face. His hands moved to the frogs that fastened her riding jacket, undoing them nimbly. In moments he found what he sought. With the layers of linen laid back and her camisole unlaced, her breasts were bared to his touch . . . to his hungry kiss.

Lavinia experienced a strange elation born of the feel of sunshine and open air on her skin. Even though they lay deep within a sheltering grove of fragrant cedar trees, the idea of making love in the open had an exotic allure to it simply because such intimacies were normally confined within the privacy of the bedroom. The strangeness of being watched by birds and the burning eye of the sun was soon lost on her, however. As Damien's wonderful hands caressed her and his lips and tongue paid homage to her flesh, all else fled her mind. She was attuned only to the hot rush rising within her, seemingly drawn to flood height by his gentle sucking. Her skirts and stockings felt suffocating against her flesh. Her whole body longed to breathe the fresh air and feel the sunlight teasing it as Damien's tongue now teased her naked, aching breasts.

Sensing her need but never ceasing his other attentions to her for a moment, Damien maneuvered her skirts downward and soon divested her of all she wore. Then he rose suddenly—she thought to undress himself. Instead, he stood over her, gazing down with eyes so hot and bright they looked fevered, and the bulge in his britches throbbing noticeably.

His gaze traveled the whole shade- and sun-dappled length of her, from the copper-bright hair spread out over the leaves to her full breasts with their dark peaks straining toward him, down the pathway of her smooth belly to the flaming arrow that pointed to his certain destination.

Slowly, never taking his eyes from her lovely body, Damien shed his clothes. Once more Lavinia marveled at the classic lines of his nakedness and the great pulsing darkness that she so desired to fill her and make her one with him.

Still standing over her, he said, "I meant to make you hate me this afternoon. You know that, don't you?"

"Yes, my love, but I don't know why," she answered in a husky voice.

He knelt beside her, letting his hands play over her body as he said, "Because I wanted you away from here. When I said good-bye at the cottage, I meant it."

Sudden realization dawned, making Lavinia brush Damien's hands away and sit up. "You weren't coming back to Thunderbolt? You never intended to?" Angry, shamed tears rushed to flood in her eyes. Her voice rose and fell with her alternating emotions. "You asked me to marry you only so you could take what you wanted from me!"

"Lavinia, I never said I'd marry you. You only assumed—"

His hand was resting on her hip. She slapped it away, glaring at him. "No, don't touch me!" she cried. She was aching inside; his words had pierced her heart. She wanted to hurt him back. Suddenly, remembering how jealous he'd been of Randy Wentworth, her thoughts flew to Sam Coltrain. A cold, baiting smile curved her lips, and her whole body seemed to beckon to him as she stretched and posed seductively. "What difference does marriage make? Go ahead, Damien. Take whatever pleasure you like. Why shouldn't you? Another man already has!"

A flush of fury rushed into Damien's face and he raised his hand in anger, ready to strike her. For a moment she lay stricken and terrified by what she had said. She'd wanted to give him pain in return for the grief he was causing her. But she'd used the wrong weapon. She hadn't meant to tell Damien Clay about Sam Coltrain, *not ever*! But just as she thought Damien was about to slap her face, his hand dropped and he laughed out loud.

"Another man, eh, Lavinia? You forget, my dear, that I was your first and had my bloody proof of the fact there in the river cottage. You aren't going to tell me now that the minute I rode away you went running into the arms of Lieutenant Wentworth? Miss Rutledge, you are good at many things, but lying is not one of them!"

"It wasn't Randy," she whispered, terrified now. "It was a Yankee officer, and I certainly did not run into his arms!"

Damien fell back as if he had been slapped. He stared at Lavinia, looking so beautiful and innocent as she lay huddled in the leaves, the sunlight trying to kiss away her tears.

"The slimy sonuvabitch! Tell me his name, Lavinia!" His

voice was so filled with vengeful rage that he frightened her more now than he had before. "*His name!* Dammit, tell me!" He was upon her, pinning her shoulders to the hard ground, hissing his demands directly into her face.

Lavinia cowered beneath him, breathing hard under his weight. "It doesn't matter," she gasped. "Forget what I said! Besides, he didn't . . ."

But her explanation was drowned out by the animallike growl that came from Damien's throat. His knee came up, forcing her thighs apart, and he sank into her so suddenly and deeply that she cried out. Any tenderness she had hoped for from her lover seemed beyond the realm of possibility now. He used her ruthlessly, as if he meant to pound the name of the other man from her. Even so, the pain of his full penetration quickly gave way to a rising wave of exquisite sensation. Her body rose and fell with his, driving hard, striking sharply. He was the battering ram, she the stubborn wall. Their passionate conflict continued until suddenly all resistance gave way and a bittersweet flood washed them both.

After their shared moment of violent ecstasy, Damien withdrew immediately. He knelt over Lavinia, raking her trembling body with blazing eyes.

"I'll find out his name," Damien said in a harsh whisper. "And when I do, I'll kill him!"

"Damien," she answered in a voice she hoped would restore his reason, "he didn't harm me."

"I don't believe you!" His tone was such that she knew at that moment that Sam Coltrain was already as good as dead.

That night Lavinia lay awake in the guest room at the Ready residence, her mind too troubled to sleep. The ride home from Stones River had been a silent trial. She was aware all the way of Damien's accusing eyes on her. No doubt he was wondering what she had done to tempt the other man. How could she admit to him that she had mentioned her encounter with Sam Coltrain only to make him jealous—to get even with him? It was a damn-fool thing to do! Certainly, he would never forgive her for it.

When they had arrived back at the Ready home they found that Mattie and Colonel Morgan had preceded them and brought happy news to all. Martha Ready would be called Mrs. John Hunt Morgan after December 14. The wedding was to be in Murfreesboro. It seemed the whole town knew already and everyone wanted to drop in and congratulate the couple, who were holding court, much like benevolent royalty, in the Ready drawing room.

Lavinia felt thoroughly ashamed of herself when she realized that the sight of Mattie's glowing face caused her an undeniable pang of envy. Just a few hours earlier she had thought that she might wear such a happy smile herself. But never mind! She refused to allow her own misery to blight Mattie's special day. Lavinia put on a brave face, then kissed them both and offered her congratulations. But when a new circle of friends closed in, she slipped up to her room, telling Mrs. Ready that she needed a nap after their exhausting ride.

"My dear, that might be wise," the woman said. "You do look a bit peaked and pale."

There was no need to make her excuses to Damien. He had seen her to the door and left abruptly, pleading "business at camp." They were his only words to her, and their brusqueness cut her to the quick. She knew for certain that he only wanted to be away from her as quickly as possible. Would she see him again before Morgan's Raiders rode away? She had no idea. She wasn't sure she could bear to. But how could she bear not to see him?

The bell in the church steeple had tolled midnight long since when Lavinia heard a sound outside her door. It couldn't be Helen-of-Troy. She was sleeping out in one of the cabins with some of the Readys' serving women. Perhaps Mattie was too overwhelmed with excitement to sleep and was paying her a midnight call to talk. No, the two women didn't know each other well enough yet for that sort of thing. Who, then?

The doorknob turned. Instinctively, Lavinia pulled the sheet up around her and damned herself for shedding her nightgown in the April heat. Her dressing gown lay over the chair across the room. She watched, holding her breath, as the door opened and a dark form stepped into the room. Then she heard the door close and the lock click. Still, she had no idea who the intruder might be. She tried to speak, to demand an explanation for such an invasion of her privacy, but her throat was so dry with fear the words wouldn't come. The dark shadow moved toward the bed. She drew away to the far side, trying to force herself to scream.

Then out of the darkness came a quiet voice: "I'm sorry, Lavinia."

"Damien!" she cried, weak with relief and unable to contain her joy. "Darling, you've come!"

He was there beside her, kissing her face so tenderly, so lovingly. "I was almost too ashamed to come to you," he said. "And I don't deserve such a sweet welcome after the way I abused you this afternoon, my love. I know I have no right to ask, but can you ever forgive me?"

She pulled him to her, reveling in the feeling of his arms around her and his lips, soft upon her own. Happy tears streamed from her eyes, and she was conscious of the dampness on his cheeks as well.

"Damien, my darling, let's don't ever quarrel again. *Please!* It hurts too much!"

When he shed his clothes this time, there was no threat in his naked presence, only the gentle promise of her strongest needs about to be satisfied by her lover's tenderness. She lay in his arms, quivering with pleasure as he stroked her with knowing fingers, causing her breath to quicken and her veins to run hot with desire.

"Oh, please!" she cried. "*Now*, darling, *now!*"

Lavinia lay beneath him, feeling both consumed and filled by his strength and love as he took her with a worshipful passion. The afternoon's prelude of pain made their ecstasy, when it came at last, all the sweeter. They lay in each other's arms for a long, tender time after their climb to the heights, her lips against Damien's neck as he continued to fondle her silky breasts.

Dawn was streaking the black sky with the faintest hints of apricot and lilac when he whispered, "Darling, it's time for me to go. Sh-h-h!'' he said in anticipation of her objection. ''Listen to me. I do love you, Lavinia Rutledge! Furthermore—''

''I won't go, Damien! You can't make me go back to Thunderbolt!''

He silenced her with his lips. ''You *must* interrupt, eh? Well, if you'd hold still long enough, you'd find out you have no need to protest. I was about to say, furthermore, I want you here when I get back!''

A little gasp of surprised pleasure escaped Lavinia and she hugged him tightly.

He kissed her deeply one last time, then said, ''Sleep now and dream of me.''

She slept, and dreamed as ordered.

Chapter Fourteen

Cheer, boys, cheer! no more of idle sorrow;
Courage! true hearts shall bear us on our way;
Hope points before and shows a bright tomorrow,
Cheer, boys, cheer for the new and happy land!

Out of the golden spring dawn came the sweetest tones ever to reach Lavinia's ears. She was wakened from her sleep by the sound of a chorus of deep male voices singing, soft and mellow, the strains of "Cheer, Boys, Cheer," a favorite among all lads in gray, but especially those who hailed from Kentucky and Tennessee.

Drawing on her robe and pulling the lace curtain aside, Lavinia gazed out toward the public square. There, John Hunt Morgan had formed his squad, three hundred and fifty strong, for a farewell serenade. Their deep voices rang clear on the fresh morning breeze. The sound sent a melancholy shiver through her and brought tears to her eyes.

"Come in," she called when a knock sounded at her door.

Mattie and Alice, their eyes soft from sleep, hurried in to take their places on either side of her at the window.

"My darling Jack!" Mattie murmured, shaking her head in wonder. "What will he think of next?"

"That's one of Jack's five younger brothers, Tom, singing

172

the solo, Lavinia,'' Alice explained. ''Isn't he handsome? And he sings like an angel.''

Lavinia took note of the tall young man Alice mentioned and of Colonel Morgan, his gloved hands raised, leading the chorus. But her tear-blurred eyes quickly shifted back to the long-haired soldier second from the left. Damien, his dark eyes trained on her window, was singing his heart out for Lavinia alone. Her own heart swelled with pride and love. She could almost feel his gaze caressing her.

When the song ended and Colonel Morgan shouted the order to move out, the men offered one last salute. They split the morning's silence with their collective Rebel yell. Horses reared and snorted. Plumed hats waved high in the breeze. Then the squad wheeled and pounded off, riding north toward Nashville.

Lavinia strained her eyes, trying to watch Damien's figure as long as possible. But soon he was lost to her in the rolling wave of uniforms, horseflesh, and swirling dust.

For several moments the three women in the room remained silent, listening to the retreating thunder outside. The echo of the horses' hoofbeats thudded in Lavinia's heart. She felt strangely empty, and more alone than ever before in her life.

Mattie Ready slipped an arm around her shoulders and said, ''It's always hard when they leave, but you'll get used to it in time, Lavinia.''

''Never,'' she murmured.

''We'll both have to if we plan to marry our soldier boys. There's no other way for a cavalry officer's wife. We may have to suffer frequent partings, but, believe me, the homecomings make all the pain worthwhile.''

Lavinia only half believed the other woman's words. ''How long will they be gone, Mattie?''

Martha Ready frowned in spite of her encouraging words of a moment before. ''That's hard to say. Jack and his men are undertaking a difficult journey this time. Kentucky's an unstable state, aligned with neither North nor South, but filled with partisan groups for both sides. They'll be cheered and feted along the way. But they're bound to run into resistance as well.''

* * *

The resistance Martha Ready spoke of to Lavinia did not wait for Morgan's Raiders to reach Kentucky, however. The sons of the bluegrass ran headlong into an angry hive of blue-jackets at Lebanon, Tennessee, the morning of May 5.

Morgan's arrival in the town the day before was greeted warmly by Southern sympathizers. Tending first to their dust-clogged throats, the Raiders crowded into the town's saloons, where all drinks were on the house to Morgan's men. Around dark, rain began to fall. The weary cavalrymen were taken into homes, given accommodations and food. Even the few pickets left outside of town to watch for Federal troops soon accepted invitations to come in out of the rain. The celebrating, with Morgan and Damien Clay in the thick of it, went on till well past midnight. No one gave much thought to the fact that they were inside enemy lines, only thirty miles from Federally held Nashville. Lebanon was such a friendly place!

After their hard ride and a night of feasting and drinking, Morgan's Raiders deserved a bit of respite, their leader reasoned. The colonel gave no orders for early rising.

"Let them rest," he said to Damien. "We have a long ride still ahead. And this weather . . ." He cursed the rain soundly before he dropped off to sleep.

Dawn was considering whether or not to break when one alert picket sighted the Union troops bearing down on Lebanon. The guard spread the word as quickly as he could but lost his life for his efforts. Confusion and splitting headaches reigned. Half-naked men jumped on the first available horses and sped away in all directions with the Yankees, two thousand strong, in hot pursuit.

In the chaos, which would forevermore be called by Morgan's Raiders the "Lebanon Races," Damien Clay, Morgan, and about a hundred of his men roared off down the road to Rome and Carthage. Twelve hot, furious miles later, Morgan found himself with only a dozen soldiers on the north side of the Cumberland River, while blue uniforms swarmed over the far bank. The small ferry boat used in their escape would not accommodate their horses. Sadly, John Hunt Morgan watched from the far side as Federal troops confiscated their mounts. He last saw Black Bess as she was ridden away, a Yankee soldier triumphant in her saddle.

"The total count?" Morgan demanded of Damien some hours later when his remaining forces had regrouped. Morgan's face was dark with depression and grief.

"We lost one hundred and eight men all told," Damien answered quietly. "Seventeen killed, twenty-six wounded, sixty-five captured, Colonel."

"Damnation!" Morgan swore, slamming a gloved hand down on the war chest that still contained the precious gold to finance his expedition. "No men, no horses! Now what?"

"Then we'll be turning back?" Damien knew what Morgan's answer would be, but he had to ask, to prod his commander out of his deep depression.

Jack Morgan turned eyes gone almost black with anger on his friend. "Turn back?" he blazed. "Blast you, Clay! If that's what you think we ought to do, go fetch your petticoats and ball gown! You're not fit to wear the bluegrass green! *Turn back!* Ha! I'm going to give those damn bluebellies a taste of their own medicine. We'll take Kentucky by storm, roll through the whole state like a thunderbolt shot out of a night sky!" Morgan was on his feet now, arms flailing, eyes flashing, his voice booming through the night like cannon fire. "No, goddammit, we're not turning back! Spread the word, Captain Clay! The Second Kentucky is going home! We're off to the land of bluegrass and the Green River!"

Word of the "Lebanon Races" reached Murfreesboro in a matter of hours, shrouding the town in a pall. Nowhere was the sorrow felt more deeply than in the two-story house on Main Street just off the public square. The courier who brought the news assured the two anxious women that Morgan and Clay were unharmed. The young messenger, wounded himself in his dash to break through Union lines, brought quickly scrawled messages to both Lavinia and Mattie. But it seemed nothing could allay their fears.

Martha Ready, her tears given way to angry frustration, strode about the front parlor, clenching and unclenching her fists.

"If I were a man!" Her voice rose as she continued. "If I were only a man, Lavinia, I tell you, I would be in the thick of the fight so fast! I'm half tempted to go anyway. I could tend the wounded, cook for Jack, hold the horses if need be. *Anything* would be better than this interminable waiting and wondering!"

Lavinia nodded but said nothing, her mind busy—leaps and bounds ahead of the other woman as she schemed.

"Suppose you did want to go to Colonel Morgan, Mattie. How could you find him? You know he was at Lebanon, but that was days ago. He could have gone anywhere."

"Not *anywhere*," Mattie replied, taking down a map from a shelf and unrolling it on the marbletop table. "You see this blue line? Those are the Federally held locations. I know my Jack. He's headed for Kentucky. They're probably about here now, regrouping." She pointed to a dot on the map very near Sparta. "My guess would be that he'll turn northwest, recross the Cumberland River, and head for Cave City to hit the Louisville and Nashville line running through there." She tapped a front tooth thoughtfully with a fingernail while she studied the map a while longer. Finally, she bobbed her head. "Yes! That's what I would do if I were leading the men!"

Lavinia stared at the map, memorizing the roads and symbols. "Cave City," she murmured.

"Yes, he'll definitely go to Cave City," Mattie replied with almost military authority in her voice.

Just then the door banged open and Mattie's father, his face flushed with excitement, rushed in. "Ladies, I thought you might find this of interest." He spread a newspaper over the map and jabbed a finger at one column. "Mattie, your Colonel Morgan's made the news again. By God, the man is giving those Yankees fits! Look here! This correspondent refers to him as a 'swashbuckling blood-about-town.' But here's the big news—a letter written by Andrew Johnson to Representative

Horace Maynard. Oh, he has them riled! And fit to be tied, I'll vow!''

Both women scanned the newspaper silently.

> Morgan's marauding gang should not be admitted to the rules of civilized warfare, and the portion of his forces taken at Lebanon should not be held as prisoners of war. I hope you will call attention of Secretary Stanton to the fact of their being a mere band of freebooters.

"Freebooters!" Mattie cried. Well, I never! How can they get away with printing such a pack of lies, Father?'' Her cheeks flamed with indignation and she tapped her dainty slippered foot furiously.

"Mattie dear, your Jack's a hero!" Charles Ready explained. "He has them all panicked. He's the worst possible threat to the Union Army. He strikes without warning, dashes off into thin air, then is back snapping at their unguarded heels like a rabid bulldog the moment they let their guard down, confident that he's far away. Don't you see, my dear? Colonel Morgan has the entire Union Army jumping at shadows, firing at ghosts! The toll he's taking on the blue army's morale is at least as great as the destruction he's cost them in supplies and railroad lines.''

Lavinia's knowledge of the military came only from her few days as a private in the Confederate Army. But from talk she had heard among the men of the Wiregrass Rifles, she knew the fate of men taken in battle who were not offered protection as prisoners of war. Privates were hanged, officers shot! The mere thought made her shudder.

"Can they do that, Mr. Ready?" she asked.

"Do what, child?"

"Declare Colonel Morgan and his men *land pirates*, as I've heard them called? Can they take away their honest rights as prisoners of war?"

The excitement drained from Ready's face. He looked from Lavinia to his daughter and back. "I'm afraid they can," he said quietly. "Abraham Lincoln is Commander-in-Chief of the

Union Army and he can be a hard man. If Stanton, that mad-man, takes it in his head to press this point, Colonel Morgan and every man riding with him can be branded an outlaw, sub-ject to punishment accordingly.''

''Oh, Father!'' Mattie cried, running into his arms.

Lavinia, her heart clutched by cold apprehension, said noth-ing. This was not a time for words but a time for action.

Throughout the rest of the afternoon and evening Lavinia kept her own council. She'd thought everything through very thoroughly. At first she had considered enlisting Martha Ready's aid in her plan, but then decided against it. She had no right to involve anyone else. When dinner was over she ex-cused herself early and said a casual good-night to the Ready family as if she fully expected to greet them again over break-fast. No one must know her plan and be given the chance to head her off.

But, as usual, Helen-of-Troy was one jump ahead of Lavinia Rutledge. When she entered her bedroom, Lavinia found the servant waiting.

''Well?'' Helen-of-Troy demanded. ''Where we off to now, missy?''

Lavinia tried not to meet the woman's gaze. She moved about the room as if preparing for bed and finally climbed in, pulling the covers up before she answered.

''I haven't the faintest idea what you're talking about!''

''Um-hum! That's exactly right, and a peach ain't got no fuzz neither!'' Helen-of-Troy responded sarcastically. ''You might just as well come on out with it. I knew we's going. I just don't know where to, that's all.''

Lavinia felt totally frustrated. Could she keep nothing a se-cret from Helen-of-Troy? She lay in bed, pretending to ignore her servant and feigning sleep.

''You ain't a-foolin' me, Miss Vinnie! And I ain't leaving this room till you answer me!''

Lavinia tumbled out of the bed with an impatient sigh. ''You're not going this time!''

''Am too!''

"Helen-of-Troy, I say who does what around here!"

The servant drew up to her most imposing stature, the towering, hands-on-broad-hips stance she sometimes had to resort to when Colonel Rutledge was in his cups. "Now you listen to me, young lady! I done promised your daddy I'd look out for you. There ain't no way I mean to break my word to that man. And I sure can't keep an eye on you with me here and you run off to Lord-knows-where! So it's settled!"

"Oh, very well!" Lavinia relented, knowing she had no choice in the matter.

They waited quietly together in the bedroom until everyone else in the house was sleeping. Then Lavinia, dressed in buckskin britches and a loose shirt, tiptoed out into the hallway.

"The coast is clear," she whispered, motioning for Helen-of-Troy to follow her.

Before the moon had sailed much farther across the sky, Lavinia and her faithful servant were in their buggy, headed up the Nashville Turnpike. When they reached the fork in the road where the Wilkinson Pike branched off, Helen-of-Troy pulled back on the reins.

"Now you going to tell me where we're going, Miss Vinnie? It gets a mite hard to drive a team when you ain't got no directions!"

"Give the horses their heads, Helen-of-Troy! We're bound for Kentucky and, from what Damien says, any horse worth his flesh will sniff out that bluegrass and go right to it!"

Helen-of-Troy was still blustering and sputtering over the answer she'd received, when a rider, dark against the lightening sky, moved out of a copse of cedars just up the road and came slowly toward them.

"Oh, Lord, help us!" Helen-of-Troy moaned.

"I'm not at all sure He will," the rider said in an all-too-familiar voice. "But I'll watch over you, Lavinia. Just as I have these past weeks. You'll be safe from everything, everyone."

Lavinia felt a tingle of dread run along her spine. She'd had a feeling someone was watching her ever since she arrived in

Murfreesboro. She'd heard things in the night, but thought she had only dreamed them. Still, that was the reason Damien's appearance in her room had frightened her so the night before he rode away.

"Why have you been spying on me, Sam?" Lavinia asked in as even a tone as she could muster. She had thought . . . she had *hoped* . . . that Sam Coltrain was out of her life for good, even though she knew the night they had shared would haunt her forever.

"Spying, Lavinia? I wouldn't call it that." He edged his horse closer as he spoke to her. "I've thought of myself more as a bodyguard than a spy. I'm afraid I fell asleep on the job one day, though. My arm was paining me after the long ride up here and I took some morphine. I awoke just in time to see the two of you together."

"You mean Helen-of-Troy and me?" She frowned, trying to think when that might have been.

"No," he answered coldly. "The man who took you out to Stones River. That hurt me deeply, Lavinia."

She gasped. Sam Coltrain had watched, had listened . . .

"It was good of you to try to protect me," Coltrain continued in that same oddly cool voice. "But you might as well have confided my name to him, Lavinia. He'll find out soon enough. The two of us are destined to meet someday, some *bloody* day. That hour will be his last."

Lavinia was trembling, though the air was warm with the approaching dawn. Coltrain's voice sent a chill through her with the diabolical certainty in its tone.

"Sam, I don't know what you can be thinking of, following me this way. What about your men?" She must find some way to distract him from this mad mission as her "protector." "Who will lead them if you aren't there?"

"I ride alone now, Lavinia. My men have gone their separate ways. Most of them have headed back to their homes and families."

"And you'll be returning, too?"

He didn't answer. He only stared at her, and through the faint, first light of dawn, she could see the cold glow of his eyes. He seemed to be trying to make a decision. He breathed heavily as his gaze caressed her. Lavinia sat stock-still, waiting for him to speak.

When he did, he voice was barely audible. "Is that what you want, Lavinia?"

"What I want isn't important, Sam," she replied in an even tone. "It's what's best for you that I'm thinking of. You can't sit a fence in this war. You'll have to choose one side or the other if you stay here. Otherwise, both sides will be after you. Can't you see that?"

A strange smile twisted his mouth. "Do you really care what happens to me?"

"Of course I do!"

"Then you're the only one. I really would as soon be shot by one side as by the other. Life simply isn't worth the bother any longer."

"How can you say that?" Lavinia cried, horrified that any human being could be so cynical.

"If I promise to go, will you come and walk with me for a time first? I need to talk to you, Lavinia."

She hesitated. What did Sam Coltrain have in mind? It didn't matter, she decided at last. She could handle him. And, besides, the only way she knew she'd be free of him was to convince him that he should go home.

"Hold the horses here, Helen-of-Troy," she ordered, starting to climb down.

"Miss Vinnie!" the servant objected.

"I won't be long."

Major Coltrain dismounted and tied his horse to the buggy. He took Lavinia's arm and led her away from the road to a nearby copse of trees. When they were safely obscured from view, he turned her gently and slipped his arm about her waist.

"You're a brave woman, Lavinia Rutledge," he whispered huskily.

"Hardly," she answered.

"How do you know I won't take advantage of you now that we're alone?"

She stared solemnly up into his eyes. "I trust you, Sam. I don't think you'd do anything to harm me."

Suddenly, he pulled her tightly against his chest. "Lavinia, Lavinia," he moaned. "You are too trusting. What if I were a different sort of man—a fiend who would brand you with his lust?"

"You've branded me already, Sam, with a scar I'll carry all my life. But it would be wrong for you to take me now, when you know I don't want you!"

He had been acting in such a rational manner that Lavinia thought she was safe in speaking bluntly. But now his face changed, contorted. He clamped his arm around her waist in a more powerful grip, bracing her hard against his chest. His mouth came down over hers, forcing her lips apart, searching viciously. She struggled against him, but he would not be denied. Panic rose within her. She had misjudged his intentions. Now she was trapped.

When he released his hold on her lips, his eyes held a maniacal light. "If I've scarred you so already, whatever I do to you this time can't make that much more difference."

His strained, angry voice grated along her nerves. Still, she was not afraid. There was no way a one-armed man could take her against her will, she thought. She could escape him, given half a chance.

But a pine tree behind her worked as Sam Coltrain's ally. Forcing her backward, he used his body to pin her against the rough trunk while he pulled at her britches with his hand. His lips cut off any cry she might have uttered. Her whole body tensed against his, straining as if to force him away. She twisted and thrashed, but there seemed no escape.

When she felt the morning breeze on her thighs and his urgent hand smoothing down her belly, her fear rose to a new pitch. He *would* take her! She was powerless to stop him!

Just as Sam's first sharp but poorly aimed thrust stabbed into her thigh, a voice made him jerk away from her.

"You leave off pesterin' her or, swear to God, I'll blow your balls off!" Helen-of-Troy stood beside them, wide-eyed, with

Lavinia's pistol aimed point-blank at the area of Sam Coltrain's anatomy she had threatened.

He gave another, futile thrust, and she said in a deady voice, "I ain't joshin', mister!"

Sam pulled his mouth away from Lavinia's and stared into her face with a twisted grimace. She half expected him to continue his attack unless Helen-of-Troy pulled the trigger immediately. Madness and anger blazed in his eyes. A nerve twitched and throbbed in his neck. Slowly, he released Lavinia and backed off, raising his one arm above his head.

"That's good! Now, you just stand easy right there!" Helen-of-Troy ordered.

Still holding the gun on him, she edged over to Lavinia and lent a supporting arm. "You all right, honey lamb?" she asked.

"Yes." Lavinia's voice was little more than a quivering whisper.

"Come on, then."

The two women backed out of the woods while Sam Coltrain stood watching them.

"Lavinia, don't leave me!" he commanded, but she didn't answer him.

"You get yourself into that buggy!" Helen-of-Troy ordered. "We're gettin' out of here. Fast!"

They did exactly that, taking Major Coltrain's horse along with them. Helen-of-Troy considered shooting the man. "Reckon there ain't no bastard I know deserves killin' more!" she told Lavinia. But in the end she decided simply to leave him in the woods. More likely than not, a Confederate patrol would pick him up, or the Federals would catch up with him and have him shot for desertion. Either way, he would be out of their hair for good, the servant reasoned. And the penalty for a slave woman killing a white man was too stiff to run the risk.

Lavinia, too shaken to talk for some time, rode on in silence. Helen-of-Troy, sensing her mistress's need to sort things out in her mind and to calm her nerves after the frightening experience, respected the privacy of her thoughts.

They were miles down the road before Helen-of-Troy

reached over and squeezed Lavinia's hand, saying, "You feeling better now, honey?"

"Yes, I think so," Lavinia answered shakily. "Thank you, Helen-of-Troy. If you hadn't come when you did . . ."

"Never mind that now. It's over and you're safe."

"I feel like a fool. I really trusted him. He can be very kind in his own odd way."

"Don't you worry your pretty head about him no more. He's a crazy man, that's all! Wasn't no way you could have guessed what he had in that twisted-up mind of his. Folks like him, they don't think like the rest of us."

"I only went with him thinking I could convince him to go home. He needs help. He's sick."

"He's sick all right! But his kind of sickness takes more than a doctor to cure. Now, let's just forget about that Sam Coltrain!"

That was easy to say, but Lavinia found it far from easy to do. As they rode on, Sam's horse still tied to their buggy, she found her thoughts straying back time and time again to the man, wondering when he would intrude upon her life again. She knew he would. She only hoped she'd be able to handle it when he did.

Chapter Fifteen

Lavinia knew they were in Kentucky. What she didn't know was exactly where. Several days had gone by since their encounter with Sam Coltrain. They had followed the roads as best she remembered them from the map Martha Ready had shown her. But somewhere along the way she feared they'd taken a wrong turn. Now, with night coming on and their supplies running as low as their spirits, they bumped along a narrow, rutted cart path. Both women had been silent for some time, each dreading to ask the other what they should do.

"I'm sure it's not far now," Lavinia offered in a hopeful voice.

"*What* ain't far? That's the question, missy!" Helen-of-Troy replied glumly.

"Cave City. I'm sure if we just follow this road we'll find it."

"Well, that's good, 'cause we sure ain't got much choice in the matter."

Helen-of-Troy was right, Lavinia thought miserably. They hadn't passed a turnoff all day. Not a house, not a farm, not a living soul had they seen. All they could do was travel on through the dense woods, following this meandering calf path, which seemed to lead absolutely nowhere.

"Do you think we ought to pull over for the night?" Lavinia asked.

"Pull over *where*? I ain't seen a wide place in the road for hours! Course, as much traffic as we's met, I don't reckon it would hurt nothing to stop the buggy right here in the middle."

"I don't know if that would be safe. If we sleep out in the open, anybody might happen by and do Lord-knows-what to us."

" 'Tain't likely!" Helen-of-Troy argued.

Just then both women sat up straighter, strained their eyes, and sniffed the air.

Yes, she did smell it. Lavinia was positive!

"Smoke!" she cried joyfully. "There must be a house near here, Helen-of-Troy! Maybe they'll give us a bed for the night."

The servant clicked at the horses, urging them to pick up their plodding pace.

Damien Clay's corset itched. And the ruffles inside his bodice had scratched all hell out of his chest in the heat of the day. Damn, he needed a place to stop for the night! But this part of Kentucky was wild and almost unpopulated. He'd hoped to find bed and board with some Southern sympathizer tonight. But that hope was growing as dim as the twilight. And he dared not drive his horse on after dark. The narrow road was pitted and rocky. One misstep and his mare could break a leg. Then he'd really be up the creek.

He began to curse himself for being a damn stupid fool. Sure, he didn't like caves—never had, never would! They made him feel like the walls were closing in on him, and the thought of being underground made his skin crawl and his stomach tighten up. Still, that cave entrance he'd passed a couple of hours back would have been the perfect shelter for the night. Thunder was rumbling now. He'd probably have to sleep out in the open and get drenched in the bargain, all because he had a silly aversion to tight places and being underground.

"And I do hate soggy petticoats!" he said aloud in the most simpering feminine voice he could muster. Damn, he was disgusted!

He'd seen no sign all day of the Yankee patrol he'd been sent out to locate. Too bad! He didn't mind his Annie Flowers disguise half so much when he got a chance to put his act to good use. And dressed in gray or blue, a soldier was a woman-hungry man. He'd been looking forward to a bit of sport with that bunch of bluebellies. Besides, Morgan desperately needed to know what Federal moves were afoot in the area. And it was Annie Flowers's job to get that information.

He settled back in the saddle, trying to force his mind to pleasanter thoughts than the rain about to drench him and the long, lonesome night ahead. "Lavinia," he sighed aloud. "I wonder what she's doing right this minute."

His mind painted a pretty picture of her, lying naked and lovely in her bed at the Ready house. She might have been an innocent when he met her, but she was one of those wonderful women born to give and receive love. He'd marveled at the speed with which she learned from him. He could see her now in his mind's eye, her limbs pale and shapely against the sheets, her long, graceful legs invitingly spread just enough to entice him without making her seem wanton. He imagined the taste of her breasts, sharply sweet like warm honey, and it made his mouth water. And the smell of her silky hair . . . like *smoke*?

No! He didn't imagine that smell! It drifted to him through the forest on the rising wind.

"By damn!" he said aloud, spurring his horse. "I may not have to sleep in the rain tonight after all!"

He spotted the house in a small clearing around the next bend in the road. The ramshackle old cabin of notched logs chinked with mud and straw might have been the finest hotel in all of Kentucky, he was so delighted to see it. The canvas-covered windows showed a welcoming glow from within, and he was sure he recognized the tantalizing aroma of venison roasting on the fire.

As he drew nearer he slowed his horse, staring more closely at the tiny dwelling. At first he couldn't make out what the stacks of boxes about the place were. They looked almost like ammunition crates. Could this be a secret enemy arsenal hidden away in the woods? He dismounted, his ears pricked for the slightest sound from the surrounding forest. If this was an ammunition dump, guards were sure to be about. But as he approached on silent feet, he identified the boxes and shuddered. *Coffins!* He might rather have spent the night in a cave than accept the hospitality of a coffin maker.

Lavinia took the reins from Helen-of-Troy, eager to hurry the horses toward shelter for the night.

"You'd best slow down, Miss Vinnie," the wide-eyed servant cautioned, holding on to the board seat with both hands. "You're going to tip us over if you hit one of them potholes!"

"Don't worry! Josiah and I used to race this old buggy through the meadow at home. I never took a single spill. I'm in perfect control."

But as the horses rounded the curve, Lavinia very nearly lost the reins. At first she believed the dim twilight was playing tricks on her eyes. She thought she saw a woman walking toward them, leading a horse. What would a lady be doing all alone at night out in the middle of nowhere? Then her heart swelled with recognition. That was no lady! That was the man she loved!

"Damien!" Lavinia cried shrilly, frightening the horses. "Damien darling!"

"Lavinia?" He quickened his step, staring, not quite believing it could be true. "Lavinia, what in God's name are you doing here?"

She leaped down from the buggy, leaving Helen-of-Troy to calm the horses. She ran toward Damien, her eager arms outstretched. Finding him this way was more than she had dared hope for. She had to touch him before she could believe that he was real. Repeating his name over and over again, she kissed his hands, his face, his lips, in a frenzy of excitement and relief.

Finally, he held her away and looked down at her, smiling and shaking his head. "I swear, I never in all my life met another woman like you, Lavinia Rutledge! Have you ever thought of going into bounty hunting as a profession? You've got the instincts of a bloodhound and a will like a steel bear trap!''

She drew her lips into a pretty pout. ''You're angry with me again, aren't you?''

''Hell, no!'' he said, drawing her close once more and feeling a sudden swell beneath his skirts as the touch of her warm breasts scorched his chest. ''How could any man be mad when his woman chases all over creation just to be with him? But how'd you know where to come looking for me?''

''Mattie guessed that Colonel Morgan would be heading for Cave City. I memorized her map before I left. But, Lord, I thought we were lost today! I don't have any idea where we are right now.''

Damien Clay chuckled softly and said, ''You women! Second-guess us every time. It's lucky for us the Yankees aren't as smart as you are.''

''Then Mattie was right?'' Lavinia couldn't keep the note of triumph out of her voice. ''You are headed for Cave City?''

''Right as rain!'' Damien replied. ''Morgan and the others should get there sometime tomorrow. I'm out on reconnaissance, checking on where the Yankees are so we won't run into any more surprises like we encountered at Lebanon.''

''You mean there might be Yankees around here?'' Sudden horror gripped Lavinia as she realized that they must have been riding through Federal territory most of the day.

''Well, we thought there were. But I haven't seen a sign of one. Maybe they've left this area for the time being.''

A heavy rain poured down so suddenly that Lavinia and Damien were both drenched before they could reach the cabin. They laughed like children as they started their dash, but sobered when it came time to thread their way through the coffins to reach the front door.

Lavinia shuddered against Damien and he said, ''They're only wood and nails. Just think of them as pine boxes.''

''You're sure they're all empty?''

''Of course, they are, darling!'' But Damien couldn't help wondering what they would find inside the cottage.

He knocked, but received no answer. Cautiously, he eased

the door open and called, "Hello? Anybody home?" Only the crackling of the cookfire and the sizzle of roasting meat answered him.

"Should we go in?" Lavinia ventured.

"Might as well. Whoever lives here must expect to return pretty soon. He left his supper on the spit. And I'm sure he wouldn't want us standing out in the rain, catching our death."

Lavinia shivered at his unfortunate choice of words.

"Come on in," Damien urged. "It's not a bad place."

She entered hesitantly, but had to agree. The single room was rudely furnished with a rope bed and a rough pine table and chairs, but the fire's glow made it seem comfortable and welcoming—if one could ignore the coffin set up in the corner.

"Come here, woman!" Damien growled playfully. "I've been wanting to get you alone for a long time."

She went into his arms. When Helen-of-Troy bustled in the door, having seen to the horses and carried in dry clothes for Lavinia, she caught them clinging together, their deep, satisfying kiss stretching on and on.

"Ahem!" She cleared her throat loudly, waited, then repeated her interruption, adding more volume.

"Oh, Helen-of-Troy," Lavinia said dreamily, "I forgot—"

"You forgot I was here! I know. But it don't matter. I brung you some dry clothes. Shuck them wet things and change. Right now! I'll just go see to the horses." Then Helen-of-Troy took herself back out to the tiny stable, discreetly offering her gift of privacy to the love-starved couple, closing the door softly after her so as not to disturb them further.

"Well, you heard the woman, Lavinia. *Shuck them clothes!*"

Damien began the process for her, kissing her as he slowly unbuttoned her wet shirt. Lavinia sighed into his open mouth as his hands tenderly fondled her breasts, bringing her nipples erect and the rest of her to a point of burning awareness of her need for him. Soon she stood before him, stripped to the waist, the firelight turning her damp flesh to glittering gold.

"My God, you're a lovely sight!" Damien breathed, feasting his eyes on her. "Come here!" He caught her about the waist and began unlacing her britches while he nibbled at her neck and earlobe.

"What if the owner comes back, Damien?" But only her words offered him protest.

She felt his strong hand slide down over the bare, goose-pimpled flesh of her buttocks as he slipped her britches off, at the same time drawing her body to his.

"We'll ask him to wait outside until we finish," he said in a moist whisper into her ear.

"Finish *what*?" She asked her question in the most innocent voice she could muster, though she was already working at the fastenings of his costume. His soggy gown fell away, leaving only the straining fabric of his riding britches between them.

"Finish *this*!" Damien growled, catching her up in his arms and capturing her lips once more.

He placed her gently on the worn hooked rug before the fire and lay down beside her, propped up on one elbow. Slowly, agonizingly, his fingers played over her flesh. He stroked her neck, tracing down to her breasts. There he paused to play with one pulsing nipple and then the other. Her hips thrashed slightly at the feelings he was arousing. Letting his palm slide down her body, he fanned his strong fingers, pressing down on her belly to hold her still. The pressure of his hand made her insides burn to know another sort of pressure.

"Damien," she pleaded.

He leaned over her, teasing her lips with the tip of his tongue. Her hungry lips captured it, sucking it into her mouth. While he distracted her with this tongue-to-tongue battle, Damien released his hold on her belly, letting his fingers slide downward until his hand parted her thighs. Slowly, tormentingly, he stroked her. He teased her to new heights of need. Lavinia felt as if she were on fire as he continued his gentle manipulations of her body. She could feel the tender parts he stroked pulsing at his touch, turning instantly to melting heat, her flood of desire taking physical shape to drench his fingers in a flow of warm juices. When she thought she was about to scream her need, he left off his loving torture, sliding his hand, damp now with her moisture, down the insides of her quivering thighs. She relaxed.

His hand caressing her legs felt good, but not so good that she couldn't stand it. Perhaps she would not die from wanting him. She let her concentration shift to their kiss, still warm and deep and wet. Her head felt light with the taste of him. She strained forward, craving more. Then, when she was most aroused by his kiss and most vulnerable to his touch, his fingers rushed back to her most vital spot, charging her body with new sexual electricity, stroking her toward insanity fostered by passionate need yet unsatisfied.

Lavinia tore her lips from his and cried out. Her hands fought with the buckle of his belt, the buttons, and then . . . hot, pulsing, demanding flesh touched hers. She stroked it, glorying in the fullness of him and the heat of his desire that almost burned her palms. He lay still as a statue beside her, as if he feared to move while her hands possessed what seemed at this moment to be his very life. When she leaned forward to touch him with her lips, Damien wailed her name in a desperate cry.

The next moment he was over her, seeking entry. Lavinia held her breath. She had wanted him for so long and he had manipulated her to such a fever pitch that she almost dreaded for the anticipation to end. He remained poised, his hips not touching hers as he bent his head to kiss her breasts. It was almost as if he knew exactly what she wanted. Then, when she could bear his gentle sucking no longer and thrust her hips high to meet his, he sank into her with perfect aim. She tightened her muscles, drawing him in until she possessed his full throbbing length. For a time he lay atop her, his eyes tightly shut, not moving a muscle. The only movement between them was his pulsing deep inside her, like a distant drum beating its message of desire. Lavinia held her breath once more. Never had she felt anything like this—so fragile, so tense, so all-filling and all-consuming.

Damien began to move inside her, drawing back slowly, thrusting quickly. Her body felt shattered with sensation, a broken rainbow flung before the winds. Then the bright pieces began to draw together. As he rode her down their magic path of passion, she felt herself glowing, her skin tingling, her mind glittering with colors, warm and cool. When their moment came it lingered on and on, filling them both with heavenly joy and exultation.

They descended slowly from their rainbow world. The hues left only a warm afterglow in Lavinia's mind and heart. She lay in Damien Clay's arms, marveling at this man. *Her* man!

They were dressed, Lavinia in the fresh frock Helen-of-Troy had brought her, and Damien in his britches and shirt, when they heard a commotion outside. They stopped their flirtatious afterplay—touching, kissing, nibbling—and turned solemn and alert at the sounds.

"Miss Vinnie! Open up!" Helen-of-Troy was pounding on the door.

"What is it?" Lavinia cried as Damien pulled the door open wide.

"Yankees, Miss Vinnie!" The servant's eyes were like twin moons in her terrified face. "They's comin' this way, too!"

"How many?"

"A whole passel, Mr. Damien! I don't know exactly, but there's a bunch of them. I heared 'em a while back and sneaked off down the road to see if it was the owner of this place coming back."

Damien reached for his gun. Lavinia caught his hand and cried, "No! You can't go out there—one man against so many!"

"If I don't, they'll soon be here. We both found this place and you can bet they will, too! I have to go, Lavinia. Now, turn me loose!"

Helen-of-Troy, frantic that Lavinia and Damien were wasting time arguing, ducked back outside to see if the Yankees had come into view yet.

Lavinia's jumbled, frightened thoughts began to sort themselves out. Uppermost in her mind was the determination not to let Damien face these men. He'd be killed for sure! She glanced about, trying to think of a plan. Her eyes lit on the open

coffin and saw a shovel standing near it. She looked again at
Damien. His back was turned to her as he loaded his pistols.
She didn't allow herself too long to think about what she was
going to do. She might change her mind.

In one swift move she grasped the shovel, raised it, and gave
Damien a resounding whack on the back of the head. He crumpled to the floor without a sound, but Helen-of-Troy, hearing
the sickening thud of metal against skull, dashed back in. She
saw Lavinia bending over Damien's still form and her hands
flew up to cover her mouth.

"Miss Vinnie, what happened? He ain't dead, is he?"

"Dead enough!" Lavinia replied in a stony voice. She
grabbed Damien beneath the arms, dragging him toward the
waiting coffin. "Give me a hand here!"

"What you going to do, child?"

"I'm going to save Damien Clay from his own bullheaded-
ness." She was breathing hard with exertion while her heart
pounded with fear. They had to get everything set before the
Yankees arrived. "Get hold of his legs. Help me lift him up
into the coffin."

"Lord, Lord," Helen-of-Troy muttered under her breath. "I
ain't never in all my born days!"

"Hush up, Helen-of-Troy! Use your strength to lift him. We
don't have any time to waste!"

In a matter of moments Damien was laid out fine as you
please. Lavinia spit on her palm and slicked his hair back.
Enough of the rice powder from his Annie Flowers disguise
was left on his cheeks so that he really did look pale as death.
She glanced about and, spotting a tall candle in a brass holder,
lit it and placed it at his head. Then she smoothed her dress, hid
their other clothes, and worked herself into suitable tears of
mourning.

Helen-of-Troy stood by, her eyes wide and uncomprehend-
ing, thinking that her young mistress must have lost her mind.

Lavinia's next words to her seemed to confirm her worst
fears. "Go out there and attract their attention. Tell them your
mistress's husband just died and she's in mourning. Beg them
not to bother me."

"It won't do no good, Miss Vinnie!"

"I know that. But you have to get them in here so that I can get them out—*fast*! Before Damien comes around."

Helen-of-Troy hurried out. While she waited, Lavinia watched Damien's still face for the slightest flicker of movement. She prayed he'd stay unconscious long enough. If not . . . She touched the handle of the shovel, ready at her side. The sound of horses' hooves in the yard alerted her. She forced more tears, wailing her pretended grief for all to hear. A moment later the door opened. A tall Yankee captain, hat in hand, stepped quietly inside.

"Ma'am, I don't mean to disturb you," he whispered. "Your woman told me of your bereavement. I stopped in to offer my condolences and see if my men and I could be of any service."

Lavinia keened loudly before answering, "That's very kind of you. But there's nothing anyone can do. He's gone! My husband is dead! Please, just leave us to ourselves."

The captain started to turn and leave, then all but stopped Lavinia's heart as he changed his mind, advancing toward the coffin to pay his respects. Lavinia kept her tear-blurred eyes on Damien, willing him not to recover consciousness just yet.

"Ma'am, at least allow my men to bury him for you."

"No!" Lavinia gasped, with more horror in her voice than she'd intended. But she forced herself to answer calmly. "No, thank you, Captain. I'll tend to it myself. If you'll excuse me now. I'd like to be alone with him."

The stubborn officer stood his ground. "Ma'am, begging your pardon, but he won't keep. It's been dreadful hot these past few days. I really must insist!"

Before Lavinia could object again, the officer strode to the door and called, "Burial detail!" which brought six other soldiers tramping into the tiny cabin.

"One of you nail the lid on. You other men go out and dig the grave!"

A burly, red-bearded private advanced toward the coffin. Lavinia prostrated herself across the pine box, crying, "No! Don't come near him!"

The captain came forward and gently pried Lavinia's hands loose. "Now, ma'am, we're only trying to help you." He restrained her while saying to the private who was waiting, hammer and nails in hand, "Give her a few minutes, O'Leary. Then I'll take her out of here while you nail it shut."

Lavinia gasped and gave a real sob when she heard his words. But there was nothing she could do. If she explained that Damien wasn't really dead, they'd want to know what he was doing stretched out in a coffin. When the truth came out, as it was bound to, they would arrest him, if they didn't shoot him on the spot. He was, according to the Union Army, a dangerous outlaw. All Lavinia could do was hope they would hurry and do the job before he awoke, then pray they would leave so she could dig him up before he really was dead from suffocation.

"Please," she said to the captain in a calmer tone, "can't we get on with this? You're right, of course. He should be buried immediately. It's been two days since . . ." Lavinia floundered momentarily over the supposed cause of his untimely demise, then blurted out the first thing that came to mind. "Since the stack of coffins fell on him and killed him."

"Oh, that explains all the pine boxes out front. Your husband made them?"

She nodded, feeling a new dread creeping through her. Where was the real coffin maker? What if he returned to find this odd assortment of people in his cabin, one of them using his merchandise without paying first? She'd just begun to ponder this problem when she glanced toward Damien and saw a muscle twitch in his eyelid. Oh, sweet Jesus! He was waking up!

"I beg of you, Captain, do tell your men to hurry! I've had as much grief these past two days as I can stand. I can't bear to see his poor, lifeless face any longer." She wailed loudly, convincingly.

"O'Leary, nail it shut," the captain ordered quietly.

Lavinia uttered a soft sob as wood scraped against wood and her lover's face disappeared from her view.

* * *

Damien Clay couldn't think straight. He couldn't remember where he was or what had happened. Something warned him not to open his eyes, that the light would split his head right open if it weren't cracked wide already. Every heartbeat brought racking pain. Then suddenly, a deeper, thicker darkness closed in around him. He could feel it, a tangible force pressing down on his chest, cutting off all light and air. With great effort he forced his eyes open, but remained blind in the dark void. He gasped for breath, bringing on a dizzying attack of vertigo. With no light to help him focus his vision, he lost all sense of horizontal and vertical. He felt as though he were spiraling downward into a bottomless pit, its sides closing on him at a suffocating rate.

He forced himself to breathe more slowly. There had to be a reason for this strangeness. Where was he? As if through a heavy fog he recalled that the last he knew he'd been in a cabin with Lavinia. *Yankees!* They'd been coming! Then something had hit him hard. Yes, that was why his head hurt so. But that still didn't explain where he was or what was happening right now.

A sudden jarring, like hammering, shook him, sending bright sparks of pain from his head to ignite his whole body. He reached out his hands to steady himself against the continued jolts. His fingers, sweating and trembling, touched smooth lathed wood. He tried to rise, but banged his head sharply on more wood pressed down just above him. He moved his arms but found only bare inches of space in any direction. The pounding from outside continued. He was sweating, gasping, trying to call out. But his vocal cords seemed frozen or severed. Suddenly, he knew where he was. The *coffins!* He was in one of them and the lid was being nailed shut over him. He beat at the wood until his knuckles were raw, but no one seemed to hear.

Lavinia heard. He was awake! She eyed O'Leary as he hammered the last nail in place, securing the lid. Didn't he hear, too?

"If I didn't know better, I'd swear he's hammering back, Captain Flagg."

"O'Leary!" the captain warned sharply. "That will be quite enough!" He cast a glance toward Lavinia, cautioning the man not to upset her further. She was once more convulsed in loud hysterics.

"Call the others now to carry the coffin out," the captain ordered.

"Yessir!"

The Yankee captain insisted on saying a graveside prayer over the deceased. By the time he finished and his men started shoveling dirt in over the coffin, Lavinia felt sure Damien had, indeed, departed this world.

Damien himself was beginning to wonder. He'd done a lot of un-Christian things in his lifetime. Maybe whatever hit him had killed him outright. And since the worst fear he'd ever had was of being closed up in a tight place with no air and light, he supposed that this must be his punishment in the hereafter. Yes sir, he'd died and gone to Hell, sure as rain! Damien had never figured he deserved wings and a golden harp, but he was damned if he was going to accept spending eternity in these close quarters! Even Hell had to have a less disagreeable punishment! When he heard the first shovel of dirt hit the top of the coffin, he once again beat at the lid with his fists.

Lavinia heard the drumming from inside the pine box and her heart leaped with joy. Damien was still alive!

She let out her most heart-wrenching wail and threw herself into Captain Flagg's arms. "Please, leave us now! I can't bear anymore. I want to sit through the night with him before he's covered up forever."

Helen-of-Troy bustled over and took the weeping woman into her ample arms. "Captain, sir, I can handle her. If you and your men will just go on now. I thank you kindly for all your help. I'll see to my mistress and to the burying, too, when she's ready to let go."

"Well . . ." The captain looked doubtful but finally motioned his men away from the grave. "Mount up! We can't spend any more time here. We've still got to locate that devil Morgan!"

The moment the men left the clearing, Lavinia hauled up her

skirts and jumped down into the grave. "Hand me that shovel, Helen-of-Troy!" she cried. "And be quick about it!"

"Help me!" came a strangled voice from inside.

"Hang on, Damien! I'll have you out of there in two shakes!"

"Lavinia? Better make it one!"

With the edge of the shovel she pried at the lid, using all her strength to loosen the nails. She forced it up a small crack, giving her more leverage. "Push, Damien," she ordered.

She strained and he pushed upwards until finally the lid flew off with the sound of splintering wood. Lavinia fell on Damien where he lay, kissing him and sobbing, feeling him all over to make sure he was all right.

"What in hell happened?" he gasped out, fending her off with some effort.

"Oh, Damien, it was the only way I could protect you from those Yankees, my love!"

He sat up, his head still spinning with pain and vertigo and his lungs burning for air.

"Do me a favor, will you, Lavinia?"

"Anything, my darling!"

"Next time just let the Yankees have me! I'm not sure I could survive any more of your protection!"

While Damien sat in the coffin, gingerly rubbing the goose egg on the back of his head, a shadowy figure stepped out from a nearby stand of pines. He'd watched the whole proceedings from hiding but still couldn't puzzle it all out. Now he edged into the clearing behind the cabin, his squirrel gun trained on the two women and the man who had risen miraculously from the grave only moments before.

"Damien," Lavinia whispered in warning. She touched his arm and nodded, alarmed, toward the bearded gnomelike figure approaching them.

Damien looked in the direction of Lavinia's fixed stare. The little man with the big gun wore long white whiskers. His skin was leathery brown from working out of doors and his arms bulged with muscles from shaping pine to his will. His squat, bowed legs gave him a comical gait, but there was nothing laughable in the quick black eyes glaring at them.

"You must be the coffin maker," Damien said quietly.

Keeping his rifle at a steady aim, the man nodded. "Yep!"

"We didn't mean to intrude."

"I reckon you did, though. Ruint one of my best coffins, too."

"We'll pay for whatever damages we've done," Damien offered quickly.

"I ain't carin'," the coffin maker answered, Kentucky parlance for "By doggies, you'll pay or I'll take it out of your hide!"

Appeased with more than enough greenbacks to cover the cost of the coffin, which he knew he could repair anyway, Noonie Crenshaw finally lowered his rifle and invited the trio back into his cabin, hospitably offering them a roof over their heads for the night, some of his venison roast, and plenty of good Kentucky 'shine to wash it down.

"We're mighty grateful, Mr. Noonie," Lavinia said, seated cozily by the fire while thunder and lightning crashed outside and torrential rains lashed the cabin.

He grinned at her, licking his fingers clean of the venison grease and using his long beard as a towel.

"Hellfire, little lady, 'tain't nothing. I wouldn't send a knight out on a dog like this!"

The jug passed 'round and 'round while Damien and Noonie swapped tales. By the time Lavinia's eyes began to close, she'd been listening for nearly two hours as the little coffin maker filled them in on all the Federal movements in and around the area.

Annie Flowers' mission was a success.

Chapter Sixteen

The mournful whistle of the southbound Louisville & Nashville passenger train careened off the rocky Kentucky hills and reverberated down through the green valleys. All seemed peaceful and calm, as it should be on such a gentle spring day.

But the chief engineer didn't like it. No sir, not one bit. He shoved his cap back from his grimy forehead and swabbed his face with a sooty red bandanna.

"You see anything, Sparks?" he yelled to his fireman.

"Nothing right now," the man called back, shielding his eyes against the morning sun's glare and squinting at the horizon, off toward Cave City. "But I could swear I saw smoke up ahead a while back. Could be some farmer burning off his fields."

The engineer refused to dignify that dumb statement with an answer. They both knew better than that. Farmers didn't burn off their fields this time of year. No, if there was a fire in these mountains, he had a sneaking suspicion that murdering horse thief John Hunt Morgan was carrying the torch.

Why *me*? he wondered. And why, of all times, when he was carrying a trainload of Federal soldiers, their officers and wives, *and* that strongbox in the baggage car?

"Damn!" he cursed softly. "And this wasn't even supposed to be my run!"

* * *

Back in one of the coaches, Mrs. Major Coffey was holding court as wife of the ranking officer on board the train. Gowned in a fashionable traveling suit of mauve faille, the pert brunette sipped tea and regaled the six younger women with tales of her triumphs and travails as the wife of a professional soldier.

"Oh, I do hate all the traveling," she moaned, "but, my dears, the places I've seen. Why, you just can't imagine! The forts out west are truly an abomination—the heat and dust, and *savages* always lurking about!"

Mrs. Coffey gave a very visible shudder, which seemed to the other women an outward indication of her horror. In truth, her mention of savages had brought to mind a certain handsome brave named Bold Rider. Her blood warmed at the thought of him. He had ridden her all right, as boldly as you please!

"Dear lady," Major Coffey interrupted, "you'll have these young women frightened out of their wits any moment. Don't dwell on your abduction." A general, horrified gasp went up from the ladies. "Tell them about the balls . . . the time you met President Lincoln . . . and when you danced with my old friend John Hunt Morgan."

Another collective gasp filled the coach.

"My dear Major, how can you still refer to that infamous outlaw as your friend? Why, our very lives are probably in danger at this moment because of that man!"

"You needn't worry about your safety, love," the major replied. "I've never known Jack Morgan to kill a woman." He laughed softly, remembering some of their escapades as young men-about-town. "Though a few may have thought they would die from a broken heart after an encounter with him. He's always been quite the ladies' man, you know."

The young women twittered among themselves, exchanging John Hunt Morgan tales they'd heard, their cheeks flaming pink with excitement and a certain feminine stirring deep inside, thinking what it might be like to be taken prisoner by such a bold villain.

"Oh, I'd just die of fright if we ran into him!" the youngest and most volatile of the women cried.

Major Coffey was becoming annoyed. Why did Morgan always have this effect on women? And why didn't he himself? It would be nice to have females, even his own wife, swooning and sobbing over him for a change. He was sick of all this talk about the "handsome, dashing, virile" Colonel Morgan. He decided to divert the conversation.

"Now, ladies, I must give you fair warning." The women, hearing Major Coffey's serious tone, grew silent at once. "If by some outside chance we should happen upon Morgan's Raiders before we reach Nashville, there is one among his band whom you should truly fear."

Having the women wide-eyed and dangling on his every word gave Major Coffey a satisfying feeling of power. Maybe he'd even embroider just a bit.

"There's a very dangerous woman riding with Morgan!"

"A *woman*?" they exclaimed in unison.

"One Annie Flowers! If we should come upon her, don't be taken in by her pretty face and pleasant airs. Believe me, she is capable of anything . . . *even murder*!"

The cries and squeals of horror warmed Major Coffey's heart and brought to mind a shocking rumor he'd heard in Louisville. He decided to claim the story as his own.

"Hear me well, ladies! Not a month ago I was traveling by stage between Lexington and Harrodsburg, my fellow passengers including another gentleman not of my acquaintance, his wife and daughter, and a young lady traveling alone. Unbeknownst to me at the time we boarded, she was this same Annie Flowers. We were not more than an hour on our way when two riders hailed the driver and, presenting arms, ordered him to stop the stage and throw down the mailbags. At this point Annie Flowers whipped out a pistol from beneath her skirts and ordered us out of the coach. The two riders, Morgan's men by the plumes in their hats, were obviously in league with Miss Flowers. While they dumped the mailbags and searched the interior of the coach, Annie Flowers relieved us of our valuables then ordered the other male passenger and me to disrobe!"

"*Major Coffey!*" his wife cried. "I don't believe our young friends want to hear this!"

He patted her cold hand, enjoying himself immensely. "It's

for their own good, my dear. As I was saying, that horrible woman ordered us at gunpoint out of our jackets and trousers right there on the road, in plain view of the lady and her daughter. I'd sooner have gone into battle unarmed! Then, unhitching one of the horses from our team, Miss Flowers hiked up her skirts and rode away with the two outlaws, firing back as she left, barely missing me, and wounding our driver. So beware, ladies! John Hunt Morgan offers little threat compared to this vicious woman who rides with him!''

On down the track the ''vicious woman'' of Major Coffey's tale was out of uniform. Instead of the petticoats he wore for spying operations, Damien Clay had donned more masculine attire, anticipating action when he reached Cave City. He was not disappointed.

With Lavinia and Helen-of-Troy in tow, Damien hooked up with Morgan's Raiders early in the morning of May 12, just outside of Cave City. The little town, eighty-five miles south of Louisville, was still sleeping when the men arrived. With a quickness and ease born of long practice, they headed straight for the freight train standing on the tracks beside the station north of town and set fire to the string of cars.

Lavinia sat in the buggy, where Damien had warned her to stay, and watched with a mixture of fascination and horror as the engine exploded. He soon rode out of the thick haze of smoke, his grin wide and white against his blackened face. He urged his horse toward the buggy, leaned down, and kissed Lavinia's lips quick and hard.

''Well, what do you think?'' he demanded, as if asking her to judge some part he had just performed onstage.

She couldn't think at all for a moment. Her mind was confused with thoughts of the rights and wrongs of actions in wartime as opposed to those taken during peace.

''Why, Damien?'' she managed at last.

He sat straighter and stared at her. ''*Why?* Because that train would be carrying arms and supplies to Union troops by tomorrow. Because those L and N bastards are working against us every way they can. Why, Lavinia? You know why as well as anyone!''

He turned and rode quickly back to join the others, leaving her to mull over his words. She wasn't given long to ponder them. A wailing whistle from the north drew her attention. Her eyes followed the puffs of smoke in the distance. She could make out a passenger train moving toward Cave City. A sudden coldness froze her heart. She had thought of war as glorious, exciting. Now she could only picture that train and those people onboard going up in flames that would leave a second charred and smoldering wreck before her eyes. She had to stop it from happening!

Hiking her skirts up about her waist, Lavinia leaped from the buggy seat to the back of Sam Coltrain's horse.

''Here, what you doin', child?'' Helen-of-Troy cried out. But she received no answer. Lavinia gave the horse a firm kick with her heels and rode into the thick of Morgan's Raiders.

Her mind was set. She would not allow them to harm the people on that incoming train.

''Lavinia! What the hell . . . ?'' she heard Damien yell, but she never turned to look.

Leaning close down on the horse's neck, his mane whipping her face, she steered him toward the little station house, following the tracks from there out of town. When the train rounded the last bend, she galloped onto the tracks, waving and yelling.

The engineer saw her full well. But it was too late to stop. Not enough track remained ahead for him to brake his iron horse and throw it into reverse. Still, he gave it a futile try, sending sparks flying from the wheels with a sound to set teeth on edge.

''Damn!'' he swore to himself as the train continued sliding forward. Turning to his fireman, he warned, ''Better get your shotgun. There's a welcoming committee waiting up ahead.''

''Morgan?'' the other man asked in a quavering voice.

''Well, by the looks of that burnt-out freight, it ain't Saint Nicholas!''

Lavinia barely had time to spur her mount off the tracks before the train came hurtling past. The hot wind whipped her skirts and hair, and cinders bit into her face. She turned the horse and raced along beside the train, trying to catch a glimpse inside. She spotted the gleam of gold against Federal blue. Yankees! So it was a troop train after all. There would be no civilians caught in the middle. That relieved her mind some until she saw a woman's face peering out at her through the smoke-glazed window.

When the first shot rang out up ahead, Lavinia ducked instinctively. Someone on the train had fired at Morgan's men. Apparently, no one was hit. She didn't hear a cry of pain. But one of the Raiders answered the shot with two of his own. Soon a regular volley was ricocheting back and forth. And Lavinia was riding right into it.

Out of nowhere a strong hand grabbed her horse's reins. "Dammit, Lavinia! Are you trying to get yourself killed?"

Sure enough, it seemed that someone on the train had chosen her as a target. Even as Damien steered her horse away from the tracks, farther back to supposed safety, the bullets continued whistling past, too close to be wild shots.

"Dirty bastards!" he ground out between clenched teeth. "Leave it to Yankees to shoot at unarmed women!"

Only after he spoke did Damien see Lavinia pull a pistol and commence firing back. He smiled. She would do!

"Hold your fire, men!" Morgan barked.

The shuddering engine ground to a halt on the tracks. Tension crackled through the morning air as they waited for the passengers to detrain. Lavinia realized to her amazement that her uncertainties concerning the right and wrong of things had resolved themselves quite naturally in her mind. The first shot that had whizzed by her head had brought with it the understanding that this was the enemy. Her own allegiance was as clear as the blue Kentucky sky. She was a Confederate, her Southern sympathies running clean to the core!

"No one's hurt," Damien observed as the crew and passengers came down from the train. "It's a damn good thing we can say the same for ourselves! Still, I mean to find out who was shooting at you, Lavinia, and make the sonuvabitch pay!"

She scanned the troops and their officers, but her eyes soon came to rest on the women. To the last one, they were all staring back at her, their expressions ranging from horror to disdain. The woman in dusky pink, clinging to the senior officer's arm, looked at Lavinia as if she were some sort of filth. Yes, Lavinia thought, this woman had to be her attacker.

"Coffey, you old so-and-so!" Morgan shouted with a laugh. "How long has it been?"

"Not long enough," the grim-faced major answered.

The major's wife rushed forward and laid a supplicating hand on Morgan's arm. "Oh, Colonel! You aren't going to harm our husbands, are you?"

Lavinia watched as Jack Morgan's blue-gray eyes examined the woman intimately, resting for some time on her full, heaving bosom. His gaze remained locked there as he answered, "Why, Mrs. Coffey, you must take me for some sort of villain."

"Then you'll only take us prisoners?"

His chuckle was deep and husky. "Now, that might be an interesting proposition, ma'am." His gaze swept on down the line, lingering just long enough on each woman to make her quiver with delicious dread. "But not being equipped to handle prisoners at this time, I'll write paroles for the lot of you. Your husband will be *your* prisoner for the duration of this conflict."

Some of the Yankee privates, hearing Morgan's remarks, grinned in spite of themselves. They knew what parole meant. They would be sent home, no longer allowed to fight. Those who had seen battle already knew that this would be a nice war to sit out.

"Search the train, men!" Morgan ordered.

The officers and their wives moved back into the shade of some tall trees and watched as Morgan's Raiders swarmed over the train like an army of blue-green ants. Some of the women wept. The men looked embarrassed, uneasy.

"Come on, Lavinia," Damien demanded. "I'm going to question them, to find out who shot at you."

"Damien!" She caught his arm, stopping him where he stood. "There's no need. I know who it was." She nodded toward Major Coffey's wife.

Seeing them staring at her, the woman tossed her head and raised her nose in a gesture of contempt.

"Let me talk to her alone." Lavinia, shoulders squared and a most commanding look on her face, approached the group of Yankee officers. They fell silent, all eyes watching her. She walked straight to where the dark-haired woman stood and stopped not two feet in front of her. Mrs. Coffey avoided her eyes, pretending she didn't see Lavinia at all.

"Why were you trying to kill me?" Lavinia demanded.

The woman didn't answer.

"I was trying to warn you," Lavinia said. "Some misguided sense of justice, I suppose. But why did you shoot at me? I'd really like to know."

"Humph!" Mrs. Coffey sniffed. "Warn us, indeed! I know who you are! And you're a disgrace to womankind. I only wish my aim had been true!"

"You know me? I don't understand. I'd never laid eyes on you before I saw you peering out at me through the train window."

"Maybe we haven't met in person before this. But you can't say you don't know my husband . . . *intimately*!"

Lavinia looked at Major Coffey. He was tall, lean, not bad-looking, but a total stranger. At the moment he looked quite uncomfortable, running a finger inside his collar as if to keep it from strangling him.

"My dear, please," he cautioned in a pained whisper.

"Don't try to silence me!" she snapped. "Maybe you were willing to, but I won't take any abuse from this whorish beast!"

Lavinia's hand flew up to strike the woman, but she stayed it, saying in a harsh whisper, "You take that back!"

"I most certainly will not! Any woman who does the things you've done, Annie Flowers, deserves to be called what she is!"

"Annie Flowers?" Lavinia said, staring in disbelief.

"Yes! *Annie Flowers* . . . harridan, strumpet, floozy, *slut*!"

With each name she was unjustly called, Lavinia could feel her blood rising to color her face as fiery as her hair. The last epithet did it. She flew at the woman, screaming like a banshee, nails clawing, teeth biting, feet kicking. They hit the ground with a body-jarring thud, rolling and tumbling in the dirt. Lavinia felt the woman's teeth sink into her arm. She screamed and grabbed two fistfuls of hair, yanking as hard as she could. Then she heard the woman's yelps and felt clawlike hands tearing at her bodice.

"Ladies! Ladies!" someone was shouting, but they fought on.

A moment later Lavinia felt rough hands grasp her waist and pull her up. Her opponent lay panting in the dust, her coiffure a tumbled tangle, her face smeared, her lovely rose-colored gown dirtied and ripped. Even though Lavinia was no less a sight, she took smug satisfaction in the other woman's disarray.

Damien Clay, who had pulled her off, clamped a firm arm around Lavinia's waist and hauled her away from the scene. He took her inside the little station house, where he found a pail of water. Tearing a piece from his shirttail, he washed her face and dabbed at the bloody tracks down her bosom left by Mrs. Coffey's nails.

"She got the worst of it," Lavinia said proudly.

Damien answered her with a reproving stare before he said, "What the hell was all that about, Lavinia?"

He was angry, she could tell.

"She's the one who shot at me."

"That's no excuse to make a spectacle of yourself! Honestly, you jumped on her like some trashy guttersnipe!"

Lavinia felt tears welling up in her eyes. How could he talk to her this way? "I was only defending you!"

"Me? How could that be? I don't even know that she-devil out there."

"Well, not you exactly, Damien." Lavinia hesitated, feeling light-headed suddenly, a delayed reaction from one of Mrs. Coffey's left jabs. "She took me for Annie Flowers and called you some awful names, Damien."

"Like what?"

She pursed her lips and glared up, annoyed suddenly. "I'm

not going to repeat those words! What kind of lady do you take me for?''

Damien had to stifle a chuckle at her question as he gazed down at her hair, which looked like a storm-tattered bird's nest made of red silk thread, her filthy gown gaping open at the bosom, and her beautiful angry face streaked with dirt, blood, and tears. What kind of lady, indeed!

"Anyway," Lavinia continued, her hands on her hips and a defiant scowl on her face. "nobody calls my man a . . . a *floozy* and gets away with it!"

The incongruity of it all struck them both at the same instant. Lavinia's grimace trembled into a smile and then she began to giggle. Damien guffawed loudly and closed his strong arms around her, smothering her against his chest. They held each other, laughing uncontrollably, for some minutes. Slowly, their mirth died down to an occasional snicker from Lavinia, prompting another spasmodic chuckle from Damien.

"You're really something!" he whispered just before his mouth came down over hers, silencing all sounds save the quiet, moist whisper of lips and tongues caressing.

With one well-aimed shot John Hunt Morgan blasted the lock off the strongbox, then kicked the lid back with the toe of his boot. The sight inside was greeted by a chorus of low whistles and excited chatter. When the money had been counted out, it came to eight thousand dollars in Federal currency.

"A bloody fortune!" Morgan breathed. A delighted smile made a white path between his mustache and beard. He raised his arms in an expansive gesture. "Ladies and gentlemen!" he shouted to his prisoners. "Since you've been so kind as to *donate* this handsome sum to the Confederacy, I'd like to invite you, one and all, across the way to the hotel for lunch."

The ladies twittered and exclaimed excitedly. Wouldn't this be a tale to tell once they got back home! Even Mrs. Coffey left off nursing her wounds to smile delightedly and order her husband back onto the train to find her trunk so she might change. Morgan had informed them already that due to the heat and to his desire that the ladies experience as little discomfort as possible from their unfortunate situation, he would spare the train so that they might all return to Louisville.

The luncheon was a gay affair, and the food and wine, the best the house had to offer. Lavinia, in a fresh frock of nutmeg brown trimmed in spring green, found herself seated at the far end of the table from Mrs. Coffey.

"A good thing!" she told Damien.

He squeezed her hand under the table and cautioned, "Temper, my darling!"

Morgan's men, flushed with victory, celebrated with bottle after bottle of the good Kentucky bourbon and were soon casting longing glances at the officers' blushing wives. The Union men sat stiff and frowning, uncomfortable in their predicament but unable to do a thing. When Morgan felt their tempers rising to the boiling point, he stood, thanked them all for coming, and suggested that his parolees be on their way. The officers whisked their ladies out of the hotel and onto the train as quickly as possible, relieved to be parting company with Morgan's Raiders.

Damien was escorting Lavinia back to her buggy when Morgan called, "Wait up, you two!"

"Here it comes," Damien whispered to Lavinia. "He's going to give you what-for, not that you don't deserve it!"

Lavinia framed a suitably curt reply but never had the chance to utter it.

"Miss Rutledge!" Morgan boomed. "Well done! I've seen some feisty ladies in my day, but you top them all. I congratulate you! And now I have a proposition for you. Are you interested in hearing it?"

The silver glitter in his eyes fascinated Lavinia. "By all means, Colonel!" she answered.

"The rest of us are going down to Chattanooga, where General Bragg is putting together a brand new Army of the Tennessee. I have a feeling that after today I'll be able to convince him to lend reenforcements to the Second Kentucky so that we can plan a real raid into the Bluegrass State. I want to take these boys home . . . to Lexington. But I need to know, before we get started, just what the Yankee movements are in that area.

Would you be willing to go along with Clay on a scouting mission for me?''

"Hold on, Colonel!" Damien objected. "That would be too dangerous for Lavinia. I won't stand for it!"

"And just what business is it of yours, Captain Clay?" Lavinia demanded. She added pointedly, "You're not my husband, after all!"

Taking her by the arm and turning toward a little church down the street, he said, "I can fix that quickly enough!"

Lavinia's heart soared, then plummeted. As much as she wanted Damien for her husband, she would not marry him only to be dominated. She jerked her arm away and stood her ground. "Nobody said I'd marry you!"

"By God, you will!" he bellowed. "I demand it!"

Morgan stood by chuckling, enjoying Lavinia's defiance immensely. Yes, she would be perfect for what he had in mind.

"Are you finally *seriously* asking me to marry you?" Lavinia said in a softer tone.

An expression of uncertainty flickered across his features, then turned to surprise. "I—well . . ." Damien had been carefully skirting his true intentions for some time now. His feelings were clear enough: he loved her. But *marriage*? From the beginning he had felt that he and Lavinia Rutledge were both too strong-willed ever to live happily together as man and wife. But her near-fatal encounter with Mrs. Coffey's bullets had changed all that. Like it or not, Lavinia was a part of him already. He couldn't imagine life without her. His surprise turned to resolve. *"Yes!"* By damn, she'd marry him or else!

"I accept!" she said quickly, before he could take it back.

Damien threw a desperate glance at John Hunt Morgan. The man only smiled at him and nodded. He'd asked her, she'd accepted, and there was a witness. *Trapped!*

'I'll marry you, Damien," Lavinia added seriously, "but only *after* you and I return from this mission."

His brown eyes narrowed and a muscle twitched in his neck. What the hell kind of woman accepted a man's proposal of marriage in one breath and made demands in the next? He opened his mouth to say just that, but Lavinia stood her ground, daring him to refuse her. Tension charged the air between them and for moments it seemed that the engagement might be terminated before it could even be announced.

"Well, Clay, what are you waiting for?" Morgan's booming voice broke through the tense silence. "Kiss your intended, man!"

Damien did kiss her—with force and command, to show Lavinia Rutledge who was boss once and for all.

She surrendered happily, knowing that the victory was hers.

Chapter Seventeen

Lavinia marveled at the way things had worked out and once again wondered if Helen-of-Troy's second sight had rubbed off on her. Hadn't she often thought of riding off to war with Damien, posing as Annie Flowers' sister? Indeed she had! And now she was doing that very thing.

Colonel Morgan's plan was beautiful in its simplicity. Too many people knew about Annie Flowers now. Any woman traveling alone was suspect. But *two* women—sisters—out in search of their lost brother Josiah would be a different matter.

"Especially if one of those sisters is lovely enough to be diverting," Morgan said, smiling at Lavinia, "and the other, Damien, is older and somewhat homely."

"I beg your pardon!" Damien objected. "Annie Flowers has been called 'charming . . . a winsome beauty.' I find your remarks highly insulting, Colonel!"

"I know of Annie Flowers' charms. And so do too many others. That's why your new disguise will include powder to gray your hair and a few age lines about your eyes and mouth. And you'll have to come up with a new name."

Lavinia, laughing at Damien's bruised vanity, suggested, "Why not call yourself Re-bey-ah-ca?"

He only scowled in her direction.

Morgan wished them well, promised to see Helen-of-Troy safely back to Murfreesboro, and then left them. He rode south. Lavinia, and Damien in his new disguise, rode north. Their mission was to scout the territory around Louisville, Frankfort, and Lexington, the main pocket of Federal activities in the Bluegrass State, and to pinpoint troop locations, determining the Yankee's strength before reporting back to John Hunt Morgan.

They rode for a long time over back trails, Lavinia feeling exhilarated in spite of Damien's sour mood and gloomy countenance. He was an actor who did not enjoy being upstaged, she decided. Never mind! She could endure his temperament as long as she was close to him. At least she wasn't stuck back in Murfreesboro with Helen-of-Troy, pacing the floor and worrying like Mattie Ready.

The late afternoon sky was thick with ragged gray clouds before Damien finally spoke a word.

"I think we ought to go ahead and get married!" he snapped.

"We will, darling," she answered sweetly.

"When?" Now that his mind was made up, he was impatient to get on with it.

"Whenever you like, if you're in such a hurry. But I haven't seen a sign of any church or preacher in these parts. Have you?"

They rode on in silence for another mile before Damien said in a more cordial tone, "There's a place up ahead that I want to show you. I remembered it just today. I'd thought we might honeymoon there, but since we aren't married . . ."

Lavinia hadn't been able to keep her mind off certain intimate phases of their relationship all day, not since he had kissed her in the station house after her fight with Mrs. Coffey.

"Please show me, Damien," she whispered, feeling a blush warm her cheeks and lowering her eyelashes in an unaccustomed maidenly fashion.

Suddenly, Damien reined in his horse and put a hand out to stop Lavinia's mount. "Did you hear that?" he whispered.

Her skin prickling, she shook her head, straining her ears to catch the slightest sound in the thick woods about them. All she heard was the faint static of summer lightning off in the distance.

"I guess I was imagining things," he said finally, a relieved smile lighting his face. "Don't worry about it."

But Lavinia did worry. The smile he offered her was too bright, his voice too anxious to reassure her. She didn't like these woods, especially now that the gathering clouds were casting an eerie yellow-green light over everything. And most of all, when someone told her not to worry, that was when she most often did.

The rain started slowly, fat, heavy drops that made plopping sounds as they hit. Damien, riding slightly ahead of Lavinia, spurred his horse and urged them both to more speed.

"It's not far now," he called against the rising wind.

She never would have noticed the little-used path off to the right. Damien turned his horse onto it and she followed. In the distance she heard water falling, louder than the rain, making a rushing, musical sound. A moment later they broke into a clearing beside a pond at the base of a steep hill.

"How do you like my secret place?" he asked, smiling back at her.

"Oh, Damien!" she cried. She scanned the scene with wide eyes. The pond was deep and as clear as glass, magnifying the smooth brown and black veined pebbles on the bottom. Across the miniature lake a waterfall crashed down from the rocky side of the hill, frothing into stark white foam at ground level.

"Come with me," he ordered, dismounting and leading the way to the waterfall.

Long before they reached the falls, Lavinia could feel the fine mist on her face, cool and refreshing as silk on a hot day.

"Damien, it's so beautiful! How did you ever find this spot?"

He tied their horses and took her hand, leading her around behind the falls to a sheltered overhang of rock, where a cave ran back into the hill.

"I had to outrun some Yankees in these parts once and just happened upon it. I call it the Garden of Eden. I swear I think we're the first humans here since Adam and Eve."

Lavinia could almost agree with him. The alcove at the cave's mouth was made of smooth, clean rock, high and dry.

But only a few feet away the water poured over the lip, plunging and foaming in a mysteriously lovely display. The edges of the pond were cloaked in lush cinnamon fern, dipping its tapering fronds into the clear pond. And close by, tall trees stood watch over this tiny piece of paradise.

"Oh, Damien! Let's explore the cave!"

He moved up close behind her and rested his hands on her hips while his lips pressed the pulse at the side on her neck. "I'm glad you like it, but let's don't explore the cave. I hate being underground. Besides, I know better things we can do," he whispered. A moment later his hands crept up to her breasts, cupping them firmly. He sighed and a tremor ran though his body. He tried to press close to her, but there were too many clothes between them.

"Adam and Eve in petticoats." He laughed. "If you don't mind, Adam is about to strip down to his fig leaf!"

Damien released her and quickly shed all his feminine apparel down to the riding britches he always wore under his skirts. Lavinia watched as he hauled off his boots, then ran, fleet-footed, up the hill to the rock ledge. For several moments he stood high above her, his back straight, his arms out for balance. Then with a graceful leap he dived into the pool. Lavinia watched the explosion of bubbles as his trim form knifed through the water, skimming the bottom before he burst to the surface once more.

"Try it!" he called. "The water is nice and cool!"

Lavinia knew how to swim, though Helen-of-Troy deplored her love of the sport. And on a few occasions she had even tried diving off a bridge over one of the smaller rivers back home. Tempted, she glanced up at the rock above. It was a long, frightening way down to the pool.

"Come on!" he called, floating on the calm surface. "You can do it, Lavinia!"

"I don't know, Damien."

"I dare you!"

Well, that did it! No one ever dared Lavinia Rutledge without her taking up the challenge. Quickly, she stripped off her frock and petticoats—right down to her pantalettes and camisole. Not allowing herself to think about what she was going to do, she hurried up the rocks until she was perched on the ledge above the falls. It was indeed a long way down, but it didn't look as far as she had imagined. She steeled herself for the plunge.

"Want me to catch you?" Damien called up to her.

"You just stay out of my way!" she called back.

The rain shower had passed, and the last light of the afternoon gilded the clearing. Damien, his body tingling with the feel of the water and his longing for Lavinia, stared up at her, poised there high above him. The sun's rays caught her in a pool of liquid gold, shining through the thin batiste of her underthings to offer a hint of dark nipples and the triangular shadow between her shapely thighs. He swallowed hard, feeling desire throb through his body.

Then she took wing, gliding through the air, her body in a perfect, graceful arch. She straightened the moment before the water rushed up at her, and needled into the surface with hardly a splash.

The soaring freedom of her fall set Lavinia's skin tingling. The sharp impact stung her, but a moment later the water soothed away all other feelings. She felt Damien's hands on her even before she surfaced for her first gasping breath. When she drew that breath, it came directly from his lungs as his mouth possessed hers. He held her close, only the water and her thin, soaked garments between them. They clung to each other hungrily, treading water as best they could. But Damien's hands had better things to do. They slithered over her wet shoulders, drawing the straps of her camisole down, freeing her breasts to his touch. Lavinia shivered with pleasure when her nipples puckered for his fingers. He eased her back into the water until she floated on the surface. With expert hands he stripped away the pantalettes and camisole and tossed them in a soggy heap upon the bank, where his britches lay already. Then slowly, tantalizingly, he touched her, stroked her, set her flesh on fire.

When their legs thrashing in the water made any further progress in their lovemaking an impossibility, Damien steered her to the bank. Night had fallen while they played in the clear pool. A million stars twinkled overhead and the moon cast a silvery glow in the clearing. The air was warm, but she shivered as he carried her from the water.

"I'll build a fire," he said.

She huddled against the smooth, warm rocks and reached out to take his hand and draw him back to her. "You already have, darling."

He eased down upon her until their bodies were kissing from lips to toes. His throbbing member lay locked tight between them. The hot flesh pulsing against her stomach filled Lavinia with a new kind of desire. She raised her hips, urging him to enter. Slowly, he lifted himself from her, pausing, looking down through the darkness.

"Take me now, Damien, *please*!" she begged.

He didn't answer, but sat back on his haunches between her legs, letting his hands dance over her aching body—a stroke here, a caress there, a pinch, a tickle, a flick. Her body writhed beneath his hands. She gasped and cried and begged. But no quarter was granted. When his hands had done with her, his mouth took over the task—licking, sucking, biting ever so gently until her body flamed for him.

Lavinia had never known such delicious torture. Her mind whirled with bright images in a kaleidoscope of vivid, hot colors. She imagined her own body glowing a pulsing, burning red, scalding to the touch inside and out. Only he could quench these deep fires.

When he sank into her at last, her first feeling was relief. But his own heat added to hers, bringing them both to the melting point. He stroked her slowly but deeply, each plunge seeming to encounter a new and more sensitive part of her depths. She could feel her flesh inside trembling against his. As he drew himself out of her, inch by agonizing inch, Lavinia moaned and her body clutched at his but failed to hold him. He took himself completely away, his tip poised, barely touching her tender opening. Spasms racked her body. She tried to hold still, afraid of losing even that slight contact with his flesh. For long, silent moments he tormented her, holding his position while he teased her aching breasts until she wept with need.

When next he thrust, easing in his full, hard length, it set up a shattering reverberation through her body. Like a droplet in the pond, the sensation moved outward in waves, reaching farther and farther until she felt it in her fingertips and toes. At that same instant he matched her climax, shuddering and clutching her trembling body to his. They never moved, soon falling into a deep, exhausted sleep in each other's arms.

It must have been near dawn when Lavinia awoke. Damien was not beside her. She sat up, alarmed, and glanced about. He was by the mouth of the cave, making a fire. He smiled, blew her a kiss, and said, "Go back to sleep, darling."

She was too weary not to obey him. But only moments later, it seemed, she awoke again, startled out of slumber this time by the crack of a pistol. She cried out, clutching the thin blanket he had spread over her earlier.

"Damien?"

Lavinia glanced about, frantic now, but there was no sign of him. She was all alone. The first glints of dawn cast eerie light into the clearing and filtered through the rushing waterfall, making it look like a glowing tower of glass. The fire Damien had been building when she awoke earlier had died to gray-crusted embers. The silence about the place was too thick, too absolute. She shivered and whispered his name again, feeling some unknown dread clutch at her heart.

Suddenly, a distorted shadow fell across the light from the falls. Lavinia gasped. The apparition seemed to be coming toward her, but she couldn't decide from which direction.

"Damien, please! Don't play games. Where are you?" she begged.

"He won't be coming back," the shadow said from very near her.

"What? Who are you?"

A familiar, humorless laugh resounded from the falls. "How soon you forget, Lavinia!"

"Sam!" she gasped.

"Very good! You do remember." A cold hand came down

on her bare shoulder, the fingers bruising her flesh. "And now you're going to come with me."

"No, I'm not!" she yelled up at him, jerking out of his grasp and trying to flee. "Damien!" she screamed. "Damien, help me!"

But no one replied. Sam Coltrain clamped his strong arm about her waist, dragging her toward the cave's entrance. Tears came to her eyes as she heard her own screams echo pitifully through the yawning cavern.

"He can't help you now. I'm the only one who can, Lavinia. And I am a forgiving man, so don't be afraid."

"*Forgiving?* What have I done that you should forgive?"

"You ran away with *him*! You left me, stole my horse. I'm sure you hoped I was dead by now," he told her.

"I never wished you dead!"

"Never, Lavinia? Well, maybe not yet."

His words sounded unnatural, diabolical. She turned to look at him. At that instant the first rays of sun crept over the horizon and their reflection flashed deep in Sam Coltrain's eyes. Lavinia gasped in horror. His gaze was like that of a dead man—empty, colorless, grave-cold.

"Sam, what have you done to Damien?" she pleaded, trying to regain her composure and some control over the situation.

"Nothing . . . yet."

"Where is he, then?"

He only smiled, his tongue coming out to smooth over his lips in an ominous gesture of pleasure.

When he shoved her into the cave, Lavinia begged, "Please, Sam. Where is he?"

"Where he won't bother us."

Damien Clay heard Lavinia's screams change tone. They had been coming from an open area. Now she sounded as if she had been swallowed up by some kind of monster. Her cry was distant and hollow.

The cave! he thought. That lunatic has taken her into the cave!

He struggled frantically against the ropes that bound his

hands, cursing himself for not paying closer attention to his own instincts. He had no idea who the one-armed man was or why he had followed them, but Damien knew that he had trailed them most of the previous day. He had heard their pursuer, but he had ignored his own ears. Now Lavinia was the one paying for his carelessness.

Shortly after he had awakened and built the fire, Damien had heard a sound from the far side of the pond. Not wanting to startle Lavinia, he covered her and left her sleeping while he went to investigate. The man, whoever he was, might be insane, but he wasn't stupid. He had used every trick in the book to lure Damien to exactly where he wanted him. One false step was all it took. The animal snare tripped, and Damien found himself dangling upside down several feet off the ground, a rope secure about his ankles while his useless arms flailed the air. His gun, falling from its holster, had discharged when it hit the rocky ground below.

Thinking back on it, Damien almost felt fortunate. The stranger could have left him dangling for all eternity. But the man had wanted to talk to him, tell him that he had no right to Lavinia, that she was spoken for by deed if not by word.

While this Sam Coltrain, as he'd said his name was, gagged Damien, trussed him thoroughly, then lowered him to the ground, he had explained his claim on Lavinia, telling Damien of their night together in shockingly intimate detail. Before, Damien hadn't really believed that Lavinia had been with another man. Now he did. The only thing Sam Coltrain's explanation failed to make clear was why.

Another scream pierced the cool morning air. It didn't matter why she'd chosen to be with this one-armed lunatic before, as Coltrain had claimed. What mattered to Damien was that she obviously did not choose to be with him now. He strained against his ropes, rubbing them back and forth on the sharp edge of a rock, feeling the razorlike granite slice into his wrists though his bonds held. Forgetting in his panic that he was gagged, he tried to call out to her, but only faint gurgling sounds rewarded his efforts. He worked harder at the ropes, ignoring the pain.

* * *

Had the circumstances been different, Lavinia would have enjoyed seeing the cave with its crystal formations and sculpted, lime-white stalactites and stalagmites. As it was, she hardly noticed the natural fairyland.

Sam Coltrain gave her a torch to carry, reserving the use of his one hand to hold the pistol at her waist. "I'd probably die myself before I'd shoot you, but then one never knows," he said.

Lavinia decided not to try anything just yet. *Especially not with a madman's finger on the trigger,* she thought.

On and on they wound their way through the rooms of the cave, at times having to bend under the low ceilings, while other passages were almost too narrow to slip through, though they seemed to have no ceilings at all. Lavinia felt herself growing dizzy with their twisting and turning. How would she ever get out if Sam Coltrain decided to leave her here? The answer was simple: *she wouldn't*! Even more frightening was the thought that perhaps he had no idea where they were going or how to get back. Maybe in his mind, seemingly as twisted as the route they traveled, he felt that this was the one way to keep Lavinia for himself. He would simply lose them both in the bowels of the earth where no one could find them. They would die here together, moldering away to twin piles of bones. She tried not to think about it.

"We'll rest here," Coltrain announced when they reached a large, high-ceilinged room with a pool in the center from which bright blue light emanated.

He took the torch from her and set it against one wall. Moving toward her, he smiled and reached over to touch her face. Lavinia drew away, clutching the blanket more closely about her. Never in her life had she felt so helpless, so all alone in her peril.

"You really have no reason to fear me, Lavinia," he said in a voice so calm and sympathetic that he sounded almost normal. "Relax, my dear. I'm not going to harm you."

His face was very near hers; his lips parted, anticipating her kiss. She couldn't bear to look at him. To avoid eye contact, she focused her gaze and her thoughts on the pretty pool. Where did the light come from? The rest of the cave had been totally black except for the illumination from the torch.

"Ah, the water," he said, following her staring eyes. "You like to swim. I watched you earlier. You're a very good swimmer, too. Would you care to now?"

"No!" Lavinia cried, feeling his hands tugging at the blanket. Then, her mind working on plans of escape, she relented. "Maybe it would relax me."

"That would be good." He smiled and took the blanket from her shoulders, sliding it over her skin slowly, sensually, while he smiled down at her.

Lavinia cringed inwardly, conscious of his eyes devouring her naked flesh, playing over her as Damien's hands and lips had done such a short while ago. Eager to be away from him, she hurried to the side of the pool. The edges were slippery with waving strands of hairlike lime. The water was very warm. She eased her body in, trying to find the bottom with her toes, but the pit of water seemed bottomless. She dived deep, swimming toward the glow in the depths, but could not reach it. Still, the light grew brighter the deeper she went. The mystery puzzled her. When her lungs were near bursting, she surfaced for air.

"That's enough. Come out now, Lavinia," Sam Coltrain ordered, his face grim and his pistol aimed at her breasts.

While Lavinia swam, Sam Coltrain had shed his shirt and britches. He stood before her now, a bull-like figure, completely ready to take her.

The ropes snapped suddenly, freeing Damien's wrists. He yanked away the gag and almost shouted Lavinia's name. But no! His only hope of rescuing her lay in the element of surprise. Quickly, he unbound his ankles and searched the grass for his pistol. It was there. He would have a sporting chance, at least. He needed more than that, though, if he was to save Lavinia from this madman.

He stalked quickly and soundlessly around the pond. Now the greatest test of all came. Lavinia was somewhere deep inside the gaping mouth of the cave. He would have to go in, bury himself alive, in order to find her. Taking several deep breaths, Damien steeled himself, willing his mind to blank out his irrational fear.

"Light," he said aloud, taking strength from his own voice. Though the morning was now warm pink and gold, the cave mouth yawned black and forbidding. He grabbed up a glowing stick from the fire and blew on it until it flared. Then, taking one step at a time, he forced himself inside the cave.

"There! You did it!" he encouraged himself. "Now, easy, watch for their tracks, listen for sounds."

He could feel the force of gravity pulling the ceiling down on his head at the same time that the walls pressed in on him. The sensations set his heart thundering and made breathing a near impossibility. When he caught himself gasping for air, he slowed his pace and forcibly measured each breath he took. His pulse calmed. He moved ahead.

Lavinia and Sam Coltrain were not difficult to track. It was almost as if the man had wanted to be followed and apprehended before he could do Lavinia any permanent harm. The thick powdering of lime dust on the cave's floor bore their distinct marks—Lavinia's barefoot tread, partially obscured by a trailing corner of the blanket, followed by the man's booted imprints. Ignoring the tightness in his chest and the disorientation he felt, Damien hurried on, praying that he would find them in time.

"Sam, please!" Lavinia begged after pulling her lips from his. "I can't breathe!"

"I'm sorry, my dear. If I seem overeager, it's only that I've been thinking about this moment for so long. You'll never know what our night together meant to me. I've thought of only you since then. And now I have you here, close enough to kiss, to touch." His shaking hand strayed to her breasts, fondling her too roughly.

"Sam, why are you doing this?"

He stared at her, his eyes glowing in the torchlight. "Lavinia, Lavinia! How many times must I explain it to you? We *belong* together! I think we must have loved each other in another life. I feel I've been searching for you down through the ages. And now . . .'' He caressed her face with his hand, forcing her lips toward his. ''Now we have found each other at last. I'll never let you go again.''

There was no way she could fight him. Once more he held a death-lock grip on her throat. He forced his way into her mouth with his tongue, battering hers, stealing her breath and pulling her body hard against his.

He tore his lips away as violently as he had kissed her. His words came in an impassioned rush. ''Don't you understand, Lavinia? *I love you!* I would give my life for you!''

''Sam, I'd never ask that of you,'' she said softly, hoping to dissuade him from his set course. ''All I ask is that you take me back, leave me to my own life.'' She hesitated, wondering what reaction her next words would bring, but then she rushed on. ''I can't love you, Sam. Not the way you love me. I've told you that before. Damien Clay is the man I love. He means everything to me. Without him I would be better off dead!''

The moment she said the words, she realized her mistake. Sam Coltrain's face turned granite. His eyes flared with anger.

''That could be arranged!''

When Damien took the turn into the next corridor and saw them there together, his body refused to obey his orders and the blood froze in his veins. They stood naked, the two of them, chest to breasts, with Sam Coltrain now pressing the barrel of his pistol to Lavinia's throat, even as his erect member pressed into her abdomen. One false move from Damien and he would have nothing left to take in his arms but a bloody corpse. He held his breath, once more feeling the cave press in around him.

''Sam,'' Damien heard her say, ''you can't kill me!''

He jabbed at her throat with the pistol and she cried out.

''No, Sam! Wait!''

''What for?'' he growled. ''You don't want me. You want *him*!''

"But you killed him, didn't you?" She steeled herself for the answer, sure that she would get the truth this time.

"No! I should have! But I had in mind to go back and get him. I'd planned to make him watch while we made love." His laugh echoed hollowly through the cave. He pressed closer, forcing Lavinia against the cave wall with his hard, muscled body. "Maybe I still will."

"No, don't!" she cried. "He couldn't stand that! It would kill him quicker than any bullet! You can't be that cruel, Sam."

Lavinia's fingers slithered up Sam Coltrain's back, twining through his hair. Damien bristled.

"Oh, can't I, my dear?" her captor said.

When Coltrain thrust Lavinia away from him, Damien found the opening he'd been waiting for. He rushed forward, knocking the man aside and aiming at him with his pistol, point-blank.

"No, Damien!" Lavinia cried.

Both men—Damien standing beside her, and Sam Coltrain sprawled on the floor of the cave—looked at her as if she were demented.

"Don't kill him," she said lamely. "Let the cave have him."

Damien's finger was already tightening on the trigger to put an end once and for all to Sam Coltrain and his mad lust for Lavinia. But her words stopped him. He lowered the gun, not out of mercy but out of vengeance. What better fate for such a demented villain than to have his despicable life ebb slowly away deep in the foul, lonely blackness of his own grave? Yes! The drama of it appealed to Damien.

After kicking Coltrain's pistol into the pool, he threw the blanket around Lavinia and shepherded her back the way they'd come. Suddenly, Sam Coltrain was upon them. He snatched the torch from Damien's hand and tossed it into the pool as well. His own light was soon doused in the same manner.

"Damien!" Lavinia gasped.

Without a torch to see their way they would never find the

trail they had followed into the cave. Eerie laughter filled the void, reverberating off the damp walls about them.

"So, the end has come!" Sam Coltrain chortled. "My darling Lavinia, I had much sweeter things in mind for you."

"Quickly, Damien, into the pool!" Lavinia whispered. "There has to be an opening letting that light in."

Side by side they dived. Deeper and deeper they swam, their lungs burning, their heads aching from the pressure. A million thoughts drifted through Lavinia's air-starved mind. Still, she followed the light. Down, down, ever deeper, ever nearer. Blackness began to replace the bright light. It was all over. The light faded. Only Sam Coltrain's demented laughter echoed in the watery silence.

"Why does there always have to be a damn snake in the Garden of Eden?"

Damien's voice seemed to Lavinia to come from an ocean away as the blackness cleared from her soggy brain. She was lying on dry grass, the sun warm on her face. She raised her hands to look at them. She needed to know that she was real, alive, and safe.

Seeing her eyes open, Damien leaned down and kissed her. That was her proof. Kisses like this, she thought, do not take place beyond the grave.

"I thought I'd lost you," he murmured.

"I thought so, too! Didn't I drown?"

She sat up and pounded her temple with the heel of her hand until the pressure in her ears eased.

"You tried to," Damien said, "but I wouldn't let go. We've come too far for me to go on alone."

Her arms snaked up around his neck and she drew his warm lips down to hers once more, kissing him tenderly, passionately.

"You'll never be alone again, Damien Clay. I don't intend to let you out of my sight from now on."

Suddenly, his face darkened. "What about him, Lavinia?" He jerked his head toward the opening from the cave. "Why

didn't you let me put an end to him? Some sentimental attach-
ment for a past love?''

"Is that what you really think, Damien?" Her voice was totally without emotion, though her heart pounded in her breast.
How could he imagine such a thing?

"I don't know what to think. I just feel in my bones that I
should have pulled that trigger. Now Sam Coltrain's still a
threat to us."

Lavinia shook her head. "I don't think so. Without a torch
he'll never find his way out of that cave."

"He could swim out. We did."

"With only one arm? I doubt that, Damien," she said
quietly.

"I guess you're right. It was a tough pull. We just barely
made it."

"As for why I asked you not to shoot him . . . well, it's a
long story. Sometime, when we have nothing better to do, I'll
tell you about it. I sort of owed him a favor, in spite of everything."

"Well, you're paid up in full now. Let's forget him. Sam
Coltrain is a closed chapter in our lives."

But even as Damien Clay spoke the words, a weary figure,
blind in the total blackness below them, was clutching at a thin
thread, following it back to the cave entrance.

Chapter Eighteen

The next few days proved blessedly uneventful as the "sisters" rode north toward Louisville. Gone were the stormy spring afternoons of April and May that had threatened tornado winds and delivered damaging hail down through the thick yellowish air. Now Kentucky breathed the fresh, warm summer breezes. The narrow trails Lavinia and Damien traveled were dappled with shade and canopied in lush green. Wildflowers bloomed and cardinals flashed, brilliant red, through the limbs.

Having lived all her life near the water, Lavinia could sense the great Ohio River before she actually knew how near they were to it. She sniffed the air like a sleek hound on the scent.

"We're coming to the ocean," she said delightedly.

Damien laughed. "Remind me to buy you a map when we get to Louisville and show you what's what. We're nowhere near an ocean. That's the river you smell—the mighty Ohio. We're almost where we're going."

Lavinia stretched in the saddle, feeling her muscles ache and her stiff joints creak. "That'll be a relief," she sighed.

"Too much for you, eh?" Damien cast a sidelong leer at her. He'd been needling her the whole trip, hinting, though he never said it outright, that this work was too strenuous for a woman. "Had about all you can take?"

She settled back into her usual riding position and smiled at him as if she were thoroughly enjoying every bounce and bobble her mount made under her. "Oh, I'm fine! You don't have to worry about me. I'm only thinking of this poor horse. He must be ready to drop. And I'm sure he has saddle sores by now." The very mention of such an affliction made her own chafed bottom ache.

"The horse—of course. I should have figured you were concerned about him, you being such an animal lover." Damien grinned at her, letting her know she wasn't fooling him for a minute.

They rode out of the woods a short time later and spotted a town in the distance.

"Is that Louisville?" Lavinia asked.

"Nope. Portland." He didn't miss the pained expression that passed quickly over Lavinia's face. She'd thought they were at the end of their journey. "It's right next door to Louisville, though. And come to think of it, we might be better off finding a place to stay in Portland. It's a shipping port, with lots of strangers in and out. And, too, most of the military is concentrated in Louisville. I think we'll feel freer to move about if we aren't right in the city. What do you think?"

Lavinia was already visualizing a hot bath and a soft mattress—the sooner the better. "Sounds reasonable to me." She had trouble pretending to be casual about it.

Following a maze of narrow streets in the eastern part of town, Damien soon led them to the main thoroughfare, Rudd Avenue. It followed the river, and Lavinia found herself torn between watching the wide, busy shipping port and taking in the unusual architecture on the other side of the street. The whole area bustled and rumbled with activity. Rivermen and soldiers along with servants and civilian pedestrians jostled one another for elbow room. Lavinia thought to herself that even Savannah wasn't as busy a place as this. There might be just as many people, but they all moved more slowly in the oppressive Deep South heat.

"Here we are," Damien announced.

He dismounted and looped his horse's reins over a hitching post in front of what looked like a private home. It sat back from the street with a tiny lawn in front. Pink petunias bordered the stone front walk.

"Who lives here?" Lavinia asked.

"I don't know, but they're asking for visitors." He pointed to a neatly lettered Room to Let sign in the front window.

As they started up the walk, she got a better look at the house itself. It was a small white clapboard structure with lace curtains frothing at the windows, a porch swing, and rocking chairs where a person could sit and watch the world go by.

"I never saw such a homey place," Lavinia said.

"And never will again anywhere else, my dear. Around these parts we try to make our guests cozy and comfy." A neat, round little woman with a red face and cotton-white hair smiled from the front door as she spoke to Lavinia. "I saw you two ladies coming up the walk and figured you must have seen my sign. Do come in."

She ushered them into the cool, shadowed hallway. Lavinia glanced about. The woman's house looked like her—everything perfectly in order but slightly overstuffed and overfluffed.

"I'm Mrs. Campbell," their hostess offered.

"Miss Lavinia Rutledge, ma'am, and my sister, Rebecca." Lavinia had warned Damien to keep his mouth shut and let her do the talking whenever possible, especially to other women. She had told him that women were not as easily hoodwinked as men. Actually, she just didn't want to put temptation in his path. He was one to clasp a pretty woman's hand longer than need be when he was in disguise and could get away with it.

"Oh, that's fine," Mrs. Campbell replied. "If you're sisters, then the one room will do you nicely. It's all I have at the moment. I wouldn't be letting it out—it's my boy Andrew's room and he's away at war—but being a widow woman, I do need the income. I hope you'll find it to your liking."

"A room to share will be a blessing, Mrs. Campbell," Damien answered in spite of Lavinia's warning. "My little sister's afraid of the dark, you see, and she's never slept alone."

Lavinia narrowed her eyes at him, silently vowing to get him for that later.

"Well, my dear, you certainly have nothing to fear while you're in my home. The only other guest is an officer attached to a unit over in Louisville."

Damien touched Lavinia's arm, signaling her to make their excuses and refuse the room. Getting information from the Yankees was one thing, but living under the same roof with one was quite another. Lavinia ignored him.

"I'm sure this will be perfect for us, Mrs. Campbell. And I'm not such a silly as my sister would have you believe. She just thinks I need protecting noon and night.

The landlady smiled at Lavinia and nodded approvingly at Damien. "You're sister is absolutely right, my dear. A pretty young thing like you needs someone older and with a wiser head on her shoulders to look out for her. Come along, now. I'll show you the room."

Damien tried to find something wrong with it, but it was in no way lacking. Curtained windows opened on both sides, giving a wonderful view of the river and fine cross-ventilation. It was spotlessly clean. And the wide brass bed looked utterly inviting. He glanced at Lavinia, then at the bed, and gave her a meaningful grin. She frowned reprovingly back at him.

"This will do nicely, Mrs. Campbell. Thank you." She paid the woman in advance, just in case they had to make a quick getaway.

"Anything you want, my dears, just give a call. My room is right below yours. So if you should need me, even during the middle of the night, just stamp on the floor. I'm a light sleeper and I hear every little sound from this room."

She bustled out, promising to have her serving girl bring water up for a bath as soon as it was heated.

"Damn!" Damien said under his breath as soon as the door closed after Mrs. Campbell. "What in hell are you thinking of, Lavinia? This is no place for us, with that Yankee staying right here."

"Quiet, Rebecca," Lavinia cautioned, grinning mischievously. "Remember, Mrs. Campbell hears all! I think this is the perfect setup. It should be easy as pie for me to get to know our housemate and probably get worlds of information from him. How is it you say you always work—'with a smile and a flutter of eyelashes'?''

"Dammit, Lavinia! I won't have you flirting with that Yankee bastard! It isn't decent!''

"Oh, calm down, Damien, for heaven's sake! He's probably old as the hills and has a wife and fifteen kids. I expect he'll turn out to be more your type than mine.''

A knock at the door silenced them both.

"That'll be our bath water,'' Damien said, going to open the door.

"Oh, Miss Rebecca,'' Mrs. Campbell said when her knock was answered. "Is Miss Lavinia presentable? I've caught Lieutenant Waring about to go out and told him all about your charming sister. He's most eager to meet her before he leaves.''

Lavinia hurried forward at the mention of her name.

"Here she is, Lieutenant!'' the woman exclaimed. "Didn't I tell you? A real beauty and sweet as they come.''

Lavinia smiled. Lieutenant Waring was certainly not old as the hills. He was, she guessed, near her brother Josiah's age, tall, fine-boned and -featured, with golden hair and tawny eyes. He was perfectly handsome!

"Lieutenant Waring,'' Lavinia said, offering her hand, which he pressed warmly. "I'm so happy to meet you.''

"And I you,'' he answered, smiling directly into her eyes. "I hope you and your sister will be at supper tonight. I have to dash right now, but I do want to get to know you both.''

"Oh, yes,'' Lavinia answered. "That would be nice. I'm sure we'll see you later, Lieutenant Waring.''

His smile lit his handsome face like the sun breaking through the clouds. "I'll count on it. Ladies,'' he said, bowing his farewell.

Mrs. Campbell rolled her eyes, then winked at Lavinia. "Oh, isn't he just the most darling boy!''

By the time Lavinia closed the door, Damien was steaming. He looked primed to kill, she thought.

"Whatever is the matter with you?'' she demanded.

"Oh, nothing! Nothing at all,'' he seethed. "I thoroughly

enjoy seeing *my* fiancée being fawned over by every Yankee that comes along!''

''I didn't think he was fawning.''

''*You* wouldn't! You were enjoying it too much!''

''Damien darling, you're being ridiculous.'' Lavinia went to him and put her arms around him, laying her head on his chest. ''You know you're the only man I want.''

His anger eased some. How could he stay mad when she was this close, when he could smell the perfume in her hair and feel her heart beating against his? He lifted her chin in one hand and brought his lips down hard on hers. She responded to him eagerly. He was inching them toward the bed when the serving girl's knock wrenched them apart at last.

Supper that night was a trial for Damien Clay. In spite of his protests, Lavinia had insisted upon wearing a daringly low-cut gown of pale yellow lawn. Lieutenant Waring couldn't keep his admiring eyes off the soft rise of creamy flesh nestled so delectably in her ruffled bodice. And for that reason, Damien had trouble keeping his eyes off the all-too-eager young officer. He had no idea what he ate at Mrs. Campbell's well-burdened table. All his concentration was on the courting and flirtation going on between Waring and Lavinia.

Just wait, he thought, till I get her upstairs!

''I realize this is sudden, Miss Lavinia,'' Waring said, drawing Damien's mind back to the conversation, ''but there's a regimental ball next week. Would you do me the honor . . .''

''I'm afraid that's impossible, Lieutenant!'' Damien cut in abruptly. ''My sister never goes anywhere without me.''

Waring smiled beguilingly at the older Rebecca, at the same time thinking what a sour old maid she was. ''Of course we'd expect you to accompany us, Miss Rutledge. If you would like, I could even arrange for an escort for you.'' Waring almost chuckled aloud. There was a certain dowdy major he wanted to get even with. What better punishment than saddling the old lech with Miss Rebecca for an evening?

''That would be grand,'' Lavinia enthused. She cast a warning glance in Damien's direction. ''You'd enjoy that, wouldn't you, Sister?''

As much as Damien hated to admit it, this was just the sort of setup that proved most efficient when it came to gathering valuable information. He and Lavinia could find out more in an hour at one of these social gatherings than they could in a week of casual gleaning around town.

"Well, Miss Rebecca, shall we call it a date, then?" Waring asked.

"Oh, I suppose," Damien answered resignedly.

Lieutenant Waring wanted to show Lavinia Mrs. Campbell's garden after supper. But there was no way Damien was going to allow her out in the moonlight with that grinning Romeo! Thanking their hostess for the delicious meal, he whisked her up the stairs to their room and bolted the door behind them.

Lavinia knew he was angry again, and she was getting tired of his jealous rages. Backing away from him, she warned, "You can't yell at me, Damien. Mrs. Campbell will hear you."

Tearing at the fastenings on his dull gray gown, he stalked toward her. By the time he reached her, he was down to the real Damien Clay. His hands came up, grasping her bare shoulders.

"I don't plan to yell," he said in a quiet voice. "I only plan to remind you that there's a starving man lurking under Rebecca's petticoats. Remember me, Lavinia?"

His hands slid from her shoulders across her chest and down in the low neckline of her gown. Her breasts trembled in his firm grasp. She swayed against him and caught her breath. A moment later her gown slid to the floor and his mouth sought her nipples. Lavinia was as starved as he. They grappled in the darkness, fighting for possession of each other's bodies. The need for silence lent a delicious danger to their lovemaking. The sounds they dared not utter manifested themselves in passionate action.

They couldn't use the bed, with its creaking springs, for anything more active than sleep. So they stood in the center of the room, touching, tasting, loving each other with a fury. Lavinia clung to Damien for support as a welcome weakness overcame her. When he had reached the ultimate, throbbing point of need, he grasped her buttocks in both hands and lifted her, sliding into her with ease. Legs wrapped about his hips, she set the pace while her lover stood strong and still, supporting her. When their time came, their lips were locked together as tightly as the rest of their bodies. They muffled each other's cries of release.

Afterward, the old brass bed sighed only softly with their gentle stroking and nestling. They lay awake for a long time, whispering to each other as sisters will do. If Mrs. Campbell heard the muffled sounds of their quiet pillow talk, she thought nothing of it. But had she been able to hear their exact words, she would have been appalled.

Lavinia and Rebecca made regular trips to Louisville and scouted the surrounding areas during the next few days. They explained their sorties to Mrs. Campbell as shopping expeditions. After all, Lavinia couldn't wear one of her old gowns to the ball with Philip Waring. "Of course not!" their amiable landlady agreed.

Lavinia did buy a gown in one of Louisville's fashionable Main Street shops, but what she got for free there was far more valuable. She happened upon the very dressmaker used by most of the Yankee officers' wives. They, too, were being outfitted for the ball and gossiping while they were measured, pinned, and basted. Though Damien roamed other sectors of the Federally occupied town, his gleanings were far inferior to the inside information Lavinia overheard from the ladies.

Only a few important details of troop movements in the offing remained to be uncovered by the night of the regimental ball.

"We really don't even need to go tonight," Damien insisted as he worked at the tiny buttons up the back of Lavinia's gown.

God, she looks gorgeous! he thought. *Too* gorgeous! He didn't want her at that ball, dancing in Philip Waring's arms. Not wearing satin that had the same pale rose glow as her skin that showed off her slim waist and high breasts, that made a man think of wedding and bedding just to look at her.

"Don't start that again, Damien," she answered. "You know we have to get all the information we can. Morgan needs it! You'd better get dressed now. Philip and Major Zollicoffer will be here any moment.''

Damien turned a sudden, furious look on Lavinia. "I'm not going to dance with him! I refuse!''

Lavinia suppressed an amused smile. "How will you get out of it? This is a ball, you know.''

"I'll tell him I have a clubfoot.'' He limped dramatically across their bedroom, demonstrating his affliction.

"Philip knows better.''

"I won't do it!''

"Don't dance, if you don't want to. But just watch yourself and don't give us away,'' Lavinia admonished him.

As it turned out, there was no problem about the dancing. The short, thick-trunked Major Hyman Zollicoffer had no intention of making a spectacle of himself in the hotel ballroom. Besides, he'd been shystered by that fresh twerp Waring. The "charming lady'' he'd been promised turned out to be a tall, unattractive crone with a limp. Rebecca Rutledge belted down Kentucky bourbon like a man, talked politics and military tactics, and seemed far more concerned about her baby sister, who was the belle of the ball, than she was with entertaining him. So be it! Zollicoffer thought. He'd get drunk as a lord and forget this whole stinking mess of an evening!

Damien knew he had to take it easy on the bottle the fat little major kept passing to him. He was feeling a buzz already, and a drunk spy was as good as a dead spy. One slip of the tongue was all it took, especially in a ballroom filled with Yankees. Still, he was so furious he could hardly think straight.

Lavinia had apparently made it her goal to dance with every damn bluebelly in the hall. They were lined up, waiting their turns, for Chrissakes! And she hadn't been over to speak to him for two solid hours. In fact, she'd hardly glanced his way all night. She was having a grand time. He hated it. He bet she wasn't even bothering to try to find out anything. She was just dancing right through her new slippers and lapping up all the attention. *Women!*

Lavinia's head was whirling, but not from her hundreds of turns on the dance floor. She'd crammed so much information into her brain that it felt like it was about to burst. She could hardly wait to tell Damien. Philip Waring hadn't been much help at all. He was tight-lipped and far more interested in getting her off in a dark corner than in talking about anything. But all these others . . . Well, it just made a girl's head spin. All she had to do was act coy and cute and ask dumb questions and they spilled the beans on any subject she wanted to know about. She bet if she asked what size drawers General Grant wore, one of his officers would come up with the answer promptly and correctly.

"Lavinia, my dear, you seem miles away," Philip Waring whispered close to her ear.

"I'm rather tired actually, Philip. This has been a marvelous but an exhausting evening. I don't believe I've ever danced so much in all my life."

"You've only danced with *me* three times. I'm terribly jealous." He punctuated his statement by squeezing her waist and planting a kiss on her cheek.

Damien didn't miss Waring's maneuver. Fury boiled up inside him like a volcano gearing up to spew hot lava in all directions. He was about to charge the dance floor when Major Zollicoffer, so drunk now that even Rebecca Rutledge looked enticing to him, flung an arm around Damien's shoulder and enveloped him in a smothering clench, at the same time puckering up to steal a kiss. Damien, shocked for an instant by the major's all-out attack, stared at the man's puffy red face. As the lips approached him Damien drew back his fist and landed a solid punch on the officer's jaw. He watched Zollicoffer's eyes go wide with surprise. An instant later they closed. The major slumped in his chair, then slid to the floor—out cold. A few shocked cries went up, but no one had actually seen what happened.

Damien raced to the dance floor and tore Lavinia out of Philip Waring's tight embrace.

"What's wrong?" she cried.

"Major Zollicoffer is dead drunk! I will not stay a moment longer. Come, Lavinia!"

Before Lieutenant Waring could react, Damien whisked Lavinia out of the hotel, hailed a hack, and they were on their way to Portland.

Less than an hour later—before Philip Waring returned to Mrs. Campbell's—they were in the saddle and headed back to Louisville.

They would have to find a new place to stay and lay low while they waited to hear from John Hunt Morgan. They had their information, but they needed their marching orders from their commander before they could leave the area. In the meantime, it would be to their definite advantage to steer clear of Lieutenant Waring and Major Zollicoffer, and that was exactly what Damien Clay intended to do.

Chapter Nineteen

By the first week in July, Morgan's Raiders were on their way home. The disgrace of the "Lebanon Races" was long forgotten in the face of approaching victory. The refurbished Second Kentucky, almost a thousand strong, left Knoxville following the old Walton Road laid out across the state in 1799. Sparta, Tennessee, would be their final stop in that state before fording the Cumberland River and heading into Kentucky at last.

Military men from all over came to join the famous Morgan. His brother-in-law, Basil Duke, returned from sick leave, bringing with him a squad of Texans and their commander, Captain R. M. Gano. John B. Castleman joined up, volunteering his forty-one Kentuckians. Bringing a letter of introduction from General Robert E. Lee himself, Englishman George St. Leger Grenfell arrived, telling Morgan that since his mother country was not presently at war, he had to find another country to fight for. And riding all the way from Canada, telegrapher George Ellsworth arrived to add his lightning to Morgan's famous thunder. As chief telegrapher with the Second Kentucky, Ellsworth's cunning and expertise would be much prized and long remembered.

The entire Second Kentucky took on a whole new look—they sported the latest in Confederate uniforms and a special weapon designed exclusively for their purposes. Henceforth,

241

Morgan's Raiders would be armed with the Enfield rifle with the barrel sawed off. As for textbook tactics, "Forget the book!" Morgan ordered. He and his commanders made up their rules to fit the situation. It was a whole new war for Morgan's Raiders, and Lavinia and Damien were eager to join it.

Damien in particular became increasingly impatient to get back in the saddle. Their work was finished. They had the numbers and troop locations Morgan needed. Now all that remained was for John Hunt Morgan to send a message recalling them. Why didn't he?

Damien paced the small sitting room of the boardinghouse suite where they were hiding out in Louisville, staring at but not seeing the bird-and-rose pattern of the wallpaper. It was raining. The day had been long, and still it was only mid-afternoon.

"Damien, why don't you come take a nap?" Lavinia called from the bedroom.

"I never sleep in the daytime," he snapped.

"Well, you certainly haven't been sleeping much at night lately either," she said lightly. "You'll be worn to a frazzle when we do get the word to ride."

He stormed into the bedroom and glared at Lavinia. "Do you plan to continue needling me all day? My God, the way you go on, you'd think we were married already!"

Lavinia pulled the covers up over her bare breasts and drew her lips into a hurt pout. She was just as bored as he was! After the excitement of gathering their valuable information, just hiding and waiting was almost unbearable. These last days had weighed heavily on them both. Her nerves were worn thin, her temper nearly as short as his.

And she had a lot more on her mind than he did. Though she'd inquired everywhere she went, she was just butting her head against a stone wall trying to find Josiah. Then, too, she'd had no news from home for weeks. Anything could have happened at Thunderbolt. As for their coming marriage, Damien couldn't possibly be any more eager than she was to secure the bonds once and for all. But they certainly couldn't get married in Louisville. The marriage certificate with their real names on it would also be their death warrant. No, they both had to just sit tight and endure until Morgan recalled them.

"Where are you going?" she asked sharply when he pulled off his shirt and began donning Rebecca's costume.

"Out!"

"Out where?"

"You're neither my commanding officer nor my keeper, Lavinia." He swung around, glaring at her. "I don't have to account for my every movement to you! If I want to go out, I'll go! It's none of your damn business where!"

His angry tone brought stinging tears to her eyes. He'd been so patient and loving most of the time that they were in danger, except for occasional jealous flare-ups. Now that they had a few days to rest, relax, make love whenever they liked, Damien Clay was like a caged beast, lashing out at her constantly.

"I only thought," she said quietly, "that if a message should come while you're out, I would need know where to reach you, darling."

"I'm sorry." He muttered the words so quietly that she had to strain to hear them.

"Well?"

"There's an old friend of mine in town. I thought I'd go over to Woods Theater and say hello."

"Oh, he's an actor?"

Damien avoided answering by giving her a quick nod.

"Won't he think your costume a bit out of the ordinary? I'm not sure it's safe, Damien. What if he should tell someone of your disguise? We're not out of danger yet. Lieutenant Waring might find out we're still in Louisville."

"Oh, for God's sake, Lavinia!" he exploded. "This person isn't going to tell anyone!"

"He's a *close* friend, then?"

"Very close!"

Damien hurried to finish dressing and left without even kissing Lavinia good-bye. She lay in the bed, feeling empty and alone, sorry that she had nagged, even sorrier that they had quarreled. Oh, well, she would make it up to him as soon as he came back.

Suddenly, a thought struck her. Damien had forgotten to tell her his friend's name. Odd! she mused.

Naturally, he had forgotten to tell her. Quite often when men go off to see former lovers, they fail to mention their names to their sweethearts or wives. Damien Clay was no exception to that rule.

It wasn't just boredom that had been preying on him. Now that all the excitement was over, he had long, calm hours to think. And think he did! Mainly about Lavinia's other admirers—Philip Waring and especially Sam Coltrain. The idea that "Lavinia's other lover," as Damien had come to think of Coltrain, might still be alive and searching for her nearly had him crazy. He'd seen a one-armed soldier on Market Street just yesterday, and it had been like seeing a ghost.

Not once since the day at the cave had Lavinia mentioned the man's name. But to Damien's way of thinking, that only proved her guilt. She had promised to tell him about this great favor Sam Coltrain had done that prompted her to beg for his life. But she had yet to enlighten him. The pictures that Coltrain had put into his mind with his spiteful words gnawed at Damien the way a worm bores into rotten wood. There was no assuaging his jealousy.

No way but this! he thought to himself, silently planning his revenge. He hurried to Woods Theater, eager to find Pauline Cushman before he changed his mind.

It would have been easy enough, had he been dressed in boots and britches, to slip the doorman at the theater a few dollars to let him in to watch *La Cushman* rehearse. But as the prim spinster, Rebecca Rutledge, Damien faced a new challenge. Raven-haired, black-eyed, voluptuous Miss Cushman was not the sort of actress proper ladies paid to see.

"Sorry, ma'am, but Miss Cushman don't allow no one in during rehearsal," the doorman growled out of one side of his mouth, the other being filled by a soggy cigar butt that bore all the attraction of an unsightly growth. "You'll have to come back later."

"But I *must* see her, sir. I beg you! I've come all this way from New Orleans to find my dear niece."

The man squinted a suspicious, watery eye at Damien. "Your niece, huh? Her ma's sister or her pa's?"

Damien quickly combed his memory. He recalled that Pauline's mother was French and her father Spanish. They were Creoles with thick accents and quick tempers. He guessed that he must look more like the Spanish side of the family.

With expansive gestures and a suddenly acquired accent, Damien answered, "Her *padre* is my *hermano* —my brother. *Sí!* Now, *por favor, señor,* I must speak with her. It is most urgent!"

"Well, I 'spose it'll be all right, you bein' family and all. Go on in. But don't you make a sound till she finishes! She's mite touchy when she's rehearsing."

"A mite touchy, period!" Damien muttered to himself, remembering the soft Creole voice that belied Pauline's fiery Latin temper.

Damien eased into one of the back seats, hoping she wouldn't notice him. He wanted to watch her for a while, to think about their past times together so he could work himself into a suitable frame of mind for what he was about to do.

There she was in all her garish glory! With her heavy-lidded eyes and the full red lips of a born temptress, prancing about the stage like a sexy pixie in purple tights, only a paisley piano shawl draped about her torso to hide the intimate hills and valleys of her luscious body. Ah, how well he remembered its delightful secrets!

He closed his eyes, letting her surprisingly sweet voice lull him, thinking about that night in the French Quarter. Pauline had been his leading lady. Their final love scene on opening night all but brought down the roof of the St. Charles Theater. And there was little wonder! Although the audience had no way of knowing it, they probably were witnessing more realism onstage than they had seen before or ever would again. Between the lines meant for audience consumption, Pauline was whispering her own special lines for Damien's ears alone. Such titillating vulgarities he had never heard from a woman's lips!

And while she aroused him verbally, she used her hand, hidden from view, to do equally fascinating things to his crotch. By the time the curtain came down on the final act, Damien would have been ready to take her to bed even if she'd been fat, ugly, and diseased—none of which Pauline Cushman was.

Sitting there in Woods Theater in the dark, her voice caressing him in much the same manner that her hand had at the St. Charles, his thoughts traveled on to her spirited performance in his hotel room later that night and he groaned aloud.

"Who is that back there?" a grating voice shouted from the stage. "I demand to know what you are doing here!"

Damien sat up quickly to see Pauline, her face flushed with temperamental fury, shade her eyes against the footlamps, trying to get a better view of him.

"You there in the back row, answer me! I will not have this! Do you hear me, Louie?" she yelled at her manager. "I will cancel my performance unless that person is removed this minute!"

The burly manager, aided by the doorman, started toward Damien. He had to do something fast.

"Pauline, my dear child!" he cried, rushing down the aisle with arms outstretched. "Don't you remember your old aunt Rebecca? Your own papa's beloved sister?"

Pauline squinted through the stagelights, trying to get a better look at the woman. Something about the voice struck a chord. But her papa had no sisters. So who could this tall, uncharming creature be?

Suspicion gripped her. Pauline had to be extra careful these days. She was in a precarious position, a supposed Rebel sympathizer in a Federally held city. Only one or two key officers knew that she was not what she seemed, that she was, in fact, spying for the Union. Any peculiar happening such as this set her teeth on edge and brought up her guard immediately. But what was this person saying?

"Oh, Pauline, my little *Laughing Breeze*!" The woman knew her Indian name! Almost no one was privy to that secret. "My love, my pretty child!" Another name from her past. Someone had called her that . . . some lover from long ago.

She had laughed at him and laid to rest any delusions he might have had concerning her childlike innocence. It was coming back to her. New Orleans . . . the St. Charles . . . an actor she had never seen since . . .

Damien had failed. He knew it the moment the two men grabbed his arms and began hauling him toward the door. Hell-fire! He couldn't do anything right, not even cheat on Lavinia! Might as well go back to the boardinghouse, confess what he'd meant to do, and then see if she wanted to make up. Maybe he'd even bring up the subject of marriage again. That always put her in a good mood.

"Wait, Louie!" Pauline cried suddenly from the stage. "Don't handle my dear aunt so roughly!"

The two men stared at Damien, who gave them what he hoped was his most convincing "Aunt Rebecca" smile.

"Sorry, ma'am!" the doorman said, releasing Damien.

"Show her to my dressing room," Pauline ordered from the stage. "Auntie, love," she called in a husky voice, thick with sensuality, "I'll be right there. I can hardly wait! It's been *so* long!"

A sudden frog found its way into Damien's throat while an army of butterflies set up camp in his stomach. She remembered him! He was sure of it! Oh, Lord! What had he gotten himself into?

Lavinia felt perfectly miserable. Back at the boardinghouse, in bed all alone, she thought back over the last couple of weeks. She'd been a real pain in the saddle sores! Damien had every right to be angry, hostile, even downright mean. Why hadn't he just hit her? That would have put an end to her nagging, at least for a time.

Never mind! She was going to make it all up to him. No more harping and complaining. When he got home she'd be ready to greet him. Yes, sir, she'd plan a homecoming that would snap him out of his boredom all right!

She heated water and took a long, soothing bubble bath, carefully powdering and perfuming her body afterward. The soak relaxed her and made her feel utterly feminine and ready to be loved. She tried to find something suitably alluring in her trunks to wear for him, but everything she owned looked too dowdy or too girlish. Then she remembered that Damien had a few of his old costumes packed away. Pawing through his things, she came upon a red satin gown the likes of which she'd never seen. She slipped it over her head and gasped at her image in the mirror. Without benefit of a corset or any under-things at all, the gown fit her like a second, flaming scarlet skin. The neckline dipped nearly to her navel, and there simply was no back at all. A froth of bright ostrich feathers softly out-lined the deep plunge. Her nipples puckered like hard little peb-bles within the fabric and she could feel that familiar, welcome warmth spreading through her.

"No," she breathed in a husky voice. "Damien won't find this boring!"

Suitably made up to match the wanton style in which she was gowned, Lavinia sat down to wait. She fidgeted and twisted. Where could Damien be? He'd been gone hours!

"You have to find something to do," she told herself. "Ah, the paper!"

She hadn't yet read today's *Louisville Daily Journal*. That would take some time off her hands. When she opened it up, a small item in the theater news caught her eyes. "Woods Thea-ter . . . one-woman revue opening . . . Pauline Cushman, the Toast of New Orleans . . ."

"Pauline Cushman," Lavinia mused aloud. She'd heard the name before. But where? Then it struck her! Damien kept a scrapbook in one of his trunks, old clippings and reviews of plays.

She ran to the bedroom and searched frantically until she found the leather-bound book, then flipped hurriedly through the pages. There it was! New Orleans, the St. Charles Theater, Damien Clay playing opposite Miss Pauline Cushman. The re-viewer remarked at length on the final scene of opening night. "Such shocking realism . . . two women fainted while watch-ing the scene . . . the voluptuous Creole Jezebel . . . Mr. Clay putting more into the role than called for by his direc-tor . . ."

Lavinia threw the scrapbook across the room with a furious cry.

"Close friend, eh, Damien? I'll show you!"

Damien paced Pauline Cushman's dressing room, waiting, thinking, doubting, wondering just what in hell he was doing there. So Lavinia had made him angry. So what! Was that any reason to go running off to another woman? He glanced about him. The dressing room blazed with flashy costumes, provocative with their glass beads and feathers, eye-dazzling in their purples, scarlets, and puce. He felt sudden disgust for himself.

"My Lavinia wouldn't be caught dead in clothes like these. She's a lady!" he said aloud.

Then he caught sight of his pained face in Pauline's mirror and nodded to himself, saying, "And here you are, about to put the woman you love through a passel of grief, just for a few minutes with a . . ."

He didn't say the word out loud, but he thought it. And Pauline Cushman would have been the first to agree with him. She had no delusions about what kind of woman she was. She used her sexuality to get what she wanted. To her mind it was as much a part of an actress's life as learning her lines and making curtain calls. "And after-curtain calls," he said to the mirror. Still, he couldn't fault her for it. But at the same time, it wasn't fair to either woman to use Pauline to punish Lavinia.

His mind was made up. He winked at his image and said, "Exit stage right, old boy!"

"Dah-ling!" came the husky whisper from the doorway.

Damien swallowed hard. He was trapped!

"Pauline!" he answered with a nervous twitch in his voice. "I just happened to be in Louisville and I thought I'd drop in and say a quick hello. To tell the truth, I wasn't sure you'd remember me after so long."

She tossed the paisley shawl aside dramatically and opened her purple-clad arms to him. "Dah-ling boy, don't be silly. Pauline could never forget the greatest love of her life. Come!"

Damien went. What else can I do? he asked himself. And he

had to admit that the feel of those huge, purple bosoms smashing warmly into his chest wasn't at all unpleasant.

"Kiss me, love!" Pauline ordered, offering full, carmine-colored lips, parted and waiting.

By the time she finished with him, Damien was sporting a full erection. He cursed himself soundly but silently.

"Pauline, I really can't stay long. In fact, I'd better go right now."

He started for the door, but she caught his hand and brought it to her lips, nibbling at his thumb suggestively.

"My dah-ling, of course you'll stay long enough to have a glass of champagne and explain to me what you are doing in that outrageous costume. Is there a farce playing at one of the other theaters in town?"

Damien, feeling utterly ridiculous suddenly, thought that if there were, he should certainly be cast in the roll of the lead fool.

"It's a little complicated, Pauline. I don't want to bore you. Really, I think I'd better—"

She shoved him down to the bed and crawled up next to him, breathing into his face as she purred, "Bore me, dah-ling, *please*!"

While Damien made up a wild tale about a bet with buddies who didn't think he really knew her and would never get into the theater, much less into her dressing room, Pauline flicked at his face with the tip of her tongue. Meanwhile, her hand successfully subdued his petticoats and crept up his thigh toward his pulsing crotch. When she found what she was searching for, Damien moaned, "Oh, God!"

"Ah, yes! I do remember you now, dah-ling!" she cried suddenly, as if this were the only absolute means of identification. "We made the most horrendous love in that dingy little hotel room in the French Quarter after our opening night together." She leaned close to his ear, tracing it with her tongue, then whispered several ribald suggestions to him, identical to the words she had used onstage that night. He immediately felt the buttons of his fly straining under renewed pressure.

"Pauline!" he gasped. "How about that champagne?"

She gave him one last squeeze and laughed before she stood and brought the bottle of wine. Damien sat up, straightening his gown.

She handed him a full glass and said, "So what are you really here for?" She frowned and tossed her long hair with impatience. "Forgive me, but isn't your name Clayton or something?"

He had to smile. She didn't even remember his name, yet she hadn't forgotten certain of his finer points. "Right, Clayton," he answered. "As for why I came here . . ." He paused. Should he tell her the truth? The champagne he'd gulped down too quickly made up his mind for him. "The truth, Pauline? I came here to use you!"

A wide, slow smile parted her full lips. She sauntered toward him, unlacing her bodice. "I do love a truthful man," she purred.

Damien stared as her ripe, melon-sized breasts popped free. The nipples were large and exceedingly dark. The next moment he found his face pressed between them in smothering contact. The scent of heliotrope cologne and hot female flesh filled his nostrils. She held the back of his head, pressing his face against her.

"*Use* me, Clayton dah-ling," she cried.

He was shaking all over. He tried to pull away, but she held him fast. In his struggle he did manage to turn his head to one side, making breathing tremendously easier.

"Oh, yes!" she moaned. "Don't be shy, dear boy. I adore a forceful lover!"

Damien found himself suddenly faced with a new problem—a large, pulsing nipple pressed firmly against his lips. He had only to open his mouth and . . . No! He wouldn't!

But he did! Pauline swayed against him, moaning ecstatically as he sucked at her with greedy lips. She did taste wonderful. Damien couldn't deny that!

"Dah-ling, wait!" she whispered. "Let me get this damn thing off." She pulled away, tugging impatiently at the tights. Naked and breathtakingly endowed, she stretched out on the bed, pleading with open arms for Damien to come to her.

"Pauline," he said in an uncertain voice, aching fearsomely with every step he took away from her, "you have to let me explain. I only came here to use you to make the woman I love jealous!"

Slowly, the wanton smile on her face distorted into a furious grimace. Her lips curled back from her white teeth. Her eyes narrowed.

"You filthy bastard!" she seethed. "You unspeakable, sexless beast! I'll kill you!"

With those words she flew at him, fully intending to do just that. He dived for the door as she lunged. Only the points of her clawlike nails caught his cheek, raking a bloody trail to his chin. Damien made his fastest exit ever, slamming the door behind him. A moment later, over Pauline Cushman's screams, he heard the champagne bottle smash into the other side of the door. Gathering up his skirts, he ran.

When Damien was several blocks away from the theater he slowed his pace at last. Taking the lace hanky from inside his sleeve, he mopped at the blood trickling down his face.

He wandered the city aimlessly for some time, trying to think up a suitable lie to tell Lavinia. If he thought Pauline Cushman had a temper, she was nothing compared to Lavinia Rutledge when crossed!

Lavinia's emotions had run the full gamut while she waited. Her initial jealous fury had turned into murderous rage after Damien had been gone two hours. At that point she had placed a chair in front of the door, loaded her pistol, taken a seat, and sworn to shoot the sonuvabitch the minute he showed his ugly, lying face! But as twilight progressed to dusk and dusk to full dark, her temper softened. He wouldn't be gone this long, not even if he were with another woman. Something had happened to him! The Yankees had him! Or maybe he had slipped and fallen into the river. Oh, Lord! Anything could have happened to her poor, dear Damien! She loved him so much. And whatever happened was all her fault. She had driven him away.

The pistol drooped, forgotten, in her hand. Tears of remorse streamed down her cheeks.

"Please, God, just let him come home safe and sound. I promise I'll mend my ways. It doesn't matter where he's been or what he's done. Just bring him back to me. I can't live without him!" she wailed. "Please, God! Oh, *please*!"

The door opened at that moment and she sat up straight.

"Just where in hell have you been?" she demanded.

Damien looked at her angry face, her eyes flashing green fire. Then his gaze shifted down to the pistol in her hand. To hell with it! he thought. Let her shoot me. It beats having to explain.

"Where?" she demanded.

"Out with another woman!"

Lavinia slumped back in the chair as if he'd hit her. She'd expected lies, and might have accepted them. She'd expected evasion, and could have dealt with that. But the stark, unadulterated truth left her breathless, with no plan of attack. All she could think of was Helen-of-Troy's threat to Sam Coltrain.

"I ought to shoot your balls off!" she hissed, aiming her pistol.

Damien grinned. He actually grinned at her as if she were making a joke and started toward her. "I wouldn't be much fun to have around if you did that, darlin'."

The next moment he was on her, wrestling the gun from her grasp, kissing her, tickling her, pinching her nipples through the sexy red satin. She screamed and fought, kicked and clawed, gasped, and finally giggled. He stood back, smiling down at her.

"I'll make a deal with you, Lavinia."

"What?" she asked warily.

"I've been jealous as hell of Sam Coltrain. What say I trade you one Pauline Cushman for one Sam Coltrain and we call it even and let the matter lie? Deal?"

She considered for a minute, nodded, then rose and went to him, insinuating herself into his arms.

"Deal," she sighed.

Their lips met, lingered, and battled for possession as they made up.

His mind and conscience clear, Damien noticed her dress for

the first time and said, "My God, Lavinia, you look like a whore!"

"Hm-m-m" was her only reply as she continued to nuzzle his cheek.

He took her face into his hands, brushing her hair back to uncover her ear. He pressed it with moist lips, sliding his tongue in suggestively, then whispered, "Let's go see if you know how to act like one."

Sweeping her up into his arms, he made for the bedroom.

Chapter Twenty

Glasgow, Horse Cave, Lebanon, Springfield, Harrodsburg, Versailles . . .

John Hunt Morgan and his Raiders took Kentucky by storm during the hot days of July. They thundered into the Bluegrass State with horses prancing and plumes waving, greeted by cheers, picnics, and, at other times, heavy Union resistance.

As one journalist wrote: "Morgan came like Zeus, hurling telegraphic thunderbolts, majestic proclamations, and gathering fresh horses and fried chicken and ham as he went."

Still, most Kentuckians loved the man. Here was a true Southern hero . . . a loyal son of the bluegrass.

At Georgetown, one of Morgan's officers, George Niles, found a print shop. Going quickly to work, Niles published a recruiting poster headed: "KENTUCKIANS!" It continued in Morgan's own words. "I come to liberate you from the despotism of a tyrannical faction and to rescue my native state from the hands of your oppressors." There followed a patriotic call to arms.

Meanwhile, George Prentice, editor of the *Louisville Journal*, was writing fiery messages to John Hunt Morgan with his flaming journalist's pen. "Again we say to you, misguided young man, as much for your own good as for ours, and more in mercy than in anger—prodigal, profligate, apostate, traitor, ingrate, and brigand—go!"

255

Morgan planned to go, but not before he rode on to Cynthiana.

There Kentuckians battled Kentuckians once more, this time for possession of a covered bridge over the Licking River. It was the bloodiest fighting the Raiders had seen since Shiloh. But Morgan came out the victor, with only eight losses and some three hundred captured horses. On these fresh mounts Morgan's Raiders rode on to Paris, Kentucky.

General Jeremiah Boyle, commander of the Federal troops at Louisville, fired off message after hysterical message to President Lincoln. "MORGAN HAS OVER 1,500 MEN!" And in another he wailed, "MORGAN IS DEVASTATING WITH FIRE AND SWORD!"

In his office in Washington City, a haggard, war-weary Lincoln called in his secretary. "Send a message to General Halleck in Mississippi," he ordered. "I want him to look into this stampede in Kentucky."

Halleck would come, but not in time to interfere with "The First Kentucky Raid," as Morgan's initial, great foray into the Bluegrass State came to be called.

It was at Somerset, Kentucky, that Damien and Lavinia finally rejoined Morgan's main force. They found the Raiders weary but in exceedingly high spirits.

Lavinia, herself in fine fettle since she and Damien had settled their differences, was fascinated by telegrapher Ellsworth's vocation. She came into the little station house at Somerset one morning to find him tapping away.

"What are you up to today, George?" she asked. "Sending a message back to Canada to your sweetheart?"

"No, ma'am, to Louisville. But old George Prentice is a sweetheart, all right!" He laughed. "He'll probably close up the newspaper and hightail it for Cincinnati when he gets this little love note I'm sending him!"

Lavinia stood by quietly, absorbed in the musical click of the telegraph key. Then she spotted the message he was tapping out, written on a scrap of paper in Morgan's bold scrawl. She read it silently. "My dear Editor Prentice, Please inform me at your earliest convenience when you will be at home to callers.

The prodigal profligate, Colonel John Hunt Morgan, would like to drop by for a visit.''

"Oh, Lord, Lightning!" Lavinia said, calling the telegrapher by his nickname. "He'll have a fit when he reads this!" She laughed merrily.

Lightning grinned up at her. "Maybe the old bastard will have a heart attack and we'll be rid of his raving once and for all!"

Damien stuck his head in the door at that moment. "You know better than that, Lightning. Morgan's Raiders don't leave anything to Providence. Colonel Morgan says, 'If you want it taken care of, do it yourself!' Here, I'll show you what I mean."

He slipped an arm around Lavinia's waist and drew her close, capturing her lips and kissing her thoroughly while Ellsworth looked on.

"Like that!" Damien said at length. "Now, you see, this woman needed kissing. Real bad, I could tell! Her lips were all soft and puckery and just waiting there to be taken care of."

"I don't follow you, sir," Ellsworth said, grinning.

"Well, it's simple! I wanted her kissed. Now, I could have waited to see if anyone else was going to do the job for me. You might even have seen to it when you finished sending your message. But I wouldn't have felt I'd done my duty if I'd just walked on past and left it to Providence to see that she got kissed." He nodded solemnly. "Yes, sometimes our tasks become a cross to bear, but a real soldier never shirks his duty, no matter how onerous the job may be."

"You!" Lavinia shrilled, giving him a sharp nudge in the ribs with her elbow. "If kissing me is such a chore, I'll excuse you from that duty from now on!"

Damien gathered her into his arms. She could feel his arousal and the tension zinging through his whole body, electrifying hers.

"You finished in here, Lightning?" he asked, bearing down on Lavinia's parted lips once more.

"Yes, sir, Captain Clay!" the telegrapher replied, jumping

up from his chair. "The place is all yours. Just try not to melt my key!"

Damien's mouth came down on Lavinia's—hot, wet, searching. He held her tightly in his arms, forcing her hips against his and telling her in actions more eloquent than words what he wanted. But when his hand strayed to her bodice, seeking entrance, she pulled away.

"Damien! For heaven's sake! It's the middle of the morning!"

"Good a time as any," he insisted huskily.

"Well, I'm certainly not going to . . . not in the telegraph room. My word! What would people think?"

His hands continued their exploration of her bodice as he said, "They'll think I'm the luckiest bastard around, to have a woman willing to do *whatever* I want *whenever* I want it!"

"*Exactly!*" she snapped. "And I don't want them thinking that!"

"You did a lot of mighty pleasing *whatever* that night in Louisville—the night you were wearing that red satin dress."

Lavinia could feel herself blushing all over, remembering that all-night session of lovemaking after their jealous battle. Much to her relief, he hadn't mentioned that night since, probably guessing that she was embarrassed by her own abandon on that occasion. How could he bring the subject up now, in the broad daylight?

He nuzzled her ear, stroking the tender lobe with the tip of his tongue. "I liked what you did to me that night, Lavinia. I've been dreaming of you doing it again. Come on, darling. Nobody will come in here. They'll all stay clear when Lightning tells them what we're doing."

"Damien Clay!" Lavinia cried in horror. "He *will* , won't he! Oh, how could you do this to me? I'll never be able to show my face in camp again!"

"Why?" came a familiar voice from the doorway. "What have you done that's so terrible, Lavinia?"

She whipped around to see Jack Morgan grinning at her. Quickly, she removed herself from Damien's embrace. Her throat seemed to close, not allowing·words to pass. Her face flamed. She dropped her gaze to the floorboards but, in passing, her eyes lit on Damien's very pronounced erection straining inside his tight britches. What must Jack think of her? She wanted to die!

"Seems to me," Morgan continued in a matter-of-fact tone, "you two would have a much easier time of it if you'd just go ahead and get married. What do you think?"

"I'm *ready*!" Damien said in a husky voice, pulling Lavinia close once more.

"Lavinia?" Morgan questioned.

Her mind was awhirl. Of course she wanted to get married. But now? Here? Why, there wasn't even a parson in the camp!

"A new man joined up yesterday," Morgan said, as if reading her thoughts. "He figured he'd be just right for the cavalry since he's a circuit-riding preacher by calling. What do you say, Lavinia? We've captured enough supplies here for a real wedding feast. The men would get a kick out of it. And what other bride can claim she had a thousand guests at her wedding? All of them Morgan's Raiders, at that!"

Her answer was typically female: "But I don't have a thing to wear!"

"I think between us we can come up with something, don't you?" Damien said, leaning close.

John Hunt Morgan left the two of them to their kiss. He was smiling, thinking of his own wedding to come. He had already decided, though he hadn't told Mattie yet, that once they were married, she, too, would be a part of his camp. Many women were joining their husbands at the front these days. Some were even fighting beside their men. The war wasn't supposed to last this long. And a man wasn't meant to endure so many months without his woman. Yes, December would come soon enough. And when it arrived, his lonely nights would come to an end. He was counting the hours.

Damien, insisting he had a tender spot in his heart for red satin, tried to convince Lavinia to wear the shocking creation for her wedding.

"The only thing you've convinced me of, Damien Clay, is

that you have a soft spot in your head! Brides don't wear flaming scarlet! They wear virginal white!''

It had been a week since the day in the telegraph room. And at the moment Lavinia agreed to marry him, she had also "slipped on her chastity belt," as Damien said without the least hint of an amused smile. Now, when she spoke to him of "virginal white," he was about ready to rip her clothes off and have his way with her in front of God and the entire company of Morgan's Raiders!

"Don't you look at me that way, Damien!" she warned.

"What way?"

"You know very well *what* way! We may have been a lot of things to each other already, but now that I'm about to be your bride, I demand that you treat me accordingly. Then on our wedding night you'll appreciate me more.''

"Oh, Lavinia!" he groaned, trying to pull her into his arms, "I *do* appreciate you, darling! Just a hug . . . one little kiss! Please let me touch you!''

His hand groped toward her breast, but Lavinia slapped it away with a shriek.

"Get out of here, Damien!"

He put his palms up in front of him. "I'll behave! I promise!''

"You'll have no choice, since you're leaving this minute! Out! Out right now!''

Totally crestfallen and painfully frustrated, Damien sauntered out of the little abandoned frame house that was being refurbished for their first night as man and wife.

John Hunt Morgan spotted his friend, head down and shoulders sagging, and called, "Damien! Come on to my tent! I've got a bottle of aged whiskey that will cure what's ailing you.''

Damien cast one last dejected glance over his shoulder at the house. The men had rigged blankets over the windows so that Lavinia could have privacy, but still he could see her silhouette. She was undressing, pulling her gown off over her head. A moment later her shapely shadow turned, presenting a tantalizing profile. He could almost imagine her peaked nipples in relief. Then she sat down, brushing her long hair with slow, sensual strokes.

"Goddammit!" he swore, feeling aching heat pulse downward once more. "Where's that bottle, Jack?" he called out. "I plan to drink a whole damn case!"

Lavinia heard Damien outside and realized suddenly that he'd been watching her undress. She leaned forward and blew out the candles. Then she rested her head on the old dressing table and wept. She wanted Damien tonight. Lord, how she needed him! She wasn't trying to punish him by keeping him at arm's length. If that truly were her purpose, then she was certainly cutting her nose off to spite her face. No, it just didn't feel right to be with him now.

She hadn't suffered any real guilt about their being together before. It had seemed right and innocent somehow. The war made old conventions seem silly and outmoded. But on the eve of their marriage, things were different. She wanted to go to him at least *feeling* pure and like a virgin again.

She cried herself out, then crawled into bed. The mattress felt unnatural with no weight sagging it to one side. She let her hand stray over the empty space, caressing Damien's place with her fingertips, remembering how his skin felt warm to her touch. The very thought of him made her ache way down inside. How long had it been? Two weeks? No, *three*! They'd had Yankees hot on their heels most of the way from Louisville. There'd been no time to stop and satisfy amorous urges. And there hadn't been any privacy in camp. Not until now.

She turned on her stomach, pressing her sobs into the pillow. They would be married the day after tomorrow, but right now that seemed an eternity to live through without him. She wanted Damien Clay here, now, holding her, filling her! Nothing else could take the ache away.

Her mind made up, Lavinia dressed quickly. She slipped out of the front door and headed straight for Jack Morgan's tent. The lamp was lit. The two of them would be there, passing the long empty hours together. She hurried her steps. She could almost feel Damien's hands on her, his mouth possessing hers, his need quenching her desire.

"Damien?" she called in a tremulous voice from outside the tent. "Damien, are you in there?"

The tent flap stirred and Lavinia rushed forward, her arms outstretched. But it was John Hunt Morgan's face she saw.

"Is Damien with you, Jack?" She tried to keep the disappointment out of her voice, but failed. "I need to . . . I just need him tonight."

For several moments Morgan didn't say anything. When he finally spoke, his voice was low, his tone guarded. "I'm sorry, Lavinia. He's here, but he's asleep."

"Well, wake him!" she snapped. This was degrading, having to come searching for him because she couldn't sleep and finding him dead to the world.

Morgan just shook his head and smiled apologetically. "I'm afraid that's impossible. I invited him in for a drink. I meant to let him have only a couple. But it seems like he set his mind to drinking the whole Commonwealth of Kentucky dry before morning. Even if I could wake him up, he'd be no use to you."

"Of course," Lavinia said. She had to say something. She was embarrassed, humiliated, and so mad at herself that she wanted to spit! She wandered back toward the house, alone, numb with disappointment, dreading the dark hours ahead.

All night she lay awake, mentally counting the minutes. How many more hours? And how could she possibly get through them?

Quite a surprise awaited Lavinia two days later. Not only was she getting married that morning, but it would be a real church wedding. Not far from the abandoned house, some of the men had come across a rundown little house of worship. Secretly, they had worked for days with hammer, boards, and whitewash to fix the place up in time. When she arrived on Colonel Morgan's arm just before noon, her breath caught and her eyes filled with tears.

An honor guard of Morgan's Raiders in their fancy green and gold uniforms, their sabers raised, formed a ceremonial arch leading to the church door. The poor country chapel, which had never known a lick of paint before in its life, now gleamed eye-burning white in the noon sun. And the gown Lavinia had fashioned from several of Damien's costumes mirrored the building's pure glow.

The regimental band played solemnly as Lavinia and Morgan came through the door into the cool, shadowed sanctuary. All the pews were filled with uniformed men. Directly ahead, Damien, looking every bit the hero, stood beside the little, black-clad circuit preacher. Morgan eased Lavinia forward to the altar railing and handed her over to her groom.

From that moment on, Lavinia lost all consciousness of her surroundings. Church, soldiers, minister, and musicians faded into a hazy background. She was aware only of Damien Clay, his hand holding hers, his lips smiling down on her, his eyes caressing her. Somehow, although her throat felt tight and dry, she managed the proper responses during the ceremony, even though she barely heard the preacher's words. Only when he had pronounced them "man and wife" and said to Damien, "You may press the bride," did Lavinia come back to earth. Conscious now of her husband's every breath, she trembled when his fingers touched the veil she'd made out of an old lace curtain. Slowly, as if he had all the time in the world, Damien lifted the lacy barrier and just as hesitantly he lowered his lips to hers.

Lavinia drank in his kiss, tasting him as if it were their first time. She marveled at the warmth of his mouth, the moist softness of his flesh pressing hers, the tenderness of his hands holding her. He seemed almost like a boy approaching his first girl and hoping that she wouldn't reject his attentions.

The sun streamed in the tall, paneless windows, freezing them in a golden tableau. Morgan, standing nearby, marveled at the sight. It almost looked as if the light were coming from within the pair, their love for each other casting out a warm, bright glow.

Suddenly, the band struck up and the magic spell broke into a celebration. Damien and Lavinia ran up the aisle, laughing like a pair of children off on an adventure. The wedding guests followed, and once everyone was outside, the party began in earnest.

The high-noon wedding progressed into a steamy afternoon of feasting, drinking, and dancing. The Kentucky boys, inordinately fond of their bourbon, used the happy occasion to drink their fill.

By the time the summer sun finally drifted down to sink behind the trees, the celebration had passed from boisterous to benign as the besotted revelers settled down to sleep it off. No one even noticed when Damien clasped Lavinia's hand and urged her toward the little whitewashed house.

"Well now, Mrs. Clay," he said softly when they were standing just outside. "Looks like I've finally earned the right to wear the pants in this family!"

"Yes, Damien," she answered demurely, casting her eyes down in feigned submission.

"So now that we're married, what I say goes around here. Right?"

"You're right, of course, Damien."

"And there won't be any more back talk?"

"Certainly not, Damien."

"You'll bring me my slippers and pipe every night?"

She flashed a mischievous glance up at him and said, "You don't smoke a pipe."

He pulled her into his arms and poised his lips over hers. "Then I'll have to think of something else you can do for me in place of bringing my pipe, Mrs. Clay."

As his mouth possessed hers, Lavinia felt his arm slip down her back. He lifted her as if she weighed nothing at all. The next moment he was carrying her over the threshold, his lips still clinging to hers, kindling warm, licking flames through her body.

At last her time had come. She was married to the man who had stolen her heart and soul with his first kiss. As he took her to their waiting bed, undressing her slowly, almost reverently, all the pent-up need of the past weeks rushed back with a new intensity. Perhaps it was the white gown she had fashioned out of bits and pieces, or perhaps it was the solemn words spoken over them by the circuit preacher. Whatever the cause, Lavinia did feel like a virgin bride when her new husband came to her.

Damien did nothing to tarnish the illusion. His kisses were gentle, loving, almost hesitant. With seeking hands, he explored her body as if for the first time, exclaiming huskily at the silkiness of her flesh while she shuddered and writhed beneath his tender touch. And when at last he entered her, Lavinia realized all her girlish dreams and womanly yearnings. From the intimate fact of his knowing her, he gave her what she longed for, stroking deeply, pausing, stroking again, until they rode the same crest to flood water, then ebbed slowly in each other's arms.

They were man and wife, two living, breathing, loving souls forged by the white heat of passion into one entity.

The next day the entire wedding party, Morgan's Raiders, rode south for the Cumberland River. Weary but happy, they fast covered the twenty-one miles to Monticello. There they were safe, beyond the reach of the enemy. A few days later they were back in Tennessee.

Morgan summed up his First Kentucky Raid for his superiors.

I left Knoxville on the 4th day of this month with about nine hundred men, and returned to Livingston on the 28th with nearly twelve hundred, having been absent just 24 days, during which time I have traveled over a thousand miles, captured seventeen towns, destroyed all the government supplies and arms in them, dispersed about fifteen hundred Home Guards and paroled nearly twelve hundred regular troops. Of the number I carried into Kentucky, I lost in killed, wounded, and missing about ninety.

He might also have added to that official report that he had accomplished what neither Damien Clay nor Lavinia Rutledge had been able to until now. He had seen to their marriage and their everlasting happiness, or so it seemed as they rode along side by side, holding hands and gazing longingly into each other's eyes.

"When will we stop for the night, Damien?" Lavinia asked softly with a flush of embarrassment, knowing that his thoughts were the same as hers.

"Soon, I hope, darling. It can't be too soon to suit me."

They had been awake most of the night before, but their thirst for each other had yet to be quenched.

"Are you tired, Damien?" Her wifely concern told in her voice.

He squeezed her hand and smiled. "Not tired—*starved*! For you."

They rode on, both wondering how many nights, how many years, it would take for them to have enough of each other.

An eternity, they both decided.

Chapter Twenty-One

Morgan's Raiders, with Basil Duke left in charge, as John Hunt Morgan was off to a council of war with General Bragg, had been settled at their old camp in Sparta, Tennessee, only a few days when Lavinia began to sense a troublesome stirring in the air. She couldn't quite put her finger on the problem. Maybe it wasn't in the air after all, but only in her own mind. Maybe being married made some changes in her that she hadn't foreseen. She had started to fret over her husband's safety and her own, and the fact that their only home was in the saddle.

Even as they lay in their own tent, alone and intimate through the darkest hours of night, her mind worried over things like a hound worries a bone. She became nervous and short-tempered, even with Damien.

"Damn, Lavinia! What's eating you?" he demanded one night when she turned away from his seeking lips.

Tears welled up in her eyes. Oh, how she wished she could tell him! This unknown burden would be so much lighter shared.

"I don't know," she mumbled through her tears.

"Well, if you don't know, then it can't be worth crying over!"

He waited a moment for her to stop sobbing. When she couldn't, he swung his long legs out of bed, pulled on his britches, and strode out into the night. Lavinia lay there—empty, aching, confused—and cried herself out.

Dawn had probed the tent flap with one scrawny gray-gold finger before Damien returned. He came in quietly, not wanting to wake his wife, although she wasn't sleeping. He eased himself into a camp chair. For a long time he sat staring at her, his fingers steepled under his chin and a frown pulling at the corners of his mouth. He wasn't happy with the decision he'd come to, but there was no other way.

When she turned over and opened her eyes, unable to feign sleep any longer, knowing that his eyes were on her, he said quietly, "I'm taking you back to Murfreesboro, Lavinia."

She sat bolt-upright in bed, her tear-swollen eyes wide, "No, Damien! You can't!"

"I can and I intend to, this very day!"

Lavinia flung herself from the bed and dropped to the ground, hugging his legs. "Please, Damien! I don't know what's been wrong with me these past days, but I'll get over it. You won't hear another complaint out of me." She looked up into his solemn face, her own cheeks streaked with new tears. "I've never asked you for much. But I'm begging now. Don't send me away, Damien! I couldn't bear it!"

He wavered in the difficult decision he'd spent all night making. He knew it was right to send her away before the fighting began again, but he was selfish enough to want her with him. Still, what if something happened to her? Could he live with himself then?

He pulled her onto his lap and cradled her against his chest as if she were a small child, rocking her and kissing her forehead.

"Lavinia, Lavinia," he whispered. "What am I going to do with you?"

She slipped her arms up around his neck and forced his face down to hers. "Love me!" she whispered.

Just before their lips met, he answered back, "I do! Too much!"

For the first time since the night of the red satin gown, Lavinia tossed all propriety to the four winds and gave up her body to her husband in a wanton and shameless fashion. Damien gloried in her abandon, reveling in her lack of modesty. *This* was his Lavinia!

As they lay back exhausted afterward, he thought to himself that perhaps he could keep her with him. For one delirious moment he let go of his worries for her safety and thought only—selfishly—of his own needs. But the moment was short-lived.

Hurried hoofbeats thundered into camp.

"Morgan's back!" Damien said, deserting Lavinia's arms and pulling on his clothes.

Those two words shot through Lavinia like twin bullets. She had felt the change in Damien as they made love. He had meant to let her stay. But now . . .

"Ho, lads!" she heard Morgan's voice boom. "General Bragg has given us our riding orders!" Lavinia squeezed her eyes shut and covered her ears, trying to block out the cheers of the men. "We're to aid Generals Bragg and Kirby-Smith in chasing every last bluebelly from Tennessee and Kentucky! Our first target is the L and N Railroad. We light out for Gállatin in two days!"

Lavinia sat on the bed, screaming silently inside. *Two days!* And this would be a major action. Damien would never let her go along.

"Dammit! Why was I born a woman?" she wailed aloud.

"Because I was born a man . . . and I couldn't have lived without you," Damien said softly from just inside the tent.

"Oh, Damien!" she cried, running into his arms.

"It won't be long, darling." He tried to soothe her. "You'll see. We'll make fast work of the Yankees. Why, we'll probably finish off the whole damn war! Then we can really begin our lives—maybe even settle down and have some kids."

Lavinia stood away from him for a moment. Slowly, a smile stole over her face. "Damien, you've never spoken of children before."

He looked embarrassed, "Haven't I? Well, I meant to. What do you think—three? Four? Or maybe just two—a boy and a girl?"

"Why don't we just work on one to start with and let nature take its course?"

"Right now? In the middle of the morning?" He used his best acting talents to look and sound thoroughly shocked, but even as he did, he took her forcefully in arms and steered her toward their cot. Their earlier lovemaking had only been an appetizer, whetting his appetite for more. Now he took her like a starving man devours a banquet.

Afterward, Damien dropped off into a deep, satisfied sleep. Lavinia lay very still in his arms until she was sure she could slip away without waking him. She hated to have to go over his head on this matter, but after all, he was only her husband, not her commanding officer. She would take her plea directly to the top—to Colonel Morgan himself.

Morgan, busy at his camp desk, waved his orderly out when Lavinia appeared at the door to his tent.

"Come in, my dear," he said with a welcoming smile. He rose to give her an affectionate peck on the cheek but decided against such informality when she came into full view.

Lavinia, dressed in a regulation uniform she had fashioned in secret, stood before her commander, saluting smartly. Only the plume on her hat quivered slightly as she stood at rigid attention. Seldom had Morgan seen such spit and polish, such perfection of military bearing.

"Private Clay reporting for duty, Colonel Morgan, sir!"

Jack Morgan suppressed a smile, but his eyes still twinkled with amusement as he returned Lavinia's salute and answered, "At ease, Private Clay. State your business."

"Sir!" Lavinia barked. "Request permission to reenlist, sir!"

Morgan frowned. What was this all about? Some sort of practical joke she and Damien had cooked up? He decided to play along.

"Previous service, soldier?"

"Company K of the Wiregrass Rifles, Colonel, sir," she answered proudly.

"Good outfit! Duration of enlistment?" He had his pen in

hand as if taking all this down. He waited. She hesitated over her reply. "Well, Private, how long were you in for?"

Lavinia's answer was barely audible this time. "Three days, sir."

"Three days?"

His stern voice and hard look made Lavinia squirm inside her uniform.

"You were wounded and taken out of action, you mean."

"No, sir." The words were a bare whisper.

"What, then? Surely you didn't desert your post?"

"No, sir, Colonel Morgan, sir!" This time her reply rang through the tent.

"Well, Private, explain yourself, then."

Lavinia's gaze dropped to the toes of her boots. "I was sent home, sir."

"A reject?"

"No," she snapped, "a virgin!"

Morgan couldn't help himself. He'd held his laughter in as long as was humanly possible. He howled and slapped his knee.

"But I'm not any longer . . . I mean . . ."

Lavinia was flustered, but determined. Morgan had to hear her out and take her side in this against her husband. Damien Clay was not the sort of man to be swayed by a woman's pleas or threats. But he would take military orders from a superior without question. As she saw it, there wasn't a reason under the sun that John Hunt Morgan could refuse to let her join the Raiders. And once she was officially under his command, Damien couldn't make her leave.

Dammit all! Why did he keep laughing that way? This was serious!

"Colonel Morgan, will you please listen to what I have to say!"

Her loud, authoritative tone stilled his mirth. He looked at her pretty, troubled face and realized that this was indeed no laughing matter, at least not to Lavinia.

"I'm sorry, Private Clay. Please continue."

"As I was saying, Colonel, I want to join up with the Second Kentucky. I know it's a bit irregular . . .''

"Irregular?" he boomed. "It's goddamn crazy, Lavinia! What's this all about? Did Damien put you up to it?" Morgan asked.

"No! He'd probably be upset if he knew I was here," she admitted.

"Try *mad as hell*, Lavinia! 'Probably upset' is far too mild for the way I feel at the moment!''

"Damien!" she cried, turning to see him at the tent flap.

"Clay, what in God's name is going on here?" Morgan demanded.

"Ask her!"

Lavinia stiffened and drew up to her full height, determined to do battle with both of them if need be. They were trying to intimidate her, staring her down. Her palms were sweating. Her heart was pounding. But she wouldn't back off. Not before she gave it her all!

"Well, Lavinia?" Morgan said quietly. "What do you have to say for yourself?"

She thought out her words carefully before she spoke. "Colonel Morgan, you're about to set out on a major campaign. You need men, and I'm volunteering. I've got a regulation uniform, my own horse and saddle, my own guns, and I can ride and shoot better than most. And I'm willing to fight. I *want* to fight! So if you'll just pass me that enlistment paper, Colonel, I'll sign my name to the dotted line, sir, and be proud to call myself one of Morgan's Raiders!''

By the time Lavinia had finished having her say, John Hunt Morgan was looking on her with a new kind of respect. As for Damien, he was so filled with pride he wanted to grab her and hug her, but he knew she wouldn't take kindly to such a show of affection at the moment. There wasn't another man he knew who had a wife with so much grit and gumption. They both realized they had to let her down gently.

Damien reached out and squeezed her hand to show her he wasn't angry any longer. She gave him a quivery half smile, then turned her attention back to Colonel Morgan, who had cleared his throat to speak.

"Lavinia, you stated the honest-to-God fact: I need *men*! If you were a man, I'd sign you up so fast you wouldn't know what hit you. But you wouldn't be a private. Not by a long shot! If ever there was officer material, you're it! You showed me the stuff you're made of at Cave City and again while you and Damien were in Louisville. Actually, your time spent doing undercover work is the real reason I have to turn down your request to enlist."

Lavinia, sorely disappointed, tried to interrupt, but Morgan held up a hand to silence her.

"Hear me out. You are too valuable to me. I can't risk you on the battlefield. The time is sure to come again when I'll need you for other special missions. You and Damien are my secret weapons. I'm not willing to tamper with the success you've shown so far. I'm sorry, but that's my final word on the subject. I want you to know, though, that your offer is a courageous and generous one. I won't soon forget what an honor it is to have you serving as a special agent to the Second Kentucky."

He rose and offered his hand as if Lavinia were his equal.

"Thank you," he said. "Now, if you will excuse me, I have a campaign to plan."

Damien started to take Lavinia's arm as they left Morgan's tent, but thought better of it. She looked and acted every inch a soldier—albeit a very pretty one. He decided to accord her the same comradeship as any other officer in the troop.

When they were outside in the sunshine, he clapped a hand on her shoulder and said, "How about a drink, Private Clay?"

Her stern, militaristic frown melted into a sly smile that made sparkles dance in her green eyes as she looked up at her husband.

"I have a better idea. How about a kiss, Captain Clay?"

Later that day John Hunt Morgan gave his consent for Damien to see his new bride to Murfreesboro, providing he would be back and ready to ride with them in two days.

"Give my pretty Mattie a kiss for me, Clay," Morgan instructed as he stood before the pair, who were mounted and ready to leave. "Tell her, if it were possible, I'd make the trip myself. Lord knows, I want to see her bad enough! But she'll understand. She knows the military. Give her my letter and tell her I love her." He turned to Lavinia and placed a gloved hand on hers. "We'll miss you, young lady! By God, you've done a fine job! But you'll be better off with the Readys. And you ladies will have a grand time preparing for my marriage to Mattie. It won't be long now." He grinned and shook his head as if he couldn't quite believe it. "Get going now. You've a long ride ahead of you."

Lavinia turned and waved as they rode out of camp. A strange hoarseness came into her throat, but she knew she wouldn't cry. She was a soldier, as good as any. Both Colonel Morgan and her husband had told her so. She saw herself as going on leave from the front. She would be back—to ride, to fight, to love—another day.

The Ready family welcomed Lavinia back into the fold with open arms and happy, smiling faces. Helen-of-Troy, so overcome with emotion that she couldn't find words, hugged her young mistress and wept oceans of thankful tears.

"Lord, Lord, Miss Vinnie," she managed between sobs, "I done figured I'd never lay eyes on you no more. I kept a-waitin' and a-prayin', but I was near out of my mind with worryin' over you."

Damien could stay only long enough to get a bite to eat and change horses. With the whole Ready family gathered in the parlor, he and Lavinia spent their final moments together staring longingly at each other across the crowded room. It seemed to Lavinia that miles separated them already. Her heart ached with emptiness.

"You're sure Jack is all right?" Mattie inquired in a worried voice. "He's usually so good about writing, but I've hardly had more than a scribbled note this past month."

"He's fine, Mattie," Damien assured her. "We've been through a hectic time. But your Jack did himself proud in Kentucky. Watch the newspapers. I'm sure there'll be detailed accounts of his triumphs.''

"He sent you a letter," Lavinia said, reminding Damien of that forgotten detail. "And he had a message for you, too.''

Damien, frowning his apology for having to be reminded, handed Mattie the folded paper. She tore it open, eagerly scanning the page. Tears welled up in her eyes, but she smiled. "And his message?" she asked.

Damien glanced about, embarrassed suddenly. Mr. and Mrs. Ready, Mattie's sisters, Lavinia, and several servants were staring at him. He cleared his throat and looked directly at Martha Ready. "Jack said to tell you he loves you," he said quickly.

Mattie rushed forward and threw her arms around his neck, kissing his cheek. "Oh, thank you, Damien! Do tell Jack that I return his affections a thousandfold.''

"Well, yes, of course, I'll do that," he mumbled, blushing in spite of himself.

Lavinia smiled, thinking how like a small boy he looked when something made him uncomfortable.

He rose, bowed a bit stiffly, and said, "I thank you kindly for the supper, but I'd better be on my way now." He glanced meaningfully toward Lavinia. She forced a smile she didn't feel and stood to walk him to his horse.

Their parting was brief, stiff, and painful. Lavinia could not say the things she was feeling. She wanted so to make him understand how much she loved him and needed him. She wanted to beg him to take care, to return to her quickly. But words seemed to have no real meaning at the moment. So instead of speaking the words to him, she told him all with her eyes and her silent parted lips.

His hands encircled her waist, pressing down on her hips as he kissed her deeply and tenderly. She drank in his kiss, never wanting it to end. How empty and arid the days ahead would be without him. She held on to him, savoring this instant in eternity. *Now* he was hers! If only she could freeze the moment—have him forever!

But the earth continued in its never-ceasing orbit and their time together was soon ticked away. The moment was lost and the next wrenched him from her. Lavinia stood alone on the porch, watching him mount, wave, blow a parting kiss, spur his horse, and grow smaller as he moved down the street and out of her sight. When Mattie Ready came out, Lavinia was standing where Damien had left her, staring through her tears down the empty length of Main Street.

Mattie took her hand compassionately. "It won't be so long, Lavinia. You'll see."

"It's been too long already," she answered, her heart threatening to break.

Martha Ready was right. The weeks did pass quickly. The two women scoured the war reports in the newspaper daily. They were not disappointed. Big South Tunnel, Hartsville, Glasgow, Richmond, Kentucky—the Confederates were rolling over the Union Army like a gray tide whipped by hurricane-force winds.

For a brief time, General Bragg and thirty thousand troops camped near Murfreesboro, a feint toward Nashville. Once more the Ready home resounded with the thud of shiny boots. Both Lavinia and Mattie felt their patriotic zeal replenished.

John Hunt Morgan, by this time, was publishing his own newspaper, flaunting the brave exploits of his Raiders and pleading for new recruits to further swell the ranks. Morgan sent Mattie copies of the *Vidette*. Together with Lavinia, she spent hours poring over every word. They especially appreciated the salute to Southern womanhood in the first issue.

"That's just like Jack," Mattie said with a bright, loving smile. "He and the other men are out risking their very lives for our Cause, and he writes of all *we* are doing!"

"I think it's sweet of him," Lavinia added.

"I won't argue that!" Mattie laughed. "I'm proud as I can be! And I think he's the dearest man alive!"

Lavinia lowered her eyes and indulged in a secret smile. How could Mattie know how dear her Jack was? They weren't married yet. Lavinia herself hadn't realized one-tenth of how much she loved Damien Clay until that sunny day back in July

when the stiff little preacher joined him to her forevermore.
Their love had grown and matured since then. And every day
that passed only made her cherish him more.

Hearing a tread on the porch, the two women looked up.
They exchanged nervous glances. They dreaded this type of
unheralded visit as much as they looked forward to it. A lone
soldier riding in with news could mean letters from Jack and
Damien. They tried not to think about the fact that messengers
brought bad news more often than not.

"I'll get the door," Mattie said in a tight, dry voice.

Lavinia sat clutching the arms of her chair, holding her
breath.

A little cry of delight from Mattie allowed her to breathe
again.

"*Two* letters! One for each of us!" she exclaimed, hurrying
back to the parlor.

Lavinia tore hers open with trembling hands. The letter was
long, written in a neat, unhurried script, from Hopemont, John
Hunt Morgan's home in Lexington.

> *Lexington, Kentucky*
> *5 September 1862*

> *My dearest love,*
>
> *I've wished you here with me every minute of every
> hour since our parting, but never more than I did yester-
> day. What a triumph! What a celebration! The con-
> quering hero returned to his boyhood home! Morgan's
> return to Lexington can best be compared to Caesar's re-
> turn to Rome.*
>
> *We camped the night before in Nicholasville, twelve
> miles from Lexington. Many of the men wanted to go on,
> but Morgan said no. He set us all to work—cleaning,
> brushing, polishing. Parade dress was the order of the
> day, and parade formation as we rode the next morning
> into Lexington. I wish Miss Mattie could have seen her
> betrothed! At the head of 900 men, he rode smartly into
> town, waving to the cheering citizenry. Somewhere a*

band struck up, marking our cadence. Confederate flags unfurled from windows and rooftops. Morgan saluted each as he passed. The whole town went wild! When the order was given to dismount, a grateful mob rushed forward to shake Morgan's hand, to touch him. The throng grew to such proportions that we had difficulty negotiating the streets to reach Hopemont.

Once we arrived at the house, the gifts began pouring in. The ladies brought a battle flag stitched with their own dainty hands. Food and wine arrived by cart and carriage. Then came an offering of silver spurs, beautifully crafted. But Mr. Keene Richards brought the grandest gift of all. Having heard of Morgan's misfortune in losing Black Bess, he made Jack a present of a splendid thoroughbred gelding by the name of Glencoe. For the first time in our long association, I saw Jack Morgan moved to tears.

A fine day, and a wonderful homecoming for our hero! But how much more it would have meant to have you riding beside me, my darling!

I cannot say when I will see you again. We are too far away at present for me to dash home overnight. But soon, my love, soon! And when I come, I hope to see you in fine fettle and red satin!

> *Ever your loving husband,*
> *Damien Clay*

Lavina, reading the letter aloud to Mattie, forgot in her excitement to edit the final sentence.

Mattie looked at her oddly and asked, "Red satin? Whatever does he mean by that?"

Her friend laughed softly, and a bit self-consciously, Mattie thought. "A private joke," Lavinia answered. "*Very* private!"

The Confederate wave was cresting, but late in September something went amiss. General Bragg, holding Munfordville, got his chance for glory, what might have been the first major battle on Kentucky soil and an opportunity to wrest the Blue-grass State from Federal hands once and for all. His thirty thousand men stood between Union General Buell's starving troops and the vast stockpiles of supplies in Louisville warehouses. There was no way out. Buell had to fight his way through Bragg's superior army or let his men waste away. Bragg anticipated the battle, but rather than stand and fight, even though the advantage was clearly his, he moved the majority of his troops out to Bardstown, leaving only a small rear guard to face the advancing Federals. General Buell pushed the few troops aside as if swatting a bluetailed fly from his horse's rump and marched on for Louisville. What promised to be Bragg's shining hour dimmed to dismal defeat.

Then General Kirby-Smith rode in to Frankfort on October 4 to see Richard Hawes put into office as the Confederate governor of the state. But hardly was Hawes's inaugural speech out of his mouth before Buell's troops entered the capital, sending the new governor and his staff fleeing for their lives. One by one the cities Morgan's Raiders had helped take were recaptured by Federal troops. Their only escape route lay to the south—back to Tennessee.

Taking his orders now from "Fighting Joe" Wheeler, Morgan suggested and received permission to seek his own route back, hitting Union supply trains and railroads along the way. Because he rode west instead of due south, Morgan missed the great and bloody battle at Perryville on October 8. Burning and fighting their way through, often sleeping in the snow, Morgan's Raiders reached Tennessee in November.

Once more Jack Morgan's heart led him toward Murfreesboro and the woman he was to marry in little over a month. By early in December, Morgan and Martha Ready were reunited at long last.

Lavinia, though she was happy for the couple, could not contain her own disappointment. Damien Clay was not with Colonel Morgan.

"He'll probably join up again any day, Lavinia," Morgan assured her.

"But where is he?" she demanded. "Hasn't he been with

you all this time? He hasn't been lost in battle, has he?'' She clutched Morgan's sleeve at the thought. ''You would tell me if anything like that had happened, wouldn't you?''

Mattie shot a concerned look at Lavinia. ''Please, you mustn't upset yourself.''

''Believe me, Lavinia,'' Morgan soothed her, ''I'd tell you. I promise your Damien is fine. Really! I expect him to turn up any day now.''

She took heart. ''A secret mission, Jack?''

He laughed aloud. ''It's secret, all right! He wouldn't even tell me what he was up to.''

A disturbing thought popped into Lavinia's mind. She tried to brush it aside, but it refused to be banished.

''Jack,'' she said cautiously, ''have you ever heard of an actress named Pauline Cushman?''

One dark gold eyebrow shot up. ''What red-blooded man doesn't recognize that name? Why, Lavinia?''

''Oh, nothing. I just wondered if she was still in Kentucky.''

Just a few days before, Damien Clay had begged Morgan's permission to don Annie Flowers' skirts and ride out alone. His mission could well turn out to be a wild goose chase, but he had to follow this lead. It would mean so much to Lavinia. Though she hadn't spoken of Josiah in some time, Damien knew that her mind often strayed to her brother, wondering where he was and what had become of him. Damien wondered, too. And maybe soon he would find out.

A Union prisoner had given him the tip, quite by accident. The private had laughed when he was taken instead of seeming concerned over his capture.

''See here, man, this is no laughing matter,'' Damien had cautioned him. ''Colonel Morgan isn't handing out paroles this trip. You'll probably end up down in Georgia, at Andersonville.''

The grinning private spit through his gaping front teeth and slapped his knee. ''I reckon your prison camps can't be no worse than ours, like say Point Lookout over to Maryland. If that Georgia feller can pull a stunt to heigh his tail out of there, I can do me the same thing.''

"An escape, eh?'' Damien prompted, hoping to get more information out of his talkative prisoner.

"Right enough! He was one clever bastard for a Johnny Reb. I'll give him that.'' He squinted up at Damien. "Ain't you heared tell of what happened? Everbody's been talking it up.''

Damien shook his head.

"Well, sir, there was some cases of smallpox at the camp. Had 'em all—prisoners and guards—scared stiff. Anybody break out in a heat rash and it was off to the quarantine hospital with 'em. So this here Georgia boy got it in his head to get hisself a fine case of the pox. See, there warn't many guards on the sick men, them being too weak to travel.''

"But how could he escape by getting smallpox?'' Damien frowned. "That seems a drastic measure.''

"Well, hell, that's what he figured on everbody thinkin'. This here boy cut hisself a length of wire—not longer than your finger, so's nobody would notice. Then he heated it up from the sunlight with a bit of broke glass and stuck that hot wire to his face time and time again. Raised some mighty ugly blisters, I'm here to tell you. A fine case of the pox!''

"Well, I'll be damned!'' Damien said, thinking what lengths men would go to for freedom. "And it worked?''

"Slick as you please! The officer in charge, he had that feller hauled off to the hospital in jig time. Then it warn't a full day 'fore he was vanished.''

Damien gave the Yankee a hard look, wondering just how much of the tale to believe. "How do you happen to know so much about all this?''

"Hell, I's the poor sonuvabitch got took prisoner by him! How'd I know he wasn't really sick? He plumb overpowered me, took my gun and turned it on me. Nobody noticed him sneakin' out by the dark of night, usin' me for cover, so there wasn't no shootin'. He just hauled me off into the woods, tied me up, and left me there. When the cap'n found me the next day, he talked hangin' for a while. Said I'd 'been instrumental in the escape,' whatever the hell that means. Had me nearly scairt to death. But then says he, 'This un ain't worth the rope to hang him! Send him to the front. Let the Rebs take care of him.'

"So here I be, big as life and twice as ornery. Hellfire! Send me to your old Andersonville. See if I give a good goddamn! I'll have me out of there in less time than it takes to skin a cat, and then I'll haul my carcass on home to Missouri. I was a damn fool to join up in the first place!"

"That Georgia boy? What was his name?" Damien knew it was a long shot, but he had to ask.

His prisoner grinned at him and spat again. "Don't rightly remember the gentleman introducin' hisself, Cap'n."

"What did he look like?"

"Tall, skinny kid. Bright red hair. Said he hailed from some place with a funny name—Lightning Strike, maybe?"

"Thunderbolt?" Damien asked excitedly.

"Yeah! That was it!"

"You don't by any chance know where he was headed?"

The prisoner squared his shoulders and looked at Damien importantly. "So happens, I just do! What's it worth to you?"

Damien felt his pockets and shrugged. "A plug of tobacco?"

"Throw in a bottle of that Kentucky firewater I seen your men guzzlin' and you got yourself a deal, Cap'n!"

Leaving the prisoner content with a chaw, a bottle, and a plan of escape by smallpox, Damien rode off, hoping against hope that he could find Josiah Rutledge.

Meanwhile, back in Murfreesboro, Lavinia had worried herself into a state.

"You've got to stop this!" Mattie warned. "You don't want Damien to come home and find you ill."

Lavinia lolled in bed, restless, weary night and day, sure that her husband was off somewhere with his fancy lady friend. She cursed herself silently for the jealousy she felt, but she couldn't seem to overcome her suspicious doubts. She had given Damien hell for the days before their parting. Maybe he'd decided that their marriage was a mistake. It had all come about so suddenly. She began to wonder if he had done it more because he desired her at the moment than because he loved her and always would. Men were such strange creatures, always wanting to strike while the iron was hot. And it had certainly been smoldering that morning in the telegraph office!

Mattie left her to herself and she lay in bed, listless and miserable. Outside, the snow was falling again. She'd loved the unaccustomed sight of snow at first, but now it only depressed her. It blanketed the familiar world in deathly white and muffled every sound. The winter had come early and promised to be severe. Right now spring seemed a lifetime away—as distant and illusive as Damien Clay's love. What she wouldn't give to see a robin, a rosebud, a single blade of grass. But most of all, to see her husband, to have him hold her and reassure her, tell her that he still loved her and needed her.

That night Lavinia suffered terrible nightmares. She was trying to find Josiah. But each time she caught sight of her brother in the distance he would vanish before she reached him. Then it seemed that she was finally about to catch up with him. She reached out to take his arm, but the sleeve her fingers grasped was empty. In the next instant Sam Coltrain was leering down at her. She cried out for Damien, but he didn't hear.

She awoke to the cold white dawn in an even worse disposition than before. Nothing seemed to matter anymore. Why had she even bothered waking up?

Then, as her mood was about to reach rock bottom, something of her old spirit revived. Who was she—warmly snuggled into a feather mattress with downy comforters tucked about her—to feel so sorry for herself? Hell's bells! She had plenty to be thankful for. Her health, her husband, her future.

Throwing back the covers, she got out of bed for the first time in three days. Quickly, she dressed in a warm woolen skirt, shirtwaist, and jacket.

Mattie knocked and poked her head in the door. "I thought I'd see what you want for breakfast, Lavinia." She broke into a delighted smile when she saw her friend up and dressed. "Well, my goodness, you must be feeling better this morning. That's wonderful!"

"I'm fit as a fiddle!" Lavinia answered brightly. "And I'm going out for some air before breakfast."

"Lavinia!" Mattie said laughing. "It's snowing like blazes out there!"

"All the better for a brisk turn around the town square. Care to come along?"

"Oh, I would, but I have a fitting on my wedding gown, and Mrs. Bascomb said she'd be here first thing this morning. Some other time?"

Lavinia plopped a hat on her head and pulled on her fur-lined cap. "I won't be long, Mattie."

And she hadn't planned to be.

Lavinia, used to gentle South Georgia winters, had no idea that she was going out to face a blizzard. At first as she walked along Main Street, the big flakes seemed to swirl about her as if she were caught in the midst of a fairy dance. The silence of the storm fascinated her. She was alone in an enchanted white world.

Up ahead the courthouse loomed, an indistinct dark shape through the falling drifts. Stepping carefully to avoid patches of ice on the walk, Lavinia headed toward the building on the square. What would be a short walk on a normal day seemed to take forever as she leaned forward into the gusty wind. It whipped her cape, sending icy chills through her.

The snow was coming down faster now, swirling like an eerie white whirlpool about her. She shielded her face with her gloved hands, feeling her nose and lips growing numb from the cold. The driving snow caught in her eyelashes, all but blinding her. She stumbled forward. If she could just reach the courthouse steps, she could seek shelter there until the buffeting gusts died down again.

Thinking more of speed than her own safety, Lavinia quickened her pace. Her feet hit a patch of ice beneath the snow and for a sickening instant she flailed wildly, trying in vain to regain her balance. She pitched forward, but a deep drift cushioned her fall so that only her dignity was bruised.

"Oh, bother!" she mumbled, thoroughly embarrassed by her clumsiness.

She glanced about as she lay sprawled on the walk, to make sure no one had witnessed her awkward fall. She needn't have worried. To all appearances, she was the only soul on the face of the snowbound earth this morning. The thought gave her a peculiar feeling. Perhaps she would give up her goal of reaching the courthouse and just return to the Readys'.

Dragging herself out of the snowbank, she turned back the way she had come. But the wind had shifted. Though she bent far forward, the blizzard tore at her cape as if it were a sail, making progress impossible in that direction. All she could do now was head once more toward the square and fight the angry elements until she could reach shelter.

What had started out to be an invigorating stroll had become a frozen nightmare. Lavinia realized suddenly how tired and cold she was. Her heart was pounding in her chest and she felt light-headed from exertion.

"Just calm down and keep moving," she told herself.

With every step she took she became more conscious of the cold. She had snow in her boots now and her feet were freezing. She could no longer feel her toes.

What if I fall? she thought. There's no one about. I could freeze to death in sight of the house!

The storm was getting worse. Wind-lashed snowflakes sliced at her face like icy knives, blinding her. Still, she trudged on. What else could she do?

Then she stumbled and fell again. This time the landing jarred her badly, sending pain shooting through her cold-numbed limbs.

"Help me!" she cried weakly. She was sure she'd never be able to get up this time. But no one answered her call.

Inch by painful inch she dragged herself up until she was sitting. Then, carefully, she got to her feet. She was almost afraid to chance another step. The ice was there. She knew it. But where? The snow covered everything. She looked back toward the Ready house, but she could no longer see it. The snow had turned the day into a murky brown twilight. Another gust hit her, threatening her balance. She leaned into it, forging on toward the square.

She was within a few yards of the courthouse steps when she spied a figure approaching her. Her heart gave a sudden joyful lurch. She hadn't realized until this moment how very frightened and alone she'd felt.

"Please," she called. "Could you help me up the steps?"

The man was no more than a dark shape against the backdrop of white. He turned, stumbling through the deep drifts, hurrying to her. Lavinia made her way, as best she could, to meet him. Some of her panic fled. Now she was no longer alone. There were two of them in this snow- and ice-locked nether world.

She gave a thankful cry and flung herself at him. She held on to him, sobbing with relief. A comforting hand came up to touch her freezing cheek.

"Lavinia?" a familiar voice said.

A numbness far more dreadful than any the storm could produce closed in on her. She pushed away from him.

"No!" she gasped. "Stay away from me, Sam!"

He caught her with his arm, clutching her to him.

"Lavinia, please. I only want to . . ."

She had to get away. Panic consumed her. She didn't even know at the moment if Sam Coltrain was real or a ghostly shadow come to take her to the grave. She fought him, finally wrenching free. Unmindful of the treacherous ice and wind, she tore toward the courthouse steps. If she could only climb them and get inside she would be safe from the storm, from Sam.

"Lavinia-a-a!" His voice wailed in her ears, whipped to distortion by the wind. The sound spurred her uncertain step.

Higher and higher she climbed, never daring to look back. He was coming after her. She was sure of it. Just a few more steps. Her heart was pounding painfully. Her lungs burned. Her head throbbed. She could no longer feel her feet and legs. Just a few more steps. If only she could . . .

"Lavinia, be careful!"

She was falling suddenly. Down and down and down. Her

body felt the sharpness of each step as she plummeted earthward. Then a blinding pain shot through her head. Her ankle throbbed. Her arms refused to move. Darkness was closing on her. The instant before the blackness claimed her, she saw Sam Coltrain's ice-blue eyes as his face hovered over hers. But was he real or only a figment of her imagination in this painful, freezing white dream?

Mrs. Bascomb had come and gone, and still there was no sign of Lavinia. Mattie began to be truly worried.

"I'm going out to look for her," she told her mother. "The storm's getting worse by the minute."

Cold swirling winds whipped Main Street, trying to freeze Mattie's cheeks, but she leaned into the gusts and forged on. The whole world seemed frozen in place this morning. An eerie brownish-yellow light sifted through the flying flakes. Not a soul moved anywhere—no horse and wagon, no mongrel dog, no child on a sled or carrying skates. This was staying-in-by-the-fire weather if ever she had seen it. Still, Lavinia was out here somewhere. Mattie tried calling, but the wind lashed her words back into her mouth. Only the howl of the gale could be heard.

Going was slow, but she finally reached the square. She glanced about but saw no one. Step by step she inched on against the storm, scanning the blanket of white, while snowflakes froze on her dark eyelashes. Her heart thundered in her breast. Where could Lavinia be?

Then a movement in the snow a short distance away at the foot of the courthouse steps caught her eye. She tried to hurry toward the quivering form but lost her footing on a patch of ice and fell.

"Lavinia!" she wailed, and a pained cry returned to her.

When she reached her at last, Mattie found that Lavinia was still breathing, but her lips were blue and her body buried in the snow. She tried to get her to her feet, but it seemed an impossible task. Lavinia was only barely conscious. Mattie struggled to lift her until the breath burned in her lungs, and her fingers

ached with numbing cold. She couldn't leave her friend to go
for help. By the time she returned it might be too late.

"Get up, Lavinia!" Mattie wailed. But it was no use.

Suddenly, a hand touched Mattie's shoulder. She turned
with a start, staring up into a dark, bearded face and strange
ice-blue eyes.

"Can I help?" the man asked.

"Oh, please! She's almost frozen."

Mattie watched, amazed, as the stranger threw back his cape
and with one arm lifted Lavinia as if she weighed nothing at all.

"Follow me," she instructed, hurrying as best she could
through the deep drifts.

The time it took to get to the house seemed an eternity to
Mattie, but in reality it was only a few minutes. Lavinia was
aware of nothing at all. The bare thread of consciousness she'd
been clutching for so long slipped from her grasp when she felt
herself being lifted out of the snow by a strong arm.

Later, as she drifted back upward through the cold, gray
wastes, she heard Mattie's voice.

"How is she, Dr. Farnsworth?"

"Even with everything that's happened, she's a lucky young
lady. The snow saved her. It it hadn't been coming down so
hard, she might have frozen to death before you found her. As
it is, she's going to make it. She's young and strong. A
fighter."

The man's words faded. Then she heard other voices, bits
and snatches of disjointed conversations. She heard Mattie's
voice, then Damien's, and—glory! Could it be? *Josiah's!*

She tried to pull herself to the surface of the spinning whirlpool that was dragging her down, but it was no use. She was
lost! Dying or dead already. Her fingers gripped like claws into
the white counterpane, then her hands relaxed, trembled, and
slid to her sides.

"Damien," she whimpered. "Damien?"

Only the angry scream of the storm answered her. Then all
was blackness.

Chapter Twenty-Two

"Damien, help me!" Lavinia cried, struggling out of her deep sleep to face the uncertain gray dawn. For nearly a week she had lain at death's door.

A cool hand stroked her forehead. "It's all right, Lavinia. Damien will be here soon, I'm sure. No, don't try to get up! You must rest. You've had a terrible time of it."

Mattie's face wore a grave expression. Though she and Helen-of-Troy had spent long days and nights heating and reheating bricks to warm Lavinia and spooning hot tea and warm broths between her pale lips, her hands were still like ice. And her face was the same color as the snow that had almost claimed her life. Add a badly sprained ankle from her fall down the stairs to her near brush with being frozen to death, and it was understandable that Lavinia was so ill.

"Where is Damien?" Lavinia demanded, trying to raise her head from the pillows once again.

Mattie shook her head. "I don't know, Lavinia. But Jack and some of his men have ridden out to try to find him."

"You don't understand," Lavinia insisted, wild-eyed now. "He was here! I heard him in this very room." She saw Mattie's nervous frown. "Wasn't it Damien who carried me back to the house? I'm sure of it!"

"No, Lavinia. You're mistaken," Mattie said gently. "You've been delirious. You only imagined you heard Damien's voice. As for the man who saved you, he was a total stranger. Odd, too, the way he brought you in and then just vanished. He never even told me his name. I wish I'd taken more time to thank him. He saved your life! And him a poor, one-armed soldier.''

Lavinia's mind had been drifting as Mattie spoke. But hearing that a one-armed man had rescued her, her thoughts snapped back to the present. So she really had seen Sam Coltrain, not his ghost.

''Was he a dark-haired man with pale blue eyes?''

''Why, yes! Do you know him, Lavinia?''

For a long time Lavinia didn't answer. She lay back with her eyes tightly shut, trying not to imagine Sam Coltrain's face. What was he doing here? And how had he gotten out of the cave? Some perverse part of her was glad he was still alive, but she desperately wanted him out of her life for good.

''Lavinia?''

''Yes, I know him. But I thought he was dead. Please, Mattie, I don't want to talk about it anymore.''

''You rest. I'll go and make a pot of tea.'' Mattie smiled brightly at her friend. ''You have to get your strength back. We have a wedding to get ready for!''

Yes, a wedding. Lavinia lay very still, thinking. All four of them—Damien and she as much as Mattie and Jack—had looked forward to this happy event. Would only three of them be on hand when it actually came to pass? Where could Damien be? Lavinia gave a weary sigh. She had no idea. All she could do was trust that fate would bring him home safely. It was beyond her power to do anything more.

It had been a long haul. The information Damien got from the prisoner concerning Josiah Rutledge's destination was only partly correct. The Missouri man had told Damien that the Georgia boy had said he meant to head for Chattanooga, Bragg's headquarters. Damien had ridden hell-bent-for-leather toward Lookout Mountain.

Arriving there, he questioned the rough-hewn sentry on duty and was told, ''Hell, yeah, he was here! Near about scared us foolish, riding up looking like he was bringing the pox into camp. Left in a right big hurry, though. You ain't missed him by more than a hair—couple of hours maybe. Rode off to the south, he did.''

Making a calculated guess, Damien struck out toward Thunderbolt. At nightfall, somewhere in the North Georgia mountains, he spotted the smoke of a campfire in the distance. It could have been anyone—a deserter from either army, a hunter out scavenging for game, a family burned out of their home. But it wasn't just anyone—it was Josiah Rutledge.

Now Lavinia's brother, his face blotched with healing "smallpox," rode next to Damien on their way to Murfreesboro.

"Married, eh?" Josiah said for about the twenty-seventh time that day, as if he still couldn't quite believe it.

"Yep! These past five months."

"By damn, you're a brave one, Damien Clay. It isn't just any man who'd take on the likes of Lavinia Rutledge!"

"I wouldn't trade her for a passel of prim schoolmarm types!"

"She's going to be mighty surprised to see us," Josiah commented.

Damien laughed. "It's a good thing I found you. You're my peace offering. If I'd turned up this late and empty-handed, like as not she would have taken the broom handle to me. She still may! That sister of yours is one hellcat when she gets riled."

Josiah nodded his agreement. "Always was, and I reckon she always will be. But who'd have her any other way?"

Damien let his mind hurry on ahead. In his thoughts he was already at the big house on Main Street, taking Lavinia to their bedroom, coaxing her toward her wildest, most abandoned lovemaking. She could be a hellcat in bed, too. And, as Josiah had said, he wouldn't have her any other way.

Damien spurred his horse along the icy road, more than eager to see his Lavinia. God, it had been a long, loveless time!

* * *

John Hunt Morgan was superstitious about Sundays. He always said, "Every one of the most important things in my life happened on the Sabbath."

On this particular Sunday—December 14, 1862—possibly the best and most important thing of his entire life was about to take place. He was about to make Martha Ready "Mrs. John Hunt Morgan." And what a wedding gift he had to offer her! A brand-new promotion to brigadier general, coming on the heels of his recent victory at Hartsville.

President Jefferson Davis had arrived in Murfreesboro on Friday. Saturday had been given over to a full-scale presidential review of the troops, culminating in the announcement of promotions. At his wedding, for the first time, John Hunt Morgan would appear in full general's regalia.

The usual Sunday calm of the Ready house was lost in a whirlwind of last-minute preparations. Mrs. Ready dithered about, turning from one task to another and issuing order after order to an army of servants. In the midst of the flurry she would stop from time to time, get a surprised look on her face, and say to no one in particular, "My stars, the president is coming!" before she hurried on to some other pressing matter.

Under her knowing guidance the parlor took on the look of an enchanted forest with its drapings of holly, cedar, and winterberries. The whole house was decked in Christmas finery, from the popcorn ropes and tinsel threaded through the greens to the wax angels gleaming their benediction from every mantelpiece and whatnot shelf. Dominating the parlor, where the ceremony would be held, stood a splendid cedar Christmas tree, lavishly ornamented and twinkling with tiny candles.

The whole place smelled like heaven itself. Mingling with the evergreen scents were the mouth-watering aromas from the kitchen—turkey and hams roasting, mince and pecan pies cooling on the racks, fresh Christmas breads ready for slicing.

"Lord, Lord!" Helen-of-Troy muttered through a wide grin as she iced the fragrantly steaming plum pudding with hard sauce. "Smells so good, makes a body wish they had four stomachs like a cow!"

Lavinia, still recuperating but out of bed and dressed in her green crepe de Paris gown for the occasion, viewed all the excitement and preparations with mixed emotions. She had never seen anyone as happy as Mattie Ready. The bride's cup of goodwill brimmed over, spilling on everyone around her. Lavinia wasn't any exception. But still there had been no word from Damien. The grim thought that something terrible had happened to him followed her every minute of every day like a dark cloud above her head that never allowed the full sunlight of happiness to shine on her. Still, she put on a brave face, not letting anyone know that she was suffering from a touch of melancholia or that her ankle hurt like the very devil. As for the emptiness that refused to be banished from the pit of her stomach, regardless of how many gallons of tea and broth Helen-of-Troy forced down her, food and drink were not the answer. Only her husband could take that ache away.

All day long the house bustled with comings and goings. The wedding, a brief respite snatched from the very jaws of war, took on a mingled atmosphere of carnival, old-time tent revival, family reunion, and holiday celebration. The large rooms of the Ready home seemed to shrink with the number of friends, relatives, and soldiers arriving and departing all through the day. Finally, a cordon of Morgan's men were stationed outside to hold down some of the traffic in and out. But as the sun went down and candles and lamps flickered on inside, an expectant hush fell over the setting.

Lavinia sat in Mattie's room, helping her pass the final hour before the ceremony.

"I'm terrified, Lavinia!" Mattie confessed. "I feel as if I don't even know Jack Morgan. A general's wife— *me*! Why, it's outrageous! I'll never be able to handle it."

Lavinia smiled gently at her friend. The confident shine of Mattie's deep gray eyes belied her words of misgiving.

"Oh, you'll do, Mattie!" Lavinia assured her. "If ever a woman was perfect for the role, you are."

"I do hope so!" Mattie sighed. "But what if St. Leger Grenfell and those others are right in saying that Jack shouldn't marry at all? What if having a wife makes him soft and ruins his career, as they seem so sure it will? I couldn't stand that. Neither could he!''

Lavinia sat up straighter and an angry green fire leapt in her eyes. ''St. Leger Grenfell is a pompous British know-it-all! He's only jealous because no woman will have him! Don't worry your head over his prattle, Mattie. Jack loves you! Don't you know that? He says that taking you as his wife will make him the stronger for having a share of your strength. And General John Hunt Morgan is never wrong. He told me that himself!''

Both women giggled, then laughed out loud.

''What a thing for him to say!'' Mattie replied, still laughing. ''Jack Morgan, now there's a pompous one for you!''

''Maybe so, but he has every right to be. Martha Ready, you're about to marry a *hero*!''

Mattie went all dewy-eyed and dreamy suddenly. ''Oh, Lavinia, I know that, and I do love him so!''

''Then you have nothing to worry about.''

Mrs. Ready knocked and looked in. ''It's about time, girls.''

Lavinia helped Mattie on with her long white veil and smoothed the lace of her wedding gown. For a moment she thought of the ''make-do'' dress she had worn to get married in. She smiled. Mattie's might be finer and newer, but Lavinia was sure Martha Ready was no happier a bride than she had been on her special day. Oh, how she wished Damien were here!

Three regimental bands were in attendance for the occasion. Two of them remained outside to entertain the hundreds of soldiers crowding the street while the other one took its position inside to provide wedding music.

When these favored musicians began to play softly, Lavinia kissed Mattie's cheek and said, ''Time for me to go. I'll see you downstairs.''

A few moments later Lavinia watched through the obligatory wedding tears as Martha Ready, a vision in delicate white lace, made her way down the staircase on her father's arm. The parlor below was filled with ranking brass—all of Morgan's favorites. The candlelight cast myriad reflections off the gold of their uniform trappings, making the whole room glitter and gleam.

Lavinia glanced about. President Davis looked thin and somber in his frock coat, trousers, and boots of black. He stood in a place of honor, near the mighty figure of General Bishop Leonidas Polk, who, over his Confederate uniform, wore the vestments of his office as Episcopal Bishop of Louisiana to perform the ceremony. He resembled a towering saint with his serene face bearded and capped in silver. John Hunt Morgan's groomsmen—Bragg, Hardee, Breckinridge, and Cheatham—stood at attention, their collective gaze on the lovely bride. When Mr. Ready placed Mattie's small hand in the general's, everyone moved in closer. The music stopped, and a hush descended.

Lavinia listened to General Polk's words with a bittersweet ache in her heart. It seemed such a short time since she and Damien had spoken these very promises to each other. But in another way it seemed so long ago. Where was he now? If only she knew! She was glad when they were all asked to bow their heads in prayer so that she could hide the tears streaming down her face.

"Amen!" the bishop boomed.

Lavinia looked up, wiped her cheeks, and looked again. Could it be? Or were her eyes playing tricks on her? There in the hallway just beyond the parlor door stood two desperately bedraggled men. They were dirty, unshaven, and their clothes were a far cry from Sunday best. Lavinia had to force herself to stay where she was and not run to them. The ceremony seemed to be lasting an eternity as Damien caught her eye and grinned. He poked Josiah and nodded toward her. Her brother, his smooth face strangely pocked, smiled at her, too.

General Morgan was still pressing his bride when Lavinia hurried through the throng of guests to let her husband do the same to her. When Damien's arms enfolded her, Lavinia felt a new spark of life surge through her. The long, empty days were at an end. She was whole again, vibrant and alive with the knowledge that she was loved. Whatever else might happen in the coming days and years, she could face it as long as she had the assurance of her husband's abiding affection.

"Don't I even get a hello?"

"Josiah!" Lavinia cried. "Oh, I just can't believe you're really here!"

He embraced her, smoothing a hand down her hair as he had done when they were both children—so long ago, it seemed.

"Where have you been?" she demanded of her brother. "And how did you find me here?"

Josiah offered her a broad smile. "I had my doubts about this fellow of yours when we first met, but he's truly one of the family now. He rode across two states to locate me and reunite us. I've been in a Yankee prison, but I escaped. I was headed home when Damien caught up with me. I'm still going back to Thunderbolt, but I had to see my little sister first."

"Oh, Josiah! I'm so glad you're safe!" she said, squeezing him tightly. Then she turned her flashing eyes on Damien. "So that's why it took you so long! You might have told someone where you were headed!"

Damien shielded his face with his hands in mock fear and whispered loudly to Josiah, "Is she going to hit me?"

"It would serve you right!" Lavinia scolded good-naturedly. "Taking off to who knows where and not saying a word to anyone! It's just a good thing you brought Josiah back with you, Damien Clay!"

Both men laughed, and Damein slipped an arm about Lavinia's waist. The next moment they were caught up in a throng, spearheaded by the bride and groom.

"Damien!" Mattie Morgan cried. "You're home at last!"

"High time!" Morgan put in. "Another couple of days and I would have had you shot for a deserter if you dared show your face again."

Jack Morgan grasped Damien's hand firmly in a gesture of close friendship. But they were hardly given a chance to say hello before the wedding feast was announced. Damien and Josiah excused themselves to clean up quickly.

For the next hour the wine flowed freely, complementing the well-laid board of turkey, duck, ham, venison—anything and everything that a Southern kitchen can so deliciously provide. After the guests had finished the last morsel they could put away, the regimental band played for dancing.

As Damien swept Lavinia onto the floor, her thoughts were transported back to the ball at Mulberry. It seemed a lifetime ago. He steered her carefully through the waltz, trying not to put too much strain on her tender ankle. It didn't matter as long as she was in his arms. His cheek against her forehead felt smooth and warm, sending familiar little thrills to her heart. She sighed and closed her eyes, drinking in his nearness with her other senses.

"I've missed you," he whispered. "Every night while I was away I thought about how much I wanted to be holding you close. This isn't just Jack and Mattie's honeymoon night. It's ours as well. Can we slip away soon, darling?"

For the first time Lavinia was glad she'd been ill. Her convalescence offered the perfect excuse for her to go up to bed before the last of the guests left.

She looked up into Damien's eyes, savoring their warm brown depths. "I'll make our excuses to Mattie," she said in a husky whisper. "She'll understand."

But the war intruded even upon the wedding. With so many generals in attendance, a strategy meeting seemed called for. Lavinia sat staring at the door to the smoking room as an hour, then two dragged by. Would they never be done with their war council?

Little did she or any of the other guests realize how important this planning session was. The war was about to come to their very doorsteps. Federal General Buell had been replaced by a more determined commander, Major General William Starke Rosecrans. "Old Rosy," as he was known to his men, even at that moment had Murfreesboro in his sights. If he could rid that Tennessee town of the Confederate Army, he could place at the Union's disposal the main road and rail routes to Chattanooga. The next step, of course, would be total Federal control of the entire state. Lavinia might not have guessed all this, but the wedding guests locked away behind the smoking-room door were as certain of Old Rosy's intentions as they were that tomorrow would follow today.

The hour had crept past midnight before Lavinia and Damien could be alone. The last guest had departed, the servants and family were all abed, and somewhere in the big house on Main Street, John Hunt Morgan was lovingly stealing his bride's virginity, a theft Martha Ready had dreamed of for too long a time, she felt.

Once Lavinia and Damien could be alone together, the necessity to hurry their lovemaking seemed to vanish. For long moments they stood in the center of the dark bedroom clinging to each other, but there was no desperate haste in their long, languid kisses, no frantic need to rush the ultimate act. When they had their fill for the moment of each other's lips, Lavinia lit the lamp. Damien stood a few feet away, staring at her as if he meant to fill his mind with the sight of her.

"How have you been, darling?" he asked quietly, but not in a casual manner.

Lavinia was taken aback. She had told him of her sprained ankle but had passed lightly over her ordeal in the snow and her slow recovery. Now she gave him the details, trying to make her near-brush with death sound almost like an amusing adventure. She carefully omitted Sam Coltrain's name from the account.

"By damn! You do get yourself into some fixes, Lavinia! Who was the chap that hauled you in out of the blizzard?"

Lavinia had been laughing, caught up in her own comical-sounding recounting of the accident. But Damien's sudden, unexpected question turned her solemn in a flash.

"What's wrong, Lavinia?" Damien asked, his own mirth dying as well.

"I hadn't meant to tell you." She hesitated.

Damien strode to where she stood and took her upper arm in a firm grip. "Dammit, Lavinia, I won't have you keeping secrets from me! Has something been going on while I was away? Who was the man? I demand to know!"

She couldn't face him as she answered, "It was Sam Coltrain."

For a moment Damien was stunned speechless. When words came they sounded bitter and tormented. "That unholy bastard!"

"He saved my life, Damien." She covered her mouth quickly with her hand. She hadn't meant to say anything like that.

"What do you mean?"

"Well, it's just that it was snowing so hard that day. With my sprained ankle I couldn't have made it back to the house, not even if I'd been conscious."

"You mean you were lost out there in a snowstorm, injured and unconscious! My God, Lavinia, you didn't make it sound that serious!" He pulled her into his arms, crushing her against his chest. "I could have lost you!"

"Yes, but Sam Coltrain saved me." Before his anger could flare again, she hurried on. "Don't you see? I'm sure it was fate that prompted me to beg for his life in the cave. If you had shot him, I'd be dead now too!"

He stared down at her with a puzzled frown on his face. "Do you really believe that, Lavinia?"

"Yes, I do, Damien."

"Well, if it's so, I'm glad I spared him. But I can't honestly say that I'll be comfortable knowing that he's still lurking about."

"But he's gone now, Damien. He must be. I haven't seen him since. I'm sure he's far away, probably headed back north."

"I hope so, for his own sake! I can't promise what I'd do if I had a second opportunity to aim at him and fire."

Suddenly, Damien's eyes took on an expression that was unmistakable to Lavinia. There was a certain liquid heat smoldering deep down beneath his half-closed lids. He was finished talking. The time for action had come. Lavinia watched as his hands reached out, grasping her rib cage gently and sliding down the thin fabric of her bodice to encircle her waist. She stood very still, feeling a lovely weakness sweep through her.

In one easy motion Damien drew her toward him, burying his lips in the soft fragrant curls that framed her face.

"I've missed you so, Lavinia!" he sighed into her ear. "You'll never know."

But she did know. She had ached for him, cried for him, prayed for him, while he was away. She had been only half a being without him.

"Damien . . ." she bagan, but his lips stopped her.

He kissed her with slow, deep determination to make her understand his fathomless need. While his lips possessed hers, his hands strayed about her body, stroking her back, fondling her neck, and finally pressing her breasts until they ached for more intimate exploration. By the time Damien broke their embrace, Lavinia knew that she must have him *soon*.

In a miracle of dexterity her husband whisked her out of her gown, lifting her into his arms to kiss the satiny nipples his hands has teased erect moments before. Lavinia gave a ragged sigh and arched her body toward him. He laid her on their bed, quickly stripping off his own clothes.

She took quick inventory of his naked body. Yes, it was still strong, unscarred by battle, and more than ready to join hers. She smiled and raised her arms to him. Damien sank down beside her with a grateful sigh. He kissed her all over, seemingly unable to have enough of her.

"Oh, love," he whispered, "you don't know how I've suffered waiting for this moment!"

She never got a chance to tell him she knew his suffering exactly, for the next instant he covered her, entered her, and brought her to the very brink of ecstasy. All thoughts were lost in a wonderful, soul-tingling barrage of sensation.

Chapter Twenty-Three

Something had to be done about General Rosecrans. He couldn't be allowed to sit comfortably in Nashville, such a short distance away, stockpiling arms and supplies all winter in anticipation of a major Federal attack come spring. Braxton Bragg knew it; Jack Morgan knew it. Every man who had been involved in the council of war the night of Morgan's wedding fully understood that fact. But it was the bridegroom himself who came up with a possible solution.

"If we cut the Federal supply lines from Louisville south to Nashville, Rosecrans will be too hard-pressed finding food for his troops to worry about planning attacks," Morgan told Bragg soon after the wedding. "I propose another raid into Kentucky. My men can be ready within the week. We'll turn the L and N tracks into nothing more than a useless collection of 'Morgan's Neckties.' "

General Braxton Bragg agreed.

Two days after the wedding Mattie and Lavinia had their pretty heads together making plans for the holidays.

"I think a Christmas ball would be the very thing," Mattie enthused, her silver-gray eyes all aglitter.

Lavinia could hardly disagree. Her own husband cut a fine figure on the ballroom floor. She loved the envious stares of the other women whose husbands or beaux were neither so graceful nor so handsome. And the thought of spending an evening in his arms anytime, anywhere, had its own vast appeal. Yes, a ball it would be!

But much as he usually responded to the siren song of Terpsichore, Damien frowned when Lavinia told him the happy news about plans for a holdiay ball.

"What's wrong? I thought you'd be delighted, darling. And I was so looking forward to seeing you decked out in your new major's uniform."

"Oh, you'll get to see that soon enough, Lavinia," Damien answered cryptically. In response to the quizzical look on her face, he said, "There's to be a full dress parade on December twenty-first."

"Here?" she asked, feeling an uneasiness growing inside.

"In Alexandria, Tennessee."

"Oh, that's only a short distance away," she said, relieved.

Damien Clay let the subject drop. If Lavinia didn't know that troops were moving out, that must mean that Mattie Morgan had no knowledge of it either. He hoped her husband would inform his new bride soon. Until the official word was out, he didn't feel it was his place to discuss Morgan's planned Christmas raid into Kentucky with anyone, not even with his wife.

At the same moment that Lavinia was quizzing Damien in their bedroom at the Ready home, John Hunt Morgan had Mattie in the parlor downstairs alone. For the first time the gallant Raider was faced with the exact predicament some of his friends had warned him of. His duty lay with planning and leading the raid. But in his heart he dreaded having to tell Mattie that he would be leaving her so soon. As yet he hadn't worked up the courage.

"A regimental review on Sunday!" Mattie cried delightedly, clapping her hands in glee. "Oh, my darling, what a wonderful idea for your men to put on a holiday show for the citizens of Murfreesboro."

Morgan couldn't meet her eyes as he said, "It won't be here, Mattie."

Her smile faded. "Not here? Where, then?"

"Up in Alexandria."

Mattie was frowning now, as much from confusion as from displeasure. "I don't understand, Jack. What is it you aren't telling me? Why Alexandria instead of Murfreesboro?"

Wanting to soften the blow he was about to deliver, Morgan pulled Mattie into his arms and kissed her quite thoroughly before answering.

His kiss only heightened her fears. At length, she drew away.

"Tell me, Jack. What's going on?"

"It's nothing really, Mattie." He tried to sound nonchalant. "Just a brief foray into southern Kentucky. The L and N has repaired the South Tunnel already. We need to ride up there and do a little damage to stop the supply trains from reaching General Rosecrans in Nashville. I'm moving men to Alexandria to get ready. A couple of days there, then we'll make our strike and ride right back. We won't be gone a week."

Mattie looked at him askance. "I've heard *that* before!"

He shrugged. "There's a war on, Mattie."

"And what about my Christmas ball?"

"I promise I'll be back in time." She looked unconvinced. "Really, Mattie! Trust me!"

She moved into his arms and leaned her head against his chest, fighting to keep control of the jealous feelings she harbored when making war took precedence over making love.

"I do trust you, Jack," she murmured softly. "And I love you so much!" She looked up into his worried face and gave him a brilliant smile. "The day in Alexandria will be wonderful! If the snow keeps up, we'll take the new sleigh. We'll pack a banquet lunch complete with champagne!"

His lips came down to caress hers.

"You're a wonder, Mrs. Morgan," he said softly.

"I have to be," she answered. "I married a hero!"

Sunday, December 21, dawned bright sapphire-blue. It was one of those rare winter days made for being out of doors after weeks of foul weather. Cold and brisk, but with a hint of warmth to the sun's golden gleam, it was a perfect day for a sleighride. Morgan and Damien had ridden down to Murfreesboro the night before to escort their wives to Alexandria for the regimental review. This was to be the grandest show Morgan had ever produced.

The two couples snuggled close in the shiny red sleigh, tucked cozily inside fur robes while the jaunty vehicle sped over the glittering ice-crusted snow. Down roads lined by leafless trees, the sleighbells jingled merrily, giving the entire setting a holiday atmosphere.

"Oh, it's going to be a grand day!" Mattie enthused. "Seven regiments! Can you believe it?" She turned, asking the question of Lavinia and Damien, who were huddled close in the back seat.

Lavinia, in spite of the dread she was feeling at the thought of Damien's leaving, couldn't help being infected by her friend's excitement.

"How many men in all, Mattie?" she asked.

Mattie looked to Morgan, but he was busy guiding the snow-white team over a treacherous patch of ice.

"Four thousand!" Damien volunteered. "The most your husband has ever commanded."

Mattie hugged Jack and cried, "Oh, I'm so proud of you, I could just burst!"

"Hey! Hey! Curb yourself, woman!" Morgan warned, laughing. "You'll have us pitched into a snowbank, surprising me like that. Now, if we had more time, I'd pull over and let you show me just how proud you are, but, alas, duty calls."

"Jack," Mattie whispered in a shocked tone, "what will Lavinia and Damien think with you talking that way?"

"I don't know. Why don't we ask them?" Handing the reins to his surprised wife, Morgan turned in the seat and said, "What about it, Clay? Shall we pull over for a bit?"

"You're in command here, General," Damien replied, grinning from ear to ear as he gave Lavinia's breast a firm squeeze beneath the carriage robe. "But you know me! I'll follow wherever you lead, willingly and enthusiastically!"

Taking the reins back in hand, Morgan urged the horses off

the road. He headed toward a copse of evergreens a few yards away.

"Jack," Mattie whispered. "What are you doing? I won't be hauled off to the woods like this! It isn't ladylike. Why, it isn't even civilized!"

He leaned down to peck at her cheek. "You never said that when I took you to the woods before we were married."

"Well, that was different!" She sat up straighter and smoothed the robe primly, her mouth set in a pout.

"Different how, darling?"

"For one thing, you weren't a general then."

"Oh, I see!" Morgan replied with an exaggerated nod. "You'll let a colonel haul you off to wherever he pleases, but not a general!"

"Now you're making fun of me! I meant only that such cavorting about is beneath you now."

Morgan leaned down very close so that the other pair couldn't hear his reply. "The only thing I want beneath me, my precious love, is you!"

Mattie gave a horrified cry, but at the same time his words started a hot pulse beating deep inside her. They were in the woods now and Morgan pulled back on the reins to stop the horses. He leaned down to steal a kiss from his wife. She objected only momentarily, saying, "What about Damien and Lavinia?"

Morgan glanced over his shoulder. Their two companions were all but lost in the tangle of bear robes and each other's arms. He didn't even bother to answer Mattie's question but took her into his arms and pressed her back against the red leather seat, searching her mouth with loving thoroughness.

If anyone at the parade ground in Alexandria noticed that Mrs. Morgan's cheeks were a brighter pink than normal or that Mrs. Clay's hair was mussed a bit, they undoubtedly attributed both to the ladies' twenty-five-mile sleighride. No one would have guessed that the two officers' wives had been involved recently in some heavy petting with their husbands, nor would they have mentioned such minor imperfections in the lovely pair.

The reviewing stand was crowded with officers and their wives, decked out in their holiday togs for this grand occasion. General John Hunt Morgan took the seat of honor with his bride of a week at his side. The crowds cheered him when he arrived and continued their shouts and Rebel yells for some time.

Mattie touched Jack's arm, leaned close, and whispered, "They love you almost as much as I do, darling."

Morgan smiled down at her. Their time in the woods had mellowed her "general's wife demeanor" considerably. He liked her this way, all soft and feminine and adoring.

Lavinia and Damien, sitting in the seats next to the Morgans', were lost in their own world. The few intimate moments stolen in the back of the sleigh had served only to fan the flames inside them. Lavinia clung to Damien's arm, feeling his taut muscles beneath the fabric of his uniform. At the same time, she was conscious of his eyes on her, watching every move she made. He had tried to make her stay in Murfreesboro, afraid that Sam Coltrain might still be lurking about.

"I'm not afraid of him," Lavinia had insisted. "And I won't be cheated out of our last hours together before the raid. I am going to Alexandria! That's final, Damien!"

Wanting to be with her every bit as much as she wanted to be with him, Damien had spoken to Jack Morgan about a military escort for their wives' return to Murfreesboro.

"A fine idea!" Morgan had replied. "I can't be too careful now that Mattie and I are married. Those Yankees are unscrupulous bastards. I wouldn't put it past them to take my wife hostage to get at me. Consider it done, Clay!"

So now they would have their last night together. Secretly, Damien wondered just how long he would be away. Morgan might have his bride convinced that they would be back in Murfreesboro for the holiday gala, but Damien wouldn't place any bets on it.

Lavinia glanced up and caught him still staring at her. Their eyes met and held. Then slowly his gaze slipped down, kissing her lips visually, stroking her lace-encased throat, fondling her full breasts through the amber-colored velvet of her dress. Lavinia felt his burning look as surely as if his flesh were pressing hers. It sent a delicious tingling sensation rippling through her.

She smiled and blew him a kiss. "How long will this last, Damien?"

He heaved a sigh. "All day, I'm afraid."

They settled back for their long wait. Soon the blare of bugles signaled the start of the review. For hours on end Lavinia and Damien watched as horses pranced by, flags waved brightly in the crystalline air, and firearms glittered in the warm sunshine. They knew the end was approaching when John Hunt Morgan left his seat in the reviewing stand. A few moments later a roar went up from the thousands of soldiers and spectators. Down the field came the leader of the Raiders—General John Hunt Morgan himself. He sat Glencoe like a centaur while the thoroughbred high-stepped the length of the parade ground. When he reached the reviewing stand, Morgan doffed his plumed hat and swooped it toward his bride in salute. Glencoe reared high, pawing the air while the handsome general waved and smiled. The crowd went wild. Rebel yells split the air once more. Feet stamped and bugles chorused. How could anyone think of war as terrible when it offered patriotic moments as grand as this?

By the time Morgan reached the end of the parade ground, women all about were tugging lacy handkerchiefs from their sleeves to dab at heartfelt tears of Southern pride. And not a few of the soldiers were surreptitiously sniffling right along with the women.

"Oh, Lavinia!" Mattie sighed, not even trying to hide her happy tears. "Isn't he wonderful!"

Lavinia glanced up at Damien, feeling a tug at her own heartstrings. "He certainly is!" she replied, and slipped her hand into her husband's.

Damien shook Lavinia gently. "Time to get up, darling. We move out at dawn."

Lavinia snuggled her naked body closer to her husband's

abundant warmth and made a purring sound in response. He let her stay a moment longer while he stroked her shoulders, back, and thighs. She arched closer still, obviously ready for more lovemaking.

Damien stared at her through the semi-darkness of predawn. This was the picture he wanted to carry in his mind until he could be back with Lavinia once more. She lay on her side, facing him, with her hair spilling in a tumble of dark reddish gold over her arm. Her lips were curved in the slightest smile, her eyes closed. With the edge of his hand he traced the soft rise of her hip. She responded to his touch, moving the lower part of her body in a wavelike manner. Finally, his hand reached her breasts, fondling the nipples, which looked like wide eyes against her pale skin. Lavinia sighed, licked her lips, and lay back.

Damien hesitated. The bugler had blown the morning call some time before. But how could he leave her like this? He leaned down and took her lips. Her body bowed upward against his and a moment later he took all the rest of her.

This shared ecstasy was made all the sweeter by their knowledge that it would be their final intimacy for a time. Damien lingered over his caresses. Lavinia held back, savoring the tender pleasures of their closeness, not wanting the soul-tingling, earth-shattering climax to come in a sudden flood.

But at last there was no holding back. The sweet deluge came. They clung fiercely, feeling the melding of body and soul, heart and mind.

Afterward, they dressed quickly. The troop was assembling and almost ready to leave. Dawn was just breaking, but for a soldier the morning was well along. When they reached the parade ground, the first regiments were moving out.

"Damn your hide, Major Clay!" Morgan called. "I was about to leave without you. Why are you late?"

Lavinia, her gown buttoned wrong in her haste, clung to her husband's arm, fighting back tears. Damien turned and kissed her quickly. Their good-byes had already been said.

"Sorry, General! I was delayed by . . ." He paused for a final glance at Lavinia. "By family matters."

Morgan chuckled and leaned toward Damien. "I know what you mean. I was almost late myself."

Mattie found Lavinia and came to stand beside her, taking her hand. Together the two women not only watched but felt their husbands' departure for battle. The sound of sixteen thousand hoofbeats rumbled through the early air, blocking out all other noise. They stood there long after the men had disappeared over the horizon, still listening to the rolling thunder in the distance.

"They're gone!" Lavinia said at last in a trembling voice.

"But they'll be back!" Mattie assured her.

Damien was back sooner than expected. Just before midnight on Christmas Eve, Annie Flowers came roaring up Main Street on a horse that was winded and lathered.

"My Lord!" Mattie exclaimed. She had been standing at the front window, praying for a message from Jack. "A woman on horseback is coming this way, riding like the devil himself is on her heels!"

Lavinia, who had been trying to concentrate on the latest war sketches in *Harper's Illustrated*, threw the magazine aside and ran to look out.

"It's Damien!" she cried, tearing for the front door.

When she flung it open, her husband—a bedraggled-looking woman who obviously needed a shave—came stumbling into her open arms.

"Thank God, you're all right!" were his first gasping words.

"All right? What do you mean?"

She led him into the parlor, where Mattie was already pouring a tumbler of brandy.

"It's Rosecrans!" he said between gulps. "He's planning an attack!"

"Now? In the middle of the winter?" Mattie was incredulous. "Why, that's foolish in this weather!"

"That may be, but he's moving his troops onto the pike tomorrow, headed for Murfreesboro!"

Both women gasped aloud.

"Where's Jack?" Mattie demanded. "Why did you ride in alone?"

"Jack's in Kentucky. He doesn't know anything about this. He's gone ahead with his plan. The Raiders should be in Glasgow tonight if all has gone well.

"We captured a deserter from Rosecrans's forces our first day out and he gave us some jumbled bits and pieces of information," Damien explained. "None of what he said made much sense, but all of it sounded highly suspicious. So Jack sent me to Nashville to see what information Annie Flowers could pick up. By the time I uncovered the entire plan from a rather overamorous sergeant, the Raiders were too far away for me to alert them and then get back here to tell General Bragg in time. So they'll just have to go on with their Kentucky raid and we'll have to make do without them."

"So this is really serious?" Mattie asked.

"*Damn* serious, if you'll pardon the expression!"

"What'll we do?" Lavinia asked.

Damien took his wife's trembling hand in his and brought her fingertips to his lips. "You'll have to do just like everybody else—pack up to evacuate and pray you don't have to go through with it. There's a good chance we can drive Rosecrans's troops back up the pike. If not, we'll have to hold them at Stones River."

"And if you can't do that?"

Damien didn't answer Lavinia's question. They all three knew what would happen if Bragg couldn't hold Rosecrans. It was too depressing even to discuss.

Lavinia, once she got over the shock of Damien's news, let herself rejoice for a moment in his safe return. Her thoughts turned to spending her first Christmas with her husband. But it was not to be. Damien stayed at the Ready residence only long enough to change clothes, gulp down some cold cornbread and bacon, and then he was off once more. Again Lavinia was left to wonder where he was going and for how long.

As any patriotic hostess would, Mattie Morgan immediately canceled her Christmas ball. Then, sending servants flying with her orders, she whipped the household into evacuation status. Never a tear from her or an uncertain move, she was all cold command, the general's wife to the core.

On December 26 General William S. Rosecrans moved his force of forty-seven thousand out of Nashville, headed southeast to strike a blow at the Army of Tennessee, Braxton Bragg's troops, which numbered fewer than thirty-eight thousand with Morgan still in Kentucky. But weather and Joe Wheeler's cavalry were against Old Rosy. Over the next four days Rosecrans had to fight hard for every one of the twenty-five miles of turnpike he took. Cold rain and fog retarded his progress, and at each turn in the road, it seemed, "Fighting Joe" Wheeler was waiting.

It was late on Monday, December 29, when Rosecrans halted his troops at their destination. Directly in front of him lay Murfreesboro and all routes south. To get to the town, however, he had to first fight his way through Braxton Bragg and the icy waters of Stones River. He vowed to attack at dawn.

Although the silver and crystal were packed, and the wagons were ready for a quick escape as soon as the fighting started, the first shots did not budge the stubborn Ready family.

"Bragg will hold!" Mr. Ready declared. "Our leaving would only show our lack of faith in his ability. So I plan to remain exactly where I am to welcome our conquering army!"

"I agree totally, Father," Mattie said.

"Now, see here! I don't mean for you girls to stay. You need to get your mother away from here. All this noise and excitement. It's bad for her heart!"

But Mattie refused to go, and Lavinia couldn't leave until she knew Damien was all right.

Word reached town by messenger late on the thirtieth that Bragg had routed the Yankees.

"Gall darnedest thing you ever saw!" the cold, wet private told the Readys and Lavinia. "Old Rosy figured he was pulling a pretty smart bluff on us, built a bunch of camp fires last night way off to the right where he didn't have no men. General Bragg, he fell for it, thinking we'd have to swing wide to get around their lines. He sent us on around that way, but there wasn't no troops. Just fires. 'Fore we knowed what was happening, we was clean around the flanks and closing from the rear and front all at once. Old Rosy's plan had plumb backfired. You never seen such a panic. Them fool Yankees was hauling tail ever' which a way! Yes, siree! We got 'em on the run!''

The country the men were using as a battleground consisted of cedar forests, and generally level fields marked with limestone outcroppings and small hillocks. There were a few buildings about—the Cowan house, the Griscom place, and the Widow Smith's. But nobody was home when Rosecrans knocked. So the Yankees helped themselves to the leftover cotton still standing in the boles in the widow's field, stuffing it in their ears so they wouldn't have to hear themselves shooting and getting shot at.

But the people in town didn't have cotton wool in their ears. They heard, and they knew that Bragg might have won the first battle, but he sure as hell hadn't won the war. Not yet, anyway.

At noon on the last day of 1862, while shots still rang out in the distance, Lavinia made her decision.

"I'm going to find him, Mattie! I can't just sit here wondering any longer."

Mattie Morgan eyed her friend with a brave, proud smile, even though she had tears in her eyes. Lavinia stood before her in the most outlandish outfit Mattie had seen since Damien Clay rode in on Christmas Eve. They were a pair! she vowed.

"Where on earth did you get the Zouave's uniform, Lavinia?"

"Made it myself the first time I joined up!" Lavinia said proudly. She leaned forward and scooped her long hair into a hat, then saluted and said in a deep voice, "Private Vinnie Rutledge, Company K of the Wiregrass Rifles, at your service, ma'am!"

Mattie ran forward, hugging her friend, laughing and sobbing all at once. "Do take care, Lavinia!"

"Don't you worry about me none, ma'am," Lavinia replied

in her best South Georgia drawl. "This here soldier-boy plans on taking mighty good care of hisself!"

It was almost dark by the time Lavinia rode into the lines. The shooting had slacked off. The wounded were being tended. And out there in the gathering shadows she could hear the dying calling out for help. A cold shudder ran through her. She wandered aimlessly for a time, searching for Damien, then when that seemed hopeless, looking for someone in charge.

"You there, soldier!" a gruff voice called.

Lavinia turned and saw that the medical officer meant her. "Yes, sir?"

"If you aren't wounded, you shouldn't be in the hospital zone. Where's your company?"

"I don't have one, sir. I'm on special duty, assigned to Major Damien Clay. If you could tell me where to find him, I'd be mighty obliged."

It was one chance in a million that the surgeon would even know Damien's name, much less where he was at this moment. She held her breath and offered up a prayer.

"Major Clay's over there in the general's tent," the doctor said, then he turned back to this patients.

Lavinia picked her way carefully among rows of wounded lying on the ground. Those that were conscious called out to her and raised their arms, pleading to be tended. There was nothing she could do. She tried not to look at their bloody clothes and gaping wounds.

An aide stood outside General Bragg's tent. "State your business!" the soldier demanded when Lavinia approached.

"Special assistant to Major Clay," Lavinia replied importantly. "Is he with the general?"

A moment later Damien Clay poked his head through the tent flap. He was frowning, obviously unaware of who his "special assistant" might be. The moment he spotted the over-sized Zouave's uniform, the frown turned into a grin. An instant later he had "Private Vinnie" in his arms, planting a firm kiss on her lips as Bragg's astonished aide looked on.

"Damn your hide, Lavinia, I should have known I couldn't trust you to stay put!"

"Hell, no, you couldn't! I've about had all I'm willing to take of these separations. From here on out I'm your wife 'for better or for worse.' If that means taking my chances on a battlefield, I'm willing. What I'm not willing to do is sit back home, stewing over whether you're alive or dead. Now, I mean it, Damien! Don't you try to give me any back talk! I found you and I mean to stick to you, close as a chigger to a hound dog. So just don't you start talking ing about sending me back to Murfreesboro, because if you do . . ."

Lavinia never got to finish her tirade. Damien's lips swallowed whatever else she might have said and he kept her clamped in an embrace for so long that when it ended she came up breathless.

"Well, now! Does that settle the matter to your satisfaction?"

Lavinia grinned at her husband. "Damien, do you mean it? I can stay? *Really?*"

He pulled her close enough to let her feel his erection through her Zouave's britches.

"Damien!" she protested softly, since the aide was still all eyes. But she soon forgot the nosy man. If anything he saw shocked him, it was his own damn fault for eavesdropping, she decided. She let herself sag against her husband, luxuriating in the feel of his heat.

"I think you'd better stay," he whispered. "Ever since I left you without so much as a teaser on Christmas Eve, I've been having an awful time sitting my horse!"

The two didn't have much time for showering affection on each other, and found no privacy at all. By full dark Bragg's troops were drawn up close to Stones River. Just over the water they could see the campfires of Rosecrans's men. It was New Year's Eve, the final hours of 1862, a long and bloody year. Both armies had their minds on what the coming year would bring. Every man wondered if he would still be around this time next year . . . or even this time tomorrow.

The night was cold and heavy with mists and expectations.

General Bragg had announced to his men, "God has granted us a happy New Year." He was sure of Rosecrans's defeat.

Across the river the Northern generals gathered together for a council of war. "Pap" Thomas, a tough old warlord who had been in the thick of the fight all day, leaned back in his chair and drowsed off while the others talked. General Rosecrans was in complete agreement with General Bragg. He figured he was licked. His main consideration now was pulling back with as few additional casualties as possible. The word *retreat* wormed its way from Rosecrans's speech into Thomas's light slumbers. Pap roused himself enough to boom, "This army can't retreat!" then dropped off again. The others took his word for it. There would be no retreat. They would stand their ground and fight, by God!

Just before tattoo the regimental bands on both sides of Stones River began playing. Lavinia lay cradled against Damien's shoulder, staring up at the frosty stars. The music soothed her and set her dreaming of happier days back home in Thunderbolt. A tear dribbled out of the corner of her eye. Damien leaned down and kissed its silver trail.

Midnight was at hand. The men were restless, some in pain, all thinking of home and loved ones. Low humming moved like a wave down the line, then here and there a voice broke out in song.

Suddenly, the night came alive with music. From the far bank the Billy Yanks blared out "Yankee Doodle." The Johnny Rebs battled back with "Dixie."

Damien and Lavinia held each other and sang at the top of their lungs: "Oh, I wish I were in the land of cotton/Old times there are not forgotten/Look away, look away, look away, Dixie Land!" Tears were streaming from Lavinia's eyes now and her heart was beating with the same thunder as the drums.

A Yankee volley of "Hail Columbia" soon drowned out "Bonnie Blue Flag." Back and forth the battle raged, musical shot answering musical shot until it seemed the night had burst forth with brass and percussions.

Suddenly, somewhere along the line—it could have come from either side of the river—the mournful cry of a harmonica cut thinly through the brass barrage. The sweet strains of "Home Sweet Home" floated tremulously on the misty, cold air. The bands hushed. The voices died. Only the lone mouth organ filled the night with a bittersweet melody.

The singing began slowly—a lone voice here, a chorus there, until thousands of voices raised the familiar refrain. The bands on both sides joined in. Lavinia felt goose pimples crawl along her flesh, and she was beyond putting a halt to her flood of tears.

For the briefest time on that New Year's Eve, all separating lines disappeared. There was no Blue, no Gray—no Yankee, no Rebel—no black, no white—*no war*!

Long after the last strains faded and the last voice died, the momentary truce lingered in their hearts much like the after-glow of a lover's heartfelt kiss. Lavinia and Damien lay in each other's arms, trying to hold on to the feeling.

"Will the world ever be sane again, Damien? Will you and I ever have a 'Home Sweet Home'?"

He kissed her tenderly before he answered. "Yes, my darling. Soon, I promise you!"

But the only promise that hideous night offered was death. Orders passed down the line that no campfires were to be lit. A thick, frigid mist seemed to drift down from the sliver of pale moon overhead. The fog shrouded the landscape—freezing the dead, the dying, and the waiting in the mud where they lay. Lavinia stayed all night in Damien's arms, shivering as much from the agonized cries filling the night as from the marrow-deep cold in her bones.

So this was war! A freezing, muddy nightmare of fear and darkness and anguish. Why did men bother? she wondered. Where was the glory?

She watched the sun rise, red and bloody through the mists. Dawn came and went, but the cold remained. Some men's fingers froze to their triggers, and it seemed that General Bragg was frozen into inaction. Instead of attacking at first light, he let his moment pass. Rosecrans, pleasantly surprised when he was not called upon to defend himself before he was ready, made no move to retreat, but awaited his opportunity to take the offensive.

"Damn!" Damien cursed to Lavinia. "What can Bragg be thinking? He's wired Richmond that we've won, but he refuses to secure the action with a final attack."

"Why don't you tell him, darling?" Lavinia asked in all seriousness.

He gave a humorless laugh. "Generals don't take orders from lowly majors, my love. If only Morgan were here!"

But John Hunt Morgan was far away in Kentucky, winning the battles he waged. He did not even know about the debacle taking place at Stones River.

On January 2 Braxton Bragg finally decided—too late—to push. Rosecrans was ready for him, crushing the Rebel forces with ease. That night Lavinia and Damien were among the ragtag army caught up in the Confederate retreat.

"We're not licked yet," he told her as they rode hard back toward Murfreesboro.

But Lavinia, her heart heavy, could tell by his tone that Damien wasn't convinced by his own words.

Chapter Twenty-Four

Damien Clay proved a great help in evacuating the Ready family from Murfreesboro after Braxton Bragg's untimely defeat at Stones River. This most recent Union victory was the third in Tennessee, coming on the heels of Fort Donelson and Shiloh. The Confederacy could ill afford such major losses.

With haste and horror the family fled forty miles east to McMinnville, while Bragg retreated to Tullahoma. John Hunt Morgan, returning from a glorious two-week victory in Kentucky, rode on to join his wife, wondering what would happen next.

The winter wore on, severe and depressing. The civilians who had fled Murfreesboro were short of supplies and shelter. The soldiers of the Confederacy were lacking in food, equipment, and ammunition. Still, Mattie Morgan and Lavinia, living in log huts in Morgan's camp, were blissfully happy with their men always at their beck and call. Some of Morgan's detractors claimed that he stayed too close to his wife, that his appetite for battle had waned with his marriage. But Mattie let all that go over her head.

Writing to her sister, Alice, who was in Nashville, she said, "My life is one joyous dream now, from which I fear to awaken. I know my leige-lord is devoted to me, and each day I am forced to love him more."

Lavinia wrote similar glowing sentiments to her father at

318

Thunderbolt. Her communications with the family had been spotty at best since she had left. She now hungered for news from home, and wrote long letters to Rambeau Rutledge, pleading with him to answer back with the lastest family happenings. In May, a letter from her father finally caught up with Lavinia.

Thunderbolt
February 2, 1863

My dearest Vinnie,

I cannot begin to tell you how Josiah's return gladdened my heart! If only you were home with us, life would seem almost normal and complete once again. But I understand from your brother that you are well, happy, and intent upon remaining at your husband's side. So be it!

You surprised me greatly with the letter reporting your marriage to Captain Clay. You have my blessing, Vinnie, though I had hoped to see you married here as your mother and I were, and (now it is my turn for surprises) as I shall soon wed Sara Wentworth! I asked the dear lady to become my wife at Christmastime and—Glory be!—she said yes. So when you return, you will find some changes in the family.

As for the other existing member of the Wentworth clan, it seems your leaving played havoc with the poor boy's brain! You were hardly away before Randolph came home on leave and took to dropping by, as he explained, 'To keep Mallard company.' Turned out, though, that he was sneaking into the pantry with Miss Sammie Sue every chance that presented itself. She came up before long ripe as a melon in season! Mallard was fit to be tied! Had it not been for his injuries, he would have called young Wentworth out. As it was, Randolph and Sammie Sue lit out together and no one's seen hide nor hair of them since. (Don't dare tell Mallard I said so, but I think he's well rid of that prissy little baggage!)

Mallard left a few weeks ago to join his brothers in

Virginia. Jake sends word when he can. All the boys are hale and hearty. Elijah took a bullet through the hand back in December, but he's fine now. Just like him, too! He got shot reaching for a second helping from the cookpot!

Miss Sara and I are planning our wedding for the first of August. I'd be mighty proud and pleased if you could be here, honey. Josiah plans to stay until then. He needs a mite of fattening up after that prison camp. But he's raring to get back to the war as soon as he can.

Do take care of yourself, and tell my new son-in-law howdy for me. I send love and kisses.

> *Ever your affectionate Papa,*
> *Rambeau Rutledge*

P.S. How's that uppity wench, Helen-of-Troy? Give her my regards and tell her she'd better be getting on home now. I don't see how I can get through this wedding without her!

Damien came into the cabin just as Lavinia was folding the letter after reading it. The tears streaming down her cheeks alarmed him.

"What's wrong, darling?" he asked, kneeling beside her chair and taking her hands in his.

She sniffed, smiled, and answered, "Oh, nothing really. I guess Papa's letter just made me homesick."

Damien reached up and brushed a tear-dampened strand of hair back from his wife's cheek. "It's understandable that news from home would make you a little blue. You've been gone over a year now, darling. Wouldn't you like to go to Thunderbolt for a visit? I hate your having to live this way, in a drafty log cabin with only the bare necessities. You should have a real home."

Lavinia leaned down and brushed his forehead with her lips. "Damien, my dear, when are you going to get it through your head that my only home is whatever shelter I share with you?"

"I feel the same way, Lavinia," he said quietly, staring into her eyes with a tenderness that caused a quickening deep inside her.

"Papa does want Helen-of-Troy sent back, though. She's needed to help with the wedding."

"Wedding? Who's getting married? Josiah?"

"No!" she laughed. "Papa and Sara Wentworth."

"Why, the old scamp!"

"She's loved him for years," Lavinia explained. "But Papa would never allow himself to believe it. He was so set on the fact that I was going to marry Randolph someday."

Before Lavinia could tell Damien about Randy and Sammie Sue, Jack Morgan knocked and strode in.

"I need to talk to you immediately!" he said.

"Do you want me to come over to your headquarters now?" Damien asked.

"No! We can talk here. Both of you are involved in this."

Damien and Lavinia exchanged curious glances.

Morgan pulled up a chair and straddled it. There was a glow to his face that neither of them had seen all through the long, dull winter. Something was definitely up!

"I've just been in conference with Bragg," Morgan began. "He believes that with the Raiders' help he can retake eastern Tennessee. It will involve another raid into Kentucky. We need to throw Louisville into a panic." He gave a great laugh. "That should be a simple enough task. Of course, we'll pay our usual respects to the L and N along the way." He leaned close and glanced over his shoulder before he continued. "This is going to be the big one! We're going to move this war right into Yankeeland! I'll take Louisville all right. But then we'll head farther north. I plan to cross the Ohio River into Indiana."

Damien frowned. Lavinia caught her breath.

"Bragg approved this?" Damien asked.

"Not yet, but what he doesn't know won't hurt him. Besides, the Raiders are my men. They take their orders directly from me!"

"How do we figure in all this?"

Lavinia was glad Damien asked the question. Her curiosity was as powerful as Stonewall the cat's.

"You two did your sister act so well in Louisville before that I want you to do it for me one more time. I'll send a man along with you to pass information back to me. I want to know every move the Yankees are making in and around Louisville—numbers, troop movements, supplies, and any rumors you happen to pick up."

"When do we leave?" Damien asked, squeezing Lavinia's hand in his excitement.

"As soon as possible!"

Lavinia felt her emotions warring within her. She, too, was affected by the excitement of a new assignment with her husband. But she had hoped against hope that she might get back to Thunderbolt for her father's wedding. Still, that was several months away. Maybe they would finish in time.

"Then it's all set!" Morgan said, rising. "Get packed and be on your way—*yesterday*!" He paused at the door and looked back at them. "Oh, and one more thing. When you're done with this job, I want the pair of you to take some time off. You will have earned it."

Damien and Lavinia prepared for their journey in less time than even John Hunt Morgan would have thought possible. By mid-afternoon, the "sisters" were gowned and in the saddle, ready to ride. The farewells said by Mattie and Helen-of-Troy to Lavinia were spoken with enough tears to drown an army.

"I'm gonna see you back at Thunderbolt come wedding time, Miss Vinnie?" the servant asked. She had just started packing for her own trip back to Georgia.

"Count on it, Helen-of-Troy!" Damien answered for his wife.

"Do be careful, you two," Mattie cautioned. "I'm still going to have that Christmas ball—just as soon as this war's over. And of course I want you there!"

Lavinia leaned down and hugged her friend one last time, then she and Damien were off.

Their traveling companion and courier was a young corporal who'd been born and brought up on a farm just below the Falls of the Ohio from Louisville. Hollis Shyrock knew the territory and he had connections by blood and marriage all over Jefferson County and its environs.

"Yes, sir, Major Clay, there ain't a soul up that way don't know some of my kin—that is, if they ain't kin their own selves."

"You're a good man, Shyrock!" Damien praised him. "I'm sure you'll be a great help to us."

Hollis was a good "man," though he was barely seventeen years old. He proved his worth in the next few weeks, leading Damien and Lavinia to parts of Louisville they wouldn't have thought of as being militarily important, and opening doors with his family connections that would have remained closed to the two "sisters." With his open, boyish face and innocent, outgoing personality, Hollis Shyrock did more than his duty. And long after Damien and Lavinia fell into their boarding-house bed, too exhausted even to make love, young Hollis was riding through the night, sending messages on their way back to John Hunt Morgan.

Early one morning in June, Hollis returned from a meeting with his courier contact, bringing a note from Morgan addressed to Damien Clay. Damien and Lavinia were awake, but not receiving at the moment as they rode passion's wave—destination, ecstasy!

They heard the pounding at their door, but waited to answer it until they had reached the heights.

Damien, naked and still aroused, climbed out of bed with a disgusted snort. Pulling on a robe, he leaned down to kiss Lavinia's throbbing breast and said, "Hate to leave you like this, darling, but it seems either duty or the landlady always calls at the most inopportune times."

Lavinia snuggled into the pillows and drifted back to her pleasant dreams. She had such a lovely surprise for Damien! She'd meant to tell him this morning. But it could wait.

"Great news!" Damien shouted from the doorway, waving Morgan's message in his hand. "We're going home, Lavinia!"

She sat up in bed, hardly able to believe her ears. "Home?" she breathed.

They planned to go—immediately. If Hollis Shyrock's third cousin twice removed hadn't told him about a band of Yankee deserters over in Bradenburg who wanted to join Morgan's Raiders, Lavinia and Damien would have left Kentucky that very day. But as it was, they only left Louisville.

"This will be our crowning achievement, darling," Damien told her as they rode toward Bradenburg later that day. "Can't you just see Jack Morgan's face when we ride back, bringing fresh recruits with us?"

Lavinia wasn't as excited about this maneuver as Damien and Hollis seemed to be. Things hadn't gone right all day. First, Hollis's interruption, then she'd had to run for the slop jar when she got out of bed, and now this detour on the road home. She had half a mind to tell them both either to take her to Tennessee right now or just to go to hell! But she didn't. She rode on feeling queasy in the stomach and light in the head, wishing they'd hurry and get to Bradenburg and have done with it.

They were riding through beautiful country. Lavinia, trying to forget her discomfort, scanned the landscape about them. Tall hickory, oak, and maple trees canopied the narrow road they traveled on through the hollow. The scrim of early-morning fog was just burning off. On either side of the road lay neat fields of burley tobacco. And dotting those fields stood barns where the green leaves would later be sorted, stripped, tied, and cured to a mellow gold. The lovely June fullness of the land seemed to stretch out before them like a painting on canvas as the red road wound toward Bradenburg.

But they never made it there.

"Major Clay," Hollis said in a peculiar, whispery voice, "something ain't right."

"What do you mean?"

"I ain't sure. I got a creepy feeling down the back of my neck. Spells trouble ever' time!"

Just at that moment a dozen or so Home Guards, their guns

blazing, came swooping down on them from a grove of trees up the road.

"The barn!" Damien yelled, shooting back as he spurred his horse toward a mud-chinked tobacco barn across a nearby field.

Lavinia's heart was in her mouth. Bullets were whizzing past her head. She leaned far forward, gripping her horse's mane to hang on. This was the first time she'd been under direct fire since the incident with the train at Cave City. She heard a sickening thud and a cry of pain behind her, but she dared not look back. The barn door stood open. She dug her heels into the horse's sides and sped into the hot, aromatic building. Damien and Hollis were right behind her. She heard the barn door bang shut even before she dismounted.

"Help me!"

Lavinia turned to see Hollis sliding, wounded, from his saddle. He collapsed on the ground, blood pumping from a wound in his chest. She tended him quickly, making a bandage out of strips of her petticoat while Damien held off the Home Guards, firing from a small window. Once Hollis was as comfortable as she could make him, Lavinia took up her gun and her position across the barn from Damien, blasting away when their tormentors rode too near.

"You all right?" Damien shouted to her in a brief moment of calm.

How should she answer that? She was anything but all right.

"I'm just fine, darling," she called back, and leveled her aim at an approaching rider.

All day they sweated it out. The Home Guards had them surrounded, and it was obvious that Hollis was gravely wounded. He lay unconscious on a stack of gunny sacks, bleeding heavily and suffering in the suffocating heat. The mingled sharp-sweet odors of sweat, blood, and tobacco inside the closed barn made Lavinia queasy. Her head pounded. How would they escape this time?

Damien took her aside finally. "You've got to get out of here. Go for help. It's our only chance. Maybe you can find those men in Bradenburg. I'll draw the Guards' fire to cover you and when I open the door, you ride like a bat out of hell, darling!"

"Damien, no!" she cried, giving way to a moment of feminine panic. "I won't leave you!"

Lavinia's voice intruded on Hollis's delirium and he moaned, "Oh, please! Don't leave me!"

Damien's jaw was set in a firm line. His face was drawn and grim. "Lavinia, do you want to see all three of us wind up dead?"

"But Damien . . ."

"No buts! You're our only hope. Saddle up!"

She caught him around the neck and hugged him, then kissed him deeply. This was her greatest challenge ever. They'd come through a lot, she and Damien. They'd fought the elements, the Yankees, their own jealousies and doubts. She wasn't about to give up now! Damien saw her determination when he looked down into her glittery green eyes. He smiled his encouragement and love.

"That's my girl! You can do it, Lavinia!"

Her shoulders and body protected by gunny sacks stuffed with tobacco, Lavinia, hugging her horse's neck, pounded to freedom while Damien drew the Home Guards' fire. She rode her mount to a lather, never daring to look back. Lungs aching, heart hammering, she made good her escape and sped toward Bradenburg.

She found the men who wanted to join Morgan's Raiders and they hurried back to the barn with her. Even as she approached, a cold hand gripped her heart. Why had the shooting stopped? As they reached the field she gave a small cry of horror mingled with disbelief. The barn door stood wide open and there was not a Home Guard in sight. She rode inside. All was dark and silent. The bloody sacks gave testament to the fact that this was the right barn. Broken tobacco poles strewn about showed evidence of a struggle. But there was no sign of Damien Clay or Hollis Shyrock now.

"Sorry, ma'am," one of the big Kentuckians said. "Reckon we're a mite too late. Ain't nothing we can do here. Might as well head south and hook up with General Morgan."

"No! You can't leave!" Lavinia cried hysterically. "You've got to help me find him. I can't do it all by myself! I want my husband back!"

The large blond-haired man shook his head sadly. "Won't be no problem to finding your husband, ma'am."

Lavinia brightened.

"They'll have taken him on to Louisville to the military prison."

"How long will they hold him for questioning?"

The Kentuckian she'd been talking with exchanged uneasy glances with one of his buddies before he answered somberly, "Won't be for questioning, ma'am. Begging your pardon, but like as not he'll hang!"

Back in Louisville, Lavinia checked into the boardinghouse. Methodically and in a daze she went about a normal daily routine, while in secret she scoured the city for leads. None of her contacts seemed to have any news of Damien, Hollis, or any prisoners recently brought in by Home Guards. Even the newspapers made no mention of the capture. It was as if they had vanished. She grew more restless and anxious with each passing hour.

By the third day Lavinia was sick with worry and frustration. And topping off everything else, she was sure she'd seen a one-armed man following her back to the boardinghouse the evening before. Could it be? Or was she only getting paranoid in her loneliness?

Lavinia was awakened by hammering at sunrise on the fourth day. Rising slowly from the protection of sleep, not wanting to face another day alone, she had trouble at first getting her bearings. The pounding continued, and finally she realized it was not inside her head but outside in the street.

She rose and looked out. Several workmen were busy building something down in the old fairgrounds. She watched for a time, wondering what it could be and why the men were at work so early. Then the structure began to take shape. *Gallows!*

Words that seemed to come from another lifetime drifted into her mind: *"Like as not he'll hang!"*

In a whirlwind of motion, frantic knowing that time was running out, Lavinia threw on her clothes and hurried to the military prison at the corner of Tenth and Broadway. One way or another she was determined to find out about Damien.

The sergeant on duty at the prison glanced up when she walked through the door. He took in her appearance at a glance—rumpled gown, mussed hair, but a beauty even if she was well-used. He hadn't seen this one walking the streets. She might be worth taking a shot at. She even looked comparatively clean, a rarity in women of her profession. He liked the way she edged up to his desk kind of shy-like.

"Excuse me, sir, but could you tell me if there's going to be a hanging today?" Lavinia's heart thundered in her breast. This was a trying enough experience without that grisly-faced soldier sizing her up as if she were his next course at dinner.

His ugly laugh made her cringe. "Maybe, maybe not!" He reached out and grabbed her hand, saying, "Enjoy a good hanging, do you, miss?"

"Maybe, maybe not!" she replied, pulling away from him.

"Oh, a feisty little wench, ain't you! I like that. Makes for a good time in the hay, if you get my meaning."

She ignored him. "I saw the gallows."

"Well, then your question don't need no answer, does it? Don't reckon we'd be paying a crew to build the scaffold and trapdoor if we wasn't figuring on dropping somebody through it. It'll happen about the middle of the afternoon."

"Who're they going to hang?" Lavinia asked, holding her breath.

"Ain't you the nosy one!" He leaned forward and winked at her. "If I tell you, will I see you there? Afterwards, maybe you and me could get together."

Lavinia averted her eyes. "Maybe, if you tell me who."

That ugly laugh again. "A *woman*, that's who!"

Lavinia's heart all but stopped. It had to be Damien!

"Just one?"

"Goddamn! How many you want? You ain't just nosy—

you're bloodthirsty as a wood tick! Sorry to disappoint you. They brung in a boy with her, but he up and cheated the hangman—died last night.''

Poor Hollis! Lavinia thought. But there was no time to mourn for the dead. It was the living who needed her.

Damien Clay sat in the hot stuffy cell, cursing his luck and the Yankees and thinking back over the past two days. If only they hadn't decided to go to Bradenburg . . . If only he'd been as alert as Hollis on the road . . . If only he'd been carrying more ammunition . . .

He shook his head and let it fall to his hands. *If* and *only* were mighty damn useless words now. And mere words weren't going to save him from the hangman's noose.

At least Lavinia had gotten away. His ammunition had run out, allowing the Home Guards to move in on the barn not an hour after she escaped. He'd put up a good fight when they burst in on him, but one man didn't carry much weight against a dozen or more. And poor Hollis, well, he'd been no use to anyone by then.

His trial, once they got back to Louisville, had been a farce. They'd hauled him before a hastily assembled military tribunal without allowing him council or witnesses in his defense. It seemed like his death warrant had been signed beforehand. In fact, one of the guards, laughing, had told him that was so.

They'd accused him of all sorts of outlandish crimes and treated him as an outlaw and a whore instead of a military prisoner. He'd stood there before the court in his dress with a white prisoner's sack over his head. And now he was to be hanged like a common thief instead of accorded an officer's right to a firing squad.

Well, he would have the last laugh, even if he wasn't around to enjoy it! Those fools thought they were hanging a woman. What a shock they'd be in for when they prepared his body for burial!

Damien hadn't realized he was laughing hysterically until one of the guards rapped on the bars and growled, ''Think it's

funny, eh? Well, we'll soon see if you can laugh in the hangman's face, missy!''

Damien stopped laughing. His head drooped lower. If only
he could see Lavinia once more before his time was up. Where
was she now? Did they get her, too? No! He couldn't let himself think about that.

Suddenly, it was too late to think about anything. They were
opening his cell door, tying his hands before him, leading him
out to ride his last mile.

Lavinia put in a full day before hurrying to the fairgrounds
for the four o'clock hanging. She still wasn't sure Damien was
the ''woman'' about to be executed, but she had to be ready
just in case.

She arrived early, but already a mob had gathered, bringing
along children, old folks, and family pets for the outing. They
lounged about on the grass, their picnic lunches spread. Occasionally, a false alarm—''They're coming!''—would ripple
through the crowd. Necks would crane and voices die down.
When nothing happened the crowd would return to their
lunches, their laughter, their fun.

But as the hour drew near, food was packed away in wicker
baskets and the throng moved nearer to the gallows, everyone
wanting a ringside view of the grisly spectacle. Almost smoth-
ered in the crush of the mob, Lavinia felt faint. She couldn't let
go now. She'd had a long, exhausting day, but it would be over
soon. She used a reserve of strength to push through the hot
bodies pressed close to hers.

Just a little longer, she told herself silently, gritting her teeth
and trying to calm her jangled nerves.

All of a sudden a whisper of anticipation hushed the milling
throng. Thin, faraway musical notes drifted on the stifling afternoon air. At first Lavinia thought she was imagining it. But
with each moment the sound grew louder and more distinct.
The somber notes of the ''Death March'' rolled down Broadway. The people around her oohed and aahed, bristling with
morbid curiosity.

''Fine day for a hangin'!'' she heard a man near her say.

"Damn right it is! Last one I seen, I got soaked to the skin watching. But I wouldn't of missed it for the world."

Lavinia cringed and looked away from the two grinning spectators.

"Here, Lem, boost little Ralphie up onto your shoulders so's he can see."

Lavinia stared in horror as the farmer hoisted up his little boy—no more than four—at his pretty wife's insistence.

"You hang on to Papa real tight now, Ralphie," the boy's mother cautioned. "I'm going to see can I get right up there and snip you a souvenir from the condemned."

Aghast, Lavinia watched as the woman brought a pair of scissors out of her apron pocket. She felt another wave of dizziness sweep over her. Perspiration beaded her forehead. She clenched her fists, determined not to give way to the weakness. Tears blurred her vision, but she swiped them away angrily.

The late-afternoon sun glinted off the polished brass instruments of the regimental band escorting the prisoner to the gallows. They were smartly uniformed, bringing back visions of Morgan's dress parades. The carriage with the prisoner inside finally rolled into view. At first Lavinia couldn't see as the mob thronged in, gaping and jostling. But the soldiers soon forced the people back.

Then Lavinia saw clearly. It was Damien! Her heart raced wildly.

She pushed her way through the crowd almost to the foot of the scaffold steps, where a soldier barred her way. "Back off now!" he growled at the crowd. "Give the prisoner room."

A moment later Damien Clay was escorted up the steps. He passed so close that Lavinia could almost reach out and touch him, but he looked straight ahead, never seeing her.

She felt hot and dizzy. The sun blazed down on her. She carried a parasol, but it was closed and at her side. It had a more important function to serve than to shade her from the sun.

Damien refused the white hood that the hangman offered. He stood tall and proud—the perfect lady.

"Any last words?" the attending minister asked.

"Wait!" Lavina cried. "Oh, please wait! You're making a mistake! My sister hasn't done anything!"

Damien's head jerked up and his eyes met Lavinia's. A soldier was restraining her at the foot of the steps.

"Could I embrace my little sister one last time?" Damien asked of the chaplain.

"As your final request," the minister replied.

"Oh, sister!" Lavinia cried, rushing to Damien.

She threw her body against his and whispered urgently, "We're getting out of here!"

Faster than the eye could see, Lavinia whipped the knife out of her parasol and cut Damien's bonds. Then, reaching under her skirt, she produced two pistols. She fired several warning shots into the air.

"Clear a path!" she yelled. "We're coming through!"

The stunned soldiers did as she ordered. Racing down the scaffold steps, Damien and Lavinia ran for the nearest horses. Everyone was still in shock. The screaming mob, dashing hysterically in all directions, further aided their flight.

But just as they were about to mount up and make their escape, a figure dressed all in black stepped toward them. The gun in his one hand was leveled at Damien's heart. He said not a word, but his intent was clear. Damien Clay might have escaped the hangman's noose, but he had not escaped death!

"Sam!" Lavinia gasped. "Please, no! For the love of God, don't do this!"

Sam Coltrain's eyes looked so cold and colorless that Lavinia's heart all but stopped. This stranger who haunted her now held Damien's life and her future in his one strong, unpredictable hand.

"Why don't you ask me for the love of *you*, Lavinia? For your love, we might bargain." Sam Coltrain's voice was ghostly quiet, chilling Lavinia with fear.

The three of them seemed frozen in time and space—Damien and Lavinia poised in mid-flight, Sam Coltrain holding them there. Lavinia couldn't find her voice. She could only plead silently with tear-filled eyes.

"Dammit, you men, get the prisoner!" the officer-in-charge commanded.

Time had run out. Sam had to shoot or let them go *now*. Lavinia stared directly into his eyes and begged, "Please, Sam, if you really love me . . . if you want me to be happy . . ."

Just then, one of the guards rushed forward, his gun aimed at Damien as well. Lavinia saw the indecision in Sam's face change to sudden painful realization, and then to resolve. He whirled, shielding Damien's body from the soldier's bullet. At the same instant he fired his own pistol. The soldier dropped. For a moment Sam Coltrain stayed on his feet. He looked stunned, but not seriously hurt.

"Thank you, Sam," Lavinia whispered.

"Hurry!" Damien urged. "More soldiers are coming!"

Damien and Lavinia leaped into their saddles. Their horses reared and charged off down Broadway. An instant later blood rushed from the wound in Sam Coltrain's chest and he crumbled to the ground.

"For love of you . . . be happy . . ." Sam gasped as he fell.

Lavinia neither heard nor saw what happened. Already their horses' hooves were eating up the road. They headed for the river at breakneck speed. There they would board the barge Lavinia had rented earlier in the day. Once they were in open water they would be safe.

Although the river was not far from the fairgrounds, the road seemed endless. She thought they would never make it. When at last the Falls of the Ohio came into view just ahead, she shouted, "Hallelujah!"

Damien added his Rebel yell to her benediction.

Hours later, as the mighty Ohio rocked them gently in its watery arms, Lavinia lay back in her husband's embrace, watching summer lightning knife through the dark clouds, turning them momentarily from purplish black to silver. They both felt spent after the day's anxiety and danger. But they were too happy to be back together, safe, and on their way home to want to sleep. Damien held his wife tenderly, kissing her from time to time, fondling his favorite parts of her.

"Papa's going to be real proud when we get back to Thunderbolt," she said with a secretive smile.

"You mean because of his wedding?"

"Oh, that, too."

"What else?" Damien asked, nibbling at her lips while one hand strayed inside her bodice.

She sighed and snuggled closer, luxuriating in his touch.

"He's finally getting something he's always wanted."

Damien laughed. "A son-in-law who wears a dress!"

"No, silly! A grandchild!"

Damien sat up straight, staring at the moonlight reflected in Lavinia's eyes. "You're sure?"

She nodded, shy with her husband suddenly.

"Well, I'll be damned! You really did it!"

"*We* did it, darling."

He was all over her, kissing, hugging, and murmuring love words. Suddenly, he released her and sat back on his heels, grinning.

"Which do you suppose it will be, Lavinia? A boy in skirts or a girl in britches?"

They fell into each other's arms, laughing their fool heads off. Then their mirth turned to a more flammable passion. It had been a long time. But there on the barge, cradled by the gentle river, they had all the time in the world.

Summer lightning flashed again, shedding silver on their naked bodies entwined in love.

AUTHOR'S NOTE

In the fall of 1983 I received an interesting newspaper clipping from Dr. Whitney McMath of Macon, Georgia. Her accompanying note said that since she had found the Confederate spy Antonia Ford a fascinating historical character in my recent novel, *Rainbow Hammock*, she thought that I might do something with the enclosed article about another secret agent from the same period. The clipping concerned a monument about to be erected in Louisville, Kentucky, to Marcellus Jerome Clarke over a century after he was hanged on that spot. I had hardly finished reading the clipping before a plot began to form. The result is *Summer Lightning*, a fictionalized account of Clarke's exploits.

Unfortunately for Confederate Captain Marcellus Jerome Clarke, alias Sue Mundy, his true story had no happy ending. Captured on Monday and tried on Tuesday, Clarke was hanged in Louisville on Wednesday, March 15, 1865, at four in the afternoon. He was not informed of his impending execution for spying until noon of that very day. It was during his final minutes that he penned the note to his sweetheart that appears in the front of this book. His lover's identity—kept secret by the minister who delivered Clarke's message—is now lost to us.

Captain Clarke also wrote this final testament to his innocence: "I am a regular Confederate soldier, and have served in the Confederate army for four years. I fought under General Buckner at Fort Donaldson, and belonged to General Morgan's command when he entered Kentucky. I have assisted and taken many prisoners and have always treated them kindly."

Like my fictitious character Damien Clay, Marcellus Jerome

Clarke often dressed as a woman to carry out his missions. A contemporary daguerreotype shows Clarke to have been a handsome young man with a smooth face, dark hair to his shoulders, and brown eyes. In this likeness, he sports the plumed hat of Morgan's Raiders.

Clarke, born in August 1845 in Simpson County near Frankfort, Kentucky, was returned to his birthplace after his death. His aunt, Mrs. Nancy Bradshaw of Franklin, had him buried in the old Clarke graveyard, next to his father, Brigadier General Hector Clarke.

While in Kentucky doing research, I ran across the interesting fact that a biography of "Sue Mundy" is currently being written by Richard Taylor of Frankfort.

Three other characters out of history caught my fancy while *Summer Lightning* was still in the embryo stage. The beautiful Creole actress Pauline Cushman had a colorful career in the theater and in the war. A Federal secret agent, she used her female charms and talents against the Confederacy. At one point in 1863 she was arrested and handed over to John Hunt Morgan as his prisoner. It is recorded that Morgan did not find *La Cushman* displeasing.

After the war Pauline, whose real name was Harriet Wood Dickinson, returned to the stage. She toured New York before heading to San Francisco and then covering all of the West. Dressed in a uniform of blue and gold, she regaled her audiences with tales of her wartime exploits, both military and romantic. When she died at an advanced age, the veterans of the Grand Army of the Republic remembered the pretty spy and gave her a military funeral with full honors.

General and Mrs. John Hunt Morgan shared one of the great romances of the Civil War. But theirs was not to be a happy ending either. In the summer of 1863 Morgan, leaving his wife expecting their first child, rode off on another raid, this time into Ohio and Indiana. He was arrested and placed in the penitentiary in Columbus, Ohio, where he spent several months. On November 27, 1863, he led a daring prison escape and was home with Mattie for Christmas. But the strain of fearing for him during his imprisonment cost Mattie her child.

On June 1, 1864, Morgan led his last raid into Kentucky. By September he was on his way back once more to join his wife. Stopping overnight in Greeneville, Tennessee, at the Williams farm, Morgan was ambushed and killed on September 4. Contemporary newspaper reports state that his whereabouts were given away to the enemy by the owner's daughter-in-law, Mrs. Joseph Williams, who rode eighteen miles through the mountains to tell the nearest Federal troops of Morgan's plans. Additional newspaper accounts tell of Mrs. Williams's death at the hands of one of Morgan's followers some weeks later.

Seven months after her husband's death, Mattie Morgan gave birth to his child, a daughter, whom she named Johnnie Hunt Morgan. Several years later Mattie married Judge James Williamson, and they reared Johnnie at Green Hill, Tennessee. Mattie died on the very eve of Johnnie's wedding to Joseph W. Caldwell, a Presbyterian minister from Selma, Alabama. Shortly after their wedding Caldwell had to attend a church conference in England. While he was away his young bride died of typhoid fever, leaving John Hunt Morgan with no direct descendants.

A number of people deserve my heartfelt thanks for their help in researching this book. Of course, it would never have been written had Whitney McMath not taken the time to clip that item of interest and send it to me. But the seed for a Civil War story set in Tennessee and Kentucky had been planted several years earlier by Donna Bond of Hendersonville, Tennessee, when she showed me an article she had written about the Battle of Stones River. Her vivid prose made me see the place and I could almost hear the Union and Confederate bands battling it out on that New Year's Eve so long ago.

My thanks, too, to my Louisville connections—my sister, Sara Creed, who enjoys roaming through graveyards in hailstorms every bit as much as I do, and to her husband, Dave, who went beyond the call of duty in resurrecting Sue Mundy for me.

A special award should go to my parents, my Aunt Vesta, and daughter, Caroline, for keeping all my cats, dogs, fish, and plants while I went traipsing off to the battlefields of Tennessee and Kentucky. And, as always, thanks to husband, Hank, and son, Vincent, who traipsed right along beside me.

Becky Lee Weyrich
Unicorn Dune
St. Simons Island, Georgia
December 1984

ABOUT THE AUTHOR

Becky Lee Weyrich, a native Georgian, was born on Margaret Mitchell's birthday, in a hospital that later became a library, and she is named for Daphne Du Maurier's *Rebecca*. So it seems only fitting that she should be a writer!

But before taking pen in hand, she spent her early career as a professional Navy wife and mother of two. For seventeen years she moved with her pilot husband from base to base, living in such diverse locations as Maine, Florida, California, and Naples, Italy.

In 1969 she took a job with a Maryland newspaper, writing a weekly column. Since then she has contributed to several other newspapers and magazines. She wrote, illustrated, and published two volumes of poetry. And since she turned to fiction in 1978, eight of her novels have seen print, including, from Fawcett, *Rapture's Slave*, *Captive of Desire*, *Rainbow Hammock*, and *Tainted Lilies*.

Becky Lee Weyrich now makes her home on St. Simons Island, Georgia, sharing her old beach cottage with her husband and son, a dog, and thirteen cats. Her hobbies include golf, bowling, beachcombing, clogging, and collecting Victorian antiques.

Watch for her next book from Fawcett, coming in April 1986—*Gypsy Moon*.